Pale Flame

Jasmina Coric

LITTLE LION PRESS
First published in the United Kingdom by Little Lion Press
www.littlelionpress.co.uk

ISBN 9781838484392

First hardback edition October 2022

Book design by Jasmina Coric
Cover art by Tom Roberts

To Eliza and Courtney,
my champions;
if my books bring me nothing
more than your friendship then
I am a truly fortunate woman

Each of us is born with a box of
matches inside us but we can't strike
them all by ourselves.

- Laura Esquivel

Table of Contents

Beings of Earth and Sundalev

Dragovik: a species of dragon shape-shifters.

Angeleru: a species imbued with some of the powers of the angels that live on Earth.

Caeletai Umea: a faction of the angeleru with all the powers of the angels.

Jacitsi Bataruce: the children of the caelitai umea, who exert control over deabrueon.

Deabrueon: the children of the jacitsi bataruce, who come in various forms.

Graemar: a type of hound-like deabrueon with wings.

Siug: a large millepede deabrueon.

Bellatoja: a faction of the angeleru who have increased strength and speed, making them the warriors of the angeleru.

Vyrium: a faction of the angeleru with photographic memories.

Avika: a faction of the angeleru with the ability to distort reality.

Onyevaras: the governing body of the dragoviks on Earth.

Hirutere: the governing body of the angeleru in Miesarinda.

Vaerdiexes: the god of fire, whose familiar is the phoenix.

Alastor: the god of water, whose familiar is the basilisk.

Yima: the god of sky, who has prophetic visions.

Kora: the mother of Vayna and Turoman, who died upon their birth. She is now a ghost that haunts Yima's garden.

Vayna and Turoman: twin gods of chaos.

Pritovis: the first god who created the angeleru and rules over angels.

Illarion: the former king of Dragovicia, whose actions resulted in the creation of the dragoviks.

Vernis Lanin: a grouup of dragovik insurrectionists run by Thaddeus Velemir.

Part I

Chapter I.

It didn't start with fire and blood.

It started with a corpse, cooling and whitening on the lawn.

It started with knowing I could love him anywhere, even in the land without memory.

***

"Jump! What are you afraid of."

The second part of the statement is phrased like a question and intoned as a taunt. I have heard this call before, in the voices that have spoken to me since my sanity began to slip through the cracks made by all that's been done to me. But in this time in which my dream takes place, those voices have not started speaking yet. I am still too young to know that madness' claws are dug deep in my mind, sharp as the hooks of mortality.

I lean back on my heels and cast my gaze across the river, which is rushing high and fast now it's glutted on the spring melted snow. The water torrents through a bottle neck between two massive rocks into a vast pool that we like to swim in through the summer and even into the cooler early autumn months. On one side, the boy stands, not yet wet from the water, having swung across from the riverbank on the rope that is knotted on the branch above me. There is a patch of snow on the hill behind him. It is the last to melt.

"Jump!" he calls again.

I take a few steps back then run, hurling my body into the air. Flailing my arms, I reach out. My hands meet the rope, allowing me to swing from the shore to the rock, and I hoist myself up. But my upper body is shocked by the heft of my small frame. I scramble to keep a hold of the rope, swinging like a pendulum, back and forth. The boy is shouting at me to drop myself onto the rock he stands on, but I can't think clearly through my shock. Eventually I slip and plummet into the hungry mouth of the river.

If the water level hadn't been so high, the snowfall so great that year, I would have died then. Split open like a too ripe fruit on the rocks. My blood would have run red, then turned to nothing, diluted by the river. I would have dissipated faster than the snow in the budding spring's warmth.

Instead, I am swept along into the churning water, pulled into the pool a little ways down. This is the one we swim in in summer months, when the sun dashes through the trees to warm the pool all the way to its depths. But instead of the warm, still waters I am used to, I find only currents. Like a vacuum, they draw me down. The water slips over my head like a suffocating blanket and I can only make out the cavernous dark blue around me. My body is sucked towards the bottom of the pool, then is pushed up along the edge, only to be dragged back down. It won't spit me out. I claw at the soft riverbed, at the hard rocks, but nothing gives way to my grasp.

Again and again the river forces me to do this dance, spiralling my body with more grace than I inherently possess. I move like an angel on the back of the wind, move like a ballerina caught up in her dance. Only I don't want this, this violent show of water's mastery over my body. I don't want to be swept away into the current, forced to dance for whatever might be watching me from the water's depths. I can only distinguish the bottom of the pool from the top by how much light filters down to me.

My head begins to spin. The water begins to fade to black all the way through as my eyes shut, growing heavy from the lack of oxygen. I have been beating against the water with my arms until now, but they've begun to feel leaden and tired. There is no use fighting; there never is.

Somewhere out there, I know he's screaming. The boy whose name I can't remember.

Somewhere out there, they are rushing from the house to dredge my cold body up from the river. My lips will be blue before they reach me.

There is a single patch of snow.

It is still melting.

***

I jerk upright. My hands swing out into the dark, searching for something to grab onto as they had in my dream. I come in to contact with my bedside table, grazing my elbow on its sharp edge.

"Fuck," I grumble, cradling my arm to my body. I look down at it, but can't make out the shape of the injury in the dark. It can't be worse than I've faced before. But I've grown so accustomed to being coddled and safe, even this sharp scratch hurts me now. I've forgotten how to go numb.

"Pansy."

The knife from my bedside table is already imbedded in the doorframe where the person who just spoke stood moments before. If it had been anyone else, they would be dead. Even after these years of inactivity, my muscles don't forget their arts. How to throw knives, how to wind my hands around a throat and choke someone, liberating them from their bodies.

"Dominic, don't scare me like that," I hiss, scrambling to switch on the lamp.

It flickers to life, illuminating the little bedroom and the tall black-haired figure leaning against the wall. I sit curled up on my mattress on the floor and feel somewhat diminished in his towering presence. His eyes have already found my face in the dark, accustomed as they are to this time of night. I, however, have managed my impeccable throw only by knowing the orientation of my small apartment even in the dark and with my heightened dragovik senses. I blink a few times, adjusting to the light.

"Not my fault you're so easily startled. And honestly Mallory, pathetic aim," he adds, wrenching my knife out of the wood.

He knows it wasn't pathetic, only that he's faster than the dagger. But he loves to tease me and I can't say I don't find it comforting. He spins the dagger in his hand before putting it back on my bedside table. He returns to the doorframe, inspecting the damage. Even from here I can see the fissure running through the grain of the wood where the dagger hit it.

"There goes my deposit," I mutter.

"Well, there goes Lindberg's deposit," Dominic corrects.

"True. Fringe benefit of being a maladapted freak from a school for assassins: they pay your rent once you move out."

Dominic laughs, but it's a sound that still doesn't suit him after all these years. It's as though it rattles up through his chest, which is hollow save for that fleeting amusement. As if he doesn't have a heart, though I know full well he does. I've managed to adapt to these human acts much better than he, but then he only half lives in the human world. I've completely submerged myself in it since leaving Aplin Hollow that summer. How disparate are the lives we lead and yet identical were our starts.

"You know you could fix this easily, right?" he says, indicating the doorframe.

"You know I don't use magic anymore, right?"

He knows I hate the subject, avoid anything to do with the Academy or what I am. It's part of living my human life: denying my past completely. I feel as though, if I cast even one spell, the distance between me and my past will grow so small that, if I reach out a finger in the dark, I will feel my old skin, waiting for me to slip back into it. He shifts from one foot to the other, aware he's derailed the conversation. At least this much of human interaction he can interpret: awkward silences.

"What were you dreaming about?"

This, however, is something Dominic missed the memo on: smooth segues.

I shrug, drawing my knees to my chest. I feel my heart pound against my thigh, the dream of drowning so like a memory. It's not the first time I've experienced something like this. It feels as my dream of Thaddeus killing Regan did. The detail with which the dream is composed, the richness of the sensations in my body as I drown. The sound of that boy's voice. When I wake, it's as though I've actually stopped breathing and I gasp to catch my breath. Could my subconscious really make all that up?

"Oh yeah, that's the body language of someone who has nothing on her mind."

He sits on the edge of the bed and I feel an odd sense of relief. Not from having him close to me, but from having him on my level rather than towering over me. Of the two of us, Dominic still wears his past life as an assassin like a cloak that lets him steal in and out of human life unnoticed. It's been three years since we were reunited in Aplin Hollow and, even though he's visited my apartment almost every night since, he still hasn't told me what he did after leaving the Academy or what it is he fills his nights with other than seeing me. I don't really want him to; he's wholly entitled to his privacy, but not knowing scares me all the same.

"The same nightmare," I sigh, looking up at the ceiling.

Our silence is filled with the sounds of sirens and cars rushing by, my apartment being towards the front of the building on Sullivan Street. I can hear all the bustle of MacDougal one block over. It's a Thursday night, but the place will still be packed with tourists and students alike.

Dominic slips off his shoes and shifts his weight around on the bed until he's right next to me. Wrapping one arm around my shoulders, he rests my head on his chest. I hear the thrum of his heart. This, this is how I know he has a heart. This and all the acts of kindness he bestows upon me. It beats, steady and at ease around me. That's how friends should be together. Not like the erratic beat of my own whenever he gets close to me. I blush furiously, grateful he can't see my face.

"Well then let's take your mind off of it," he offers. "How's school?"

"Schooly."

I glance up as he raises his eyebrows. I roll my eyes, even though I'm truly grateful for the distraction and he knows it. My dreams have always stalked me into my waking hours, troubling me even in the middle of the day. The one in which I drown has been occurring more and more frequently. I was once told that my dreams were a gift, my subconscious trying to warn me of something. But in the dream, I'm a child. This can't be the future, can it?

"I have an essay due next week. Intergenerational witness trauma and the graphic novel," I finally add.

"Comics?"

"No, the graphic novel."

"Yeah, I'm sorry but that's just comic books with a fancy name," he says, stroking my hair. I begin to shut my eyes. "What about your friends?"

"They're good. We're going to this party tomorrow. Feel free to stop by if you want to watch young women get drunk and puke on themselves."

"Wow so tempting. That's a true aphrodisiac. I'm sure they'll have no trouble picking up guys."

"The ease is less to do with the vomit, more to do with the

guys' willingness to bang anything that moves," I say and he laughs again.

It sounds more at ease now, moving from his chest to his mouth without catching on his edges. The more time we spend together, the more he seems able to reconcile himself to his sense of humanity. I wonder what it is he does during his waking hours that draws him from it again so that, each time I see him, I must reel him in from the darkness I used to live in too. I lean closer against him and wrap my arm around his middle, giving him a firm squeeze. This is the safest place in the world for me.

"How about you? What's up in the world of Dominic?"

"Oh, you know, Dominicy things," he teases.

Every time we see each other I ask and every time he avoids the question. I hate to think of him alone, waiting for me to get home, watching over me to ensure that no creature finds me as I go about my life. To ensure Thaddeus doesn't find me. I shudder. Were it not for Dominic's constant protection, no doubt Thaddeus would have found me long ago. I don't doubt he still harbours the obsession he's carried from the first moment he laid eyes on me, the obsession that drove him to follow me to Aplin Hollow and kidnap me that night, all those years ago.

"Thank you."

"For what?"

"Three years ago, when you found me, I had no idea where I'd end up. I had just lost the only family and friends I'd ever had aside from you and Lilith. Then Lindberg got me this apartment and you've been watching my back this whole time so I can go to NYU without constantly looking over my shoulder. I would never be able to live my life like this without you. So thank you."

"You really needn't keep thanking me for that. I could never live like you do, completely human. But to enable you to do so, that's the most I can ask for out of life."

I swallow, grateful again that he can't see my cheeks, flushed with pleasure at this last comment. If he only knew how saying those things makes me fall in love with him even more. How, when my friends at school ask if there is anyone I'm dating or am interested in, I think only about him. But I know he can't see me like that. No, he still sees me as a child. Scared little Mallory, the one he had to protect when we were out killing. The one who couldn't open her eyes when throats were slit, even as she was doing it.

We sit in silence, him petting my hair, me with my eyes closed. The streets begin to quiet and I know the morning will dawn on us soon.

"Mallory?"

"Hm?" I ask, sleep almost upon me. I could rest forever in the cradle of his arms. I know that, with him here, I will sleep dreamlessly. I wish I could ask him to stay every night, to keep the dreams at bay, but I don't want to take over his life entirely. He leaves mine before I wake, so I know he must be doing something with his time.

"Tell me you're happy."

"I'm happy."

And I think I am. I think this time I mean it.

The image of my lifeless corpse flashes behind my eyelids and I shiver. I feel as cold as a body dredged up from a lake so deep it seems only darkness exists within it.

Chapter II.

"From its inception, America has been concerned with the making, proving, and erasure of the individual. Not just in society, but in literature too. Is writing self-making or self-effacing? Does the author gather him or herself, or disperse their self instead through the act of writing?"

Professor Baker glances at her watch and every head turns to look at the clock on the wall. Except for mine. I make a note of her last comment. It could come in handy for my next essay, even if there's only one left before the semester ends. Everything Professor Baker says is genius though, so it's no wonder I have a notebook almost completely full from the class. I'm so grateful she let me join this class, even though it was already full. A fringe benefit of being dubbed a teacher's pet I suppose.

"And on that riveting note, you're all free from my clutches until next time. Have a good weekend."

I slip out of my seat, sliding my copy of *Fun Home* into my bag with care. Most of the students had already packed up their bags at five to four. Professor Baker is a great teacher, but there's not much love for any class that finishes at four on a Friday, especially when Noah is throwing one of his infamous house parties.

"Thanks professor," I say, giving her a wave as I walk towards the door, satchel slung over my shoulder.

"Mallory, I was going to email you to arrange some office time for us to have a chat, but now seems as good a time as any. Hang back a moment?"

I glance towards the door where a couple of friends are waiting. They giggle to each other, then beckon me. One of them, Alice, texted last night saying a major catch up was necessary regarding her date on Tuesday. Evidently it went well because I haven't seen her smile like this since her breakup. I guess that will have to wait until tonight though.

"I'll see you guys later," I assure them, giving them a wave.

"Good because there's only so much catching up one can do in a classroom with attentive ears nearby," Alice says, nodding towards her ex, who has his shoulders squared as he walks out of the classroom. He casts her a sulky look. The two broke up only a month ago and he's still trying to win her back, to no avail. "See you."

She blows a kiss then leaves the room and I hear her loud laugh ring out as she walks down the hallway with Leila. I met Alice in my freshman year and, while at first I was unnerved by her constant bubbly demeanour and intent on befriending me off the bat, I eventually caved to her kindness. Our friendship was only solidified when we both decided to major in English Literature, which was about when we met Leila.

I wait for the room to empty out and Professor Baker peers over the top of her glasses at me. I try not to shift uncomfortably under her gaze. Even after all this time, it makes me anxious to be scrutinised like this. If this conversation couldn't wait until next week, it can't be good. I prepare myself for the worst. She could say my paper is plagiarised, even though I know damn well it isn't. Yet it happens all the time. Universities are hyper aware of that, now more than ever, finding plagiarism where there is none. Or she thinks I haven't contributed enough in class discussions for the past few weeks. I've had that nightmare on my mind and it's rendered me quieter than usual. I'm not always the first to jump in when she opens the room to discussion, but often have something to add. That hasn't been the case of late. The most I can muster up is the concentration to take notes.

Removing a stack of papers from her bag, she roots through them and draws one out. I spot my name on the top of it. So, it's about my essay. I try and spot the grade scrawled on the top, but she holds it from my sight.

"Your paper was, to put it in as few words as possible, inspired," Professor Baker says. I blink a few times, shocked by the sudden turn in her demeanour. What had seemed a withering stare moments ago now conveys itself as studious curiosity.

"Oh! I thought it was going to be bad news," I laugh. "Thank you, that means a lot coming from you."

"Please Mallory, when in the three years that I've taught you has it ever been bad news? Your essays are always thoroughly researched, drawing parallels and conclusions a PhD candidate would envy. But this goes above and beyond."

"Wow, I really wasn't expecting that," I say, tucking my hair behind my ears.

I have to resist my go to nervous habit of biting the insides of my cheeks. I'm used to the academic praise from afar, receiving good grades and feedback, but this amount of attention from anyone still puts me on edge. There's always that niggling thought in my mind: what if they know what I am? What if some aspect of my beastliness has begun to shine through the façade of humanity I've grown so used to keeping up?

"You should have been, it was phenomenal. I think you should seriously pursue getting this published. I'd be happy to help with some contacts."

I perk up when she says this. Getting a paper published as an undergraduate is not only exciting, but an incredible opportunity to shine as an academic. It would be something to put on my CV at the very least.

"If you wouldn't mind, that would be an amazing opportunity."

"More than happy to. You deserve it. And, if I've said it once I've said it a hundred times, you should look into a career in academia. It's the spring term of your junior year, you've declared your major, and you'll want to start considering who will write your recommendations for applications to Master's programmes. I assume it goes without saying that this is me officially throwing my hat in the ring."

A Master's? Despite Professor Baker's regular comments on the matter, I haven't considered it seriously until right now. Literature is something I love; I spend what free time I have between school, a social life, and Dominic, doing extra reading. And it would be nice to have some concrete plans for after university. Somehow, though, I'm not sure Doctor Lindberg's generosity will extend to paying for a Master's degree. Hopes for my future as an academic wither and die as fast as they had bloomed. But I nod and smile to appease Professor Baker. There's no harm in talking to Doctor Lindberg later.

"Absolutely."

"There are lots of grants and scholarships if money's an issue," she says kindly, clearly noting the change in my demeanour. "Again, I'd be more than happy to sing your praises for those as well. It's rare I come across a student of your calibre at such a young age."

"I'll definitely look into that before the spring semester ends," I assure her. "You'll be the first to know when I start applying."

"Wonderful. Let's arrange a meeting at a later date to discuss what programmes might best suit you. If you could do some research beforehand and see if there are any that interest you, do let me know. Though I'll remind you we have a great programme here, which includes a course taught by yours truly. Alright, I won't keep you any longer. After all, you have some catching up to do." She winks and goes back to filing her papers away in her bag.

All but glowing from her praise, I make my way down the three flights of stairs, crowded with students who are keen to kickstart their weekends, and exit onto Greene Street. It's a pleasant warm spring afternoon and a gentle breeze is wreaking havoc with my short hemline. I tug my dress down, trying to keep it from flaring up over my hips.

"Save the Marilyn Monroe impression for the party. That'll get all the boys."

I glance up and spot my friend Lena leaning against the outside of the building, two coffees in her hands. She walks over and hands me one. Reaching to the back of her head, she shakes her short hair loose from its ponytail, the golden tones hidden amongst the brown glowing in the sunlight.

"Who says it's the boys I'm trying to get?" I say, pouting at her.

"I know you're obsessed with me Mallory, but you've got to give up on this infatuation," she sighs, taking a sip of her coffee. "What kept you? Baker trying to wife you again?"

"She's not trying to wife me. She's just encouraging me."

"To what?"

"Submit my paper to publications and apply for a Master's programme," I reply, sipping the cappuccino.

"Of course she was. The academic goddess that is Mallory Thiel would be told that. Meanwhile I'm tanking my political theory paper and I think my only valid lifestyle choice is to marry rich and old, let him die, then get an aviary."

She glances at the coffee in my hand then bats her eyelashes.

"Ah so this would be bribery, not just a friendly gesture," I laugh, following her down Greene Street in search of a taxi.

"Basically, if you would edit my paper, I'd be eternally grateful. It's a jumble of word vomit with a few tangents thrown in for good measure."

"Well it wouldn't be a Lena essay without a few tangents."

"Please? There's more caffeine in it for you. Caffiend," she teases, tilting her head back to catch the sunlight. Lena is singularly beautiful, with slanted almond shaped eyes and warm perennially sun-kissed skin. Beside her, I'm a washed-out pail of milk. But it never really bothers me. Lena is well suited to the spotlight: boisterous and bolshie, with an attitude some might see as rude, but I understand is a defence mechanism for her low self-esteem. I wish I could lift her out of that pit she wallows in sometimes, the one that has her calling me at three in the morning, in tears, when both her parents are away. They're often out of town and, even if they weren't, they're not really attentive enough to notice that she's struggling, let alone rush to her aid. So it falls to me instead, a role I am all too happy to fill for my friend. I go to her house any hour of the night, just to hold her and remind her she is loved. I know she'd do the same for me, though I'm too afraid to ask it of her. I'm too afraid to ask it of anyone, even Dominic.

"Anything for you, my love."

"You're an angel!" she declares.

Well actually I'm a dragon witch hybrid, but you'll never know that. Don't confuse me with those so-called angel bastards.

She kisses me on the cheek before hailing a passing taxi. The all too familiar nickname makes my stomach do a flip. *My little angel.*

"Four forty-three Greenwich Street," she says, sidling into the back seat. I follow suit, pulling my bag into my lap. "My mom is at our place in Barbados and dad is on a work trip so you can crash. Not that it would matter if they were here; mom adores you. You're the perfect daughter she never had."

"Come on Lena, she loves you to bits. She just wants you to be your best."

"That's the only way to excuse a parent coming down on me as hard as she does: she just wants the best for you. Please, we both know if she could trade me for you, she'd do it in a heartbeat. If you were still under eighteen, she'd probably adopt you too."

Not many people at school know I'm an orphan. I didn't like

the pity it engendered or, worse, the hostility it bred when people perceived me as getting free handouts due to my orphan status. It was all the more irritating as I genuinely work hard for everything I come by at school. Aside from a few freshmen year friends who fell by the wayside, Lena is the only person I've told. She, on the other hand, has no issue smugly letting people know she was adopted by ridiculously wealthy parents. It's odd because, despite the common territory, it was not the shared loss of our parents that brought us together. Whatever is between us is magnetic, inevitable.

"So, why's your mum gone to Barbados this time? Another stressful Botox experience?" I joke. There was quite the incident last year when she had Botox and her face bruised like a peach left at the bottom of a bag.

"Liposuction," Lena replies, dead serious.

"Must be rough."

"And she tells me to go to the gym to lose weight."

"You're a stick!" I exclaim, knowing exactly what to say to bolster Lena's confidence. Besides, it's not untrue. Lena has a super model's body: long legs, narrow waist, and a perfect heart-shaped face.

I glance out the window as we zip down Broadway. It will be nice to stay at Lena's tonight. Lena's parents are almost always gone and staying at her penthouse makes for a nice change from my box sized apartment. Not that Doctor Lindberg didn't offer better, but I'm happy with a Spartan existence. Most of the time. Not to mention the snack situation is unparalleled at Lena's house. For three people who are either scarcely around or hardly eating, they have the perfect assemblage of snack foods. It makes for excellent movie nights.

In the late afternoon, just before rush hour, it doesn't take long to arrive outside Lena's. She swats my hand away when I try to pay the cab driver, both of us knowing that the fare is the equivalent of three absolutely necessary coffees for me. We cross the courtyard, a large square fountain with an unblemished sheet of water cascading down from it in the centre, and get into the lift. It deposits us in her entrance hall on the top floor of the building, which is decorated by a series of three peculiar nude photographs, in which the woman is contorted into all manner of odd positions.

These are recent additions, taking the place of a Francis Bacon I had grown rather fond of.

"Hold on," I say, grabbing Lena's arm to stop her as she begins to head towards the staircase. "Is that…?"

"My mum?" she replies grimly. "Reminding us every day that she used to be beautiful without the cosmetic surgery. Makes me gag."

"I wish I hadn't looked at them so closely," I whisper, feigning a shudder.

We turn down the hall into the spacious living room. Either side of us are floor to ceiling windows, with doors leading out onto the balcony gardens. Everything that can be made out of glass, is: the coffee table, the bar, the liquor cabinet. The sofas are made from unyielding black leather. This is the room for entertaining company or her father's clients. Despite its bleak appearance, the rest of the house is much more comfortable.

"This way my dear. You're desperately in need of a trip to my wardrobe pre-party."

"Or you could just admit we have different fashion tastes and I prefer understated."

We both pause to take in what I'm wearing. Simply put, I did not have the party on my mind when I got dressed this morning. When I woke, Dominic was gone, and all I could think about was that blue lipped body by the river's edge. My body. I try to push the mental image out of my head. So, instead of wearing something Lena would deem party appropriate, I'm dressed in an utterly shapeless yellow summer dress, the colour of which makes me look sickly. Not Lena approved.

"Or you could admit that a lace corset, my asymmetric cut-out blazer from McQueen, and a pair of black cigarette trousers would look stunning on you. Top it off with some Louboutins and call it a day."

"I defer to your fashion genius," I sigh. She shrugs, giving me a sympathetic smile.

"You've got the school brains, now let me work my magic. But first, a little pre-party party."

I follow her into the wine cellar, where she scans the shelf. She procures an almost completely opaque bottle through which I can faintly make out a pink tinge. The label is black with pink lettering.

"Dom 2005 rose. Only the best for my bestie."

She pops the cork out, a well-rehearsed gesture, and pulls out champagne flutes and raspberries from the fridge. Dropping a berry in each glass, she tilts them and fills them to the brim. I watch as the bubbles multiply rapidly.

"You've had way too much practice doing that. Besides, this is utterly wasted on me. You need to stop spoiling me."

"Never, you're the only person in the world I know who's worthy. And don't worry. My mum ordered a ton of the stuff before she started her teetotal diet last month. It is not going well by the way."

"The diet?"

"Being sober. Now she's stopped drinking, she kind of has a personality again."

"Scary."

We head back out into the living room and up the stairs to Lena's room. Unlike the rest of the pristinely white house, Lena's room is painted a garish shade of red, no doubt just to spite her mother's taste. Her canopy bed is surrounded by heavy curtains and entering it always makes my stomach turn a bit. It makes me think of… Kyle's house in Aplin Hollow. My heart plummets. It's something I do my best not to think about. His face the last time I saw him, so happy as we planned our future together. And how it must have looked after he had found out I left. After everything he did for me and everything protecting me cost him, I abandoned him. I wonder how he's doing, but I already know. You don't come back from that sort of hurt, that sort of betrayal. I had promised him a future together then pulled the rug from underneath him. It's not something you forgive or forget.

I quickly swig back my glass before taking the bottle from Lena and refilling. The bubbles don't sit well in my empty stomach, but I don't care enough to ask Lena for something to eat.

"That's my girl," she says, patting me on the back, mistaking my upset for enthusiasm. All the better that she does.

We cross the room to her walk-in closet, which is larger than my small Greenwich Village apartment, and I take up residence on the chaise longue while Lena makes the rounds. First, she collects the pieces for my perfectly co-ordinated outfit, which she's no doubt been planning during class, before gathering her customary three options for herself.

"You know if you spent less time thinking about what we're going to wear to parties, you might not need my help with the essay," I suggest, as she considers two near identical gold dresses.

"Yes, but it's not as fun. Besides, you're so good at editing my papers, why would I deprive you of the opportunity?"

"My goodness," I say in mock awe, pressing a hand to my chest, "such a selfless woman I have never met before."

"Can it. Ready for a fashion show?"

Kyle's face is still in my head, my imagination taking it in turns as to which emotion it paints on his face: betrayal, hurt, misery. I'm ready to be walloped over the head with a brick if it will distract me.

"Show me what you got."

She first tries on a red bandage dress, followed by a plunging gold dress, before finishing with a flapper dress covered in an alarming number of sequins.

"Jeez are you a disco ball? Absolutely not," I scoff, finishing my drink.

It's getting late by now so I get off the chaise longue, depositing my drink on the vanity. I remove my clothes and start slipping into the ones she's provided. The corset is a little tight and the shoes pinch a bit, but the booze will help with that. I walk over to the full-length mirror to look at myself. It still feels weird, looking at myself as though all I am is this body and not the toxic mess that is my mind. I try not to find my own eyes in the mirror, surveying the outfit instead. My aversion to mirrors is mostly gone, but there's something about seeing those eyes, so inhuman, that still plagues me. My jaw drops as I take myself in. Lena giggles at the expression that crosses my face.

"I look like a gothic renaissance wench," I say, indicating my all but overflowing boobs in the corset.

She bursts out laughing.

"You look sexy, go with it, okay? The boys, or the girls, will be falling over you. I wouldn't know which you prefer because you never date anyone."

I shrug, as is my customary response when she brings up my dating life, or lack thereof. I know this is her way of asking if there's anyone I'm interested in, but I don't reply. I can't even begin to explain Dominic, and Lena is too inquisitive to let me get away with minimal information. She would want to meet him, see whether he's up to her standards. She sighs, moving back to the all-important subject of clothes.

"Okay, so, red or gold?" she asks, holding up the dresses.

"Red. I think the gold is more 'I'm going on a date with a movie star' than 'I'm going to a NYU house party'."

"Red it is. You look flawless as usual, tits notwithstanding."

"All thanks to you," I say, giving her a twirl. I almost topple over in the shoes. "I will never get used to heels."

"You just need to wear them more often."

"So my feet are permanently contorted into this position? No thank you."

I pick up my drink and take another sip. It's going down smoother, my stomach less upset now I don't have Kyle on my mind.

"Okay," she says, examining me after she's changed back into the red dress. "Let's just do something about that hair."

She comes over and leads me to the vanity where she seats me. Crouching down so her head is beside mine, she studies me in the mirror. She plugs in her straightener and waits for it to heat up.

"Oi, what happened to flawless?" I ask, swatting at her hand as she nears me with the straightener. She sets it down.

"It never hurt flawless to wear some sapphire and white jade earrings," she says, slipping them into my piercings, which I only got at her request. "Or to straighten her hair and have a slick ponytail."

"I'm just a living doll to you, aren't I?"

"Pretty much. You've got the curves, I've got the legs. It's fun to dress you. Harlot," she says, poking my boob. She begins separating my hair into layers to straighten.

"The things I let you do to me."

* * *

A girl is already doubled over, puking outside the apartment building, by the time we get there. My head's a little fuzzy from the champagne, but I have sense enough to pause to hold her hair back. Lena seems more concerned about her shoes being directly in the splash zone. She grumbles in displeasure as I take the girl's phone and call the friend whose name the girl gives me. I get the friend's address and help the girl into a cab.

"Why do you have to be everyone's guardian angel?" Lena demands, as I wave goodbye to the girl.

"Because there are people like you who would let her fall asleep in a puddle of her own vomit."

"I would not! I'd at least give her a glass of water."

"Okay, and then you'd let her fall asleep in her own vomit."

"Possibly. Depends how drunk I am myself."

We follow the slow trickle of people heading inside and get in the elevator. I keep waiting to hear the thrum of music as the elevator creeps upward, but it isn't until the doors slide open that the sound hits me like a wall. My hands leap up to cover my ears, but Lena pries them away. The room is cavernous, all hard angles washed with white paint. It would seem soulless were it not for all the people packed into the room. Even after all this time, it always takes me a moment for me to adjust to these large social situations. I take a deep, steadying breath.

"Come on," Lena urges, pulling me after her.

Already I know she's on the hunt for the party's host, Lena's on-again-off-again boyfriend, Noah. But she won't go up and talk to him right away. No. It will be hours of us enjoying the party in his direct line of sight until he can't stand the sight of another guy hitting on her and they hook up. Guess I'll be going back to my flat tonight after all. And I was so looking forward to our hangover brunch tomorrow. I start looking around for the third to our little trio, Wesley, but I don't spot him. It's not like him to miss a party, so I know he must be around here somewhere.

"Is Wes here?" I ask Lena.

"What?" she shouts back over the music, her eyes surveying over my shoulder. They stop and I glance behind me to catch sight of Noah, chatting with some of his friends. He's leaning against a doorframe, beer in his hand, pretending to be utterly oblivious to Lena's presence. Of course, how could anyone miss her? A group of guys nearby certainly hasn't. Their eyes rove over her gorgeous figure, making me want to lob something at them. I notice Noah's eyes flicker to her in a moment of distraction before he sees me looking, and is quick to turn away.

"Is Wes coming tonight?" I ask, turning back to Lena.

"Yeah, he said so when I saw him in class. He should be here somewhere."

She draws me towards where people are dancing and slips her arms around my neck. We begin to dance, chatting a little bit and catching up on the day's events. Every now and then her eyes flit towards Noah, and I know she's only half listening to everything I say. I don't really mind for my own sake, but I do worry about her with Noah. She adores him, but he only ever seems to be using her. They'll get together and she'll be ecstatic for a day or a week until he doesn't call or text. That's when I get the three in the morning phone call to come over. And I always do. For now, though, I won't say anything. But we do need to talk about this at some point. It's not good for her. Better to let their routine play out for tonight or she'll just be upset for the rest of the night. Besides, it won't be long before she heads to the bar to pick up some guy.

"I'm going to go get us drinks," she says, confirming my suspicions.

"Sure."

I look around the room as she disappears into the crowd and, sure enough, there's Wesley, leaning close to a girl to hear what she's saying. He catches my eye from across the room and grins. It's the sweet smile of a puppy, impish even. He's the all-American boy, but then again, so much of NYU's male population is, especially those in attendance of Noah's parties. Excusing himself, Wes walks towards me, and the girl throws me a dirty look. I recognise her from a few other parties and I'm quite certain they've hooked up before.

It's some effort for Wesley to squish between people to reach me, but finally he manages it.

"Hey handsome," I say, standing on my tip toes to tousle his dark brown hair. Even in Lena's heels, I'm dwarfed by him.

"Looking damn fine yourself Thiel. Very lady of the night meets business mogul. Where's your other half?"

"Getting drinks," I say, rolling my eyes.

"Ah the classic first manoeuvre of the Noah-Lena dance: picking up a guy at the bar so he can see and get jealous. Well, let's see if we can't get you something to imbibe in the meantime."

"I'll have a beer. Because I'm a cool down to earth girl who watches sports and drinks beer. Oh, and I like chicken wings."

"That joke gets funnier every time you tell it," he says, rolling his eyes. But a grin still creeps across his face. "Let's go find the fruitiest cocktail we can."

"Deal. But I really do like chicken wings if you've got some."

"We'll see if we can't make that happen later."

I follow him to the bar Noah has had set up on the balcony, which is far less crowded than the one inside, owing to the cool evening air. Still, the inside of the apartment is so crowded that the party has overflowed onto the balcony and it's a fair bit of work to get to the bar. Eventually a group clears off and we manage to squish between a few people to get to the cocktail menu.

"Noah really goes all out on these things, doesn't he?" I say, studying the menu.

"It's weird to think he basically does this all for an excuse to get Lena over without displaying direct interest."

It's probably true. Noah keeps tabs on her from the moment she walks in and never shows interest in another girl.

"Men are weird. Pornstar martini please," I say to the bartender.

"They want your drink order, not your profession," Wes says, much to the amusement of the bartender.

"Please, my tits are way too small."

He raises his eyebrows and need not say anything to remind me of the fact they're practically hanging out of my top. I button up the blazer, eliciting his laughter.

"And I'll have a vodka soda," he says to the bartender before turning back to me.

He sweeps his hair out of his face and gives me his half grin that tells me he's slightly tipsy and his puppy crush is in fine form. He's had one since just about day one, though it took me a while to believe Lena when she told me. Wes is cute, there's no doubt about that. But could I ever be with someone who doesn't know my past, who hasn't experienced something similar themselves? I don't think it's possible. That's why it has to be Dominic. I've known that since the early days of our arrival in New York. No one will ever be better suited to me than him.

"So, how are things? I feel like I hardly see you," Wes says, realising he's lost my attention.

"Sorry, just swamped with coursework. But you're right. As of now I am yours for a coffee and catch-up date. Name the day."

Probably a bad choice of words. I've never intentionally given Wes the impression I like him, which is why he's never asked me out, but I think he reads more into my affection for him as a friend than there is. People are quick to do that. My adoration for Lena and Wes is near boundless, them being the new family I found when I moved to New York. They were my first friends in freshman year and we were an unlikely trio: the athlete, the model, and the, well, whatever I am.

"How about tomorrow, if I can pull my head out of the toilet bowl."

"Deal. Lena's going to be MIA anyway."

"Oh, so I'm runner up? That's cold."

"You're never the runner up," I laugh, "I just had plans with her before."

"Okay good. My ego couldn't take it. So, how are things?" he asks again, realising he never got an answer.

"Things are good. I got to take care of my neighbour's dogs last week. They're so cute. I can't wait to have my own place and get some pups of my own. Oh, and Baker is pushing me to do a Master's and get a paper published."

"Well of course she is. You're kind of a genius, in case you haven't noticed. You put us to shame in all our classes freshman year. Just don't go too far away for the Master's. We need you in the city."

"So not Oxford?"

"Sod the British! They all have the maturity of a scone. You're an east coast girl. Boston at the furthest."

"Well, there's always Columbia if I'm feeling like a change from NYU. Don't worry, I'm not going anywhere," I promise. This is my home now.

He pulls me into a hug that's all lanky limbs, which I know he'd never be brash enough to do when sober.

"That's my girl."

"What the hell are you two doing? You totally abandoned me," Lena demands, storming up to us, noticeably without any drinks. The bartender chooses this moment to slide ours to us, causing her nostrils to flare. "You went to get drinks? I was getting drinks."

"So how cute was the guy?" Wes asks, his arms still around me.

"Rate his butt out of ten," I say.

Wes shakes with laughter and drops a kiss on the top of my head. Lena raises her eyebrows at me, but I shrug. It's harmless and he'll forget all of this tomorrow anyway.

"Cute butt, bad teeth. I think he was English," she sighs, before turning to the bartender. "Vodka martini."

"Another strike against Oxford. English people have bad teeth," Wes says.

"But cute butts apparently," I reply.

"I have no idea what you're talking about," Lena says, picking up her martini. "Come on weirdos. Dance with me."

Lena grabs our hands and drags us back into the living room, sloshing a great deal of Wes' drink down his front. Luckily, he's too drunk to care and the drink is clear anyway.

Over the next hour, many trips are made to the bar, leaving me dancing like an idiot while Lena retains her poise. The night seems to slip away from us, yet remains held within the bubble surrounding the apartment, as if it will never end. I down my fifth drink, which Wes has only just procured for me, and lean heavily on Lena's shoulder to whisper in her ear.

"Bathroom."

She nods.

"Want me to come with?"

But her eyes are still on Noah, so I shake my head. He's been glancing at her every few seconds. Taking her away now may set her back an hour. I squeeze Wes' hand and pull away as he tries to draw me back.

"Where you going?" he demands, his speech beginning to slur.

"Bathroom. And, no, you can't come with."

I push my way through the dense throng of people towards the hallway past the bar. I'm surprised to find the party hasn't filtered into here, but there are no speakers and the music grows quieter the further I walk. I've been to Noah's apartment for enough parties to know where I'm going. I've even crashed here a couple times, back when he and Lena were almost a long-term couple. I turn the corner and spot a girl standing a few feet away. For some reason, I feel like I'm intruding. I'm about to turn back, when I recognise the dark brown curls as Alice's.

"Hey!" I call out, a little too loudly due to all the drink. "What's all that catching up we needed to do? I am ready to sit down and take these shoes off."

I suddenly notice she's standing with a guy, the two pressed close together. He gazes intensely down at her and her head is tilted up towards him. The guy from her date maybe?

"Shit, sorry, I'll just go," I start. I turn around and start back down the hall.

I hear the slick sound of metal and flesh. Whipping around, I watch as the young man draws his arm back and Alice's body crumples to the floor, sliding off his sword. I open my mouth to scream, but the music from the party no doubt drowns it out. Besides, what could anyone do? I start patting myself down in search of something to weaponise, but I don't even have a handbag on me. In two quick bounds, the man's already in front of me, his bloodied sword held out before him. He lifts the sword in his hand and strikes me with the pommel on the head. The world goes blank.

Chapter III.

My wits don't rush back to me. They claw at and crawl across the floor, a tumult of confusion trying to reach my woozy brain. My eyes are shut and I keep them so when I hear voices nearby.

"What were you thinking, kidnapping her? Do you have any idea who she is?"

"I know who she is and they were very explicit about not killing her, even if we crossed paths."

"Of course they were, it goes without saying we don't kill her. But they also didn't say knock her out and bring her here either, did they?"

"What was I supposed to do? She saw me kill that girl. It was either me or her in that moment. If I'd given her another second, she could have easily overpowered me."

"So why didn't she?"

"I don't know. After I knocked her out, what was I supposed to do?"

Cold. The stone against my cheek, the air stirring in the room. It's all so cold. My head buzzes as I come around. And here I thought I wasn't going to be knocked out anymore after I left Aplin Hollow, unless it was from a particularly boozy night out. My head throbs where I've been struck and I want to press it to the cold stone, but am too afraid to move, lest they realise I'm awake. The voices are coming from only a few feet away. If one of them is the guy that attacked me, in my current drunk state, I'm no match for him, especially without a weapon.

"I don't know. Not bring her here was probably a good start."

"So, what do we do now?"

"Well, let's ask the boss."

"What and just leave her here?"

"She'll be fine in there."

The sound of footsteps softens as they depart and I hear a door swing open and closed. Listening closely, I wait for any indication there's someone else in the room, but there's nothing. They said as much when they wondered whether to leave me here on my own. I'm alone. I open my eyes, blinking a few times to adjust to the low light. I've been confined to a small portion of the room, cut off from it by iron bars and an ancient looking padlock. This does not serve to deter me though.

"Good thing assassins need to get through locks often. And good thing Lena's a stickler about loose hairs," I mutter, procuring one of the pins from my hair.

I could murmur a single word to unlock the padlock, but I've refrained from using magic since Aplin Hollow and I'm not about to start now. I bend the pin to a right angle then slip my arm between the bars. With the flat side facing up, I insert it into the lock. It takes a minute of careful work before I hear the satisfying click that lets me know I'm free. Wrenching the lock off, I push the door open and wince as it lets out an audible groan. If there's a guard outside the door, they will definitely have heard that. But no one rushes in.

I get to my feet, but find I'm swaying in Lena's absurdly high heels. How much trouble will I be in if I abandon them here? Not exactly the kind of situation I can explain to her, so it's likely she'd behead me. Not to mention the dirt on her blazer. I groan, glancing at my arm and trying my best to dust the worst of it off.

"Great," I grumble. "A perfect end to a hostage situation."

I slip the shoes off and, letting them dangle from my hand, check the room for anything other than my heels that could be used as a weapon. Coming up empty handed, I sigh and head for the door. I press my ear to it and listen to hear if anyone's on guard outside or is passing by, but there's nothing. Peeking through a crevice between the door and doorframe, I glance up and down the hall. No one. I slip out of the room, bracing myself against the wall as I stumble slightly. Damn those drinks were strong. Normally my increased metabolism would have rendered me sober by now, but this is what I get for drinking on an empty stomach. I need to make a mental note: tacos are a must before all of Noah's party. Or burritos. I would kill for a burrito right about now.

The hall splits three ways: forwards, left, and right. I stand still and quiet, listening for a breeze to tell me which way is outside. I feel it wafting around the gap beneath my trouser legs, the peach hairs on my ankles saluting. It's coming from the right. Hopefully that's my way out of here without anyone noticing, but it's likely they'll have guards at the main door. Whoever these people are, they're organised enough to have some sort of hideout.

Raising a shoe in front of me primed for attack, I creep forward, my attempt at stealth exaggerated to ridiculousness by my intoxication. All I want is a bottle of water to help dispel the cloud that swirls around my brain. Or for Dominic to be here. I'd feel safe with him by my side. If only I hadn't told Dominic about the party tonight, he would have come over to check on me and realised I was missing. Stupid me and my oversharing. I'll say anything just to keep him at my apartment a little while longer. This also means I miss out on his nightly routine visit, which I'm loathe to do. Though I did think I'd be staying at Lena's.

I scowl at myself, passing a few more doors before I reach the end of a hall. A strange gurgling sound comes from one, causing me to jump. I wonder who, or what, is behind it, but not enough to explore. I just need to get out of here before I slip back into the ways of my old life. At the end of the hall, there's a huge corrugated copper door with a patina of blue from oxidization. I can feel the breeze coming out from beneath the door and smell salt and decaying plant matter. We're somewhere near the docks.

"I am not all the way in Brooklyn," I groan. "It's going to take ages to get home."

"Hey!"

I spin around and see the pale-haired man who killed Alice standing at the other end of the hallway. He's tall and lean, but made up of muscle. His clothes seem out of place, almost medieval, as does the sword strapped to his hip. He draws his sword and begins running towards me, faster than is humanly possible.

"Fuck."

Dropping the shoe in my left hand, I grab the door, but it won't budge. Locked. I don't have time to pick it, so resign myself to my only other option. I close my eyes and visualise the lock, it turning to my will, then hear the click of it undoing itself. Throwing open the door, I make a dash out of what I come to see is a warehouse on the docks. Across the water, wood piles stick their cylindrical tops out from where a pier once stood. I dart forwards, leaping from the dock onto one, before darting to the next. I hear his heavy feet landing on one behind me and know he's not too far. Jumping onto the piles wasn't the smartest move; if I lose my footing now, he'll catch me. But he's clearly fast, so outrunning him wasn't an option either. I can only hope he slips and falls into the water. I don't know what manner of creature he is, but my guess is he's not human. For all I know, he's faster and stronger than I am. My magic won't be strong after so long in disuse and I have no weapon other than a single Louboutin.

Veering suddenly to the right, I leap back onto the dock. I race forward, concentrating on gathering as much speed in my legs as possible. Still he persists and is gaining on me. Fuck. I feel the swish of air as his sword comes down towards me, disregarding what he'd said about not killing me. I manage to roll aside just in time, though it costs me my footing. Striking out with my foot, I knock the back of his knees so they buckle and he falls to the ground. I spring to my feet and kick the sword from his hand before planting a roundhouse kick in his face. He manages to catch my foot, getting a good enough grip to toss me clear through the air. I fall to the ground and hastily push myself up into a sitting position. Definitely not human.

He's fast too. Already he's back on his feet. Towering above me, he reaches to pick up his sword, taking time to brush off the dirt that's collected on his sleeves. He starts towards me, grinning menacingly. His teeth are sharpened to points and he runs a red forked tongue across his lips. His eyes shimmer the water's reflection as he comes to stand over me. He tilts his head to the left, studying my vulnerable body splayed across the ground. He said he knows who I am to whoever was in the room with him earlier, so no doubt he's underwhelmed with the fight I've put up. Still clutching Lena's single shoe, I throw it in his face in a futile effort to gain some time to make a break for it. He snatches it out of the air with the speed of a cat taking a swipe at a mouse.

"Cute," he says, "although I never saw the point in buying designer shoes. You just end up walking down the same New York streets covered in dog shit, cigarette butts, and who knows what else."

He tosses it into the East River. Lena really is going to kill me. If this guy doesn't do it first.

"It's a friend's," I bleat, my head still not cleared from the drink.

I scuttle back a few paces and he takes his time closing the distance between us. He knows I have no chance of escaping, caught between him, the river, and another warehouse. He spins the sword in his hand, creating a whooshing sound as it circles through the air. Show off.

"You know, I've heard about you. The great Mallory Thiel. Last of the Oviras, last of the Thiels. Formidable wordless caster, assassin from the Academy. How many little kids' throats did you slit in your time, dog?"

I swallow hard when he says this. It's not a part of my past I think about, ever. The night Lilith, Dominic, and I infiltrated that man's house. It was the only time we ever killed children and, even though I wasn't the one who did it, I still stood aside while Lilith did. The man grins again, knowing he's struck a nerve.

"But now you just look like a meek, pathetic girly girl. Living in the human world will do that to you I guess."

He raises his sword again. He said he was told not to kill me, but whatever his bosses told him while he was gone has changed that. My life is officially a viable commodity and someone's willing to buy it.

"All true, except you forgot one thing," I say.

"What's that?" he asks, hesitating, and I think I see terror flash through his eyes. My name commands some sense of fear in the supernatural world, it seems.

"Well, I'm not sure, but statistically speaking, people usually forget–oh right," I say, the realisation hitting me. I raise my hand, palm flexed towards him. "Dersutisanaraava'noventa callanedo lera aleve vema dersutisanaraava callanedo saviski vanage, destoyar kaisma korevezinarava, destoyar oelanus darava izjumar."

My power manifests in a bright ball of light around my hand, before torrenting forward in a burst of wind. It strikes the man and he goes hurtling over the edge of the dock, producing a loud splash as he lands in the water. I see his arms flail briefly before he bobs back up to the surface, his sword lost below. He looks at me with wild rage, spitting out the disgusting water that has gotten in his mouth.

"I'm a dragovik witch, dumbass," I shout at him.

I imagine a vortex in the water, pulling everything into it, as it does with me in my dreams. A whirlpool splits its lips around him, drinking him down. I keep focus, letting it whirl around and around, until I sense him go unconscious within my spell. Only then do I let my magic crawl back to my fingers, the whirlpool stilling back to a wrinkled current on the flesh of the river. The effort makes me stagger for a moment, but I quickly right myself. Drawing up to my full height, I peer down at the water to be sure he won't resurface.

"Idiot."

I turn around, only to come to an abrupt halt. There, in front of me, are six deabrueon, lumbering forwards from the warehouse we emerged from. I suppose I know what that gurgling sound was behind the door then. Their bodies are almost indistinguishable from the dark, made noticeable only by the way they shift like shadows, and let out low grumbling sounds of anticipation at the prospect of killing me.

"So, it's one of those nights," I mutter.

Within a second, a tendril of water snakes forward, handing me the man's sword from its depths. I raise it before me. I haven't used magic in a while and what little I've done has begun to take its toll, especially when coupled with the fact that I'm drunk. I'll have to fall back on my Academy training for the rest of this fight.

As they near, I dart to the one nearest me on the left and, in one swift move, decapitate it. Its head rolls with the force of the blow, plopping into the river. This sets the others on their guard. They hang back for a second before closing ranks into a triangle formation. Deabrueon working together? It seems unlikely. The only other time I've seen them join forces was when they were sent in exchange for me and Kyle when we visited Illarion. But this is different. They're co-ordinated, strategic, forming ranks to protect one another. That other times, it had just been a mindless attack. Unless… I have seen them work together one other time. When Clara commanded them. The thought of the jaeitsi sends a shiver down my spine. I can't bring myself to consider the implications of her being involved in this kidnap. That can only mean that Thaddeus has found me.

I'm dragged out of my ruminations by the nearing deabrueon. As they are, I have little to no chance of breaking through their barricade without getting injured, if not killed. And if Lena is going to be angry about the shoes, she'll never forgive me for desecrating an Alexander McQueen blazer. The alternative is casting another spell, which could leave me unconscious. In which case, someone else could come out of the warehouse and find me.

With little time to decide before they reach me, I raise the sword again. I imagine Dominic's arms protecting me, the safety I feel when he holds me, and a ball of light swells up around my abdomen. It expands, shimmering on the surface of my skin. This should hold for a while against their attacks. I dart forwards and the one at the front of their triangle formation falls on me. Its claws glance off of my protection spell and it howls with displeasure. The others converge just as I run the first through with my sword. There's a squelching sound as blood splatters the pavement when I withdraw my blade from its body. Already I can feel the toll my spell is taking on me, my hands shaking with the effort it takes to maintain. I can't hold this much longer.

I'm shoved from behind and, while the claws don't pierce my flesh, the spell doesn't keep me from being knocked to the ground. Startled by the impact of the concrete on my knees, I drop my sword and the spell. I hear the tear of the blazer and feel the slash of talons run through the skin of my back. There's a searing pain, the new wounds burning. In my moment of weakness, the creature rolls me over and pounces on my chest. Hissing, it spits in my face before letting out an unearthly yowl. The others circle around us, waiting with anticipation for their turn to toy with my corpse. I won't let it come to that.

I shove hard against the creature's chest, throwing it backwards and bowling over a couple more behind it. My sword has slipped outside of the circle they've formed around me and, before I can make a break for it, the deabrueon have gotten to their feet and encircled me once more. Fuck. I feel the dizziness that comes with the use of magic clouding my mind. Mixed with the alcohol, it has an extremely soporific effect. I can't lose consciousness now. This is not how I die. I look from indistinguishable face to indistinguishable face, each one masked with the anticipation of tasting my blood. What must it taste like to them, running with isuazko and the strength of my magic? As they begin to close in, I realise there's no way out of this.

Suddenly, I hear an unearthly scream from behind me. We all whirl around to spot a couple who have come to an abrupt stop upon spotting me surrounded by five lean yet muscular deabrueon. A sight to behold no doubt. The woman is clutching her boyfriend's arm, pulling on him to leave, but not running herself. She's too in awe to look away. I can't imagine what this must look like to an outsider. Then again, I'm sure stranger things have happened in Brooklyn.

"I'd recommend running," I call out to them, taking the opportunity to kick one of the distracted deabrueon in the back.

It tumbles forward. There's the sound of footsteps rushing towards me, but I don't have time to consider them. I punch the deabrueon standing between me and my sword, sending it reeling. Then, I dive for my sword, only to find it's already gone. Fuck. Spinning around, I see the young man from the couple has taken it up. With expert dexterity, he swings the blade upwards, splitting one of the deabrueon from navel to neck. The woman screams again, taking off back the way she came. A deabrueon comes towards me and, again, I command the water to reach out of the river, this time to snatch the beast and drown it. The man has already slain three more by the time the creature stops fighting to get back above the surface. He glances at me and grins wickedly, his face illuminated by a flickering lamp hung from the side of a warehouse.

"Killian?" I say in shock, recognising the bellatoja who freed Kyle from Alastair, before one of the deabrueon sinks its talons into my arms and throws me against the warehouse.

My vision blurs and, when I manage to regain it, I see the body of the last deabrueon fall beneath Killian's sword.

He sighs, inspecting his handywork before tossing the sword aside and swaggering over to me.

"Damn, scared my date away," he sighs, reaching out a hand towards me. "Should have known she wasn't a keeper when she said she lived in Brooklyn though."

I take his hand and he hoists me to my feet, holding me steady while I regain my sense of balance. Brushing the worst of the grime from my sleeves and butt, I raise my eyebrows at him.

"You took a date to the Brooklyn docks?"

"She said they were pretty at night. How was I supposed to

know I'd come across the last person I expected to find fighting deabrueon here? Whatever, more fish in the sea, as they say."

"Probably not in the East River though," I say, grimacing as I inspect the claw marks on my arm. I draw the wounds shut with magic, the pain vanishing and my vision darkening for a moment. No more magic.

"I don't know about that," he says. "Fancy getting something to eat?"

Chapter IV.

We wander back from the docks to Van Brunt Street, making our way through the throngs of pedestrians crowding the Friday evening. Though the night is probably closer to morning than evening by now. Still, the sky reveals no traces of the dawn, but I don't know how long I was unconscious for. I can only take comfort in the fact that, if it's still dark, it can't have been too long.

My mind soon turns to other matters. Who were those men and why did they know about me? What's more, why did they kill Alice? Was she just in their way, an innocent bystander, or is there something more to her death? A shiver runs through me as I think of my friend's lifeless body crumpling before that man. What was he? His features were almost serpentine; I've never seen anything like him.

Neither Killian nor I say a thing on the walk for a long time. We've only met once, after all, and it wasn't under the best of circumstances. Though he did set Kyle free and seemed to have no clue what Alistair intended to do to me when he told his bellatoja captain who I was. Still, he did tell Alistair about Clara, so I'm not sure I can trust him. Killian has his hands in his pockets, shoulders dropped as if he hasn't just done battle with deabrueon, and he hums quietly to himself, looking around for somewhere to go. Meanwhile, I feel completely wired and tense.

"Nice song," I say, unsure of what else to say to a near perfect stranger.

"Thanks, it's one of my own."

"Didn't know the bellatoja were musically inclined," I reply, unable to keep the iciness from my voice when I mention his kind. He may have saved Kyle's life, but most of the bellatoja I've met were not particularly likeable. He glances sideways at me and I regret interrupting the pretty tune he was humming.

"You're not just defined by being a dragovik, are you? Well, we're not one-dimensional warriors at all times. We eat, dance, play instruments, and, occasionally, go to Brooklyn. Against our better judgement. Though I can see where you'd get the impression that we're all assholes," he says, scratching the back of his head.

Does he look embarrassed over what Alastair did? I can't tell because the expression is gone almost as quickly as it comes and he starts humming that song again. I wonder if he knows the full extent of what happened at the Academy. At the very least, he cannot know what Alistair tried to do to me in the moments before I killed him. The thought of the bellatoja's hands on me makes me tremble slightly, though I play it off as a shiver.

"So, you write music?" I reply, hoping to avoid the subject of the bellatoja massacre at the Academy. If anyone could connect me to that incident, it would be Killian. He's the only one other than Kyle, Leo, Aaron, and Robyn who knows they took me there to find Clara. The only one still living that is. I shudder at the memory of so many bodies torn apart. Clara was just a child when she did that, still so young. I don't want to know what she's capable of when united with the other jaeitsi.

"I dabble. A little piano, a little guitar. Where soldier life allows for some free time. Or I read. How about you? How do you fill your normal human life? I heard you left the others in Aplin Hollow."

The comment, while friendly in nature, makes my heart sting. He must know what's become of them since then, if he's heard that I left them. I'm tempted to inquire after them, so desperate for some little piece of information that confirms they're okay, but I daren't ask how Kyle is. I have no right to be a part of his life, having abandoned him when he needed me most. Even if Leo was right and it was best that I left for their safety, I cannot forgive myself for the heartbreak I undoubtedly caused him. No, the truth is, in not asking I am being selfish. I am neither hearing that he has happily moved on nor having my suspicions confirmed that he's still completely devastated.

"I'm studying at NYU. Majoring in literary studies. One more year left then I'll hopefully apply for a Master's programme somewhere in the city."

He nods and I can't tell whether he's being polite or is completely disinterested. He comes to a stop, gesturing towards a grungy looking dive bar I hadn't even noticed. I must wrinkle my nose, displaying my evident disgust, because he laughs. The sound is a relief after tonight's events, as if some normalcy can be restored.

Despite my general resentment of bellatoja, Killian seems so calm that it's hard to be ill at ease around him. It seems unlikely he's about to spring a trap inside this dive bar.

"Trust me, the pulled pork sandwiches are a thing of beauty. And the fries? Divine."

"And here I thought you were anti-Brooklyn. Come here often?" I ask, following him in.

"Good food is worth the trek."

Inside it's quite dark, the people clustered at tables mere shadows. The bar is decorated with multi-coloured fairy lights that flash obtrusively in the eyes of the customers seated along the bar. They all look slightly too tipsy to care. Killian leads me through the bar to the back door and into the outdoor seating area, which is populated by rusty chairs and worn wooden benches, most of which are occupied. There are more fairy lights strung from posts, illuminating the somewhat dank and dirty outdoor dining area. We sit at a table in the corner next to a mural of a pig holding a can of beer. It leers at me from its place on the wall. I glance at Killian.

"Classy joint. I can't believe you didn't sweep your date off her feet given your choice of venue."

"Oh, I don't take dates here. This is sacred territory."

"Well then I'm honoured."

A waitress brings over a couple menus, winking at Killian, who grins back.

"Thanks," he says, sweeping his dark hair behind his ear. It's grown out in the years since I last saw him. It almost reminds me of John.

Thaddeus. John. The man I almost loved. Again, I shudder. How close did he come to finding me tonight? It seems likely that whoever that man who attacked me was, he was working for Thaddeus and Clara. The alternative, that someone else supernatural out there wants me, is more than I can stand to think about.

"Okay so I'm thinking chilli cheese fries to share, onion rings, and two pulled pork sandwiches. Couldn't you just eat a horse after a good fight?"

"It's been a while since I've had a fight and I can't say I've ever had a good one. But yes. One horse please." He snorts and leans back in his chair, surveying me.

"So, what got you caught up with a group of deabrueon tonight? Yearning for the good old days?"

The waitress returns just then, so we order our food before I recount the night's events, leaving out my drunkenness, which has at last begun to fade. Our sandwiches and fries arrive just as I finish telling him everything, and Killian frowns.

"Six shots of tequila please," he says to the waitress before seeing the unimpressed look on my face. "You need them."

I sigh, nodding my assent before digging into the fries.

"Damn those are good," I say, pulling another one free from the already congealing cheese on top.

"Told you. Weird though. What do you think a supernatural being wanted with your friend?"

"Apparently to kill her," I say, surprised after I speak by my own blasé attitude regarding the death. It's been so long since I've been around death and dragoviks, but already it seems the status quo again. Killian doesn't seem to notice, however, chewing intently as he is on a mouthful of his sandwich. "I hadn't really thought about it. I was so drunk from this party, all I could think about was getting out of there and not destroying my friend's clothes which, whoop-dee-doo, I managed to do."

"I'm sorry. I just watched you kick deabrueon ass with magic and you're worried about repairing a jacket?" he says, raising his eyebrows.

My cheeks flush. I hadn't thought of that. I'm so used to not relying on magic. But if there was ever a worthy cause, it would be saving Lena's clothes. I shimmy off the blazer, baring my shoulders to the gentle spring breeze. I'm fully aware of how much of myself I'm exposing to Killian's gaze, but he doesn't seem to notice, absorbed with his food instead. Turning the jacket in my hands, I place my palm against the lacerations and envision something drawing shut, something whole. The blazer's threads draw together, stitching themselves back into one seamless piece. Pleased with my work, I sling it over the back of my chair and grab a couple onion rings, which are every bit as good as the fries.

"So, what was that guy, the one I told you about? He definitely wasn't human."

"Sharp teeth, forked tongue? Raika. They're, shock and horror, snake demons. The perverse progeny of the god Alastor's familiar, the basilisk."

"I'm sorry, someone had children with a snake?"

"A god's snake," he replies, unblinking.

"Euphemism aside, that's fucking disgusting," I blurt out as the shots arrive.

He bursts out laughing, handing me one of the shots and tapping his glass against mine. I tilt my head back, downing it in one. The familiar warmth running down my throat puts me at ease. I hadn't realised how tense my body had been since the fight until then.

"Explains why they're near the river; basilisks are creatures of water. Chances are your raika just went unconscious from the effort of fighting your spell. They can breathe underwater."

"Just one more demonic entity to fear is coming after me," I grumble, taking another shot.

"Why'd they take you, did they say?"

"I don't think he was supposed to take me. Whoever he was talking to seemed upset he had brought me there, like I wasn't supposed to know about the place."

"They were probably nervous you'd get in the way of their plans," he says, throwing back another shot. He clicks his tongue, staring down at the empty shot glass in his hand. "A lot has happened in the past few years. Forces are gathering and this could be a base of some kind."

I catch his gaze, his thoughts imperceptible to me. Is he afraid of what this raika could portend? All mirth I felt moments ago from our banter seeps out of me. I feel cold once more, hunching my shoulders in to bar against the cold.

"What do you mean?"

It's as if all noise is sucked out of the garden. The voices of our fellow diners sound muffled through the rush of blood to my ears. Killian shakes his head, but sighs when I persist in pinning him with a look.

"Things are bad Mallory. The jaeitsi bataruce have been gathering power. We know at least two have teamed up, so their control over deabrueon has increased. There have been deaths all throughout New York. All of the City Between is on guard, worried they'll find the other two jaeitsi before we can find them. My guess is that those six deabrueon you faced off with were theirs. Deabrueon don't tend to fight in packs like that and they certainly don't team up with raikas of their own accord. Assuming that's the case, the jaeitsi are the raika's bosses. If they don't want you dead, they probably want you for something else."

I had thought it was strange that the deabrueon were fighting together, but this is beyond what I'd imagined. This is the worst-case scenario.

"Like what?" My food sits utterly forgotten in front of me.

"I don't know. Like how about a new leader of the Vernis Lanin."

I stare him dead in the eye, looking for a sign he's joking. He doesn't waver, doesn't flinch, and I know he's serious.

"Well fuck," I sigh, doing my last shot. I study the bottle green shot glass, my dishevelled reflection looking back at me. "But I would never. They should know that from my fight with Thaddeus."

"To be honest Mallory, you're something of an enigma. And a rising topic of conversation. No one knows what became of Thaddeus after you faced off with him and, with him out of the picture, you're the only threat to the Onyevaras' power. There's growing discontent with them and a lot of dragoviks would love to see a monarch in power. Provided they're sane of course."

"Why are you telling me this? Surely that makes me a threat to the angeleru as well?" I ask suspiciously. Is he trying to bait me?

He shakes his head, wolfing down the rest of his sandwich before answering me.

"I remember when I first met you, when we spoke in the library. From what I've seen of you, I know you have no interest in taking power. Not to mention the fact you've eschewed magic for the past three years and entirely turned your back on being a dragovik, even at the cost of leaving your friends behind. I trust you," he says, holding my gaze with his emerald green eyes.

"I trust you too," I reply, "albeit tentatively. You did save my friend's life, so you win some points there."

"And let's not forget I never told anyone that you were the only one who survived the massacre at the Academy," he adds.

I go quiet. So, he has put it together.

"Don't worry, I won't tell anyone. I figured it wasn't you who killed them and I can tell by the look on your face that I'm right. You may have been trained to kill, but you wouldn't have done that. Those bodies were torn apart limb from limb. Whoever did it took pleasure in the act."

"It was the jaeitsi," I reply, looking at the ground. "Thaddeus had her do it to save me from Alastair. I think the bellatoja killed most of the members of the Academy though."

I don't mention that it was me who killed Alastair. It's another piece of my past I avoid, unless it crops up unbidden in my nightmares. I still struggle to reconcile what I did out of self-preservation with what small moral compass I have.

He nods, reaching across the table to take my untouched food.

"I pretty much figured he had something to do with it. Funny that he'd want to protect you though."

I don't reply. I trust Killian not to stab me in the back, but that doesn't mean I'm going to tell him my secrets. Certainly not the ones about Thaddeus. I can scarcely admit those to myself. The night we spent together… it turns my stomach just to think of it. Killian senses my reservations and puts his hands up in the air in mock surrender.

"I didn't mean to pry. Just seems odd. But hey, dragoviks are fiercely loyal to their own kind so it figures he wouldn't want to kill you. Probably just recruit you. That way you wouldn't be a threat to him."

I appreciate him providing me with a way out of the awkward topic, but still don't reply. I'm left chewing on the inside of my cheeks for a few moments while he finishes my sandwich and starts on the fries.

"So how have you managed to lay low and stay alive so long?" he asks, leaning back in his chair.

"I've got friends," I say.

"Well now I know you're not talking about the Caverlys, Leo, and Aaron."

"How?" I ask, the mention of their names making my heart beat faster. He's piqued my interest and he knows it.

"Aside from the fact you left them? For one thing, those four hardly speak to each other anymore. Leo and Aaron are in separate teams running missions for the Onyevaras, dispatching deabrueons. Robyn is studying to become a weapons forger in Miesarinda. And Kyle's been in prison there for some months now."

I drop the shot glass I'm still holding and it bounces across the table before falling into the gravel beneath our feet. Killian's face is totally impassive, no trace of a lie or a joke on it, not hidden in his eyes nor in the smooth lines of his full lips which yield no smile.

"I'm sorry, what?"

Chapter V.

Killian looks at me, unblinking, seemingly genuinely surprised I didn't know this. But he knows I left them behind in Aplin Hollow, so how can he be surprised? Not only that, I've all but cloistered myself away from this part of my life. And Kyle, in prison? I picture my friend, the paragon of kindness. What could he possibly have done to end up there? But loss can change a person. Losing Lilith changed me irrevocably, for the better I believe. I would never betray a friend as I had done her. Where has this loss bore into Kyle's soul; what spaces has it carved out? No. This must be a mistake. But even as I think it, my heart sinks. Killian wouldn't say this to me unless he was absolutely sure.

"I knew you had lost touch with them, but I figured these aforementioned friends of yours are supernatural, so the news would have got to you. It was a huge scandal. Rising diplomatic star of the Onyevaras found hiding a gods' weapon from the Hirutere. People lost it. The Onyevaras handed him over immediately."

"What?" I ask. There's no part of this statement I'm not utterly perplexed by.

"He was hiding a gods' weapon."

"You know the funny thing about repeating what you've just said is that it doesn't actually clarify anything," I say, and he rolls his eyes at me.

"Okay, okay. Several millennia ago, a master forger made twelve weapons, which were then blessed by twelve gods. Imbued with their power, they give their wielder unique powers in battle. But not just anyone can use one. The weapon has to choose you, bond with you. Or rather, the god that blessed it has to. It will do it upon first contact. Apparently, Kyle had been hiding one for a long time. It's the only gods' weapon that's never been seen before, only known about because the forger recorded all his creations in ledgers before he mysteriously died."

"Why can't Kyle have it if he bonded with it?"

"Problem is, he hasn't. They tested him with it. The sword won't unsheathe if you're not its bonded warrior. And part of the accords between the Onyevaras and Hirutere states that all gods' weapons found by a dragovik have to be turned over to the

Hirutere so they can pair them with a bellatoja. Basically, they're terrified a dragovik will bond with one and become a threat to the angeleru," he explains, shrugging before he does his last shot. "You want some more?"

"Definitely," I say without a moment's hesitation. "I'm surprised to hear you speak critically of your government."

"Like I told you three years ago, they forced me into being a bellatoja. As one, I've seen the bad they can do as well as the good, as have you. I have my reservations regarding them, which have been growing day by day in the face of the decisions they make regarding the threat of the jaeitsi. Instead of being proactive, it's like they're turning everyone else into the enemy, not focusing on the actual enemy. Besides, it's no secret that the accords are just a tool to oppress the dragoviks because you guys would overpower the angeleru in a heartbeat given the chance."

"Would?"

"I misspoke. Could overpower the angeleru. The truth is, most dragoviks are just looking for some place to call home. And it's a damn shame the angeleru won't let them have that. There would be more peace for everyone."

Is our desire so universal? I always felt a lack of home, a sense of being nomadic, but does it really extend to all dragoviks? It would make sense to me to let us share the City Between, but, even if the angeleru were so kind, which is unlikely, it would still be their home first. So, what's the alternative, letting us back through the portal to Sundalev, our homeland? No doubt Dragovicia has been reclaimed by some other creatures now. It's no longer our home. My thoughts are a tumult, but through them one thought calls out to me. Kyle. I have to focus on Kyle.

"So Kyle definitely didn't pair with the weapon? They could just be saying that. They clearly want these weapons desperately."

"No. If he had, they can't take it from him. He'd have the right to it until he dies, provided he fights alongside the Hirutere."

"What, they'd kill him otherwise?" I scoff. Killian's utterly silent. "They would, wouldn't they?"

"They used to. Not since the accords. Now they'd likely imprison him, keeping the weapon from him."

"But if he hadn't paired with it, why'd he keep it?" I ask,

scrounging about the basket for the last few fries.

"No one knows why he kept it. Like I said, he was kind of a goody two shoes and the darling of the Onyevaras. But it looks like he's headed for the chopping block. Breaking the accords is punishable by death."

My stomach drops as do the fries I'm holding. They're going to execute him over this? Rage rushes through me first, but I have to force that aside. Kyle's life is in danger. I have to think of something I can do to save him.

"What can we do?" I demand.

"I knew you were going to ask that. Which is one of the reasons I wanted to have this chat with you post deabrueon fight. The problem is, unless we can come up with a legitimate reason for him holding onto the weapon, we've got no case."

I fall back in my seat. Why would he keep it? Kyle's fascinated by history, but he wouldn't break the accords over something like that. No, it has to have meaning, there had to have been something sentimental about it. My mind wanders, trying to make sense of my friend's decision. Then it hits me. Could it possibly be?

"What was the weapon?"

Killian gives me a peculiar look, as though I'm something utterly unexpected. Fear for my friend he might have expected, but not this line of questioning.

"A katana. Why?"

"Shit. I know how to help Kyle."

My shoulders sag in relief, knowing I now have a way to save Kyle, but I'm also tense. If this means what I think it means, this is huge.

"You do? Hey wait," he says, as I grab my blazer and slip it on. Turning the collar back down, I look at him, surprised. He saved Kyle's life three years ago, but suddenly he's completely indifferent to it. *Headed for the chopping block.* That's exactly the kind of mindless carelessness for another life I should have expected of a bellatoja. My hands fall to fists by my sides.

"I can't wait, Kyle's life is in danger! You can sit around here if you want to, but I won't," I reply, slightly too loudly.

A few people glance at me, but they must assume I'm drunk. Which they wouldn't be wrong about. As I stand, a cloud veils my brain, drawing it into its smoky haze. The tequila has done its job, quickly and effectively. As it always does.

"I'm not saying I'm not going to help, but let's pay the bill first. I'd like to be able to come back here in the future. Then I'll take you to the City Between, Miesarinda. His trial is tomorrow, so we best hurry. Where's the damn waitress?"

Gone is the ease with which he had spoken moments ago. He's alighted with the same urgency as I am. My fists uncurl. Why do I assume the worst of him?

"How will we get there?" I ask, as he flags down the waitress and asks for the bill.

"Let's see, the fastest way in will probably be through the Library Between. We can go to the Brooklyn Public Library, but it will be closed by now."

"If breaking and entering is all that stands between me and Kyle, prepare yourself to see some dragovik magic."

* * *

The front of the library is relatively bleak looking, utilitarian with its expansive blank stone walls. This is excepting the ornately decorated columns and the panelled grate above the front door. We wait by the other grate, tarnished by time, which is drawn shut in front of the door, as a few people pass, before I press my palm to the lock.

"Matkur," I mutter, recalling the spell Robyn had used before.

As expected, the lock is not protected by any magic, so yields to my simple unlocking spell. We slide the grate open noisily, before I repeat the same process on the door. Following Killian in, I take a cursory glance around the dark library.

"How will you know which book it is?" I ask.

"An angeleru will always know. Besides, what, did you think, this was my first time?" he asks, grinning at me. I roll my eyes, but can't help but laugh. "Damn it's dark in here."

"Here," I say. Holding my hand out in front of us, I focus on lighting our way. An orb of light blooms in my hand and hovers a couple inches above it. It's cool, not lit by warm fire, but a pale flame.

"Nice," he says, before taking up my other hand and leading me past the welcome desks towards the information desk.

We take a right towards the languages, literature, and fiction section, and I make a mental note to come back to this library. Even if I do have to trek all the way to Brooklyn for it, the huge library is making it seem like a worthwhile journey. That and the pulled pork sandwiches. Suddenly this borough isn't looking too bad.

As Killian's grip tightens on my hand, a thought strikes me. What if this is all just an elaborate trap to get me to Miesarinda? Is Killian taking me to the Hirutere in connection with the death of Alistair and his men? He said he didn't think it was me who killed them, but how can I believe him? He also said I'm a rising topic of curiosity; perhaps the Hirutere are finally curious enough to bring me in for questioning. I swallow at the thought. I remember what they did to Thaddeus, how they tortured him. Will they do the same to me? Or worse, have they done that to Kyle? If Alistair's actions were anything to go off of, they certainly wouldn't shy away from using such torture.

The thought of the bellatoja captain, his last moments before I killed him, makes my stomach flip. My clothes stripped from my body forcefully, the welts on my back from the whip. My hands pulling the whip tighter around his throat until it sliced through his neck, thick and muscular. All that blood. I was a different person then, hell bent on revenge. After what happened in Aplin Hollow, I lost all semblance of what had made my life normal: Chloe and Connie's friendship, Inerea's guardianship. The only part of that life that survived was the place I had managed to get at NYU. All I want now is the peace and stability of my current life. Am I really going to drag myself back into this world?

But then I think of Kyle, his life at risk, and me, the only person who can save him with what I know, and I know there's no choice here. I owe him this much, if not more. So, so much more. But I'm certain what I owe I can never give.

Tightening my grip on Killian's hand, I resolve myself. Trap or not, I have to take the chance to save the life of the man who saved mine. I would never have had this life I love so much without Kyle. Killian glances at me, nodding wordlessly to a slender green clothbound volume. He reaches out and draws it towards him. In a flash, the library drops from sight and we're standing on that eerily familiar staircase of sandstone, though I've only been here once. Still Killian does not let go of my hand and I am grateful for the support. The memories associated with my last trip here bite into my thoughts, making me anxious. Can I really trust this person? Even if he saved Kyle once, it's been three years. Time can make us entirely different people. It can heal, it can wound.

We descend the stairs, coming to the precipice of the landing.

"Shall we?" he asks, and I nod, prepared from my last trip for the unpleasant sensation of falling. We leap over the edge, plummeting for a moment, before our bodies flip forwards. Killian yanks my arm to pull me onto the landing on the other side. Up the stairs we go, reaching the massive door ahead of us. With a twist of the knob, he pushes it open and leads me inside. There's a bright light that dissolves us.

The Library Between is as it was when last I visited. Breathtaking. I feel more able to appreciate its beauty in present company, more at ease than I was with all those bellatoja. We've entered a few stories down from last time and I can see the ground floor is crowded with people browsing bookshelves and making requests at the massive desk in the centre of the room. The towering tracery windows across the room let in a flood of golden light that washes over everything. I see the dust particles floating through it, swirling in the liveliness of the library. It's far from quiet in here, people chattering away, seeming almost more like a market than a library. Then a realisation dawns on me.

"It's day here," I say, looking at Killian.

When we left New York, it couldn't have been later than two or three in the morning. It's only been a matter of moments since we left Brooklyn and yet the day has aged swiftly in those minutes. The sun is at its peak outside the window.

"Time's a funny thing. It can sometimes be skewed when travelling from Earth to Miesarinda. Looks like tomorrow has just become today. And Kyle's trial is right now," he adds, nodding to the large clock in the middle of the help desk.

"Shit."

Pulling my hand, he leads me to the nearest ladder, which we both clamber down to reach the bottom floor. Looking around, I notice a couple girls approaching us, both their gazes set on Killian. Both are exceptionally beautiful, with flaxen gold hair and blue eyes. I see the touches of the angels in the glow of their fresh-faced, dewy skin and perfectly pinked cheeks.

"Hey Killian," one says, stepping in front of us. "Who's your friend?"

The second girl casts an appraising look over me, as though she has only just noticed my presence. I'm used to looks like this from other girls. But where it's usually bred from hostility, here it's no doubt from how different I seem to them. I must stand out like a sore thumb with my black hair and pale skin in this place of golden-haired people. Her look doesn't bother me though. If anything, it spurs me on to hurry, to get out of her line of sight.

"We so don't have time for this," I insist to Killian as he opens his mouth to speak to them.

"Sorry ladies, but my friend's right. We've got somewhere important to be." He takes up my hand again, which both girls frown at, before he drags me away. "They are going to be so pissed at me."

"For having something to do?"

"For hanging out with the most beautiful girl they've ever seen. Girls can be jealous creatures. Then again, so can guys."

I'm taken aback by his forwardness, but it quickly slips from my mind in the urgency of the situation. Kyle's trial is happening right now. They could already have decided his fate, if not executed their sentence. I pick up speed until we're both running across the library floor. All around us people dart out of our way, looking around in shock, as though they've never seen someone rushing before in their lives.

"No running!" a man calls out from behind the desk, but we ignore him. I'm grateful that, like me, Killian isn't a stickler for rules when it comes to protecting people.

We burst out through the great mahogany front doors onto a cobblestone street. The buildings we rush by look like the quaint narrow houses I've seen in photos of Amsterdam. A little wonky and overcrowded by windows, they make me slightly anxious, as if at any moment one will topple over and bring the lot down with it. They're made of various hues of brick, lighting up the city like a child's too vibrant toys, with wood beams streaked across them. The street seems to stretch on as far as I can see.

The road is packed with people going in every direction and it's something of an upstream battle to get through the crowd. As we make a right turn onto a wide boulevard, the street opens up towards a courtyard in which there is a massive rotunda made up of vast, beautifully decorated pale pink stained-glass windows and Corinthian columns painted in luminous gold. Looking at it in the sunlight is blinding, but it's too dazzling to look away. I've never seen or heard of anything like it, even in all of my reading.

"Is that where we're going?" I ask, as Killian tugs me past a couple. The man glares at us as I accidentally shoulder him. "Sorry!"

"That's the Hirutere's headquarters, where all trials take place. As this is a matter of breaking the accords, the Hirutere will want to make a spectacle of it. Punishing a dragovik sends out a message. The trial will be open to the public, in one of the courtrooms."

My heart tightens. I can't imagine it, using a life to make a point. But the Hirutere have proven themselves callous and cold to me on numerous occasions, if only through how their warriors have behaved.

Finally, we squeeze through the crowd and reach the glass doors of the building, which are open wide.

"A symbol that the Hirutere are available to their citizens at all times," Killian whispers, nodding at the doors as we slow to a walk and enter the building. "They're not, of course. But governments are all false promises these days."

I look around, nervous someone may have heard him, but no one seems interested in us. How can he so openly criticise his government? Crossing the pink marbled floor veined with gold, are men and women dressed in long, emerald green robes. They wear square topped hats with golden tassels. They must be government officials. We cross the entrance to the reception desk, where Killian clears his throat. The man behind the desk looks up, his face stoic, before he spots Killian and bursts into a smile.

"Ah Master Killian," the man says, bowing his head deeply. "It's so good to see you. How are you today?"

"Well sir, and yourself?" I give Killian an irritated look. Why is he wasting time with pleasantries? He ignores me, smiling at the man.

"Well, well. How can I help you?"

"We're here to see the trial of Kyle Caverly."

"Ah yes, quite the entertainment of the day. The year even," the man enthuses, clasping his hands together.

"Yes, nothing like watching someone being sentenced to death," I say, glaring openly at him.

Killian squeezes my hand, warning me that what I've said is a mistake, but the man seems to believe I'm being sincere. He laughs and flashes me a smile. I want desperately to punch him square in the face.

"The main courtroom. The trial's already well underway and it filled up quickly so you'll want to hurry."

"Thanks."

Killian guides me down a hall to the right before hissing in my ear.

"What were you thinking?"

"I'm sorry, my friend's life is on the line, I'm too preoccupied for pleasantries. Besides, what was with the whole Master Killian thing?"

The tips of his ears turn pink and he looks away from me as we continue down the curving corridor.

"My dad's head librarian. That commands a certain amount of respect around here."

At the end of the hall is a massive set of glass doors, leading out into a courtyard full of benches. The whole place is packed so, try as I might, standing on my tiptoes to make out the stand, I cannot.

"Is he up there yet?" I ask Killian, who stands half a foot taller me. He squints, leading me through the door. We step into the large courtyard, the stone walls of which are dripping in ivy and wisteria. The air is warm and sweet with its scent, but it seems almost sickly to me, so out of place is its fragrance. Not to mention the reminder it brings of Inerea's house, covered year-round with wisteria. I wonder now if she did not keep it in bloom with magic.

"Yup, I see him."

We sidle up to the back of the crowd, unable to make our way through it for its sheer density. I stand on my tiptoes, but all I can make out are more blonde-haired people and a man on a podium with one of those green hats. His eyes flicker up to the audience as he starts to speak, picking up from where he'd left off before our arrival.

"Let the record show that the accused has no explanation for why he kept the weapon, only that it was secreted away from the Hirutere, despite his knowing the accords state all gods' weapons must be turned over to the government. The accused was holding the weapon for an indeterminable amount of time. Therefore, it is possible, in fact, that the entirety of the Caverly family has been hiding this weapon from the Hirutere since the accords were first put down, as this is the first of it that has been seen since it was forged. Perhaps they have passed it down for generations, even."

"My family had nothing to do with this!"

The sound of Kyle's voice crying out makes my heart summersault. The panic in his words settles in my chest and becomes my own. Even with his life at risk, his family's lives are all that matter to him. Time has not changed him so much that he does not worry about those he loves in the face of imminent danger. All I want to do in this moment is fall to my knees before Kyle, beg for his forgiveness. But I can't do that unless I save him.

"This matter will be put to the court at a later date," the man continues, ignoring Kyle's protest. "As for the present, it is our decision that the accused will be sentenced to death for knowingly breaking the accords, as no evidence can be presented to prove his innocence or that he had a reasonable explanation for keeping the weapon from the Hirutere. Even if he had bonded with it, it would have been necessary for him to register its existence with the Hirutere and help our just cause of defending Earth from deabrueon. This ends the case of Kyle Caverly, dragovik, versus the people of Miesarinda."

People begin to stir, turning towards the door to leave. Still, I cannot make out Kyle through the crowd, which threatens to push me back out the door.

"Do I yell objection?" I ask Killian, turning to him frantically. A man in front of me shushes us, shaking his head.

"Move out of the way," he says gruffly.

"For fucks sake woman, yell something," Killian returns, eyes wide with panic. Why does he care so much?

"Objection!"

It comes out as an unearthly cry, all my panic releasing itself in a torrent. I start to shove through the crowd, which has now stopped trying to leave, making my way to where the man on the podium stands, and people yield to my frenzied pushes. All around, people turn to look at me, eyes wide with curiosity. Finally, the centre of the courtroom is visible to me as I emerge from the audience. I see in front of me the man on the podium, his eyes narrowed in my direction. Before him is a table, on which the katana lies. It is sheathed, but I know the blade will be bare of the swirling pattern once upon it, which now lives beneath my skin. But above all of this, what I search for is a pair of familiar dark eyes, which meet mine with shock. Kyle's jaw drops open as he takes me in and I him.

His hair is a mess of long curls and his cheeks have been made gaunt by his time in prison. He looks pained as he studies me, as if the loss of our friendship is striking him anew. But what breaks my heart the most is seeing that old wound. The one I could not protect him from. The right sleeve of the too large collared shirt he's wearing hangs limp and empty by his side. Without his right hand, they haven't bothered to handcuff him, that act serving as a reminder of his greatest loss and perceived weakness. I know he is strong even where people only see weakness, but it still breaks my heart to see him so.

"And who might you be?" the man on the podium demands.

Swallowing hard, the lump in my throat like a knot of thistles, I turn from Kyle to the man. It feels an impossibility to pry my eyes from Kyle, but I know who I must play to in order to sway the court in our favour.

"Mallory Thiel."

There's a rush of whispers through the crowd, as I anticipated there would be after what Killian told me about growing curiosity regarding me. I feel as a magnet, as they all seem to lean closer to hear what I have to say. The man's lip curls back.

"A dragovik. What place do you believe you have in this courtroom?"

"I believe the voice of honesty and reason has a place in any courtroom, be it that of the angeleru or the dragoviks," I reply, needling him with a keen glance.

I am not afraid of this man and I want him to know it. Whatever fear I may have felt is overwhelmed by my protectiveness for Kyle. The man smiles at me, but I can tell there's so much malice behind that smile. He only does so to cover the seething rage at my having the audacity to talk back, lurking just beneath the surface of his amiability.

"You object to the sentence? I am afraid it is the price of his crimes," he says, shrugging at me. The audience murmurs its assent.

"Oh the sentence is heinous for so small a crime, if it can even be called that. Although that is not the matter to which I refer. I object to the charges," I retort.

"On what grounds, girl," he snarls, his irritation now evident on his face. More whispers are drawn from the audience, but I cannot distinguish one from another. I need to be focused, poised, and proper. I must play by this man's rules to win the game.

"On those that the Hirutere has no right to this weapon."

He bites his tongue and lets out a low hiss, his face glowing with displeasure. This man is the worst kind of angeleru. Full of all the rage of Alistair, but with more authority. That last bit is evident from where he stands.

"It is stated in the accords that the weapon belongs to the Hirutere. This fact is indisputable."

"Only if you believe the accords supersede the ordination of a god."

"What is the meaning of this?" he demands, looking around. "How did this dragovik get here?"

He's not even going to give me the chance to make my case. He doesn't care about justice, just making an example of Kyle. A guard descends from his place beside Kyle and starts towards me. If he thinks I won't fight him, he has another thing coming.

"I brought her, Master Algard."

I spin around, shocked. While Killian helped me get here, I hadn't expected him to make what is essentially a public declaration of an alliance with a dragovik by acknowledging me. I know he is damning himself in doing so and can only hope the grace afforded to him by his father's position will protect him from incurring Algard's wrath. I suspect Algard's wrath is great and he will not overlook this public slight.

"Killian Varys? Why?"

"She said she had information pertaining to the case. As the Hirutere believes in fair trials, I thought it only fitting I bring her to share that information," Killian says, coming to stand beside me.

Now it's Killian's turn to hold the man fast with his look. But where Algard was all rage with me, he is stillness with Killian. He raises a hand to still the guard, then takes a moment to think things over. I can see the cognitive process he goes through. Is it worth potentially enraging the head of the Library Between by refusing his son this request? The position clearly carries a great deal of import amongst the angeleru, enough that it would concern even a member of the Hirutere. Is it worth contradicting Killian's statement about fair trials and executing Kyle without hearing me out, at the expense of seeming unjust to the audience that now studies his every move? He closes his eyes for a brief moment and I know we've won.

"Very well present your evidence."

Killian opens the gate leading up to the podium and the evidence table for me. I can see the disgust on Algard's face as he watches me approach and, uncharacteristically, I delight in the fact I irritate him. I reach for the sword, but my hand is grabbed by the nearby guard. He stares at me impassively, his grip manacle tight.

"Oh, for heaven's sake," Killian says, taking the man's hand from me and stepping between us, "don't touch her."

There's a gasp through the crowd and I'm almost overwhelmed by an urge to laugh at the near pantomime way in which they respond to everything. Killian's display of loyalty to a dragovik has shocked them, as it has me. Our eyes meet and he nods to me, telling me he trusts me entirely. I look down at the katana. I hope this works. This has to work. I take a deep breath.

When I wrap my hand around the grip, nothing happens. Shit. Isn't it supposed to do something? I glance nervously at Killian, whose expression betrays his concern that he's put his faith in a complete idiot. He raises his eyebrows at me, demanding an explanation. How to give it?

"I'm sorry is there a point to this display?" Algard asks. He's smiling now, seeming to believe I have no case. And I won't if the damned thing doesn't –

Then the sword gives and I'm drawing it from the sheath. It isn't a sudden burst of light like my magic, blossoming in my hand. Instead, the green jewel inlaid in the blade illuminates slowly. There's a quiet hum as it does so, which can be heard only for the absolute silence of everyone holding their breath. From it blooms the swirling pattern I recall. It stretches in both directions, up the blade and down to my hand, along my arm where it burrows itself in the crook of my elbow. There are cries of awe from around us and I even hear Killian's sharp intake of breath beside me. Of all the possibilities, this is not what he was expecting when I claimed to have a solution. I steady my gaze to meet Algard's. The look in his eyes tell me what I already knew: once again, I've won.

"The Hirutere has no claim to the weapon because it's already paired with me. Kyle Caverly was merely keeping it for me, which he had every right to do," I declare, my voice loud and emboldened by the current of strength pulsing through me. It takes all my effort not to gasp with the sheer magnitude of it. I feel as I have only done in my dreams: all fire and power. Algard's face falls and he looks around at the audience, as do I. On all their faces the same conclusion is readable: Kyle is innocent.

"Very well. Mallory Thiel is the owner of this weapon. Therefore, let the record show that the accused is cleared of all charges and his sentence is hereby void."

I breathe out a long sigh of relief before sheathing the katana in the black scabbard. The pattern fades instantly from both it and my arm as I remove my hand from the grip, attaching the scabbard to a belt loop on Lena's trousers. It falls to my side and I feel a sense of safety and warmth with it close to me. With my display over and the trial called to an end, the courtyard begins to clear out, though people still turn to peer at me. I turn to look at the only person in the room who matters in this moment.

He looks up at me, his face now devoid of emotion, the shock upon first seeing me having faded. I sense Killian following me, a few paces behind, as I approach Kyle. Kyle rises from his seat and steps down from the podium, neither of the guards stopping him. They give us both dirty looks and I think one mumbles "dragovik scum" under his breath. It doesn't bother me. Nothing fazes me except Kyle's gaze sweeping over me once, cold as I have never seen him before. He comes to a halt a few paces away and I mirror him, knowing there is a distance between us that I cannot close, not even given what I've just done.

"I guess we're even now," he says.

Chapter VI.

A little way back towards the library, we find a café that serves, according to Killian, the best gelato known to man, angeleru, dragovik, or deabrueon. I don't stop to inquire when and where he got a testimony as to the ice cream's greatness from a deabrueon. Instead, I spend the duration of our walk and wait studying Kyle, who remains silent all the way following his quip in the courtyard. Of course, I know exactly what he's implying: he saved my life, I saved his. Now we can wash our hands of one another for good, as he believes I attempted to do when I abandoned him. I want to tell him it's not so simple as that, but I know I don't have a right to explain my actions. Whatever reason I left for, it hurt him. That's all that matters.

Killian doesn't ask what we want, disappearing into the gelato store. It's crowded, which isn't surprising given how warm and sunny it is in Miesarinda. Kyle and I wait in silence, him kicking absentmindedly at some non-existent debris until Killian re-emerges from the café, balancing three cups of gelato in his hands. He leads us to a table just as a group of girls leave, all of whom are eyeing him up, before handing out the cups.

"I always know exactly what kind of ice cream people want. It's my gift, aside from my charm, wit, and dashing good looks. You're a butter pecan and earl grey girl, and you're a honeycomb kind of guy."

He sets the cups in front of each of us before pulling up a chair for himself. I glance at Killian, hoping he will somehow bolster my nerves. And he does. The assuredness and calm on his face lets me take an even breath, the first one since we left the rotunda. He holds my gaze and nods, telling me I can do this. Then we both look to Kyle for some indication of how this conversation will pan out. I have no idea what he must think of me in this moment. The girl who just saved his life, once his best friend, then vanished into thin air. Did he look for me? No doubt he had Robyn do a tracking spell. But she would never have been able to get past the wards Dominic arranged to have protecting me at all times. If she could, anyone could have found me.

"Beats prison food," Kyle says dryly, staring at the slowly melting gelato in front of him. Killian and I exchange a look. Kyle plunges his spoon in aggressively, jabbing the ice cream repeatedly. An all too apt metaphor for what he'd like to do to my face, no doubt.

"Kyle, I know you have a million questions," I start, but his cold look cuts me off.

"Like where the hell you went three years ago? Why you left me after you promised to stay? Why you didn't stick around to pick up the pieces?" he demands. Then the rage quickly drains from his face. He doesn't have the heart to sustain it. He simply looks exhausted, his face gaunt and cast with too many shadows. "Actually, no Mallory. I don't care. I don't want to know. I just want to go home."

I open my mouth to reply, but what can I say? I've never seen him like this, never could have imagined him like this, even. He looks so broken and betrayed, his eyes cast down, and I know a great deal of it is my doing. What isn't directly my fault is indirectly anyway, in the betrayal he feels by his own government for letting the Hirutere sentence him to death. Not to mention, he never would have come up against Clara and lost his arm if he hadn't been protecting me. I asked all too much of him simply by letting him care about me and gave nothing in return.

We sit in silence, neither Killian nor I able to say anything in response to the anger that has just been made manifest in Kyle's words. He seems so like a child, lashing out at me before I have the chance to betray his trust again. I have known that hurt. I know there is no apology worthy of its forgiveness.

"Well then, I guess we'll just go," Killian finally says, rising from the table. Kyle stands up to follow him. I'm about to follow too, but in my heart I know I cannot leave things like this. So, I ask the one question that's answer I know proves he still cares, because I'm too selfish to let him go.

"Why'd you keep the sword then?" I ask.

I shouldn't probe. I have no right to put him on the spot and ask this question I already know the answer to. Kyle looks stunned for a moment, as if he's uncertain himself. We had given it to Leora in exchange for her false help. He had to have gone out of his way after I left to retrieve it from amongst her possessions. Those aren't the actions of someone who doesn't care. And something tells me, if he kept it this long, it wasn't because it was too much effort to get rid of it. It would have been cathartic, spiteful even, to turn it over to the Hirutere, knowing it was mine.

Kyle looks down at the table before scratching his nose. I hear a quiet sniff and realise he's begun to cry. I want to spring to my feet and wrap my arms around him, but it is not my place, it is not my right, to be a source of comfort to him anymore. Instead of answering me, he slumps back into his seat and digs his spoon into the honeycomb ice cream, before taking a bite.

"I am a honeycomb man," he affirms, before looking up at me. His eyes have softened and are full of tears. "Because I'm a liar Mallory. Of course I care. I knew you had paired with the katana as soon as I saw the tracery on the sheath was gone. It might not have paired with anyone before, but I had read about it in books and knew that, when it bonds with someone, that pattern transfers from the blade to the wielder of the weapon. It couldn't have been Theodore, he was dead, as was Leora. If it had been Leo, Aaron, or Robyn, they would have been too proud to keep that to themselves. The sort of glory that comes with pairing with a gods' weapon is irresistible to most. You were the only other person who had seen it, the only person who would not know what it meant and, if you did, would want none of that glory. I hoped you would come back for it one day."

My heart drops into my stomach to see him so miserable. He's embarrassed by his confession, a child praying to a god he's uncertain about the existence of. I reach across the table hesitantly and take his hand in my own. He grips my hand tightly and sighs gently. Some relief floods into his eyes and I am grateful to be the one who put it there.

"You were wrong though."

"Is now really the time to be correcting me?" he asks, stifling a laugh. He tilts his face up to look at me, the sun shining flush across his cheeks, dispelling any shadows.

"I didn't come back for it, did I? I came back for you."

He smiles, letting out a soft sob and ducking his head to hide his face. Removing his hand from mine, he wipes his eyes.

"Why did you leave in the first place?"

I sigh staring at the gelato in front of me. I'm struck by how hungry I am, having hardly eaten at the restaurant with Killian. I take a mouthful and find he's right: it is some damn good gelato. Exactly what I would have ordered myself. What sort of perceptive person can read the flavour of ice cream someone most wants? Killian is a total riddle, what between his freely offered loyalty and his gelato ways.

"Leo and I – "

"Leo?" Kyle's voice goes sharp. He scowls. "I should have known he had something to do with it after he voiced his concerns about you coming to live with me in the kitchen that day. What the hell did he say to you that got so under your skin?" he demands, his face colouring with his upset.

"Don't Kyle. It wasn't his fault."

"Mallory, he knew you would feel guilty about what happened to me and took advantage of that to get you to leave."

"He was right at the time though, wasn't he? Look at the trouble I managed to get you in without even being a part of your life," I say, gesturing to the katana. "I'm the reason so many horrible things happened, the reason you got hurt. You would never have been in jeopardy were it not for me. Besides, after everything that happened, I couldn't. I just couldn't be there with you guys. Not in the place Inerea died. Not with the people I cared about yet cost so much."

"But I needed you."

His tone is accusatory, his eyes full of blame. I abandoned him and I don't think, even if he forgives me, he will ever get over that. And I have no right to expect him to. He had done so much to help me when I needed him most, but I could not offer the same to the man I called my closest friend.

"I know. I was selfish, I'm sorry. What, between Leo telling me it was best for you and everything I was going through, I couldn't think straight. You have no idea – no idea how hard it was for me to leave you behind," I say. I don't realise I'm crying until a tear drop falls onto the back of my hand. "Please forgive me, though I know what I've done is unforgivable. Please, forgive me."

He takes a deep breath and studies me. What's going on in his head is beyond my comprehension, but I can only pray that that overly generous spirit of his has not been stamped out for good by all it has cost him.

"Are you back?"

"What do you mean?" I ask.

"I mean are you back for good?"

He pins me with his gaze and I know what he's asking me. To go back three years, take back the decision I made, and come live with him in New York. I want to, so badly. I want to undo the wounds I have dealt, but all I'd be able to do now is make scars of them. I could heal them to scars, but they'd never be truly gone. There would always linger some of the resentment he has for me now.

"I can't," I say, shaking my head. "I have a life. A good, safe life. I'm happy."

It feels cruel to say those words. *I'm happy.* To say that when I know he can't be without me. His misery for the past three years is so evident and I know I could make it go away if I just say yes. But I'm too selfish for that. If I go with him, Dominic will have to protect both of us. Thaddeus may find out where I am. I've already risked as much by coming here. No doubt Clara and Thaddeus have spies who will tell them I've been here. Not to mention, if it was them that kidnapped me, they now know I'm in New York. I can't risk putting Kyle in that sort of danger again.

Kyle drops his gaze and nods. I open my mouth to say more but, just then, I hear someone clear their throat behind me.

Turning around, I see Algard towering by our table, casting his shadow over all of us.

"Mallory Thiel, was it?" he asks, squinting into the sunlight.

"Yes," I reply in a clipped tone, irritated that he's interrupted the conversation. More so by the fact he's pretending to have forgotten who I am in the span of twenty minutes. His pretence irritates me more than it usually would, given the present circumstances and the fact he tried to sentence my friend to death all of twenty minutes ago.

"Well, thank goodness you were here today. There could have been a great miscarriage of justice without you," he says, surveying me.

"I hear there's a lot of that here," I answer.

"You should be careful what you believe of what you hear about someone." He turns away, before pausing and returning. "It's funny Miss Thiel, I don't remember hearing much about you in the past three years. Not since, oh it must have been about the time Captain Alistair died. You met him, didn't you?"

A chill goes down my spine.

"I had the displeasure," I retort, holding his gaze. He can't know, can he? Not if Killian has kept my presence at the Academy that day a secret, as he's sworn he's done.

"A good soldier though. It's a shame what happened to him. And no one to receive punishment for the murders."

"It strikes me you enjoy administering punishment more than you like to see an innocent name cleared."

"When it is what's due, nothing gives me greater pleasure."

Without giving me the chance to reply, he smiles and walks away. I look to Killian, who seems anxious and confused. I know from that look that he hasn't betrayed me to Algard.

"Do you have any idea who you were speaking to?" Killian demands.

"A complete asshole who tried to sentence my friend to death," I answer.

"He's top dog in the Hirutere. That's why they had him handle Kyle's case. You don't want to be on his bad side."

"Like you are from getting me into the court?"

I still need to thank him for that. Words don't seem to be quite enough though.

"I can take care of myself," Killian assures me.

"I want to go home," Kyle interrupts, turning to Killian.

Slightly jarred by the interjection, Killian nods without answering, still standing beside us. Gelato forgotten, we all rise. They go ahead and I fall a few steps behind the pair, my head hung. I don't push against the jostling crowd as I'm knocked from side to side. The sharp jabs of elbows in my ribs and blunt force of shoulders against mine are a small but deserved punishment for the selfishness I've just exhibited.

And what to do with this sword? I have no use for it, no want of it. From what Killian has said, it could do a lot of good in the right hands. So why did the god of this weapon choose me? I look to

Kyle. I can't ask him to keep this memento of my betrayal. But perhaps Killian will. Maybe I should just give it back to the Hirutere and they can keep it until I die. Now there's a bleak thought. I have a sense Algard would be all too happy to expedite the process.

We re-enter the library and Killian takes us back up to the platform we entered on. The delight the library initially imbued me with has now receded to a blanched hollowness. Killian glances over his shoulder at me, a sympathetic look on his face, before opening the door.

* * *

I hadn't intended on accompanying Kyle all the way to his apartment, but at no point does it seem appropriate to leave him. The word goodbye seems such an impossibility just now, as it had done that day we sat side by side in his room, the battle behind us, wounds yet to heal. Some never did. Some new ones crept upon us after that.

We're standing outside his apartment on east second street as he fumbles with the keys, one of the personal effects returned to him after he was released from custody. He fits them into the lock and pushes his weight against the door. Looking back at Killian and me standing uncomfortably shoulder to shoulder, he hesitates in the doorway. He feels the weight of those seven letters just as I do. That is all that keeps us together now: a desire not to part.

"Well, I guess I'll not be seeing you," he says, his gaze lingering on my face. He wants me to betray some sense of regret at what I've done and what I'm about to do. I'm sure he must see it, plain as it is upon my face. "Unless."

I step forward, my heart pounding.

"Unless?"

"You want a cup of tea or something. You did save my life today."

Killian opens his mouth and begins to shake his head, but I swat him in the chest to silence him.

"Ow," he grumbles, rubbing his chest.

"We'd love one."

Kyle doesn't smile, just nods and turns away from me. I cannot tell if he's pleased or not that I've accepted his offer. Perhaps he was only saying it to be polite.

He holds the door open for us as we follow him in. We trundle up four flights of stairs to apartment fourteen and he unlocks the door. The key is jammed in the lock for a moment and he grumbles to himself in frustration as he wrestles with it. Finally, it yields to him, and we enter the apartment.

It's the early hours of the morning in New York now, time seemingly rewound when we left Miesarinda. The apartment is washed by a pale light. The inside is decorated simply, with light brown hardwood floors and a white linen sofa and armchairs. A glass coffee table with a marble base sits in the middle of the living room. It would be quite nice were it not for the clothes and weapons strewn everywhere. Not to mention the various dead plants.

"My ficus!" Kyle cries out, startling both Killian and me, as well as, no doubt, the neighbours.

He rushes across the room and inspects the few leaves that remain on its branches. Groaning, he takes in the rest of the apartment.

"This is a mess."

"Really like what you've done with the place, mate," Killian says, jabbing a crossbow with his foot.

"It's not me, it's my roommate," he sighs. "This is the last thing I wanted to come home to."

"Who– " I begin.

My question is soon answered.

"What is that ungodly shouting?" Aaron grumbles, opening his door and leaning against the doorframe. He's not wearing a shirt, only pyjama bottoms, displaying his muscular torso. His caramel hair is tousled across his forehead. He rubs his eyes and yawns before taking in the scene before him. His eyes land on Kyle first, who he has likely not seen since he went to prison. Then he scans the room and sees Killian, sparking anger on his face. Finally, he sees me. There's a rush of various emotions before his jaw drops. I have never, nor never expected, to see Aaron Baeor shocked.

"What the fuck."

"It's a long story," Kyle starts.

Kyle's voice brings him back to himself. He rushes towards

Kyle before he can finish speaking and pulls him into a hug. Kyle's eyes bulge slightly at the force with which Aaron holds him. He pats Aaron's back a few times before the latter finally steps back.

"How? I thought for sure they would charge you. I would have come, but the Hirutere bastards wouldn't let me."

"It's a bit of a funny story," Kyle starts, grinning at his friend, "but it's good to see you too."

My heart softens at the smile on his face. It's good to know there is some semblance of happiness in his life since I've left. That, despite what Killian said earlier about the four of them growing apart, at least Kyle and Aaron are still together. The two had not seemed so close when I was last with them, but that was after a year of separation while Kyle was working at the Academy. Again, my guilt floods to life. I was the reason he had grown so distant from his friends and now he hardly speaks to Leo or his own sister, according to Killian.

"You're really going to have to explain this," Aaron says, gesturing to Kyle, then the two of us, "but first, coffee."

"Only if you clean the apartment," Kyle counters, eyeing a pair of boxers with particular disgust.

"I was grieving!"

"I wasn't dead yet!"

Aaron shrugs then starts picking up his odds and ends from around the room, clearing room for Killian and me on the sofa, while Kyle makes coffee. I study him. He's adapted well to his loss of an arm; none of his movements are hindered by its absence. In twos, he carries steaming mugs of coffee over to us and sets them on the table, before sitting down in the armchair opposite Killian. He doesn't look at me, but examines the mess that has been made of his apartment in his absence instead.

"It's good you got back when you did. I was about to start looking for a roommate."

"Great," Kyle replies, adding creamer to his coffee.

Aaron flops into the chair beside him and grins at me, his usual ease returning.

"Now you I did not expect to see. Not that I'm complaining."

"It's good to see you too," I reply, and I mean it.

There were times I wondered if the four of them had survived their lives as dragoviks, perilous as they are. The confirmation they're all alive is a relief, though admittedly I'm grateful I don't have to face Robyn. I can't imagine her fury at seeing me again.

"So, what happened? They wouldn't let me visit you in prison or even come to the trial. No dragoviks allowed," Aaron scowls. "Fucking angeleru. Sorry."

"No worries," Killian says, nodding and taking a sip of his coffee.

He leans back and crosses his legs, clearly so at ease despite present company and Aaron's evident loathing of his kind. Something about his laid-back attitude soothes me. If he can be calm in the presence of a bellatoja hating dragovik, why can't I calm myself around Kyle?

Because with Killian, it's not personal. If anything, he's the exception to their hatred.

"Mallory happened," Kyle answers, still unable to bring himself to look at me. "She came and reclaimed the weapon. With her as the rightful owner, the Hirutere had no right to it and it was okay that I had it. That I was saving it for her."

He swallows hard with his embarrassment at having kept that part of me all these years, but Aaron doesn't tease him about it. Instead, his eyes soften, looking at Kyle as only someone who understands his pain in its entirety could. Has he been there all these years while Kyle suffered? I'd like to think so. I'd like to think Kyle had an anchor in the storm. For all his jokes and seeming insouciance, Aaron has always cared. He was good to me in Aplin Hollow, worrying after my wellbeing and comforting me when he could. I smile at him and his eyes find mine. There's a flicker of something within them. Then he turns back to the conversation.

"Hold on, you're telling me our little baby Thiel is the owner of a gods' weapon?" he says in a mix of awe and jealousy. "How'd that happen?"

"That day at Theodore's, I picked up the sword not knowing what it was. The pattern on it lit up and passed to me. I had no idea what it meant, so I left it behind. I guess the fact it was blessed by a god explains why Leora wanted it so much," I add.

Kyle nods thoughtfully and I find it comforting to be talking about something other than my leaving Aplin Hollow. Something we can agree upon.

"So, they just let you go?"

"They couldn't do anything," Kyle replies, shrugging. "She really saved me."

"Thank Killian. If he hadn't found me last night I'd never have known. And I'd probably be dead." Both of them look at me, curious. "Deabrueon attack."

"Sorry, I thought you abandoned us to get away from those sort of things?" Kyle says, and I flinch at the bite of accusation in his voice.

"Okay, someone's clearly not over things," Aaron quips, glancing down at his hands. "Awkward."

"Like you were okay with her leaving?" Kyle demands.

"I got over it." He doesn't sound too sure as he says it though.

"My being a shitty person aside, it's not a normal occurrence. I was at this party and some guy attacked my friend then knocked me out. When I came to, I was at the docks in Brooklyn and some raika and deabrueon were after me. It's the first time I've seen any part of your world in three years," I explain to Kyle, hoping to temper the anger in his eyes. My explanation seems to assuage him a little bit.

"First they knock you out, then they take you to Brooklyn? That's just evil. Why'd they take you?" Aaron asks, leaning forward with his elbows on his legs.

Suddenly it's just like the old days, all business and formulating plans. Some small part of me yearned for it all these years, though I didn't even know it. That part of me is satisfied by the way Aaron leans towards me, eyes sparked with interest, ready for the next mission. There was a time when my whole life was the mission, when Kyle had to ask me to pursue my life as much as Thaddeus' death. In a sense, everything I have done is to fulfil that promise, the promise to live and not just survive. Killian and I exchange a look and I gesture for him to explain.

"I think the jaeitsi may want Mallory for something."

The other two still, looking to me for confirmation. I nod, grimacing.

"You don't think one of them is Clara, do you?" Kyle asks.

Gone is his coldness, replaced only by concern, and I know

the man I came to love as my best friend is still here, despite what he's been through. If only I could reach through the armour he wraps himself in and get to him. I want so desperately to put my arms around him, to press my forehead to his. I just want all this distance to melt away and to be sitting back on his bed in Aplin Hollow, cuddled up and speaking of the future. Our future.

"Who's Clara?" Killian asks. Aaron and Kyle look sceptically at Killian, but, in the past day, I've come to trust him.

"The jaeitsi who went to the Academy, the one I mentioned to you that day back in the Library Between. She was working with Thaddeus when we fought him last, trying to help tear down the governments that had allowed our childhoods to happen," I say.

Aaron scowls, displeased with having to share intel with a bellatoja, but I ignore him. He's going to have to set his loathing of bellatoja aside, at least for this morning.

"If it is Clara, and Thaddeus is still with her, he may be after you," Kyle adds.

"Why would Thaddeus be after Mallory? He didn't want to kill her before, why now?" Killian asks.

Again, there's an awkward silence as the three of us try to reconcile my trust with Aaron's general loathing of the bellatoja.

"Thaddeus is sort of infatuated with Mallory. Obsessed may be more appropriate," Kyle answers, quickly changing the subject. "How did he find you after all this time?"

"I'm sorry, he's in love with you? Didn't he rape your mother?" Killian demands.

"Sort of the other way around actually." They all look at me in awe. "Yeah, remember when I lost it in the Library Between? It's because one of the books was a record of Thaddeus' time in prison and it had been imbued with his memories. I saw what really happened and then I found out from Alistair that Thaddeus was pretty much an innocent man unless you count being completely insane as a crime. Oh, and murdering my whole family. And probably some other people. So he wasn't entirely innocent. But he only became a monster after what the Hirutere did to him, after they tortured him."

And after Vaerdiexes abandoned him. I cannot forget that, once, Thaddeus had been chosen by a god. He had been chosen to restore dragoviks to Dragovicia and yet he had held strong through that. Even after what my mother did to him and he was imprisoned, he didn't fall apart. It was Vaerdiexes abandoning him that finally did it. I bite my lip.

"Okay, I need something stronger than coffee," Aaron says.

"It's six in the morning!" Kyle protests, as Aaron heads to the kitchen. He comes back with a bottle of whiskey and pours some in his coffee before offering the bottle to the rest of us.

"Why the fuck not," Killian sighs, taking it from him and proffering it to me.

"I'm good. You guys are alcoholics," I say, raising my eyebrows.

"I prefer the term self-medicating," Killian replies, taking a sip. He adds a bit more whiskey. "Okay, so Thaddeus was sort of innocent and obsessed with you. What does he want you for then?"

"Last time he tried to take me it was because he wanted me to be his queen," I sigh. "He thought it would consolidate his power to have the last of the Thiel and Ovira line as his right hand. And there was a disturbing mention of children."

Despite the fact I have a half-brother by him. The thought makes my stomach turn again. That's not something I'm ready to tell anyone about.

"That is beyond fucked up," Killian mutters.

Just then my phone starts ringing. I pull it out of my pocket and note I have twenty-four missed calls from Lena and Wesley. The former is who is calling now. Ah shit. She's going to be furious with me for ignoring her all night. She's probably been worried sick.

"Shit, I need to take this."

The others nod, their curiosity piqued. They all watch me as I step away from the table and accept the call.

"Mallory Thiel, where the fuck have you been? Forget the fact you bailed on the party. When I realised you were gone and couldn't reach you by phone, I ditched Noah and went back to my apartment, but you were nowhere to be seen. Except your stuff was still there, so I knew you hadn't gone home. But I went over to yours just in case because I was so freaking worried. No answer. I thought, hey maybe she got so drunk she finally went home with Wes, but he hadn't seen you either. We've been trying to get a hold of you all night. Explain yourself. Now," Lena demands furiously.

The memory of her shoe being tossed in the East River suddenly seems so comical to me in light of what's happened since, I can't help but laugh.

"Are you fucking laughing at me?"

"I'm sorry, I'm sorry. I ran into some old friends and time just kind of got away from us, you know?"

I hear a sharp inhale and know this explanation has only served to enrage her more.

"Old friends? At an NYU party? Also, hold on, you told me you talked to, like, no one from your past. What's going on?"

"Yeah, we hadn't spoken in years. But circumstance just kind of threw us together and I got distracted. I'm sorry."

"And what, your phone died? You didn't say a thing? Not to mention… someone was fucking murdered at the party. I thought something had happened to you."

I can hear she's on the verge of tears and suddenly am flooded with guilt. She's been worried sick about me, probably wondering if I met the same fate as Alice.

"Oh, what really?" I reply, feigning shock.

"It's insane, we were all questioned, but no one has any clue who did it. And, get this, she was run through with what they think was a sword. Insane. It's that girl, Alice, from your class."

"Holy shit. And no one saw anything?"

"Nope. I thought you were dead in a ditch somewhere. In my clothes no less."

"Your clothes are… well, okay funny story."

"What. Now."

"I might have got mugged."

"What? But you have your phone."

Shit. Good point.

"Yes, see I ran away, but in the process had to abandon your shoes. You know I'm dreadful in heels. I am so, so sorry and I will pay you back every cent for them."

Even though it will bankrupt me to do so. Guess I'll be living off of instant noodles for the next month. I sigh. I'm really going to miss food.

"Are you okay?"

"Yeah of course, I managed to dart out of there like a gazelle on cocaine. But did you hear me? Your shoes."

"Are not important in the face of your safety. Honestly Mallory, how shallow do you think I am?" she snaps. I can tell she's been up all night worried about me by how cranky she is, and rightfully so.

"Not shallow at all. You're an angel for checking up on me and I am so, so sorry, again, I cannot apologise enough. I love you to the ends of the Earth."

"I love you too. Just, don't do that ever again."

"I promise."

She takes a deep shaky breath, as if she hasn't breathed easy since I went missing. I wouldn't be surprised if that were the case. Lena might seem cold and aloof sometimes, but we're sisters. If anything happened to me, I know it would hit her hard.

"I'll see you Monday at the library, right? You still need to edit my paper and you really owe me now."

"Absolutely. See you Monday."

I hang up and glance over my shoulder to find the other three staring at me. Aaron has a bemused look on his face whereas the other two look slightly uncomfortable.

"You love someone?" he asks, a grin flashing on his face.

"My friend, you parsnip head," I say, swatting the back of his head before I land back on the sofa. "What were we talking about?"

"Your weird relationship with Thaddeus," Killian says, his coffee cup already drained. He grabs the bottle of whiskey and fills his mug.

"I think we're going to get along just fine," Aaron mutters, watching him, and the two tap their mugs together.

"And how the hell Thaddeus found you and why he only came looking now. I get the queen thing, but why after all these years? Surely he would have found you sooner?" Kyle adds. He looks mildly concerned in the face of Aaron and Killian's budding friendship, as I suspect he should be.

"That's what I don't understand," I sigh, "there's no way he could have found me."

"Why not?" Kyle asks. How to explain Dominic?

"Well, I have this friend, from back at the Academy. He's sort of been my lookout for the past three years while I went to university. It's how I've kept hidden from, well, everyone." Including

Robyn and Kyle. "I know he wouldn't let this happen. There's no way he'd slip up."

Dominic is my rock. I have utter faith in his ability to protect me, as he has always done. If Thaddeus found me…

"Oh no," I whisper.

"What?" Kyle's brow creases in concern. I snatch up my phone and dial Dominic's number. The line goes dead.

"His phone. It's been disconnected."

Panicking, I look at my phone screen. Amongst the flurry of calls from Wes and Lena is one missed call and voicemail from Dominic. Dominic never calls me. Between our nightly visits there's nothing to be discussed. He goes about his life and I mine. So if he did call me, something is seriously wrong. I dial my voicemail and wait, my heart frantic with anxiety. I skip through Lena and Wes' messages to get to his. His voice sounds fuzzy through the line, but I can hear the panic in it.

"Mallory, whatever you do, do not go back to the apartment. I can't keep you safe there anymore. They've killed Alice, which means they'll know where to find you soon. I'm sorry, so sorry. I shouldn't have interfered, I should have just kept you safe, but I wanted to make the world better for you, I wanted– "

He's cut off by a crash and a thud, then the line cuts out.

Part II

Chapter VII.

My world is spinning, my head a cacophony of thoughts and fears all clambering to be prioritised.

"Mallory, what's the matter?" a voice asks, but I'm not sure which of the three it is that's speaking.

Alice is dead.

How does he know she was killed? How does he even know Alice to know she was killed? My head spins in confusion. Were they working together to protect me, or was she someone else from the Academy that Dominic was helping live a normal life? If so, they both managed to keep it very quiet. My whole friendship with Alice suddenly seems a fabrication. Was it only ever a means to an end with her? What else can't I trust anymore? I shake my head, as if that will clear from it the detrital thoughts obscuring what is important.

Someone has broken into Dominic's apartment and possibly hurt him. Normally I'd be assured of Dominic's ability to take care of himself, but he sounded scared on the phone. That's all that matters right now. I need to find him before… my stomach turns. I will not lose him as I lost Lilith. Now is my turn to protect him.

"I need to go," I say, trembling as I stand, having collapsed on the sofa after listening to the voicemail. Only I stumble back onto the sofa, weak kneed and shaking. Killian leans towards me, helping me to my feet.

"Mallory, talk to us," he says calmly, holding my hands still. I could collapse against him so easily.

"It's Dominic. Someone's got him or broken into his apartment, I don't know, I just know I need to get to his apartment, right now."

"Do you know where he lives?" Killian asks.

Aaron's already on his feet, grabbing a sweater and jeans. He disappears into his room and re-emerges in seconds, fully dressed. Then he scours the room for the sword he wants. He buckles it to his belt, before trying to decide between the two daggers he's picked up. He settles on both. I watch him, finding something soothing in the methodical way he is preparing to do battle.

"Yes, he lives just around the corner from me, on Bleeker Street," I say, shaking violently. I cannot lose another person I love.

"Well let's go," Aaron says.

I breathe a sigh of relief. It's what I was hoping for, though I had dared not ask this of them. I dared not ask anything of them after the debt I already owe, but I should have known that Aaron would always rise to the occasion. And Killian has also proven himself immeasurably reliable in the past few hours.

"Thank you."

He, Killian, and I start towards the door, before realising someone is missing. We turn back, looking at Kyle, who is still sitting in his chair, nursing his cup of coffee.

"Come on," Aaron says urgently.

"Absolutely not," Kyle replies. He looks past Aaron to stare at me. "If you think you can just come back into our lives on your terms and drag us into your mess, you're wrong. I won't help you just for you to leave after you get what you want."

I hear both Killian and Aaron's sharp intakes of breath. My heart stings from his words. They are not misplaced, but they hurt all the same. Aaron recovers from this blow faster than I can.

"That's not fair Kyle, she needs our help. This is what we do. Besides, this isn't just about Mallory. Someone's died over this and her friend's life is at risk."

"No," he repeats stubbornly.

I can't fault him for this. I have done nothing to deserve his aid, especially not after he just got out of prison, which he was in because of me. I want so badly to close the chasm that yawns between us, but what could I possibly do that is worthy of even scratching the surface of forgiveness?

As I study Kyle, indignance bright in his eyes, I am suddenly assured of something. As I was when I healed Elias', the grey angel's, wings that night Lilith and I attempted to escape the Academy, I am aware I am capable of things beyond other's power. Beyond what there are spells for. And I know now what it is I can do for him. I walk to Kyle and crouch in front of the chair.

You are capable of greatness.

That warm voice I had heard when I was with Illarion, which I thought had abandoned me, wraps itself like gauze around my weary mind. It has not spoken in three years, but now it fluffs its feathers, preens, like a waking bird. Like the phoenix.

"Forgive me," I say, gently, though not as a question.

We hold one another's gaze and I can see the request catches him off guard. Enough so that it presents me with a gap in the armour he has worn since he saw me in the courtroom. He sets his mouth in a thin line, trying to remain resolute, but his eyes betray that he desires nothing more than to forgive me, to close what distance remains between us.

"No."

Then you leave me no choice.

I reach up, touching my hand to his shoulder. He looks uncomfortable, shifting in his chair, but not trying to get me off of him. Taking this as his wordless assent, I grip him ever so slightly tighter.

Let me show you happiness and kindness as you did me. Let me heal you as you did me, and Robyn years before. Let me take back what I should not be able to. Though you are whole without your arm, though you will always be a complete person for how full your heart is, let me turn back time, just this once. My heart pounds and I know what this will cost me. Not just a part of me, but time. My life shrinks and contracts beneath the burden of what I ask of my magic. But it is a price I am willing to pay.

Kyle cries out, suddenly trying to brush my hand off of him, but I only hold him tighter, keeping him from leaping out of his chair. I feel the place where his arm should meet his shoulder pulsing, as if a new heart is beating beneath the skin. Cells rapidly multiply, accommodating my spell's command. The new growth pushes itself forward, filling the length of his sleeve until his arm emerges, handless, from the end of it. A palm unfurls itself, then one, two, three, four, five; his fingers appear, like a flower blooming. When the spell is done, I feel colder, but the spark of happiness at what I've done for him keeps me warm. I draw my hand away, sagging slightly by his side.

Kyle raises his arm before him. He stares in awe, holding his hand to his face and wiggling his fingers one by one.

"Holy shit," Aaron and Killian breathe in unison.

"Forgive me. Though I don't deserve it yet, I promise I will," I say softly. It takes a moment for him to look away from the miracle I have just performed, but finally Kyle comes to gaze on me, tears in his eyes.

"That sounds like you're promising to be around long enough to earn it."

"I will be," I assure him, squeezing his new hand. I truly mean it. I cannot leave him a second time, no matter what it costs me.

He kneels on the floor before me and wraps his arms tightly around my shoulders, before bursting into sobs. They rattle us both. I bury my face in the crook between his neck and shoulder, finding I cannot help but cry myself.

"I missed you."

I don't know which one of us says it, or if perhaps we both do. All I know is that home is not a place but the arms that hold us.

* * *

Half an hour, many packs of tissues, and one extreme but swift post-prison makeover later, we're on Bleeker Street. Kyle does not let go of my hand the entire train ride, resting his head on my shoulder as we're jolted along. We emerge from the station and trek over to Dominic's flat. The urgency that had pressed me back in Kyle and Aaron's flat has restored itself to its throne in my chest, causing my heart to pound away. Checking no one else is looking at us, I unlock the front door and the others follow me into the building. We file down the narrow hall to the last apartment door. I take a deep breath, praying I won't find what it is I expect.

But there it is, exactly what I had hoped not to see: traces of something gone horribly wrong.

The door has been knocked off the top hinge and hangs ajar, leaning into his living room, as though it is bowing. I push past it and groan as I take in the room. All around me is chaos. The table and chairs have been upended, there are holes in the walls where bolts protrude. Whoever it was was firing to kill or seriously injure him. My breath hitches at the prospect of Dominic lying in the other room, his overturned body on the floor, blood igniting like fire across the hardwood flooring. It stays me for a moment and the others don't dare walk ahead either.

I regain my wits, if only just. I go into the bedroom and am relieved that the part of me that is somehow staying calm was right: he's not here. There's no blood, only signs of a struggle. His bedside lamp has been hurled across the room, shattered against the wall. But this is not what demands my attention. What I find odd is the suitcase splayed on the bed, half packed. Where was he going? I crouch beside it and begin sifting through the contents. Clothes, weapons, a fake passport. Two fake passports. I flip open the first and find a photo of Dominic, though the name reads Jack. The second contains my own photo, under the name of Beth. So, he was planning on taking me somewhere. I'm guessing it wasn't a holiday to Hawaii. What was so bad that we had to leave the country to get away from it? And, surely, if it was that dangerous, nowhere on this Earth would have kept us safe.

"He's not here," I call out to the others. I hear them begin to move around the living room, inspecting the damage no doubt and looking for clues.

Rummaging about, I run my hand along the bottom of the suitcase. My hand comes up against something rectangular, which I wrap my fist around. I procure a cell phone. Funny, this isn't the one I've seen him use. I turn it over in my hand. It has an entirely nondescript black case. Now I'm certain I don't recognise it. Dominic's usual phone features a horrendous photo case I ordered for him with a picture of us. I got it as a joke, but he's used it proudly since the day I got it for him. This must be a burner phone. I hold down the power button and the screen lights up. The background image is a photo but, before I can examine it, it's quickly populated by a flurry of text messages.

Alice is dead. Warn the others.

Get Mallory, it's no longer safe for her in New York.

They're coming. Casey must be protected at all costs.

I slide the unlock button and it takes me to the home screen. I'm surprised there's no passcode. There are only a few app icons on the home screen, lending itself to my theory that this is not his usual phone. I open the message app and thumb through the messages, unsure of what I am looking for until I see Alice's name pop up. What were they texting about? Something about this feels morbid, but necessary.

Alice: *I recast the cloaking spell. That should hold for a few more months.*

Dominic: *Thanks.*

Alice: *Mallory seems to be well. Still doesn't realise I'm from the Academy.*

Holy shit. I scroll down more.

Dominic: *She can't know that we're all meeting. She'd want to help us fight the jaeitsi. All that matters is keeping her safe.*

Alice: *Could use her power though. We're still going to get Casey later, right?*

Dominic: *Tomorrow night.*

That was two days ago. I scroll down to last night's message.

Dominic: *Where are you? Is Mallory safe at the party?*

I clutch the phone to my chest. Alice was from the Academy? Dominic must have enlisted her to look out for me then. But it seems from these texts there was a whole network of them working together, all aware of my existence and relationship with Dominic. And they're working to fight the jaeitsi, all while I enjoy a normal life. How could I be so selfish and blind to what he was doing? We spent so much time together and he never mentioned any of it. Then again, I didn't exactly ask. I look down at the phone again.

All of this leads me to the necessary question: who's Casey? Why is she so important?

"Mallory?" Kyle enters the room cautiously, surveying it as he does. "Did you find anything?"

Wordlessly I hand him the phone. I hear him tap on the screen, thumbing through the texts.

"So, they knew each other. They were going to try and fight the jaeitsi?"

"Who was?" Killian asks, coming in with Aaron. "No blood out there, so it's safe to say whoever broke in took him alive."

"They must have been strong to take him," I croak, my throat gone hoarse. Kyle places his hand on my shoulder, giving it a squeeze.

"Who was trying to fight the jaeitsi?" Killian reiterates.

"Old members of the Academy. It seems Dominic was something of a lynchpin for the operation," Kyle says. "All of these texts look like mission reports. They've been running interference, preventing the jaeitsi from gathering intel or weapons. Hang on."

He frowns at the phone before handing it to me.

"What is it?"

"New text."

I look down at the screen.

Emmett: *Emergency meeting. Usual place isn't safe. Merchants Refrigerating Company Warehouse. All attend. One hour from now.*

I turn to the other three.

"Well, I guess I know where we're going next."

Killian peers over my shoulder to read the text.

"Well, there's no way we're getting on the F train armed like this," he says, gesturing at our swords.

"Taxi?" Kyle replies hopefully.

"We could always pretend to be cosplayers," Aaron suggests.

"Cosplaying what?" I ask. "Generic dude with sword?"

"Excuse me. Extremely sexy dude with sword," Aaron replies in mock offence.

Killian raises his eyebrows, but I just shrug. He'll get used to Aaron's cocky attitude in no time.

"Yes, he's always like this," Kyle sighs. "Fine, I guess we'll walk."

It's not quite two miles to the warehouse, just by Chelsea Market. Kyle sticks close to my side the entire way, but we don't speak. I'm not sure whether he's worried for my safety or thinks me a flight risk. The usually busy area seems eerily quiet given the time of day. I remember walking down the Highline from Hudson Yard to Chelsea Market with Lena just a few weeks ago. We had gone to the market to get food and gossip about everything going on in our lives. Now those little things, the humorous encounters with classmates we recalled, seem so far away, as if I'm reaching blindly through water for them. No, it is thicker than water. It's blood.

We find the entrance to the warehouse around the back of the market. It looks like it's in disuse, but, then again, that would be the perfect place for the likes of what was raised at the Academy to meet. Especially if they're trying to go undetected by the jaeitsi.

The door is unlocked, so we slip in soundlessly, one by one. The warehouse has been emptied out of any cargo and the only furniture in the room is a table and some chairs in the corner, as well as a few crates that have been gathered together into a makeshift stage. Already there is a throng of people standing around it, though none of them are speaking. They all look as I feel: ill-suited to their own skin and this world they find themselves in. These could only be the faces of Academy members. Atop the crates, two men murmur to one another in hushed tones. One of them nods to the other before descending. The second man sighs, scratching the back of his head before turning to his audience and clearing his throat.

"You all know why I've called you here," he starts.

"That must be Emmett," I whisper to Kyle, who puts a finger to his lips and draws me into the shadows. We're not supposed to be here and there's no knowing how these creatures will react to strangers showing up, especially after one of their people has been killed and another kidnapped.

"Last night, one of our sisters fell. She was killed before she could complete her mission. We have, as of yet, not heard back from Dominic, who was supposed to aid her in this most important task."

My heart seizes at his name. Emmett surveys the crowd, taking in the murmurs of concern that filter through them. They don't know Dominic was taken yet.

"With Dominic gone, I will be taking his place, assigning missions and determining our next moves in light of these horrific events. As you all know, their mission was of the utmost importance to our cause. There's no doubt why Alice was killed, meaning Mallory Thiel's location is no longer a secret from the jaeitsi either. It is imperative that both Mallory and Casey are retrieved before the jaeitsi find them. As for Dominic, we can only hope that he will meet such peace as Alice soon."

Before any of my companions can hold me back, I step forwards. My bare feet move soundlessly across the floor, but Emmett sees me emerge from the shadows. Two men either side of the stage draw their swords and the crowd spins round. I hear a few snarls and watch in awe as one member of the crowd steps forward to reveal he has horns not unlike a goat's. They begin to close ranks around me, prepared to wipe out any potential threat. I don't doubt they could do it if they were all trained as I was. But I don't bow to fear. Instead, I hold Emmett's gaze, tilting my chin up.

"You would wish for his death?" I demand.

"Seize her," Emmett commands, and the two guards begin their approach. The crowd draws back, cutting a path for them.

"Mallory," Kyle hisses, pulling on my arm, "don't question the nice man with the armed guards."

"Mallory?" Emmett asks, blinking at me a few times. He raises a hand and the guards halt. Descending from the crates, he walks towards me. I can tell from the sweep of his gaze he's sizing me up. If anyone should know that something is not what it seems, it would be a member of the Academy. "You're Dominic's Mallory. Mallory Thiel?"

"That's right," I say, raising my head proudly when he says this.

"How did you find us?"

"I went to Dominic's apartment and found his phone in a suitcase he had packed. He's missing," I add, and I can hear the hint of imploration in my tone. If they know who took him, maybe they can help me get him back.

Emmett's eyes draw to my face, trying to read the emotions that drive my plea. Does my affection so readily betray itself? I don't care if it does. I'm not ashamed of how I feel. Finally, he nods. Without looking away, he waves a hand over his shoulder. The crowd disperses at his command, breaking off into little groups but staying, by and large, quiet.

"Come with me," he says.

As we cross to the other side of the warehouse, I feel all eyes following me. The way Emmett referred to me, they seem to all know who I am. Do they think me a coward for not joining their cause sooner? Would that I could have. If I had known Dominic was putting his life in danger every day, he's right, I would have given up my life at NYU to help. Especially if it was important to him. Now, I fear, I'll have no choice but to slip into the old skin of this dangerous life.

We reach the back right corner of the room where the table has been set up with six fold out chairs. Emmett pulls back a chair and gestures for me to take a seat. The others gather around, sitting down and looking towards Emmett. His eyes are only for me though, still trying to pry me open. His stare is intrusive, trying to find the core of me, and it sets me on edge. As if I wasn't already tense enough.

"I must admit you're not what I expected."

"I get that a lot," I reply, brushing off his attempt at small talk.

"I've wanted to meet you for a long time, but Dominic forbade anyone other than Alice from making contact. He wouldn't even give us your location."

"He was your leader?" I ask.

There's a flash of displeasure on Emmett's face, the kind that only those who have been second in command too long get when their hunger for power becomes an insatiable beast. Is he pleased, then, to see Dominic gone?

"Yes. After leaving the Academy, Dominic began organising our group. It offers protection to those who need it and, more recently, thwarts the jaeitsi's plans where it can. We're successful less often than we'd care for of late."

"What's happened to Dominic?"

He raises his pale blonde eyebrows at my forwardness.

"You want to know the truth? If you didn't find him dead, he was likely kidnapped and is being tortured for information."

My heart clutches at what I know must be true. The jaeitsi are certainly capable of that and worse from what I know of Clara.

"Then I'll cast a locator spell," I say, reaching for the burner phone "I can do it using this."

Emmett shakes his head and leans forward to take my hand in a comforting gesture that is devoid of any comfort. There is an end goal in doing this, one I cannot read in his face yet. I want to recoil from his touch but sense it would be rude.

"It won't work. They'll have witches to ward off any attempts to locate them. If it were so simple, the Hirutere would have found them by now."

"Then what can we do?"

"To help Dominic? I'm afraid there's nothing that can be done for now. Our best course of action is to continue with the cause and hope a resolution to the rising conflict means the recovery of our friend."

I swallow hard, staring down at my hands. Dominic's done so much to protect me. Here I am with the chance to help him and there's nothing I can do. Nothing but help this complete stranger in whatever way I can. But I have no choice. If there's any chance helping Emmett will lead to saving Dominic, I'll do whatever he asks.

"What can we do?" I ask again.

Emmett smiles, leaning back in his chair, and there's a hint of self-satisfaction in his eyes. So that was his aim. Does he think he's successfully manipulated me for his gain? I see right through him, but I don't care. I'll do anything to help Dominic, even if it means playing into Emmett's hands.

"Dominic and Alice were supposed to carry out a mission. They were going to recover a girl named Casey Astor."

"To what end?" Aaron asks. I had all but forgotten about the others' presence at the table until then.

Emmett looks at him coolly, the feigned kindness dropping like a mask as he takes in the other three. My impression? He's not fond of outsiders, nor is he certain of how to interact with them. Though I'm a stranger, I'm a fellow Academy student, as well as someone they've taken it upon themselves to protect. These three could be anyone; they could be spies and for that they are not welcome. That much has been made clear from Emmett's failure to address them all this time. The only reason they're not being tied up by the guards is because of the courtesy extended to them on my behalf.

"Let's just say she's vital to the cause. I'm not at liberty to share more information than that at present," he says, before turning back to me. "If you want to help Dominic, find Casey. Bring her to us. We can take things from there."

"And why can't you get her?" Aaron interrupts again. I glare at him, but he ignores me. Emmett shrugs.

"I could. But if Mallory is willing to help, we could use the extra set of hands. Our people are stretched thin as it is. Besides, Dominic trusted Mallory more than anyone, which means she's the best person to take his place."

Aaron accepts his answer, leaning back in his chair and looking to me.

"What do you think?" he asks. I chew the insides of my cheeks. Am I willing to risk our lives in this vain pursuit? For Dominic, yes.

"Let's do it."

"I'll give you the address," Emmett says, taking a sheet of paper and a pencil from the table. He scribbles down the details. The others rise, preparing to leave, but my mind is caught on something.

Dominic trusted Mallory more than anyone.

What gives Emmett that impression and why did he sound so bitter when he said it? If Dominic had trusted me, why hadn't he told me about his double life?

But I should know better than to ask myself that question. He did it for the same reason he has done everything: to keep me safe.

Chapter VIII.

The address that Emmett gives us is in Williamsburg. We catch the L train and, aside from one old woman whose mouth shapes into a small 'o' at the sight of us, no one seems to care that we're heavily armed. Luckily, New Yorkers are really just worried about where they're going to next. It makes trekking across the city decked out with weapons a whole lot easier. I don't think we could have got away with this in Aplin Hollow.

"Brooklyn twice in twenty-four hours? I'm cursed," Killian grumbles.

"You went there willingly the first time," I remind him.

"Hey, she was pretty and really nice. Dumb as a post though," he adds, seemingly disappointed.

"Why'd you go out with her then?" I ask.

"She seemed alright when we talked on Bumble."

"I'm sorry, bellatoja go on Bumble?" I laugh.

"Birds got to fly, fish got to swim," he answers, shrugging.

The train stutters to a stop for a moment and I crash against Killian's chest. He catches me in his arms, holding me a moment before setting me upright. His comment about finding me beautiful floats back into my head. Is it so surprising to find that someone like him, who knows all the secrets of my past at the Academy, finds me attractive? Yes, of course it is. I never thought anyone could knowingly find me so if they knew what a monster life has made of me. Up until now, I thought only someone equally as damaged as me could ever notice me like that. Thaddeus made sure I would feel that way. But it doesn't matter. It doesn't change anything. I cannot allow my feelings to get confused. Dominic is the only person for me, the only person who could understand what I've been through. Without our mutual understanding, how could a relationship function? Killian is too at ease with the world, something I've only learned to emulate during my time in New York. At heart, I am still so scared of it.

"I'd recommend holding it." Killian interrupts my thoughts.

"What?"

"The bar," he says, nodding to the handle to our right.

"Oh, yeah of course," I mumble, blushing furiously. Why am I acting like such a moron all of a sudden?

I turn from Killian to Kyle, who, every few seconds, glances down at his arm and flexes his fingers.

"How does it feel?"

"It feels like you performed a miracle," he replies, beaming at me. "I've heard of a lot of powerful witches, but nothing like this."

I shrug as if it's no big deal, because, to be honest, doing something like this for him isn't. I'd let him draw me back into this world of magic that I so readily abandoned in a heartbeat and I'd give up part of my lifespan to bring him comfort. No, more than comfort. I've healed the constant reminder of the wounds I inflicted that cannot be seen. As much as I did it for him, it does something to ease my guilt as well. Everything I do, will it always be tainted by such selfishness?

"I just heard this voice in my head and I knew I could do it," I explain.

Aaron and Killian raise their eyebrows.

"Party of two, Thaddeus Velemir, party of two," Aaron says.

"Hey!"

"I'm just saying, you're hearing voices? That's concerning," he replies.

"I have to agree with Aaron on this one. I should do some research when we get back from Brooklyn. Of course, getting access to the Library Between will be impossible now. I've probably been blacklisted," Kyle sighs, a look of sadness clouding his blue eyes.

"I've got you covered buddy," Killian says. "We'll sort out Miss Insanity in no time."

"Why can't I be Performer of Miracles?" I demand.

"Praising you isn't as fun as teasing you," Aaron says, tousling my hair.

I seethe at Killian and Aaron silently, but, really, I'm just glad they can get along. Aaron's long-standing hostility towards the bellatoja made me worry this would be difficult. And after our last encounter with them, I can't blame him. Hopefully his time working for the Onyevaras has shown him the better side of the bellatoja.

I feel Kyle wrap his arm around me and draw me close to him.

"Hey," I say, resting my head against his shoulder.

"Hey. You know you owe me one massive catch-up session after all of this, right?"

"Oh, there might even be coffee. If you've managed to get over your addiction."

"I'm a strictly one cup a day guy now. And I've already had one this morning."

"Guess I'll have to stick around until tomorrow."

He grins and kisses my forehead. I notice Killian studying us, a small crease in his brow. Kyle steps away from me and gets off the train with Aaron by his side. I fall into step beside Killian.

"Are you just universally adored by men?" Killian asks as we exit the train. I frown at him.

"Kyle doesn't adore me. He's my best friend," I assure him. He raises his eyebrows.

"If you say so."

I try to ignore what he's said as we emerge on Montrose Avenue. Killian just doesn't understand our friendship. It's unencumbered by the usual concerns of a female male relationship. Kyle and I have put each other back together as only two people utterly comfortable with one another could have done. Whatever Killian is doing with those girls in the library and the girl on his date, it's nothing akin to what Kyle and I have. They will never have the part of Killian that Kyle and I share with one another. That much was evident when Killian chose me over that girl on his date, and then again with those two young women in the library.

I stop myself in my tracks. Am I jealous of those girls? I groan to myself.

"You okay? Chilli cheese fries not sitting well with you?" Killian asks.

"No, I could actually go for a vat of them right now. It's nothing," I assure him, my cheeks flushing from his attention. No. No way am I jealous. What's there to be jealous of, Killian's attention?

"Whatever you say boss."

Eager for a distraction, I pull out the piece of paper with the address and directions from the station on it. Emmett was very specific that we weren't to use our phones to get there in case they'd been tapped. Even the jaeitsi are caught up on twenty-first century technology it seems. We head up Mesrole Street until we reach the building. Across the road are buildings covered in graffiti and dumpsters overflowing with trash. By now the sun has begun to set over the low apartment blocks, winking out of sight. Glancing up, I see a few lights are on inside the building we're supposed to find Casey in. The absence of the usual hum of busy streets sets me on edge.

"I guess we buzz the apartment?" I say, unsure of how to proceed. Does this girl even know we're coming to get her? Emmett didn't give us any information other than that she was key to defeating the jaeitsi. Which makes her extremely important as well as being in a whole lot of danger. But we can't just walk in and expect her to believe everything we tell her. Which is practically nothing because Emmett was very cagey with the details.

"Hey, it's your mission, we're just the muscle. Well, the extra muscle, you're also the muscle," Aaron clarifies, squeezing my bicep.

I press the button next to the faded number four. No answer. Again, I hold it down, but the door doesn't give.

"Guess we'll do this the old-fashioned way," I mutter.

Just then, an old lady emerges from the building. She smiles at me and I quickly return the smile, holding the door open for her. I watch her walk a little way down the street before we enter the building.

"Why's it always magic with you?" Aaron teases, shaking his head. "Junkie."

"I think I preferred Miss Insanity. Junkie is better suited for Kyle," I call after him as he bounds up the staircase.

"I haven't had a coffee problem in a very long time."

"That's because you've depression slept your way through the past three years," Aaron calls back down the stairs.

I know he's probably joking or exaggerating, but I still hate to hear him say anything such as that about how Kyle has coped with my absence. I glance over my shoulder at Kyle, but he's pointedly looking away from me. In light of my healing him, it seems he wishes to spare me his distress. I want to tell him he doesn't have to, that I will hold his hand through all of his pain, but how can I do that with the others around? Besides, whatever I've done, I still haven't traversed the chasm between us made by abandonment and three years of separation. There's so much distance yet to travel between us, all I've done is build the bridge by which we can cross it. We trundle up the stairs after Aaron.

Aaron's waiting for us on the landing when we get upstairs and I note his hand is already resting on his pommel. He's preparing for the worst, which doesn't make me feel any better about this situation. Once we've all gathered around, he knocks on the door twice. We wait with baited breath, but no reply comes.

"What if they're not in?" I ask, pressing my ear to the door. Nothing.

"That's possible. They might be out for tacos and margaritas at that Mexican place we saw. Or whatever got to Dominic and Alice got to Casey too," Killian suggests.

They all draw their swords, metal singing through the air, and circle around the door. Only I remain with my katana still sheathed.

"So, you're thinking death trap?" I ask them, then realise they're all looking at me. "What?"

"Do the honours," Aaron says, nodding to the handle. I put my hand on it, prepared to unlock it with magic, but the door simply gives way. "Not good."

Unlike Dominic's apartment, the inside is not trashed. There are plates piled in the sink, paintings on the wall of ambiguous shapes. It seems nothing is out of the ordinary.

"We have got to start viewing some nicer apartments," Killian says.

"That's what you get for looking in Brooklyn and Greenwich Village," Aaron replies.

"Greenwich Village is really nice!" I protest.

"It's a student hell hole is what it is."

While we're arguing, Killian steps forward and surveys the room before turning back to us.

"Again, no blood. Whatever it was probably took her," he says.

"Why isn't that comforting?" I grumble.

"Because evil fallen angeleru are kidnapping powerful supernatural creatures in a bid for power."

"Oh right, that. You guys check upstairs, I'll check the bedroom," I say.

Aaron hesitates, clearly wanting to come with me. He's used to the days of having to protect me, but I'm more than capable of taking care of myself, even if I'm three years out of practice.

"She can handle herself. Trust me," Killian assures him on my behalf.

I smile at him then watch them ascend the stairs. Crossing the living room, I slide open the bedroom door, which is already partly ajar. What I see when I cross the threshold makes me scream.

* * *

Why is there always blood?

My hands are slick with it.

That body on the floor, did I put it there?

I don't remember what's happened between my opening the door and reaching the middle of the room, only that time seems, as it did when we went to Miesarinda, to have folded in upon itself. I look out the window. It's still night. Only the night is red. The moon is painted and comes up blood.

The walls seem to heave, as if I'm trapped inside a giant set of lungs. They are porous, gushing more and more of the sick red liquid. It spills across the floor in gallons, rising to my knees. I scream. It washes over the body.

Who is it though? Casey?

My sword is in my hand and I can feel the ferocity of its power vibrating through me. Is this what you do, then? Is this your power? Possess me and bend me to your will of death? As if I'm not already its servant. But the sword has not done this the other few times I've held it. Why this time; why now?

I wade across the room, the blood sloshing around my legs. I feel it begin to seep through my trousers, warm and still full of the life it once supplied to a living creature. Plunging a hand into it, I feel for the body, but come up empty handed. No, I come up red. I drop to my knees, the weight of my body collapsing emitting a splash in the deep pool. My sword slips from my hand into the pool of blood as I let it go and begin searching frantically. I feel an arm and work my fingers up to the head. I feel it then, the face, and I know whose it is.

Dominic.

The sob that comes out of me is not human. It is a guttural

bellow, the crash of distance collapsing. He is back in my arms, yes, but he is gone. Perhaps it is a sound entirely too human, used to death as dragoviks are. I draw his head above the surface and clutch him to me. The blood is war paint. The war is a lost cause.

"No, no, no," I whimper, my breaths ragged.

I bend over him, kissing his forehead. I cannot taste the copper coin of the blood on my lips. It tastes like nothing.

I hear stirring in the blood behind me and spin around, Dominic slipping from my arms.

Towering over my kneeling figure, Thaddeus looks at me, eyes pained.

"Why?" I whimper, cowering away. He has never scared me so much as he does in this moment.

"You shouldn't have chosen him over me," he says, kneeling beside me. With a bloodied hand, he strokes my cheek and the pain eases out of his expression. I have calmed the pure savagery within him. He pulls me to him and I am powerless to resist his strength in the shock of my loss.

"You shouldn't have left me," he says, as if he hadn't left me for worse than dead on the forest floor. As if, even if Dominic didn't exist, I could ever, would ever choose to be with him. My stomach drops and grows warm, a belly full of rage and hatred that I did not know myself capable of.

I throw my arms up, breaking free of his grip, and claw at his face. He cries out in pain, stumbling back. Why is he so startled that I would attack him after what he's done? In his eyes there is an innocence that doesn't belong to him. It almost stays my hand.

"You killed him!" I scream, before throwing myself upon him.

He struggles beneath my weight, but I am pure in my ferocity. Even though he is much larger than me, my strength outdoes his. I wrap my hands around his throat, pushing him beneath the surface of the blood. There's a sickening gargle before he disappears. His hands flail above the surface, trying to grab at me. I feel him writhing beneath me, trying to kick my weight off of him, but I am too strong.

"Mallory, stop!" a voice calls.

There is no sense to be spoken into this situation. You cannot reason with me to spare his life, I want to tell whoever speaks.

"Mallory!"

Suddenly there are hands on my arms, pulling me away, but, when I look, I see no bodies. I see no hands.

"Mallory, stop!"

Why are they stopping me? This man murdered my grandmother, killed the closest person I had to family, and left his body for me to find.

"He deserves it!" I cry, clawing at the invisible bodies.

I hear a sharp intake of breath as I make contact with flesh that is not flesh. What manner of creature is this that doesn't show itself? I can faintly make out their footsteps as they attempt to drag me from the room. I lunge, biting one of their ankles, and whoever it is lets out a sharp cry of pain. Scrambling to my feet, I pounce on Thaddeus again, who has only just sat upright and is gasping for breath.

"Please, stop!"

The sincerity he commands does not belong to him. Whose voice is wrapped around your tongue? You don't sound like him at all, all hunger and skin barely able to keep its bones together. You sound soft and scared. You won't lash out at me to keep yourself from harm. Why is that?

The hands are on me again. This time, they are more careful, avoiding my attempts to bite them. They pull me from the room. We're over the threshold of the bedroom now.

I blink and the apartment snaps back into clarity. The blood I felt dripping off of every inch of my body is gone. I stop fighting against the arms that hold me, falling slack, and they let me go. There's caution in the way these creatures back away from me, but I know they don't want to hurt me. I spin around, looking for Thaddeus, but he is gone. The bedroom is no longer filled with blood and the body is gone. In its place, I see only Kyle lying on the ground, his hands on his throat, gasping for breath. What?

I glance around me and see Killian and Aaron are standing either side of me, staring down in terror.

"What, what happened? The room, it was full of blood," I gasp. "Kyle? Is he okay?"

I stagger to my feet and start towards him, but my whole body feels suddenly drained. Killian catches me when I trip.

"You tried to strangle him, Mallory."

"But that wasn't him," I explain as Kyle gets to his feet and makes his way to us. "It was Thaddeus."

Kyle and Aaron exchange a look of curiosity but Killian merely mutters "Ah," quietly.

"What is it?" Aaron asks.

"Avika magic," he says.

"Of course," Kyle murmurs hoarsely.

"What's that?" I ask.

I walk to Kyle and inspect the damage I've done. I can see red marks left by my hands wound around his throat. If Killian and Aaron hadn't stopped me, I would have killed him, so convinced was I that he was Thaddeus.

"They're a faction of the angeleru that can manipulate reality to appear as they wish it. An avika must have cast a spell in that room, leaving residue magic so that whoever came looking for Casey would hallucinate what they fear."

"They knew we would come for her," I say grimly.

"They knew someone would, whether it be us or Emmett. Whoever or whatever this girl is, she's very valuable."

"Hang on. You're saying an avika is working with the jaeitsi?" Kyle inquires, seemingly shocked.

"You've got your insurrectionists, we've got ours," Killian replies. "The Hirutere has made itself plenty of enemies, even amongst its own people."

"Seems our governments have that in common," Aaron mutters, coming up beside me. "Are you okay?"

Am I? I'm still trying to convince myself that the body I saw in there wasn't real, though it seemed his perfect likeness. Dominic has to still be alive, somewhere. And I almost just killed my best friend. I can still feel the skin of his throat pressed to my hands. We're fortunate I had dropped my sword or I really would have killed him. I nod to Aaron though. I have to be okay right now.

"I'm so sorry Kyle," I say, winding my arm through his.

"It's okay. I'm feeling much better," he croaks, still rubbing his throat.

"So, what now?" I ask.

"Like Emmett said, a tracking spell won't work. The jaeitsi will have witches to cloak themselves. I don't really want to come up against this avika either," Killian adds. "They're clearly incredibly powerful. If they were to manipulate you while you had your katana, who knows what kind of havoc they could wreak."

Like killing all of them. I hold Kyle's hand.

"Don't feel bad, the exact same thing would have happened to us if we had gone in there. Though possibly with less dangerous consequences," Killian says.

"Speak for yourself, we could have turned into bloody dragons and eaten that sweet old lady from before," Aaron scoffs.

So, is there simply no hope then? We've lost Alice, Dominic, and now this girl. Without her, what's Emmett's plan to get Dominic back? I know I should be worried about the oncoming war at large, but all my thoughts spiral the drain that is the man I love.

Just then, I hear a small ping emit from a computer on the desk back in the bedroom. We all exchange a look.

"Well I'm not going back in there," Kyle says, shuddering.

"I'll do it. Just knock me out if something happens this time."

"It really cannot be good for you to be unconscious as often as you are. You're going to get brain damage," Aaron says.

"Maybe that's why I hear voices."

My katana is still lying in the middle of the floor. They'll have to be able to get to me before I can get to it or nothing can stop me. Apparently, that's a risk we're willing to take. I test one foot over the threshold, waiting for the effects of the magic to take hold.

Nothing happens.

"It must have just been enough magic residue for one spell," Killian says, following me in.

"Why only do that much?" I ask.

"You felt how strong its power was, how convinced you were of that reality. One spell could have been enough to wipe out an entire party of bellatoja should they have come looking for Casey."

I shudder thinking of it as I walk to the desk. It was so completely compelling, so utterly convincing. I was certain that it was Thaddeus who stood beside me. No. I mustn't think of that. Focus on the task at hand.

The laptop screen has lit up and, on it, the camera is still recording. Killian leans around me, brushing against my arm, and stops the recording before pressing play. A girl with ginger hair and brown eyes appears on the screen holding a guitar. She has a constellation of freckles scattered across her face and the light from the window dashes across her face.

"Hey guys, Casey here. Today I'm going to be playing a cover of Alt-J's *Breezeblocks*. Hope you like it. Hit subscribe!"

She begins picking the guitar and opens her mouth to sing when there's a bang outside the room. Her head whips around, tossing her fiery curls over her shoulder.

"Dad!" she calls out. "I'm recording. I thought you were at the farmer's market?"

No reply.

"Dad?"

I hear a faint scuttling sound, before the door slides open. Casey lets out an unearthly scream, dropping her guitar and toppling out of her chair. I can't see whatever it is that's frightened her at first. Then a pair of antennae peek in at the bottom of the screen. The scuttling creature emerges into the camera screen and my stomach knots itself in revulsion. A massive millipede like creature with veiny pincers crawls across the wall. It clicks its pincers together, making a squeaking sound, before throwing itself from the wall and pouncing upon Casey. She screams, again and again, until a slender hand reaches into the left side of the frame.

"Peace," a voice commands. Casey falls silent. "You're safe. Your friend is holding you. You want to come with me."

"The avika?" I ask.

"Must be," Killian replies. The other two have gathered around us.

Casey rises, as if in a dreamlike trance, and walks towards the woman who speaks. She follows the avika out of the room and I hear the creature scurry after them, its many legs scratching the floor as it goes. The front door closes and then there's nothing. Two hours of blank recording remain. Killian pauses the video.

"The avika had a siug with her. Must mean there was a jaeitsi controlling it. Avikas aren't known for working with siugs. I guess that confirms it was them."

"Are siugs a type of deabrueon?" I inquire. Killian nods. "So, what now?"

"I don't know," he sighs, sitting down in the desk chair. He watches the recording again before closing out of it. Suddenly, he leans in closer to the screen.

"What's that?" Kyle asks, pointing at the notification in the top right-hand corner of the screen, which must have been why it made a sound earlier.

"It's a text. *Where are you? Why does my find my friend app say you're at the docks in Brooklyn?*" Killian puts his palm to his face. "We're daft."

"How so?" Kyle asks, as Killian turns to me.

"Because the avika took Casey to the exact same place the raika took Mallory."

"Maybe should have considered that as an option before I almost got strangled to death," Kyle mutters.

Chapter IX.

Since we were last here, the place Killian and I fought the deabrueon has been cleared of bodies. There's no evidence that this is the site that saw the beginning of the end of my once normal life. This can only mean the jaeitsi are still here and, whether they're waiting for us or have no clue we're coming, we're in for a fight. The water to our right is glistening in the moonlight, a handful of diamonds scattered on liquid black. Gentle waves lap against the concrete, disturbed as the river is by the movement of boats and the current that hides itself. Surveying the warehouse, Killian and I stand shoulder to shoulder, the other two behind us.

"Surely they can't be so stupid as to not have moved since you two were last here?" Aaron says.

"It seems unlikely. But Casey's find my phone app said she was here. Praise technology," Killian replies. He looks to me. "Ready?"

"To face an unknown number of deabrueon, an avika, and potentially two fallen angeleru? If I can face my midterm for Professor Baker's class and survive, sure, why not?"

I draw my katana from its sheath and that familiar pattern unwinds itself down my arm. My body hums with power and I know I am ready for a fight. The others follow suit, unsheathing their swords.

Killian leads the charge, Aaron taking up the rear. Kyle and I stand close together between them. His new arm is shaking. No doubt he's worried about being out of practice fighting with it after three years. Even before that, fighting was never his modus operandi. Kyle has always been a man of words and wisdom, his wit as sharp as the blades his friends prefer.

"You'll be fine," I assure him, "I won't let anything happen to you."

"You mean like suddenly being choked by you? I'm not sure how we can guard against that, Mallory. If the avika is here and she targets you, or me and Aaron, I'm not sure what we'll be able to do."

He's right. If one of them shifts into dragon form, what can we possibly do to protect ourselves? Not to mention they'll have broken the accords, putting them back on the Hirutere's hitlist.

And with my magic under the avika's control, as well as the untold power of the katana, who knows what could happen.

The door is unlocked, a worrying sign I think, but I say nothing to the others. Could it be a trap? Most likely that's why they've allowed us to be led back here. I don't believe for a second that they wouldn't think to take Casey's phone from her. Walking into this building is possibly one of the stupidest things we've ever done. But the thought of Dominic and that girl being tortured somewhere in here draws me in all the same. I won't leave him to that fate or any other. He's had enough of pain for one lifetime.

Once inside, we follow the same hallway I had escaped down. It's littered with rubbish, scattered across the floor. Papers shiver in the breeze that follows us through the door. Those hadn't been here before. I spot Lena's shoe not far off, but don't bother retrieving it. The air smells thickly of salt and something rotten. It knots my stomach. Something is off. Why is it so quiet? Perhaps I'm overthinking it. The hall had been empty the last time I was here after all and, aside from those strange gurgling noises I'd heard, it had been silent too.

I beckon the others to follow me and head back to the room where I was kept. Listening carefully at the door, I hear no sound. I push open the heavy door, but find no one in the cage I was kept in. The cage door is still ajar from my escape. They must be elsewhere. Somewhere with guards no doubt. If the avika expected us to come for Casey, enough so that she laid that trap at the apartment, then she knows what Dominic and Casey mean to us. There's no way they're not anticipating this and they'll be well prepared.

"We'll split up, one pair goes to the right, one goes straight," I whisper. "Kyle, Aaron, you go together." Kyle begins to protest, but I shake my head. "You know each other's fighting styles best, you'll work better together."

"Smart thinking boss," Aaron murmurs. "Come on."

We watch them disappear to the right before continuing down the hall. I'm still unnerved by the eerie silence. Surely if this is the jaeitsi's headquarters it should be full of deabrueons? I swallow. Something is definitely wrong. Killian squeezes my shoulder reassuringly, but it only causes me to jump. He mouths an apology.

"I bet you creep up on people in cemeteries too," I murmur.

"How do you think I spend my free time?"

"Apparently on Bumble."

We reach the next door and I listen again, but hear nothing. Pushing open the door, I see what I had feared we'd find: a phone, sitting in the middle of the table, and nothing else. Casey's phone. I step into the room to be certain she's not in here as well, and Killian follows me.

The door swings shut behind us.

"Come back for your shoe?"

I spin around to come face to face with the raika I had fought earlier. He grins, baring his teeth, Lena's other Louboutin that I had thrown at him dangling in his hand. Fuck.

"Well, you know, it's so beautiful."

"Then I guess what they say is true: beauty really is pain," he says, lunging towards me and knocking my sword from my hand.

He whirls around and swiftly punches Killian in the face, sending him spilling over the table. I hear a hiss and from behind the raika emerges one of those massive houndlike deabrueon Clara had summoned in the clearing that night in Aplin Hollow. It rolls its head back and howls before throwing its weight onto its front paws and bounding towards Killian.

"Good, I wanted to fight you," the raika hisses.

"Why, you wanted your ass kicked again?"

He snarls and drives his sword towards me. Out of the corner of my eye, I see Killian dodge the deabrueon's attack as I spin out of the way, further from my sword. The raika's sword comes down again, but I raise my hand in time to create a shield of magic to deflect it. It bounces off and I take the chance to kick the raika in the groin. He hisses again, his tongue flicking out, but my kick elicits no further response.

"Funny, that usually works on guys."

"I'm not like other men, sweetie."

In the light I can make out the slick green sheen his skin has to it, like sludge gathering on the water's surface. He looks as though he's covered in a thin sheen of sweat, though I know I've not begun to tire him out, judging by the speed and ease with which he moves. His sword is slashing through the air again and slips past my shield to graze my arm.

"This is my friend's jacket," I say. "Why are you so dead set on ruining my outfit?"

I dive out of his way and grab the table, launching it at him. He stumbles back, crashing into the cage bars and dropping his sword. I hear the howl of the deabrueon behind us as Killian pierces it with his sword. Rushing towards the raika, I pin him by the throat against the bars of the cage. He tilts his head back, grinning at me.

"What are you going to do, drown me again? It won't work."

"No," I murmur. "Kaisma." A blue flame crackles to life above my palm. "I believe this is your poison."

I hold it close to his face and he growls, straining to get away from me. I hear the dull thud of the hound's body falling to the ground and Killian approaching behind me.

"To be fair, she did warn you she'd kick your ass again," he says to the raika, picking up his sword after sheathing his own. "That was your big plan? Attacking us with one deabrueon? Stupid, mate."

"You think there's just one? I'd be more worried about your friends if I were you."

Killian and I glance at each other as the fire goes out in my hand.

"May I do the honours?" he asks.

"Be my guest," I reply.

He punches the raika as hard as he can and I hear the crunch of his nose breaking. Opening the cage door, Killian grabs him by his collar and tosses him in. He slams the door shut and clicks the padlock closed.

"Let's go."

Rushing back out the door, we race down the hallway to find Kyle and Aaron. It isn't long before we can hear the sounds of a struggle. We come upon the last door in the hall, which is ajar. Through it, I see Aaron stumbling back, fending off another of those hounds, but failing to fatally wound it. Meanwhile, Kyle is engaged with keeping two deabrueon off of himself, while another one climbs back to its feet.

"About time!" Aaron shouts, noticing us as his blade slits the beast's throat.

"We had our own welcoming committee," Killian replies, jumping in beside him as they take on another of the hounds. The two move in a perfectly co-ordinated effort, both born for battle, as they turn to another of the deabrueon. It's Kyle who concerns me.

I rush to his aid before realising I've left my sword back in the other room. Conjuring up the image of a javelin in my mind, I flick my wrist and send a spear of magic straight through one of the deabrueon.

"Thanks," Kyle calls, lopping off another's arm. "How's that for poetic justice you bastard!"

"Kyle, that's not the deabrueon that took your arm, so it's not poetic justice," Aaron retorts.

"He works for the ones who did it though."

Kyle's taken no time getting back into the swing of battle, moving smoothly to fend off the last deabrueon. Panting, he looks up at me, pride streaked across his face. Now all that's left is the deabrueon Killian and Aaron are fighting.

I hear a fearsome roar and spin round to see another of the hounds barrelling towards the room.

"Graemar, incoming," Killian shouts, as if I don't see it.

I look around the room for something to weaponise, but there's nothing, not even a table to throw at it. The beast springs into the air and I dive to the floor just in time to miss it landing on me. It staggers to a halt in the corner of the room before spinning around. Its black eyes flash dangerously at me.

"Kaisma." I command my fire once more and feel it swell in my veins.

This is my element. I draw my hand towards me before unfolding my arm and directing a whip of fire towards the graemar. The flame's tongue lashes the beast's forearm and it cries out, buckling for a moment. Again, I point the fire to its target and this time it cuts clean through the beast's arm. It stumbles on the cauterised stump, moaning and dragging itself towards me with its other paw. Aaron rushes past me before he delivers the final blow, slicing right through the thick neck of the beast. Its head rolls to the right before landing with a thud on the ground. The body collapses beside it. The room is finally still and quiet, save for our heavy breathing from the exertion of the fight.

"Everyone okay?" I ask, panting with the effort of my magic.

"No limbs lost. On our side that is," Kyle corrects himself. "Is that morbid to say?"

Aaron pats him on the back, his forehead glistening with sweat. "Yes, but we love you for it."

All around me is the carnage of our fight, deabrueon bodies heaped left and right. Aaron and Kyle had managed to take out quite a few before we even arrived.

"For someone who doesn't use much magic you're pretty damn good," Aaron says, walking over to me.

"The wordless spellcasting bit helps," I breathe. "We should go back, see what the raika knows."

"You found the one that kidnapped you?" Kyle asks.

"Yeah. He had Casey's phone. It was all a trap to get us here. We stuck him in one of the cages though," Killian explains.

"Taste of his own medicine," I mutter.

They don't put away their swords as we head back down the hall. We're not so naïve as to think that there might not be more deabrueon, or something worse, lying in wait. If this is the worst of it, we've been extremely lucky. We return to the room to find the raika huddled in a corner of his cage. He looks up at me with such wild rage that what little humanity I thought I had seen in him at Noah's party has disappeared altogether. I wonder how I ever managed to confuse him with a human. Blood glistens on his face, running from his broken nose.

"We have questions."

"And I, undoubtedly, have the answers," he replies, unfolding his arms in a mock welcoming gesture. "What are you going to do about it, Academy dog?"

For Dominic?

I may be battle worn but, still, with the slight movement of a single finger, I ignite a ring of fire around him.

"What's your name." I ask the question without the intonation. It's a command to give me what I want.

"Carlisle," he replies, willing to play along. For how long, we'll see.

"Why did you want to lure us here?"

"To kill your friends and get you alone."

"Mallory, there could be more out there," Kyle interrupts.

I turn to Aaron and nod to the door. He walks over, raising his sword and standing guard. I turn back to Carlisle.

"What do you want with me?"

Carlisle grins, his lips disappearing to reveal his deadly teeth. I have no doubt he could rip my throat out with them if he got out of that cage. But he's not getting out of the cage. I won't let him anywhere near the others.

"It's not me who wants you. Though I was wrong about you. You're not so meek after all."

"Something of a teaching moment, isn't it? Maybe you've learned it's better to play nice than fight with me," I reply coolly. I raise my hand and, with it, so go the flames. His eyes widen as he takes in his predicament. "Who's after me?"

"My bosses."

"Half answers will get you no points," I warn. The flame spits out an ember which catches his trouser leg on fire. He pats it out urgently, hissing. "Oops. My bad."

"The jaeitsi!" he snarls, realising that toying with me will get him nowhere but burned to a crisp. So, it is them. Is Clara with them? Surely, if she is, Thaddeus would have insisted she take me already. What's their game in playing this out? It doesn't quite add up.

"Bonus round time. Why?"

He weighs up his options. He can betray some very dangerous fallen angeleru or enrage the girl currently threatening to burn him alive. Neither seems a very good option, but I'm not in the mood to pity him.

"I don't know everything. They sent me to kill that witch, but told me to leave you alive. When you found me at the party, I knew I had to take you. Once I reported what I had done, they said I had to either manage to bring you to them or they'd kill me."

"Yeah, well it's looking like that's your fate either way, so either you answer all my questions and give yourself a fighting chance or you die here and now."

He gulps, and now I do think he's sweating.

"I'll tell you whatever you want to know."

"Why'd they want you to kill Alice?"

"The witch? The jaietsi don't tend to give reasons, just orders. But," he adds quickly when I raise my eyebrows and the flames begin to crackle again, "I did overhear them say she was part of a threat against them. She was using her magic to keep people hidden from them, including you."

"I already knew that, so unless you've got something more interesting to say, let's have barbecued snake."

"They said she was the one casting the cloaking spells on the members of the insurgents from the Academy. So long as she was alive, they couldn't find them. She was also supposed to get the girl, Casey."

"So that's how they found Dominic," I mutter to myself. "They must have a witch to locate people then?" He nods. "What do they want with Casey?"

"I don't know. Only that she's important. More than you, more than that guy who was protecting you. They told me to kill you before I let you find her."

Kyle glances nervously around before tugging my sleeve.

"Mallory, we need to get going. Backup could be here for him any moment and if they're this hellbent on keeping Casey from us we should be worried about what lengths they'll go to to keep us from leaving here alive."

"Agreed," Killian adds.

But I'm not finished with Carlisle yet.

"One more question then. It's an easy one," I assure him. "Where are Dominic and Casey?"

He shivers.

"Please, if I tell you I'm done for."

"And if you don't," I say, nodding towards the fire again, but I can feel my magic waning. This won't hold much longer.

"You think death is all to be feared? You who has known the many torments of the Academy?"

He's right. There are worse things to endure than death, pains that can drag themselves out into an eternity. That's exactly why I have to do what I do next, to save Dominic from such a torturous fate.

I bend my arm, drawing the flame from where it flickers. It uncoils and lashes Carlisle's leg, cutting clean through it. He screams and I hear Kyle gasp.

"Mallory!"

Even Aaron looks stunned, his attention entirely on me and not the potential incoming threat. I ignore them, unlocking the cage and stepping in. My fires die away as I crouch beside the howling man. He clutches the stump, doubled over in pain.

"You are seriously underestimating how important he is to me. You won't make that mistake again. The jaeitsi are going to come for you now whether you tell me or not. So, I can either heal this so you can make a run for it or I can leave you here for them to find. Choice is yours."

He nods through ragged sobs.

"Please," he groans, barely making out the word. I draw his leg back to the place it's been disconnected, which is bright red and slightly engorged. I feel sick with the knowledge of the pain I've just inflicted, but my head is clouded, as if by alcohol, with my need to get to Dominic.

"Hold still," I command, as I rest my hand on the place they meet.

He chokes back sobs at the agony of my touch, but keeps still. I watch as the fabric of his skin reaches from either side to reconnect tissue to tissue. The fissure seals itself shut and he stops whimpering. Gone too is the pain. Even his face is covered in awe as he inspects the perfectly healed leg. He looks up at me in gratitude. This is not a mercy the jaeitsi would have shown him.

"They're at an apartment. The avika woman has her. The address, it's," he pauses, shutting his eyes as if to draw it back to his memory. He groans a moment. "36 Bleecker Street."

I glance over my shoulder at the others.

"That's right by my apartment," I say, frowning before turning back to Carlisle. "Have they known where I've been all this time?"

He nods. "They've always known, they just weren't ready for you."

I close my eyes and lower my head. Everything Dominic has done, putting Alice's life at risk to protect me, it was for nothing. Why weren't they ready for me? What's changed? I look to Carlisle again. He cowers from me now, every trace of ferocity gone.

"Thank you," I say. I take his hand and draw in my mind a

cloak, obscurity, and darkness. His skin shimmers, and he cries out, trying to pull his hand away. When no pain comes of my spell, he looks at me puzzled. "That will keep the jaeitsi from finding you for some time."

"Mallory," Aaron begins to admonish me, but I shake my head at him.

"He fulfilled his promise to answer my questions. I won't hurt him again. We've got to be better than the jaeitsi, the Hirutere, and the Onyevaras."

"Second chances are the theme of the day," Kyle muses, smiling at me. He looks proud and it brightens me, amidst all this darkness, to know I've begun to prove myself to him once more. It will take so much time, so many acts like this before he can trust me entirely again, but I'm willing to work through that. I'm willing to commit myself to any length of time to earn Kyle's trust back.

"Thank you," Carlisle stammers, looking at the others nervously.

"You'll probably want to run, before they come here looking for you," I advise.

He takes no time scuttling to his feet and rushing past me, edging anxiously past Aaron, who glowers at him. Pausing in the doorway, he turns back to me.

"Such kindnesses are not taken lightly and they are not readily forgotten," he says, before disappearing from sight.

"Love it when they say something cryptic," Aaron mutters. He looks thoroughly displeased that we didn't lop Carlisle's head off.

"We should get going too," Killian sighs, "though I do think that was a stupid move."

"Possibly. Better to have potential friends than a body count," I reply, shrugging.

"Dude almost killed you twice and then you chopped off his leg. What sort of messed up friends do you have?" Aaron demands.

"The kind whose clothes I really, really need to stop wearing into battle."

Chapter X.

After leaving the warehouse, Killian and I stop back at my apartment while the others go to get more weapons from theirs. We walk in and I'm half surprised, half relieved to find it hasn't been broken into. Everything is just as I left it Friday morning before class. A few books strewn about, Jane Eyre on the sofa where I had been curled up with it in the morning, my empty coffee cup beside it. It's something of a comfort read for me and, after that dream of drowning, I had turned to it to soothe myself. The images from my dream flash through my head. I haven't slept in so long, adrenaline keeping me going, that I haven't had a chance to dream it. It's been days now. As long as Dominic's been taken. I bite the ridges of the inside of my cheeks, holding back the tears when I think of him.

"You might want to change, that outfit's given you a lot of grief," Killian suggests, drawing me from my thoughts. I've been standing in the doorway, not letting him through into the apartment. I step inside, letting him pass.

"Probably a good idea to shower too," I say, certain I must reek after all the sweating I've done.

He nods and takes a seat on the sofa, leaning back. He picks up my book and begins to read the back of it. Something about seeing him like that feels odd to me, but it's not because he doesn't belong. It's because he fits into this scene of domesticity all too well. He crosses his legs carelessly, but holds the book with care, understanding its value and meaning without me having to say anything. It's one of my books from the Academy, the ones that Kyle had to save for me. If it was anyone else, I'm not sure I'd trust them with my books. But Killian I know I can trust. I study him a moment longer, but, when he glances up at me, I disappear into the bathroom, sealing the door shut behind me.

Despite how helpful he's been, I'm grateful for the respite from Killian's company a shower provides. I'm grateful to have a moment to myself. I feel my shoulders relax, my muscles untense as the water rolls down me. Has it only been a day since I was with Lena and Wes at that party? It feels like weeks, but sheer exhaustion will do that to you. I should text Wes, let him know I'm okay, though Lena has undoubtedly filled him in.

I tilt my head back and let slip a sigh. How quickly my world's been thrown into chaos once more. I cannot help but worry that I will never return to the life I had at NYU, but I cannot allow myself to think like that. I'm not ready to give up on my future yet. There's still hope that I can resolve this situation and rescue Dominic. Even as I think it, though, I know it's not true. If the jaeitsi are after me and they know where I am, they will not let me be. Thaddeus is too relentless. The only way to stop him would be to kill him. And, hate him as I do, I cannot reconcile myself to that act. Not when I pity him so.

I lather myself in soap, washing away the blood and grime of a day's battle. But the day's not yet done. I feel utterly diminished, having not slept in two days, yet there's no time for that now. I can't let Dominic wait a single day if it means sparing him some misery.

Once towelled off, I realise I haven't brought a change of clothes in with me. Wrapping a towel around myself, I head back into the living room, my cheeks flushing as I walk past Killian, who glances up. I keep my gaze averted as though there's nothing off about me parading past him in a towel, though I notice he quickly averts his gaze again. For all his comradery with Aaron, at least he doesn't share his perverted sense of humour. I enter my bedroom and slip on a dark blue fitted t-shirt and a pair of leggings. Best to do battle in something with a little give. Lena's cigarette trousers were not forgiving of a roundhouse kick. I fold up her clothes, which are utterly filthy, and make a mental note to see if magic can do what I already know the dry cleaners can't. I strap a thigh sheath with a parrying dagger to my leg, something Aaron has left with me. I towel dry my hair before emerging back into my small living room. While it's tiny no matter how you stack it, the apartment seems all the more cramped having Killian's tall, muscular frame in it. He's reclining on the sofa, his deep forest green t-shirt hiked up a little bit to reveal his tan lower abdomen and the smooth curves of his muscles. I see a hint of a birthmark on his abdomen, but he quickly covers it.

Do not think of how nice his body is, I admonish myself. He looks at me, his face not stained with the same weariness as mine. Instead, the day's events seem only to have enlivened him. Must be some weird bellatoja thing, getting a kick out of battle.

"You got anything to drink?" he asks.

"Are you always such a peppy alcoholic?" I retort, going into the kitchen and standing on my tiptoes to reach a bottle of tequila on the top of my cupboard. Suddenly, I feel Killian standing behind me, his hand outstretched past mine to retrieve the bottle. I hadn't even heard him approach. I spin around and come face to face with him. God his eyes are gorgeous. Emeralds like the one set in my sword, glinting with all the mischief of Aaron, but without the overt perverseness. That makes for a refreshing change. There are small rutilated flecks of gold as well, which I hadn't noticed before, which warm his eyes like honey.

"It helps with the constant adrenaline. Kind of soothes the nerves."

"That's why you're so ready to go still, huh?" Phrasing. "The constant adrenaline, it keeps you battle ready, I mean."

He lets my comment slide and I swallow hard.

"Yup. Whereas most adrenaline rushes don't last too long, bellatoja can sustain them for extended periods of time. The come down is awful though. Shaking, sweating, exhaustion, anxiety. A lot of bellatoja self-medicate," he answers, taking a swig from the bottle. "It's usually alcohol that does the trick. And our fast metabolisms mean we don't tend to get drunk. Unless we really go in for a whole bottle of whiskey or something."

"You don't strike me as a whiskey kind of guy."

"No? What do I strike you as?"

"A tequila guy. And too generous for your own good."

He looks at the floor, nodding.

"Perhaps. It has got me into a slew of messes these past few days. But better to be kind and helping others than cynical and a misanthrope."

"Some would disagree with you."

"Oh I'm sure many would," he laughs. "I don't know, maybe it's naïve. It's the only part of being a bellatoja that I can stand, actually getting to help and protect others. Not that you need protecting."

"We all do sometimes. I'm not as strong as I seem."

"Like hell you aren't. I think you may even be stronger, if only you'd let yourself believe it."

He holds my gaze for a moment and my lips part, but I'm unable to speak. I know my magic is greater than what I believe it to be; healing Kyle's arm proved that. But I am not strong. I am a tea cup, already chipped and waiting for the final blow to shatter it. I'm on a precipice, always, about to fall, about to fall apart. He takes another sip from the bottle, then offers it to me.

"Why not. We all have our albatrosses to bear I guess," I say, taking the bottle and a long gulp. It burns my throat going down and I stick out my tongue, gagging slightly. He laughs at me, taking the bottle back. We plop down onto the sofa, the intensity of the previous moment gone in light of the drink.

"You bear yours remarkably well, balancing your past, what you are, with a human life. I hope what's come to pass today won't get in the way of that."

"I won't let it," I assure him, "not this time."

But I know already that it will. Even if I find a way to stay at NYU, I'll always be fighting for my life, always be putting others' lives at risk.

"I don't know. If it comes down to fighting to keep people safe or living reclusively for your own benefit, do you really trust yourself to choose yourself over others?"

No, I don't. Not again. It was too hard a decision to make the first time around. Swiping the bottle from him, I take another drink. I know better of my own nature. I can't, in good conscious, abandon the fight against the jaeitsi just because Dominic is safe. Not when there are so many lives on the line. In the past day I've seen the enormity of my own power, and that's after years of disuse. To deny my friends and loved ones its strength when it could spare their lives is beyond my ability. Even in the face of the loss of everything I have built since coming to New York. I tilt my head back and swallow more tequila.

"Slow down, you don't want to go into battle completely plastered."

"Didn't the Vikings do drugs before battle?"

"Yeah, but do you really want to use them as your role models?"

"No, I think I'll elect Kyle for the position."

Resting his elbow on the armrest, Killian cups his chin in his palm and studies me. Whatever it is he's looking for, he can't read the answer in my eyes. I often think myself an open book, but more and more I am realising that I keep most of myself closed off. I have had to learn how to do that, how to keep the ghosts from my eyes. Plucking the bottle from my hand, he begins picking at the label.

"If he means so much to you, why did you leave him?" I glance over my shoulder at Killian. He refuses to look at me, aware he may be prying. After all he's done, he's within his right to ask questions of me, though perhaps not this one. "I'm sorry, I shouldn't have said that. It's not my place to ask. I just, I want to understand you."

And he has a right to understand the person he is fighting beside, why she does what she does and makes the decisions she does. I feel I cannot deny him an answer.

"It's okay. The truth is, I don't know. The reasons I said back in Miesarinda? Because," I pause. But was that why I left? In part perhaps. "Because I was selfish. Because I had a way out and I wanted it. Because living like that cost me or the people I loved too much. And, well there's the small matter of Leo."

"Leo Arteus?" he asks, his interest stirred.

I nod, taking another sip from the bottle to smooth the coming of what I'm about to say.

"It's weird but, we sort of had this mutual understanding. We had feelings for each other, but neither of us was really capable of a relationship or being in love so we agreed never to see each other again. I think, at the time, I was too damaged to love or, more importantly, let myself be loved like that. I didn't need a relationship back then, not when I was only finding my feet. I didn't want my story to just be about romantic love or how much I needed someone else to feel whole. I was just figuring out who I was, how being a dragovik changed what I understood of myself. It's stupid." I shake my head.

I've never admitted any of this to someone before. Even Leo and I didn't speak our feelings into being with each other. I doubt Kyle, Aaron, and Robyn ever noticed there was something between us at the time, it was so reserved. Killian stares blankly at me, swipes the bottle and takes two long gulps without flinching.

He wipes his mouth and blinks as if he's just come out of a deep sleep.

"I'm sorry. We are talking about the same Leo? Cold, calculating, and utterly indifferent to everything but whatever mission he's on?"

"My turn," I sigh, taking the bottle from him and drinking deep. "Yes, that Leo. It's hard to explain. I didn't know of anyone else from the Academy and I thought he was the only one who would ever understand… understand what it is to utterly despise yourself."

Killian is quiet for a moment. I study his high cheekbones, strong jaw. He's beautiful and every bit the angel his blonde-haired, blue-eyed compatriots are. What's more, he's caring and compassionate. He's listening to me blather on and I can't keep myself from wondering why he cares. Yet, somehow, I know he does. How does someone like that exist in our world? I'm floored by his generosity, so similar to Kyle, but without the same loyalty that demands him rising to my aid. Why, then, is Killian fighting by my side?

"That's no reason to love someone," he says finally.

"I didn't love him," I correct him, perhaps too hastily so as to give away the fact I've been admiring him. "I just don't believe you can have a relationship with someone you don't understand."

"And the person has to have gone through the same misery as you to understand? They can't just empathise?"

I stare at him, stunned by how strongly he voices his opinion on the subject. No, I don't think they have to have gone through the same pain. Kyle understands me perfectly and he was not a child of the Academy. Yet don't I, to some extent, believe it to be true? Isn't that why I'm fixated on Dominic? Our shared history is one unobtainable to anyone else. It seems an impossible chasm for anyone to cross and I wouldn't want them to. I would pity the person who could empathise with me or understand how I feel, what I've been through. Maybe Thaddeus could have, maybe he had crossed that chasm and many more, but he was too far gone for even me to understand.

"I don't know," I say, shrugging. "I've never really dated, so I suppose I don't have much of a frame of reference for how these things work. I just hooked up with this guy one time, which ended badly and that kind of closed the book on relationships for me. How about you? Seems like you've always got the ladies around," I say, trying to deflect the conversation from myself. He snorts.

"I guess. We go on dates, hook up, but it's nothing meaningful. I don't think that's within my capacity."

I'm surprised to hear this. He seems such a thoughtful person and the way he's come to my aid in the past day makes me certain he would protect the people he loves as ferociously as I do. He cares quickly for people, that much is evident from how swiftly he has devoted himself to helping us. And he's said the only part of being a bellatoja that he likes is being able to help and protect people. How could someone that generous or caring not be capable of love?

"I don't believe that."

He looks at me thoughtfully.

"For someone whose past should leave her inclined to expect the worst in people, you have an awful lot of faith."

"According to recent studies, optimists live longer and, given the fact I'm a dragovik, I can use all the help I can get."

"You mean given the fact you're a magnet for death and destruction."

He's not wrong and there's no malice in his voice, but the comment stings all the same. I bring it with me wherever I go. To Aplin Hollow and now to New York. My past is always on my heels, haunting each step, trying to reclaim me. Killian must see something of my pain in the look on my face, because he reaches out to take my hand.

"Sorry," he says, "I didn't mean that."

"It's true though."

"No, it's not Mallory. Our way of life is the magnet. You fight to prevent those things, constantly and tirelessly."

"Do I? I haven't for the past three years. I'm why Inerea died. I'm why Kyle was hurt. I'm part of the reason that Alice died. I'm also why Dominic has been kidnapped. Even if I do fight back, it never seems to amount to anything."

"Inerea's death was not your fault. Don't assume responsibility for Thaddeus' actions just because he's obsessed with you. Kyle was injured because he chose to protect you, that doesn't make it your fault either. Besides, you healed him, didn't you? And you took no time returning to this way of life when Dominic was taken. We're going to get Dominic back. I won't stop until we do."

"Why?" I ask, turning to him.

"Because it's what will make you happy, isn't it?"

I'm bewildered by this. Why does he care what does or does not make me happy? We still hardly know each other. I've spent a sum total of just over a day with this man, but already he's so willing to risk his life to help me fight for what I care about, for Kyle's life and Dominic's. I open my mouth to ask why it matters, why he cares.

"I just do," he answers, as if knowing my question before it leaves my lips. "I can't explain it. But I think you deserve someone looking out for you."

"I've got Kyle," I remind him.

"Fine, then two someones."

"I count myself a very lucky woman indeed to number you amongst my someones."

He snorts, taking the bottle from me.

"I think you've had enough of this."

"You're probably right, but that doesn't mean I'm ready to give it up just yet. Give it here," I laugh, leaning across him to take the bottle from him.

"You do that with far too little regularity," he says, not smiling in response to my good cheer as I settle down.

"What?" I ask.

"Laugh. Smile. It suits you."

My eyes lock onto his. I don't think I'm mistaken and yet I must be. It's as if, when I look at Killian, something is taking root within me, something I won't readily be able to do away with. I hold my breath, taking him in and simultaneously being taken in by him. I don't know what to say now, in light of this new flower that is blooming in my chest.

There's a knock at the door and I'm grateful for a reason to tear my gaze from Killian's. Though it's likely the other two, I draw the parrying dagger from its sheath on my thigh, just in case. Opening the door, I see a petite blonde-haired girl standing before me. I swiftly hide the dagger behind my back.

"Ellie!" I say, taken off-guard by the appearance of my downstairs neighbour amidst everything that's going on.

"Hey! Just wanted to say thank you for taking care of the dogs last week," she says, holding out a plastic bag full of cookies. I take it with my free hand.

"Awe that's so sweet. These are exactly what I need after the day I've had."

"Everything okay?" she asks, frowning.

"Yeah just, unfinished business, you know?"

She gives me a peculiar look that tells me she has exactly no clue what my cryptic statement means. Her eyes dart over my shoulder, where they spot Killian.

"Oh, you've got company. Where's Dominic?" she asks.

Ellie has assumed Dominic and I are a couple since I moved in, always asking us to hang out with her and her friends. Unsurprisingly, Dominic has adamantly refused, though I've met them a few times. To her credit, seeing him come by every night can give the impression that we're dating.

"Dominic's visiting friends," Killian replies, smiling charmingly at her. Her expression melts into a flood of warmth.

"Oh, how nice! Well, I'll let you get back to your evening. Oh, excuse me," she says, bumping into Aaron when she turns around. She looks at the sword on his hip and glances worriedly at me.

"Cosplay?" I say.

"Okay, well, have fun."

She trots down the stairs, taking one more look at the odd scene before her.

"She's cute," Aaron says, looking after her. "Is she single?"

"Yes, and I'll even set you guys up later if you keep your mind on the matter at hand," I sigh, ushering them in.

They crowd in. Killian rises from the sofa to join us. We're all standing practically shoulder to shoulder in the tiny living room.

"Couldn't you get a better apartment?" Aaron asks. "It's nice, just small."

"Doctor Lindberg pays for it, so I didn't want to ask for too much. Living in Greenwich Village isn't cheap you know, even if you do think it's a shithole. I like it here. And don't even mention godforsaken Brooklyn again," I add warningly, raising my hand to silence him when he opens his mouth. He mimes zipping his mouth shut.

"Okay, what's the plan?" Kyle asks, before noticing the bottle of tequila "Aside from getting drunk. Do you two do anything else?"

He picks the near empty bottle off the table before I snatch it away and do the last shot.

"I've been known to bathe occasionally as well," Killian quips, "like once a month at least."

"On that concerning note, which I'm hoping for the sake of your dates is a joke, the plan is breaking in. We've all grown accustomed to that recently," I say.

"How come when we do it it's okay, but when the jaeitsi have someone do it, they're the bad guys?" Aaron asks.

"Because we always bring wine and flowers," I say sarcastically, "and, oh right, we're not kidnapping people and trying to destabilise a government at the cost of thousands of lives. There's that small difference."

"Valid point."

"If you don't mind, let's get back to the rather urgent hostage situation. Any idea what we're facing?" Kyle asks.

"The avika, at the very least. Likely the siug that was with her, if not other deabrueon as well. Worst case scenario? A jaeitsi bataruce or two," Killian answers.

There's a sharp intake of breath and it takes me a moment to realise the sound's come from me. I had thought of it, but it seemed such an unrealistic prospect. Hearing Killian say it, it sounds more likely than not that we run across them. If Casey's so precious, it wouldn't be surprising to find at least one of them guarding her. It could be Clara. After how she managed to take on Kyle, Aaron, and Robyn, I know I'm right to fear her. And if it is Clara, that could mean–

"Thaddeus might be there," Aaron says, looking pointedly at me.

"Well, I guess I know who I'll be fighting," I say, displaying no emotion.

It's been three years since we slept together and still no one knows. Surely those feelings can't still be there? In that vision I had at Casey's apartment, I had so readily tried to kill him, but that was when faced with the belief he had killed Dominic. Could I really do it, unencumbered by such violent rage? Could I take the life of the man I pity so? No, I don't think I can. But, at the very least, I can fend him off, knowing he won't aim to kill me.

"You'll have the advantage if you do. We all know he won't hurt you."

"My thoughts exactly. What about the avika?" I ask, remembering the overwhelming strength of her power back at Casey's apartment. I don't have any desire to strangle one of my friends again.

"There's a spell. I had to find it, which is why we took so long. You should be able to nullify her powers, but you'll need to get a hold of her first."

Kyle reaches into his bag and hands me a weighty book. I flip to the page he's marked, but it's all in the ancient language.

"What's it say?"

"You still can't read it?" Aaron asks.

"Hello, three years of abstention from all things supernatural," I say.

"It says you'll need to make a cut on her right hand, a place where her isuazko can be summoned from her, and then a cut on your own. The spell translates roughly to: Bring forth that which gives power, draw out the roots of ancient blood," Kyle says.

"Ciestor lista pervo tiesta suyakurava okhim, vrestir avot letai roteroka ni krestar isuazko," I recite.

"It's a near impossible spell, to take away a creature's isuazko, usually requiring at least five witches, but after what I've seen you do today, I think you can manage it. Think you'll remember the words?"

"It's nice and short, not too wordy. I'll manage," I say, shutting the book.

"Can't she just, you know, imagine the thing happening and do it? Wordless caster perks and all," Aaron says.

"Eloquent," Kyle replies before sighing. "No. One can't conceptualise isuazko. Its force is beyond innate ability; it's the magic of creation itself. To take it away from someone is near impossible and drawing on the magic inherent in the ancient language is the only way to command isuazko, unless you're a god. The spell should have many more witches helping usually. I think Mallory is the only person who might be able to cast it without help."

"Lucky for us," Killian says. His jaw is set though, a tension in his face that makes me wonder whether there's something amiss with what we're doing.

"What will happen to her isuazko once I cast the spell?"

"It will be yours. What you take will make you stronger."

I'm not sure I like the idea of having this woman's dark power within me, not given that she's using her gifts to help the jaeitsi. Kyle knows me well enough though. He must know this will bother me, which means there's no other option for stopping her. He wouldn't ask it of me otherwise.

"How do I avoid being confused by her reality distortion again?"

"That's the only problem. I didn't have enough time to find anything. A shielding spell maybe? It's difficult to make oneself impervious to magic, otherwise everyone would do it. Basically, try and cast the spell as quickly as you can."

"Well let's just hope Mallory doesn't try and strangle anyone again. Or worse. Maybe you should leave that behind?" Aaron suggests, pointing to my katana.

Its scabbard hasn't left my side since Kyle's trial and I'm loathe to part with it now. There's something secure in knowing it's by my side at all times, much like that voice that told me I could heal Kyle. But he's right. I don't know the full extent of its power, but if what I felt when I wielded it in the courtroom is anything to go by, it's too dangerous in my hands with an avika in the mix. Begrudgingly, I remove it from my hip and lay it gently on the sofa. Something goes cold within me as I do so and all I want is to reach for it again. Aaron straps a belt with a thin sword he's brought around my waist.

"Between that and your magic, you'll be safe."

Is that really something any of us can guarantee, I want to ask him. Of course not. We've survived this long though, and that is some small comfort. With them by my side I am likely to survive another day. I hope.

"Let's go then."

We trundle down the three flights of stairs before filing out onto Sullivan Street. I can hear the loud Saturday night crowd one block over on MacDougal Street, the NYU students who are likely flooding the comedy clubs and bars hollering at one another. Usually on a Saturday night, after a house party, Lena and I would be hunkered down in her in-house cinema, eating as much as we could possibly fit in our stomachs and then a little bit more. Now I may never see her again. I shake my head. I can't think like that. I won't let this be like Chloe and Connie. I won't let Lena slip through my fingers. She's come to mean so much to me, having taken me under her wing since our first day at university. Even with the bite of her attitude, I'm as fond of her as I would be a sister. I never thought I'd feel that way again after Lilith.

We make a left onto Bleecker, silent with our anticipation of the battle undoubtedly to come. It only takes a few minutes before we're outside the opulent seven-story apartment building.

"Isn't this that crazy apartment building where they listed the penthouse for like, twenty odd million?" Killian asks. We all look at him. "What, I'm into real estate. Don't judge me. The brick barrel vaulted ceilings are supposed to be a thing of beauty."

"You're the most peculiar man," I say.

Kyle and Aaron exchange a look, like an inside joke, but I can't comprehend its meaning.

"Got to hand it to them, it's an upgrade from the Brooklyn docks. Shit, there's a concierge. How are we going to get past him?" Aaron mutters.

"Not to worry," I assure him and he looks bemused. I lay my hand on each of our weapons and draw a cloak around them so only we can see them. "They'll stay cloaked until you unsheathe them."

"And to think Robyn always called you a moron," Aaron says, and I think it's his way of complimenting me.

"The jury's still out. You let that raika live. He could have warned them or sent us into a trap," Killian reminds me.

"I will never hear the end of that, will I?" I ask, striding into the entrance.

"Nope," Aaron and Killian say in unison, before grinning at one another.

"Dear heavens, there are two of them," Kyle mutters.

The concierge looks up, eyeing us suspiciously. No doubt we don't look like the people who frequent this building. Would that I was still wearing Lena's clothes. At least then I might have looked the part of someone visiting. Instead, I'm in my ratty t-shirt and leggings, my hair still damp from my shower.

"May I help you?" he asks.

"We're here to visit apartment eight," I inform him. He looks at me in disbelief, cocking one eyebrow upwards.

"The inhabitants of said apartment being?" he asks, drumming his finger on his desk.

"Old friends?" Kyle suggests. The man does not look impressed.

I step forward quickly and take his hand.

Let me draw a curtain over these thoughts.

His eyes glaze over for a moment, before he shakes his head as if to clear it of dust.

"Of course, the elevator is right there."

We cross the white marble floor and I press the button to call the elevator. The others join me.

"What did you do?" Kyle asks in a hushed tone.

"I just reminded him we're old friends of the people who live in apartment eight. He's seen us a dozen times."

"You messed with his head," Kyle says reproachfully. We step into the elevator and Aaron taps the four button. "Don't you think that's a touch hypocritical given everything Inerea did three years ago?"

"Don't mention her," I warn, and the looks on everyone's faces tell me they're just as surprised by the harshness of my tone as I am. "Just, please. Don't."

I haven't heard her name on someone else's lips in so long and the pain of losing her springs up, an open well, to spill over into my heart. He's right, it is hypocritical. But this situation is different. It's life or death. One second could be the difference between Dominic dying, so I didn't have time to think of a better plan.

Kyle falls silent and the elevator pings before the doors slide open. We cross the landing to the door. What am I expecting to hear? The trample of deabrueon clamouring in the apartment? Screams of someone being tortured? This doesn't strike me as the place the jaeitsi do such business. No, this is the headquarters where the bosses go to get away from getting their hands dirty. I can only imagine what that means we're going to face. I glance at the others. They nod at me, weapons drawn. I unlock the door and, as quietly as possible, open it.

It gives way to a white hallway, which is decorated with an enormous painting that's simply three streaks of differing shades of pink. Not what I expected of a jaeitsi hideout. We follow the hall into a dining room-living room area. The soft lights illuminate the industrial windows and large, white L-shaped sofa, decorated with orange and brown cushions.

Sitting on the sofa, legs crossed with a plate of untouched cake on the coffee table in front of her, is the red-haired girl from the video. Her shoulders are hunched forward, a curtain of hair hiding her face from this angle. Casey.

I sheathe my sword quickly while the others create a perimeter around the two of us. Glancing around, I see there's no one else in the room. I rush to her side, but Casey seems oblivious to the commotion, staring blankly straight ahead, with an odd, limp sort of smile on her face. Her brown eyes seem devoid of any feeling or emotion.

"Hi Casey," I say softly, crouching beside her. She slowly redirects her gaze towards me and blinks, but there's still no life in those eyes.

"You're not one of my friends," she says, frowning.

"No, you don't know me."

"I'm only supposed to talk to my friends."

I remember what the avika said. *Your friends are with you.* Maybe Casey is still under her spell. I better prepare myself for whatever attack she has planned, if such preparation is even possible. I rest my hand on my dagger, just to assure myself it is still there.

"Are your friends here?" I ask, glancing around the room, which is still empty save for the five of us.

"They invited me over this afternoon. I was doing something and they said come over so I did. I always listen when my friends ask something of me. It's peaceful here, don't you think?"

"The avika's here guys," I confirm.

They shift around nervously. This is not an attack we can prepare ourselves for. I turn back to Casey.

"Yeah, it is peaceful. But I think your friends would rather go to a bar," I suggest, but she shakes her head.

"They made cake. But I can't eat it."

"Why?"

"They told me not to move until you got here. They said you'd be alone though."

We all stiffen, the others looking at Casey slowly. So, this is a trap. Shit.

"What did they say to do once I got here?" I whisper, aware of how loud my voice sounds in the otherwise silent apartment.

"They told me to hide."

She stares at me a moment longer before vaulting over the back of the sofa and cowering. I hear that same scuttling as I did in the video.

"Where is it?" Aaron asks, backing towards me. I glance around, but the siug is nowhere to be seen. Then I hear the sound again, coming from above.

Looking up at the brick vaulted ceiling, I see two pincers extended towards me. I roll across the coffee table towards Aaron as it drops to the ground. The plates of its armoured back slide together seamlessly. Rearing up on its back legs, the siug clicks its pincers together before barrelling towards us.

"I got this, get the girl," Aaron reassures me, stepping between me and the creature. He drops to his knees and swings his sword up through its tender underbelly. I move towards the sofa, but Killian has already reached her. He looks over my shoulder before sighing at me and shaking his head. His face is distorted, as if painted in watercolours, as if I could smear him so easily, and I frown.

"What did I tell you?"

I turn around and see, standing on the landing halfway down the staircase, Carlisle, sword strapped to his hip. He grins wickedly before springing over the hand rail. He lands in a crouch position, but is upright in no time. From behind him come another three siugs, pouring out of the woodwork of the staircase.

"Bastard," I hiss.

"Best out of three?" Carlisle says, before charging at me.

I draw my sword just in time to counter his blow. He takes a step back, but I move in with an onslaught of furious attacks.

"You. Little. Piece. Of. Shit," I say, each word paired with a strike.

He counter strikes and I narrowly avoid falling backwards over the table. I knock his sword from his hand before lunging forward and grabbing his wrists in my vice like grip. Snatching the tassel tieback from where it hangs behind a curtain, I yank it free from its hook and bind it swiftly round his wrists. Subdued, he squirms before I knock him to the floor.

"Well, that was easy," I say, turning around.

The living room is empty except for Casey who stares at me blankly over the back of the sofa. The corpse of the siug is gone, as are the other three. And my friends. Where are they? I look around anxiously. What?

"Mallory!"

The voice calls to me as if through a torrent of wind. I turn all around, but see no one other than Casey, not even Carlisle. My sword slips from my hand. Where'd the raika go? The siugs, Kyle, Aaron, and Killian. I wasn't fighting Carlisle long enough for them to take the fight elsewhere.

"You hear my friends too, don't you?" Casey says to me knowingly, righting herself from behind the sofa.

The avika.

I turn around and there, bound where I thought Carlisle would be, are Aaron, Kyle, and Killian, tied up and looking at me in a wide-eyed panic. Did I do this? They flicker out of existence again.

"Mallory!"

I kneel beside where they were moments ago and feel for them. I try to think of any spell I can. Unveil, reveal. Nothing works. I grasp at the empty air where they should be.

"Mallory, we're here!"

Kyle. Suddenly his hand is in mine and the three of them are revealed to me once more.

"Untie us," Aaron says, "before the avika screws with your head anymore."

I reach for the cords wound around their wrists and prise them apart.

"There were no siugs, no raika?" I ask.

"No, you just went berserk and attacked us."

"But," I falter. Why is she only doing this to me and Casey? Surely it would be best to manipulate us all to do her bidding.

"Mallory."

I freeze. The others look at me.

"Dominic," I whisper. Suddenly, I'm rushing towards the stairs, but can't get up them before Killian grabs me. "Let go!"

"It's the avika trying to manipulate you again. I didn't hear anything," Kyle says, helping Killian hold me back.

"Mallory."

No, this is no phantom. I hear Dominic. I know his voice. He's in so much pain, I can tell from the way his voice cracks the syllables of my name.

As we've been speaking, Casey has come up behind us. Aaron steps aside, regarding her warily. She stands directly in front of me before putting her hands over my ears. Then she opens her mouth and sings. I can't make out the notes, but see the tremor of her lips. Killian and Kyle's hands slacken and they let loose their grip of me. I hear three faint thuds before Casey removes her hands. Spinning around, I see the three of them collapsed on the floor, sprawled out in slumber.

"What did you do?" I demand.

"What my friend asked me to. She says it's the angel's lullaby and it puts them to sleep."

"Why? We're trying to help you." I crouch beside Kyle, shaking him. He doesn't stir.

"They won't wake for some time," she says.

I look over my shoulder. Casey still has that glassy look on her face.

"But you kept me awake."

"Yes. She wants to meet you. Or, rather, see you again. She says it's been a long time."

My brows dip inwards together.

"I know her?"

Casey nods, then reaches out her hand to me. I take it and allow myself to be led upstairs. I should stay, protect my friends, but I feel a magnetic pull emanating from upstairs. I need to meet the avika.

There are three doors on the landing and Casey takes me to

the last one on the right. Is Dominic in one of those other rooms? There's no time to check. She opens the door and steps in. I follow her into a spacious office with two large, wooden arch windows. The lights are out except for a lamp on the desk, which washes the wood floors in a warm yellow glow. To my left, Casey takes a seat on a red velvet divan and stares straight ahead. She folds her hands neatly in her lap, a statue. The office is so unlike the modern downstairs. Its décor is archaic, all velvet, damask, and wood. I can scarcely make out the shapes of things though, for all the shadows cast across the room.

"Did I do well?" Casey asks.

"Yes sweetie," comes a voice from a shadowy corner.

I cannot make out the person to who it belongs, but I know I recognise it twice fold. Once from the video, when the avika spoke, and once from somewhere else. No, not once. I have heard it a hundred times, a thousand, only I can't say where. A slender leg steps forward, covered in a sheath skirt that stops mid-shin. At first, I'm not sure I know the face, obscured as it is in my memory by all the false faces she wore during our time together. But there was one she favoured above all and I know now it must be her true face.

"Hello Mallory."

Diane.

Part III

Chapter XI.

My mouth hangs agape as Diane sheds the shadows she had cloaked herself in and steps forward. Her stride is smooth, assured, as if every step she takes does not claim new territory but leads her into that which is already hers. The whole world is at her command. Her hair, a violent shade of red, hangs in loose curls just past her shoulders, impeccably done by a curling iron. Her eyes glisten, the only two lights I remember seeing those nights in the octagonal room full of mirrors. How many years has it been since I've seen this woman? And still, something about her commands my silence, my obedience. I try to fight against it, summon the spell Kyle gave me to strip her of her power, but nothing comes. Her lips quirk up as if she can read my mind and is aware of the power she holds over me. She relishes in it, enjoys it. For contained in that svelte frame is an absolute sort of power, a will to dominate.

"Sit," she says and I drop immediately into the red velvet wing armchair opposite the desk. She strides slowly, with poise and grace, cutting through the still room like a knife. "It's good to see you."

I shut my mouth then open it again. But my mouth is dried out, no words found in any of its crevices. They tuck themselves safely down my throat, out of sight of her prying golden eyes.

"You can speak freely around me now, you know? I won't hurt you. I want to hear how you are, though there's very little I don't already know about your life, being, as I am, in such proximity to your little apartment. Martini?" she offers, pausing by a drinks cart and raising her perfectly manicured brows as she looks at me. Still, I say nothing. How can I in the face of the most monstrous person my childhood knew? She ruined lives, ended them sometimes. She shrugs, as if shaking off the accusations my mind levels at her. "Casey, be a dear and help your friend out?"

Casey rises and walks, zombielike, to the drinks cart. She pours gin and vermouth in a shaker over ice as if she's been tending bars all her life. For a few seconds the only sounds are those of Casey mixing the drink and Diane drawing the desk chair back to sit. She folds her hands in front of her, resting them on the desk and studying me. Casey strains the drink into a martini glass before dropping an olive in and delivering it to Diane. Then, she sits back down on the divan, blank once more.

"Look at me, having a caeletai umea bring me my drinks," she sighs, smiling with self-satisfaction at her glass. She plucks the olive out and sucks on it, her cheeks drawing inward, before chewing.

"You've always been good at getting people to do your bidding," I say. She grins wickedly, setting her glass down. It's not a sight I'm used to seeing and, while I can't say it terrifies me more than her cold looks, there's certainly something unnerving about seeing her smile.

"There's that little girl who used to speak back to me. It got you in a lot of trouble, didn't it? But, still, I always loved that about you, your will in the face of adversity. Never completely broken like the others."

"You gave it a good go though."

"Not really sweetheart. You, Lilith, and Dominic I never intended to break. Until you necessitated it."

My fists curl at the sound of my friends' names, one of whom she killed, the other of whom she has prisoner. How dare she speak of them, of me, as if we were her pets, her children, her favourites. The cruelty she showed us, now admitted as only a small sliver of what she is capable of. I know what she can do, how she drove Thaddeus mad with her power. She could have done the same to me, but she didn't. Why? She could be tormenting Dominic with such visions as she must have done Thaddeus.

"Where is he?"

"Dominic?" she asks, eyes widening in an act of innocence ill-suited to her inherently sultry pout. "Honestly, I don't know. I can assume, but I couldn't guarantee anything. I leave such things up to my inferiors. I don't really like to get my hands dirty anymore. But let's not talk about him, sweetie. It's been a long time. I want to talk about you."

"I thought you said you had been keeping an eye on me," I retort. I can feel myself shaking in her presence, both for fear and rage. I want to climb over the desk and choke her until her eyes stay set in wide eyed fear forever.

"Of course I have. It's very convenient you live so close to Noho. Such great apartments. When I found out you were moving to New York for school I thought I was going to have to live in Queens or something," she says, shuddering. Is that really what makes her shudder? Not the years of torture she inflicted on children? What is it that could scare a beast such as her? "But that would have been a sacrifice I'd be willing to make. I promised your mother I would always look out for you after she gave you to the Academy."

"Liar," I hiss. "My mother died before I went to the Academy."

"Oh, sweetie," she says, shaking her head and taking a sip of her drink, "so much you don't know. Your mother and I went way back. We met when she came to Miesarinda for, well, let's just say it was something she couldn't get without my help. She trusted me to be your guardian in the event of her death in exchange for the information she needed at the time. She knew I'd raise you perfectly."

"Into a murderer," I bite back.

"A warrior. Even without my guidance you performed beautifully in Aplin Hollow and over the past day. I'll admit, I was a bit disappointed with the detour you've been taking the past three years, but it's good to see you back in the swing of things. I knew you wouldn't be able to resist if we had Dominic kidnapped," she sighs. "Admittedly predictable, but ultimately served the greater good."

So, Dominic is alive. That fills my heart with some relief. But will they kill him now they have me? Have I put his life in jeopardy by playing into her hands? No, she said Dominic and I were two of her students she never wanted to break. He must be as valuable to her as I am. She has plans for us all. I realise then that she always has. This. This is who wasn't ready for me just yet. She's been waiting all this time to draw me back into her world, but I've always been in her orbit. I was a fool to think I ever escaped it.

"What would the greater good be?" I ask.

"The destruction of the Onyevaras, the Hirutere, and our restoration to Sundalev with a new government, of course."

She finishes her drink and sets the glass aside while I stare at her in awe.

"You can't be serious? You think I'd help you and the jaeitsi after everything you've done? You think I'd help you kill innocents and destroy the angeleru so that you can establish your own government and control civilisations? Any future you're involved with is full of bleakness and desolation. I'll have no part in it."

"Authority can breed resentment, I've realised that now. Maybe I should have been kinder to you," she muses, walking around to the front of the desk and perching on it. She's aware of my power, of my weapons still sheathed on my hip and my thigh, but fears nothing from me. I realise she's right not to. I'm too spellbound to raise a hand against her. "And after what little you saw of the Hirutere, the bellatoja, you really think they're better than me?"

I bite the insides of my cheeks. Of course, I know they're not good either. But this is a lesser of two evils situation and given the choice–

"I will never choose you," I say coldly.

"What if I make you? I have your beloved Dominic. It's really cute how you two have cozied up over the past few years but, personally, I think Kyle would be a better choice. He softens you," she purrs.

Suddenly she's standing in front of me, running the back of her hand across my cheek. Her fingernails come to rest along my jaw, exactly as they had that day in the octagonal mirrored room. She drums them twice, before smiling coyly. She's enjoying the power she holds over me. It's like a drug to her, to see me cower in fear. I go still against her touch and at the sound of her threat.

"Oh, come now Mallory, I don't want to have to do that. It would be boring for both of us. I'd much rather work together."

"Why me?"

She clicks her tongue and paces away.

"You're a clever girl, always have been."

"You want me to lead the Vernis Lanin," I say, echoing Killian's thoughts.

She presses her lips together and rocks her head from side to side.

"I suppose yes. We wouldn't call it that, bad associations with Thaddeus and genocide. Definitely in need of a rebrand. I'm thinking something more patriotic. Work Dragovicia into your title, maybe. Or have them call you 'The Phoenix Queen'. Now that's regal and calls back to the dragovik legacy."

I look at her eyes, alive with excitement, but so dead to the world. She's been anticipating this meeting for a long time. Had I not been too, in my own way? Always wondering what would happen were we to meet again. The monster that drifted away between sheets of water, slipping between the cracks when it suited her. The only mother my childhood ever knew, no matter how cruel she was. Did I not long for her return as a child, even if only as a means by which to know myself? I felt so lost in the wake of her disappearance. I needed her, like a guiding star, to find my way back to myself, even if the self I knew was only the monster she had made.

"You're considering it," she says, reading me so easily, as she has ever been able to do. I hate being an open book to her.

"You haven't given me much of a choice."

"Now don't think of it like that sweetie. You'll command armies. You'll lay waste to your enemies. You'll build an empire as you see fit with an unstoppable alliance between you and the jaeitsi. You'll return to Dragovicia and have a new home there, the home we both know you've always wanted. It will begin a new era, shaped as you see fit. With some input from me and the jaeitsi of course."

A new era. One without the prejudice the angeleru have for dragoviks. One without the injustice Kyle was about to face. I could temper the world, make it a safe place for the people I love. No longer would I have to fear for their wellbeing, that one small misstep could lead to their execution. I'm unnerved by how welcome the prospect sounds. But, more importantly, it's the only way to save Dominic that I can think of.

"Why do you need someone to lead the dragoviks? If you have Clara, you've got Thaddeus."

"I'm not too fond of the man, prone as he is to bouts of insanity."

"I hear you had your hand in that."

"I created a lot of monsters before I came to the Academy, all at the orders of the Hirutere. You see Mallory, they're not so dissimilar to what you imagine me to be. Torturers, murderers. I learned everything I know from them. You saw what that Alistair did at the Academy."

She's not wrong. With the exception of Killian, I've yet to see any angeleru who are kind, especially to the dragoviks. Alistair took as much pleasure in tormenting me as she had. The look of pleasure on his face as the whip came down. The eagerness as he had stripped me of my clothes. He was ready to enact torments that my body would never forget, whether it bore the scars or not.

"Besides," she continues, "Thaddeus is an uncontrollable variable I don't need."

"And you think you can control me?" I ask.

"No, but I think there's a reason you haven't tried to kill me yet. There's a reason you're hearing me out. Because as bad as you think I am, you know that what I'm saying is true. The Hirutere must fall if there's ever to be peace for supernatural creatures. You wouldn't let your emotions get in the way of creating a better world. Thaddeus would."

"You mean his hatred of you would get in the way."

"Possibly. And his love for you."

So, she knows. I had suspected as much, seeing as she's been keeping an eye on me all this time. She indulges in a smile and it makes my skin crawl.

"How so?"

"Oh, please Mallory. Thaddeus would be your lap dog. He would always defer to you over the cause and we can't afford that. It has to be you who does this."

I study her, all sharpness and red. Everything about her screams danger and death, desolation and destruction. How can I trust the world we would make together will be any better than this one?

Because it has to be.

I'm surprised to hear his voice now. I would not expect the one who guided me in my fight against Thaddeus, who had told me I could give Kyle a new arm, to want me to join forces with Diane. But where he has led me before has always been for the better. Should I turn my back on my instinct to follow him? No.

"I want to know some things first, before I accept."

If I do accept, will she finally love me as I had secretly longed for her to as a child? She nods, as if in answer to the question I have asked myself, though I know she could never love me. She could never love anyone.

"Is Dominic safe?"

"Yes," she sighs, seemingly bored by that line of questioning.

"And the jaeitsi, aren't there only two of them united so far? Surely we won't be that powerful without the other two."

"Now you're thinking big," she says, beaming. "Clara's almost managed to locate the fourth. Of course, she has no idea I'm a part of any of this yet, but I plan on telling her soon. That moron Thaddeus bred a real loathing of me into that girl. Most inconvenient."

I hold my breath. Thaddeus is alive and working with them. I remember what Aaron said about his feelings being my advantage. But how to use it? And the fourth jaeitsi is almost found. That means that the Hirutere are wrong and there are already three jaeitsi working together. This changes things, creating a power dissymmetry I'm not sure I will be able to measure up to.

"And I get to establish the dragoviks in Sundalev, the government run as I wish it to be? I won't be a puppet," I warn. She grins.

"I think I stopped being able to pull your strings long ago."

But she's doing it right now, winding her dream of a new Sundalev inextricably with my own desire for a home, for peace. Could we make a better world for the dragoviks and angeleru together? My compassion and her tenacity.

"One other thing."

"Just one?" she inquires, curious.

"You have to do something for me."

"I make no promises until the request is made, but go ahead."

"Hug me. As your equal. As the girl you moulded as you see fit."

Her eyes widen for a moment before her surprise reshapes itself into a smile. I've made it so easy for her to get her way, it's irresistible. This is the plea of a desperate girl, still trapped by childish desires.

"Of course, sweetie."

She stands in front of me, her arms open wide. I rise. Face to face, we're about the same height, and her in heels no less. Was she always so small? She leans forward and wraps her arms around me, a gesture she seems unaccustomed to. Was she held as a child? I have a childhood of evidence that speaks to the contrary. I smell her hair, like a bushel of apples. It's not a softness I'd associate with her.

"Does that suffice?"

"Yes. Thank you."

In one swift movement, I draw my dagger from its sheath and spin around to grab her wrist. She cries out in shock. Already I feel her power shimmering in the room, trying to obscure reality and keep me from my goal. With one quick slash, I make a small incision on her hand, before doing the same on my own. The room begins to pool with the darkness of her magic, the feeling of smoke clotting my throat. The room is bleeding again. There are dead bodies, the people I love, stacked to the rafters. This isn't real, I tell myself. I manage to spit out the words.

"Ciestor lista pervo tiesta suyakurava okhim, vrestir avot letai roteroka ni krestar isuazko."

The blood beading on her palm glows gold. The mirage her magic created dissipates instantly, revealing her standing before me, clutching at her wrist in horror. Small, shimmering particles emerge from the cut, flowing towards me. They cluster on the blood from my own hand before seeping through the small cut. I feel the sensation immediately, warming my veins as it pushes up my bloodstream to reach my heart and become part of me. The force of the spell throws us to the ground, Diane collapsing into the desk while I stumble backwards. I catch myself on the chair I had sat in, watching in awe as my veins become luminous beneath my skin. My heart pounds with the weight of the new power flowing to it. How could what's inside her be so bright and beautiful?

Just as quickly as it came, the light recedes. Diane groans. I look over at her, but she's slumped over, passed out from the collision with the desk. Glancing down at my dagger, I wonder if I could really do it: take the life of the woman who stripped me and my friends of a chance at normalcy. I reach for my dagger and creep towards her, testing the blade against her throat. Her skin is so soft, the skin of a peach ripe to burst. My hand trembles with the choice I have yet to make. Whatever I decide, I cannot undo. My hand tightens around the handle of the dagger and my resolve strengthens.

"What's going on?"

I spin around to find Casey rubbing her eyes. She blinks at me, my blade still to Diane's throat. She must be coming back to reality now Diane's magic is broken.

"Who are you?"

She seems less perturbed by the dagger to Diane's throat than she is by my very presence.

"My name's Mallory," I say softly, not daring to move towards her, but sheathing my weapon instead. She's scared enough as it is without being cornered by a stranger, one with a dagger no less.

"How, how did I get here? The last thing I remember."

She stops, her eyes widening. The last thing she'll remember is the siug pouncing on her. I recognise that wide eyed realisation from when Aaron told me what he was. And this reality undoubtedly seems more an impossibility to someone who has no knowledge of the supernatural. She looks at me in terror.

"That thing, that woman."

That woman. That's what I used to call Diane before I had a name for her.

"It's gone now and she's unconscious, but we need to get out of here," I insist, extending my hand. "I'll explain everything, but we need to get you somewhere safe."

She looks hesitantly at my outstretched hand, but one glance in Diane's direction has her on her feet. She takes my hand and I lead her back out onto the landing. Diane said Dominic wasn't here, but I don't trust her not to lie. I check the other two rooms, but they're both empty bedrooms. Dammit. We head back down the stairs, where I'm relieved to see the other three are beginning to wake from their slumber.

"Mallory, what happened?" Kyle groans, rubbing the back of his head. He sits upright and must see something of the distress over what's happened on my face. "Are you okay?"

"Dominic's not here. I'll explain the rest later, but we need to go somewhere safe," I say. "Not my apartment. And not back to Emmett, we can't risk leading the jaeitsi there."

He nods as the other two groan and right themselves.

"I know somewhere."

Have I done the right thing in leaving Diane alive? She may not have her magic, but she has other methods of hurting people. She has ways of knowing what you fear most, clawing it free from the place in your heart, and making it your reality.

Chapter XII.

"I so cannot picture you growing up here," I say to Kyle as we make our way up the stairs to his family's brownstone. "Does your family own the whole building?"

He doesn't answer, save for with a sigh. Whether it's embarrassment or not, I can't tell, but he definitely looks uncomfortable as he eyes up the house warily. I should have guessed at his family's wealth judging by the size of their home in Aplin Hollow, but it never seemed important. Nor could I have imagined it extended to a property such as this. What else has he kept from me? Not that he wasn't within his right to.

He unlocks the door and we step into an entrance hall, which is occupied mostly by a vast wooden staircase, as well as an ornate little inlaid table with a towering vase of gladiolas on it. To our right is a parlour, with a grand piano and sofas. Their cushions have not yet bowed to use, the upholstery still in immaculate condition. Much as in Lena's house, these are not rooms to live in. What do Kyle's parents do, I wonder, that means they're never here?

"Yeah, it's an old family house," Kyle finally says, "like the one in Aplin Hollow."

Who knew dragoviks raked it in enough to afford the likes of this?

"This is your house?" Casey asks.

She has been quiet all the way here, allowing me to guide her by her shoulders. I'm surprised she's allowed me to go anywhere near her, given she awoke from Diane's magic to see me with a knife to Diane's throat. Her terror is temporarily gone in the face of her awe, as she looks around at the splendidly decorated house.

"My parents', yes."

He smiles kindly at her and it brings to mind such smiles on his face when first he took me under his wing. It effuses a gentle warmth that's like a blanket around my shoulders. I can see it has the same effect on her, her tense shoulders starting to relax beneath my hands, which I finally drop from her. She looks around more freely, peering into the parlour, before her brow creases with concern.

"Are we safe here?"

"It has magical wards," he says. She frowns.

"Magic, like what that woman used on me?" She looks frightened again.

"No, she's different from us. Our magic is entirely unlike hers. And the wards are only to keep out supernatural creatures that aren't invited. They won't do anything else," he assures her.

She shudders, and I can't imagine how terrifying it must be to have Diane in your head and not understand what's happening. I want to reach out and wrap my arms around her.

Come poor thing, you're all alone.

"Supernatural creatures like me?" she asks.

"Yes, but you're with one of the members of the household and have been invited in so you can enter now and anytime in the future. It's like a safe house," he tells her. This doesn't seem to comfort her, the confirmation of her otherworldly status confusing her all the more. "Come on, let's get you some tea."

We follow him up to the second floor. Walking straight through the dining room, we enter into a spacious kitchen at the back of the house. There's a table in the middle of the room and rich walnut counters and cupboards lining either wall. I can picture Kyle growing up in here, with his penchant for cooking and baking. But in this imagining, he is by himself. Was it always so, or did he at least have Robyn to keep him company? Kyle pulls out a chair for Casey, before busying himself with the kettle. While it's boiling, he takes a tray, a teapot, and five teacups from the cupboard.

"I haven't had a cup of tea in months," he sighs, opening a cupboard and inspecting his options.

"How come?" Casey asks. The seemingly normal topic is a welcome change of pace from what's befallen her today.

"He was in prison," Aaron replies.

I can tell his intention is to throw her off, much as he did with me when we first met. Though it seems ill-intentioned, I know he only means to distract her and set her mind to something other than the fact someone just kidnapped her and that she's a supernatural being. It seems both he and Kyle have a habit of taking in strays. I snort to myself. Killian looks over inquiringly, but I shake my head. Meanwhile, Casey looks to each of us for a sign that Aaron is kidding. When she doesn't get one, her expression turns back to mild terror.

"He was wrongly accused," Killian quickly clarifies, drawing out a chair for me and himself.

"Thanks," I sigh, slumping into it.

I've had an odd sensation ever since casting the spell on Diane. While still exhausted, I also feel a strange tingling restlessness in my limbs. My body wants to test its limits with this new isuazko, but, using Diane's power doesn't sit well with me. Do I somehow become her now? Does more than just her power run through me? So much of me is already what she made, I'm afraid anymore will cost me my self entirely. If I didn't want to use magic before, I certainly don't now. And yet it calls to me. Demands to be drawn upon. Something tells me there will be plenty of time for that yet.

"Wrongly accused of what?" Casey asks, her voice an odd high pitch.

"Stealing something. But it was mine so it was okay that he had it," I say, bypassing the whole weapon blessed by a god concept.

"Oh." She looks slightly at ease again, though keeps fidgeting in her chair. "So, you're good?"

"I mean, in the sense we're not going to torture or kidnap you, I suppose so?" Aaron answers, scratching his stubble.

"Very reassuring," I snap at him. I think his humour is ill-advised at present. Casey is far too nervous for light-heartedness. "Casey, you're free to leave at any point, we're just going to try and explain what happened."

"Like why I was kidnapped by a giant millipede?"

"Ah, well see we can't really explain that one," Kyle interjects.

"Why not?"

"We're still trying to figure out why they took you," Kyle says, filling the teapot with boiling water and plunging in two teabags. He brings over the tray with five teacups and sets the pot in the middle of the table, where steam curls up out of its spout. Casey looks between us. "I was hoping you might have overheard something when they took you?"

"Don't expect me to have answers. All I remember is that thing and then, suddenly, I was coming to in that apartment and you had a knife pressed to that woman's throat."

They all round on me.

"You were going to kill the avika? Didn't the spell work?" Kyle asks.

"Yes, the spell worked."

"Then why?"

Why did I almost kill the woman who ruined my life? More like, why didn't I follow through. It's not that I don't have it in me. If Casey hadn't come around, then I probably would have slit Diane's throat, just as she taught me to do to so many others. However bound I felt when she spoke, as soon as I saw her rendered vulnerable and realised that she's just as susceptible to pain as I am, I knew I could do it. Her words though. They had held me like a spell. Our conversation flashes through our head, the power and allure that had resonated through our conversation. One thing stands out to me, something she had mentioned about Casey.

"Not important right now. Diane said something, I think it might be a clue about why they had Casey," I start, but Kyle's look silences me. His eyes are wide with horror, his mouth agape. "What?"

"Diane?"

Stupid Mallory. Of course he knows who she is; he worked with Doctor Lindberg at the Academy. I had hoped to avoid this subject for a less urgent moment, but it seems we have to have this conversation now.

"Who's Diane?" Aaron asks. Kyle does not seem capable of summing up the enormity of this question in a short answer. But, before I can reply, Killian speaks up.

"The avika," Killian says, his eyes flashing.

"And the woman who ran the Academy," I add, before turning to Killian. "How did you know?"

"Diane used to work as an inquisitor for the Hirutere," Killian explains. "Then one day, not long after Thaddeus broke out, she disappeared. I had no idea she had anything to do with the Academy. This must have been the first time you saw her since… are you okay?"

I nod, though we all know I'm lying. How could I be okay after seeing, for the first time in years, the woman who tortured me and my friends? As soon as he explains how he knows of her, it sparks recognition within me. Of course he knows of her. I had known she had worked for the Hirutere from Thaddeus' memories back in the Library Between, had I not? She had been part of the team that tortured him. I wonder what it was that made her switch sides.

"I'm sorry but you're all talking gibberish. What's the Academy? Or an avika or the Hirutere?" Casey asks.

Kyle sighs but doesn't answer immediately. Instead, he starts by pouring her a cup of tea. I can still sense Killian studying me intently, waiting for a reaction to Diane, no doubt, but I resolve my face to composure and focus on Kyle as he begins to fill Casey in. I take the cup of tea he offers me, while he tells her about what we are and the rest, though doesn't elaborate on the Academy. That's my story to tell. His tone is gentle all the way through, though that doesn't do much to soften the blow. I think to take her hand, but worry she will recoil at my touch for fear of what we are, what I am. I know that, even after all these years, the same fear still quakes in me. And now, with this newfound power, that fear is lit anew.

"Mallory," Killian murmurs as Kyle speaks. He reaches out, his hand resting on my forearm, and he rubs it gently with his thumb.

"I'll be okay," I lie, tilting my chin downwards. He leans closer, shuffling his seat towards me.

"I know you will. But, for now, it's okay not to be. What isn't okay is for you to feel any sense of shame over what's come to pass."

"I almost killed her," I say, lifting my eyes to meet his, though I'm scarcely able to.

"Find me someone who wouldn't have done the same if they were in your shoes. Find me someone who could have gone through everything you did and not have had a moment in which they considered killing her. You didn't fail today."

I could fold myself into his arms at that moment, take advantage of every comfort I know he is willing to offer and absolve myself of the responsibility of healing myself. But not here, not in front of the others. I feel my eyes prick with tears and duck my head.

Just then, Kyle finishes, leaving Casey in a stunned silence, and he turns back to me, distracting me from Killian's sympathetic expression.

"What was it Diane said?" Kyle asks.

"What?" I ask, confused as I am suddenly being yanked from a train of thought.

"You said she mentioned something?"

"Oh yeah, she called Casey a caeletai umea?" I say.

Killian's teacup crashes from his hand to the floor, shattering everywhere. He jumps from his seat before frantically grabbing at the shards.

"What's up with you? Adrenaline crash finally kicking in?" I ask.

He stops his frenzied motion, gapes at me, then Casey, and I quickly realise they're all staring at her in awe.

"What did I miss?"

"Remember how we said you were a big deal when we first met?" Aaron says, and I nod. "Yeah, big deal doesn't cover this."

"You probably don't remember, though I told you once," Kyle whispers, his eyes still fastened to Casey's confused face, though I know he's speaking to me. "The caeletai umea are a type of angeleru. When the angels notice unrest in the world below, they imbue two souls with all the powers of the angels to inhabit new-born babies. Their arrival actually portends great evil and good in that, they wouldn't be here were there no danger, but often they're able to stop it."

"So, in this case, the jaeitsi?"

"It's likely. We'll have to take her to the Hirutere. They'll want to confirm it's her with tests and start her training to do battle right away. No wonder the raika was told to kill you before he let you get to her. She's vital for the war effort."

"There's no need for them to confirm it, I saw her knock you guys out by singing. That sounds vaguely angelic to me."

"The angel's lullaby?" Aaron asks.

Killian is still crouched on the floor in severe shock. From the sounds of things, caeletai umea are like gods among angeleru. He must be in awe being in her presence. Is that a spark of jealousy I feel within me? It doesn't sit comfortably, burning in the pit of my stomach.

While we've been speaking, Casey's eyes have glazed over, much as they had done at Diane's apartment. Slowly, she begins to shake her head, her hands trembling. I'm the first to notice, but soon we're all looking at her. Could Diane's magic still be affecting her somehow?

"Casey, what's the matter?" Kyle asks, reaching for her hand. She snatches it away.

"An angel? Do battle? Vital to the war effort?" Casey repeats. "No."

Suddenly her face is panic stricken. She pushes her chair back and it clatters to the floor as she stands up.

"No, sorry, I'm not an angel. And I'm not here to stop whatever danger you're up against. No."

She runs from the room, back down the stairs. We all spring to our feet, but I shake my head at them.

"We can't let her leave, Mallory," Aaron says. I ignore him, turning instead to Kyle.

"Tell me something: does she have any chance of getting out of this war?"

"Even if she refused to go to the Hirutere, her life would always be in peril," Kyle says. "The jaeitsi won't allow her to live."

"Fine, then I'll talk to her."

"Why are you acting like you're doing us a huge favour?" Aaron asks.

"Because if anyone gets what she's going through, it's me," I say.

Kyle nods. They were all born into this world, but, after Inerea took my memories away, I had to go through rediscovering what I was. The disbelief, the fear. If anyone can get through to her right now, it's me. I follow her downstairs. I didn't hear the front door open or close so she must be down here somewhere. I peek into the parlour before I notice the bathroom door, previously ajar, is now closed. I rap on it twice.

"Casey?"

"Go away you – you freak!"

She's not wrong. I feel all the more freakish for having absorbed someone else's powers. It's like fitting an extra body into the same skin. I rest my forehead against the door and sigh, closing my eyes.

"Yeah, I guess am. Hey, call me other things too if you want. Crazy, betrayer, assassin. But you know what else you can call me?"

I can hear her breathing on the other side of the door and

know her ear is pressed to it.

"What?"

"Alive. Because when those people upstairs found me and told me what I was, I was scared, but I listened. They've saved my life time and time again. Even now, as capable as I am, I'd still be dead if it weren't for them."

"But you fought that woman off," she says.

"I wouldn't have known how to without Kyle. And Killian? He's angeleru like you. I wouldn't have made it through this past weekend without him. Aaron, now he can kick some deabrueon ass if you'll pardon the language."

She laughs and while it's admittedly half-hearted, it's still something. I press my hand to the door. There's a pause before her voice comes back through the door.

"What made you okay with giving up being human?" she asks.

"Well, for starters, I wasn't human so I didn't have that to give up. But the humanity you've learned over a lifetime isn't gone because of this. Hell, you're an angel and, irony of that statement aside, doesn't that make you more human, at least in the sense you mean? I had to come to terms with being a dragon-witch hybrid. Being an angel is way less morally ambiguous. Aside from that," I pause, trying to remember what it was that made me give up the safety of my life with Inerea, "there are people. There are always the people we love to protect, not to mention the people we don't know whose lives we save along the way."

"My dad," she whispers, and I can tell she's on the verge of tears. "Is he okay?"

"Tell you what, we can call him. I'll even go check on him tonight if it will put you at ease."

I'm exhausted and all I want to do is sleep, but I understand the importance of knowing the people you care about are okay. Thinking of Dominic still alone out there, my heart sinks. Today I've failed him. I won't let Casey feel like she's abandoned her father.

The door cracks open and Casey peeks out. Her brown eyes are wide and full of tears, which have begun to stream down her face.

"I'm going to protect you and him, I promise."

"How can you protect him from creatures like that thing that came for me?"

"Witch," I say, pointing at myself. "I'll put a cloaking spell on him so no one can track him down, then wards on the apartment so supernatural creatures can't enter. Excepting you of course. You'll want to go home after all of this."

I know very well this last part could be a lie. Casey may never go home, as I could not after Inerea died. If she's lucky, she'll survive long enough to have a new life in Miesarinda. If she's unlucky, the jaeitsi will kill her. She smiles at me though and I know my sin is worth it to bring her comfort. Not to mention, if Casey is as a formidable force as they say, we'll need her on our side to win the war.

"Can you promise me something else?" I nod. "None of these tests from the Hiru-whatever. I don't want to be poked and prodded by strangers. These guys give me the creeps."

"They're not all bad," I say, "but if that's what you want then I won't let anyone take you to them."

She smiles.

"Thank you, Mallory, was it?"

"Yeah. Consider me your new bodyguard. Sorry, that's probably not particularly comforting."

"After you fought that woman, it's the most comforting news I've had all day," she sighs, her shoulders sagging.

Just then, the front door flies open. I'm standing between it and Casey in a second, before I realise I'm probably the one who needs protecting. Furious brown eyes find me from across the hall.

"You!" Robyn hisses, before storming up the stairs. Casey cowers behind me, holding my shoulders.

"Who's that?"

"Kyle's sister. Come on."

"She's related to Kyle?"

I know she's as shocked as I was when I discovered they were siblings. After seeing Kyle's kind disposition, how could one not be jarred by Robyn throwing herself through the door, all fury.

Already I hear yelling from the kitchen. Taking the stairs in twos, I dart up with Casey scuttling swiftly behind me. I hear the sound of china shattering and the scene in the kitchen unfolds before me.

"Complete," Robyn bellows, hurling a teacup at her brother, who ducks behind the table, "asshole!"

"Robyn, please calm down!" he pleads, dodging the accompanying saucer.

"I find out from some fucking rando in my class that my own brother has got off a death sentence which, by the way, he never told me he was in prison for, because that bitch downstairs couldn't stick around to tell anyone she had paired with a gods' weapon. And now, you're cavorting around New York with her, having gotten off the charge."

"Cavorting's a bit of an exaggeration," Aaron quips. He crouches behind a chair to narrowly miss being hit by a teapot.

"If you'll just let me explain!" Kyle says.

"Complete asshole!" she shouts again.

There are no more dishes on the table so she makes her way to a cupboard and starts pulling out glasses. From there, she spots me standing in the doorway. Her eyes narrow and she tosses a glass in the air and catches it again.

"And you."

"Hey Robyn," I mutter meekly, just as a glass comes soaring at me. I turn to Casey. "Run."

Casey darts behind the dining room table as I dodge the glass.

"Don't 'hey Robyn' me. Where the fuck have you been?"

"Cavorting apparently." Her nostrils flare.

"Must have been nice, not having to deal with the aftermath of that mess you left us in. Do you have any idea what you put my brother through? He was beside himself with worry for the past three years that you'd been kidnapped or killed. Personally, I'm disappointed he wasn't right."

"Oh how I've missed this, let me count the ways," I sigh. "While your anger is, without a doubt, justified, we have more pressing matters at hand right now."

She's still holding a glass, primed to lob at my head, when I say this. Taking pause, she slowly lowers it.

"What matters?"

"Oh, you know, hostage situations, jaeitsi hunting us down, and, oh yeah, we found a caeletai umea," Aaron says, righting himself. He brushes a shard of teapot from his shoulder. "Your aim's gotten weak by the way."

"Don't further enrage the angry woman with the glass," I scold him. Robyn doesn't seem to hear what I'm saying, her face blanching.

"A caeletai umea?"

"Yup the one and only. Well actually the one of two, but you get the idea," Aaron replies. Killian flinches, still not out of the reverie he's been in since I told them what Casey is. He's been standing aside, staring blankly on during Robyn's attack. Finding out who Casey is has seriously taken its toll on him and I'm starting to wonder if he'll ever recover from the shock. He catches my eye and the overwhelming look of sadness that crashes through his features stills my heart. What has saddened him so? Robyn looks back and forth between the two of us, as if waiting for us to burst out laughing.

"Fine," she grumbles, setting the glass down, "I'll hear you out. But I am still livid."

"We wouldn't have you any other way."

Chapter XIII.

Figuring it's best to remove myself from the equation as Aaron, Kyle, and Robyn catch up, I opt to head with Casey to her father's apartment. Killian insists on coming with us, at least on the train ride, but I see the signs of fatigue beginning to crack on his face. He's scarcely able to keep his eyes open on our way to Brooklyn. He leans the entirety of his weight on one of the bars when we can't get a seat and I'm half worried he won't make it back to Miesarinda on his own.

"You should really go home," I say to him as the train arrives at our station.

"It's okay, I'll be fine," he says, stumbling forwards out of the train. I catch him by the shoulders and he sags against me, his head tilting to rest against my shoulder. I hear his shallow breaths and half think he's fallen asleep there and then. I let him lean on me for a moment before he shakes himself awake. He looks up at me with heavy lidded eyes. "'m okay."

"Absolutely not. It's an official mandate now that Killian Varys must return to Miesarinda for rest. Go. We'll be fine."

He grumbles his assent. We wave goodbye to Killian at the train station and start the short walk back to Casey's house.

The shadows seem to delight in shifting and swelling, taunting us with the threat of obscuring some creature. The closer we get, the more nervous Casey becomes, glancing over her shoulder every few seconds. Whether it's fear of more deabrueon or for her father's wellbeing, I'm not certain. Perhaps it's a mix of both. This is where she was kidnapped by Diane after all; returning here must be terrifying. When we reach the apartment, a sudden calm seems to hit her though, as if all is forgotten and she could just run up those stairs and throw herself into her father's arms, as if none of this has happened. I remember wanting to do the same with Inerea when I found out what I am. The only trouble was, she had been keeping my identity a secret. Chances are Casey's father has no idea she happened to be born a caeletai umea. To distract Casey from the urge to run upstairs, I hand her my phone to call her dad. Hers is long lost back at the warehouse. She swallows hard, realising she cannot, at least for now, return home. She dials his number. I can hear the faint ringing before he picks up and answers with a hello. Casey breathes a sigh of relief.

"Hey dad."

"Casey? Thank goodness. Whose phone is this? Where are you? I didn't know you were going out tonight."

"I wasn't planning on it. I met up with a friend and we got so caught up hanging out I lost track of time. We started writing some music together, so I'm going to stay at hers for a few days while we work on it."

"Okay, well just as long as you're alright. Love you kiddo."

"Love you too dad." She hangs up and hands me the phone. "Thank you."

"No problem. I know what it's like."

She nods.

"I guessed from how you spoke of wanting to protect someone. That guy you were asking Diane about, Dominic, is he who you're trying to protect?"

I go rigid at the mention of his name. It pains me so much to know he's one day further from safety. In that time, all manner of torture could be administered. I am grateful, at least, that in taking Diane's powers away, I have spared him from her reality manipulations. But she has other cruel arts I cannot keep him from until he's rescued.

"I didn't realise you remembered any of our conversation," I say.

"What happened while I was under her spell is beginning to come back in pieces. Mostly I remember you, like some light at the end of a tunnel, trying to draw me out of the trance she put me in."

"Oh." I still haven't answered her question though. She shifts awkwardly from foot to foot.

"Sorry I didn't mean to pry," she mutters suddenly, staring at the ground.

"You're not," I assure her, "and yes. Dominic is my oldest friend and Diane abducted him."

"Why?"

"To get to me."

Casey swallows hard, glancing nervously up at her father's window and I know what she's thinking.

"It's not going to happen to him," I assure her, placing my hand on the wall.

I draw a cloak over the building before raising an invisible fence around its perimeter to keep out the supernatural. Stepping back, I admire my work. The walls shimmer golden before fading back to brick. This should hold for a time.

"Wow," Casey breathes. "Can I do that?"

"Different species, different abilities. I don't know too much about caeletai umea. Kyle's probably the one to ask if you want the inside scoop."

"So, what kind of magic can you do?" she asks, bouncing along beside me as we walk back down the street. It's surprising to see her sudden interest, but I suppose it beats her cowering in the bathroom.

"Honestly? I don't know the full extent of it. I've been a little out of the loop recently. I'm a wordless caster, which means I can conjure almost anything I can imagine. I couldn't undo your sleeping spell though."

"Really?" If I'm not mistaken, she sounds flattered. "But you're like, really powerful."

I laugh.

"Aside from being trained to fight and my ability to cast without using the ancient language, I'm pretty much your average dragovik. You'll be really underwhelmed by me after you see what Robyn can do with a crossbow."

"I don't know, she seems sort of…"

"Intimidating?"

"Yeah."

"She has that effect on people."

"I still can't believe she's Kyle's sister. He's seems so sweet."

"He's the best person you could have by your side when going through this. He's pieced me back together a hundred times. Not literally of course," I add hastily when horror begins to dawn on her face.

"Sorry, I'm just not sure how literally to take things. Like, there are dragons, actual dragons, and– "

Aware of something moving to my left, I draw Casey behind

me and pull out the delicate sword Aaron gave me. The shadows tremble, like cloth moving across skin, before a girl emerges. She looks at me as if on an old friend, softened eyes and a smile. It takes me a moment to recognise her, it having been so long. I hadn't even been sure she was real when we met, it only being in my dreams.

"You," I breathe, raising my sword before me.

"I promised I'd come, didn't I?" she giggles.

The girl who had promised we'd be the death of one another. After I dreamt of her that night in Aplin Hollow, the night of the first deabrueon attack in the forest, the memory of her scattered like the fragments of a teacup across my mind. And I know now, that's what she'd wanted. For me to forget her only to gather her back together when we met in person.

She still wears the same dress, waterfall upon waterfall of tulle and red flowers. Her hair is a mess of brown waves reaching her waist, which is so narrow I wonder if I could wrap my hands around it and the tips of my fingers would meet. She's so petite, nearly all surface, though I know there's much inside that head of hers that I cannot fathom. This is who she is, the appearance of grace wrapping itself exquisitely around the substance of death.

"That you did. You said we'd be the death of each other," I say, remembering her words as precisely as though they were stars piercing the black fabric of the night sky that is my mind.

"And now's come the time, my life owed to you and yours is mine," she sings. "It's a prophecy see, Yima blesses me with them at times. You too, in the form of dreams. They're more colourful, full of poetry that seeps through your mind. I want to unravel that beautiful brain of yours on the sidewalk."

She walks towards me slowly, her dress dragging heavy across the road. I make to start towards her, but my legs won't budge. No matter how close she gets, I am unable to move, my arms and legs paralysed.

"Mallory," Casey whispers in a panic.

The girl reaches me and taps the side of my head. Her eyes glow as two beacons, the brightest things in the dark street, though a full moon hangs above us.

"I know that feeling, paralysed by fear. It's my gift you see. It's a curse too, but usually I can hide from that."

"Your gift?" I manage, though my lips hardly part.

It feels as though everything has fallen to atrophy. Even my lungs struggle to swell with air against my chest. I fear if this goes on much longer, even my heart will still.

"To strike terror. The other half of me does it better, but," she pauses, shivering, "you won't like him."

"You don't like him either."

I've latched on to her body language, the tremor in her voice. This other half, whatever it is, she fears it. If I can align us against him, maybe she'll spare us. She smiles.

"You can't fight him, Mallory. Maybe you could have. They say you wielded the power of a Vaerdiexes stone, were a conduit. Robyn would have died if it had been anyone else helping her conduct the power of the stone. There's no other veins it was meant to run through. And you have one, even now, though you've left it unprotected. You need to take better care of these things. But as you are, you'd stand no chance against him and we must remain enemies."

Can she read my mind?

"No, but the shape of your fears are the sad gleam in a child's eyes," she murmurs, the breeze whispering through her hair.

If I can't create an alliance, perhaps I can distract her long enough to break her spell. I draw visions of unlocking, unbinding, and undoing, but none work.

"I have a Vaerdiexes stone?"

"Everyone heard about it, though no one knew what it meant. See I was there when they were made. The gods' weapons. The smith was my father and Vaerdiexes came to our house. He could do that back then, make visitations upon Sundalev. He did not give Illarion all the stones you see, that's too dangerous, that's too much power. It could make a god," she pauses again, before placing her hand on my forehead as if to take my temperature. "He's in your head. I know what it is to have a god in your head. So did Thaddeus, but you took Vaerdiexes from him."

"You only speak in riddles, I don't understand."

"I try, I try to break my curses. But this is how my tongue ladles words into ears until they stop listening. Then they die."

"I'm listening. I have a god in my head?"

"He's chosen you for what Thaddeus couldn't do."

I hesitate, wanting to understand, but can make no sense of her meaning.

"And the Vaerdiexes stone, where is it?"

"In your second greatest weapon. He's chosen you twice fold now. You should honour your gods better, their relics too."

"The gods' weapon." That green stone.

"The Vaerdiexes sword," she says, nodding keenly.

"Your father made them. but those were made millennia ago. How is it possible that you're still alive?"

"I took something from Vaerdiexes," she whispers, glancing around before leaning in conspiratorially. "Do you want to see it?"

I nod. Her magic is loosening itself from me and I hope soon I will be able to shuffle it off entirely. Reaching to her throat, she draws out a chain from beneath her dress. At the end of it hangs a rectangular shard of mirror.

"This is how I know what it is to have a god in your head," she tells me. "This is how my other half came into being and why he cannot leave."

I peer at it. The mirror does not reflect me; it does not reflect anything. It's utterly opaque, but I'm certain I hear a faint whisper coming from it. My hand craves to wrap around it.

"It only shows me what I want to see," she says, reading my face once more, "but after him, I don't want to see anything."

She slips it back beneath her dress. This girl has a Vaerdiexes stone and is several millennia old. I've clearly underestimated what I'm dealing with. Shit. If Casey weren't here, I wouldn't be so worried, but I have to protect her too, as I promised I would do.

"If you're here to kill me, why are you telling me these things?"

"You asked. No one asks."

"Ask me something then."

"What's that?" she inquires, her golden-brown eyes lighting with curiosity.

"Ask me to help you."

She laughs, tilting her head back to gaze at the stars. She has a softly rounded face, not unlike Robyn's, and it is full of a childish glee that does not suit her promises of death.

"You cannot, I've already told you that. Powerful though you may be. You have to die. Your life is owed to me, as mine is due to you. The visions told me so."

From nowhere she draws a scythe, it's long black handle the height of her. The curved blade abuts a short dagger on the other side. Her dress shimmers and suddenly she is dressed in all black leather armour.

"Maybe if you had the Vaerdiexes sword you could have stood a chance," she sighs, "but as you stand you have no chance."

My eyes widen. She has a gods' weapon too.

"Still, I'll give you this much."

I feel the iron will that bound my limbs release them and I stumble, falling to my knees. Pushing myself up onto all fours, I stare the girl down. Her eyes glint, all mischief. They lack the malevolence she promises.

"Run Casey" I order.

"But– "

"I said run! Get back to the others."

I spring to my feet and brandish my sword. The girl laughs, delighting in the display. I hear Casey's footsteps as she dashes down the street. I lunge at the girl, but, in an instant, she's gone, rippling out of reality. I feel something blunt hit my back, knocking me to my knees once more. Rolling onto my back, I see her standing behind me.

"How?" I gasp.

"Shigami's scythe, ferry woman of the dead. She moves between this world and theirs, as can I when I wield her weapon."

She disappears again only to appear to my right, showing off her ability. I'll never see her attacks coming. Like this, I stand no chance against her. I have to think of a new plan, and fast. At least something that will buy Casey time enough to return to Kyle's. Suddenly I know what to do. I will mirror her, invoke the fear that is already there.

"That's how you hide from him, isn't it? Your other half."

She tenses, perturbed by the mention of him. Her head bobs up and down slowly, and the look on her face renders her so childlike.

"Why can't you fight him?"

"He is smoke. There is nothing of him to be caught by a blade, except maybe one."

"You said I would stand a chance if I had the Vaerdiexes sword. I know where it is. Let me get it and I can help you. Maybe owing our lives to each other isn't about killing one another, but saving each other."

Her eyes widen as I say this and she seems to genuinely consider my words. But then she shakes her head.

"The sword is gone. Besides, it's more fun this way."

She leaps into the air, disappearing, only to shimmer back into existence when her blade is poised above me. I catch it just in time with my sword, throwing her backwards.

"You're quick."

She catches the hilt of the crossguard of my sword with her scythe's handle and yanks it from my hand. It clatters across the street behind her.

"But you're still dead."

I raise my hand before she can bring down her scythe, deflecting it with a shield of magic. She staggers back beneath the weight of the weapon. I try to heat the scythe with my magic, so it is unbearable to hold, or make it fly from her hand, but it doesn't yield to my power. Looking around, I spot a fire hydrant. With a flick of my hand, it bursts open, gushing out water. A tendril whips out, snatching at the scythe, only to glance off.

"Gods' weapons are impervious to magic," she calls, as if taunting me.

"Then I guess I'll have to take it from you myself."

Now it's my turn to disappear. Summoning the strength of my magic joined with Diane's, I pull down from the sky a shroud of fog. It seeps across the street, obscuring me from sight. We sink into its blanket, neither seen nor seeing.

Show me light only I can see, I command. I feel the strength of Diane's magic, coupled with my own, obeying me in an instant. A gold orb shimmers into existence in my palm. With it, I illuminate my way to the girl, who looks around, confused. I move stealthily towards her before darting my hand out and grabbing the top of the handle. I cry out, letting go of the handle as the metal burns my hand. She spots me and sweeps the scythe's handle behind my legs to knock me down.

"So little you know. You cannot take a gods' weapon from its wielder's hand."

Shit.

I sprint back to my sword as she follows, steady steps across the street. There's not enough time. I pull my parrying dagger from my sheath and throw it, hoping it finds its mark.

She screams, the dagger striking her hand, and I hear the clatter of her scythe falling to the ground. Diving for it, I snatch it from the ground before bounding a few steps away from her. The scythe collapses on itself, shrinking down to a two-foot rod of black metal. I may not be able to use it as a weapon now, but neither can she. I find her face, the shroud of fog lifting. Her eyes widen in horror.

"What have you done?" she demands.

Suddenly, the earth beneath us trembles. She freezes.

"No," she whispers.

I look around as a flock of pigeons flies from a nearby tree. Rats scuttle away from the dumpsters on the sidewalk. The fire of my blood goes cold. Everything I fear, all that which is unknown but haunts the edges of our reality, suddenly seems possible and imminent. My body freezes in place, as if encased in ice. I cannot move for fear that the things that makes my blood go cold are coming for me. I should run. I should want to run. But I am too afraid. This power, it is double hers, no, thrice hers. It is the adamant will of the gods that holds me still. I look to the girl and she is equally bound.

"What is this?" I gasp, my throat seeming to close.

"Him."

The shadows to our right let out a groan, like some great beast awakening from hibernation. They rise, unfolding themselves to the height of the three-storey building behind it.

"Thrabr."

Huge red eyes blink into existence. Horns sprout from the head of the beast that is all shadow. It's slightly translucent, existing as it does between our world and darkness. Its skin whisps like smoke peeling off of it.

"Found you," it growls, looking to the girl. "Do you know how long I've waited to catch you without your little escape route? To take what is owed from when you forced me into being? You keep what ought to be mine, what I should have ripped from your throat the night I killed your father."

He groans, straining to free himself from the shadows, as if they were a swathe of fabric from which to cut and fashion new demons. I hear a tearing and he roars, pulling himself into the street. He leans over the girl, reaching out a claw, which he curls above her. She doesn't run, her body merely shivering like a current rippling in the wind.

"Give me the Vaerdiexes Stone and I will be a god. You have squandered its gifts far too long. Give me the stone and I will bring about a new era. Out shall go the age of man, in shall I usher the age of demons."

"Stop!" a shaky voice commands from behind me.

Casey? The creature moves to spy her, though I cannot turn to look at her.

"I told you to run," I say, "go now!"

She ignores me. Seemingly unaffected by its paralysing spell, she walks past me.

"This is my friend," she says, stepping between me and it. "I won't let you hurt her."

My arms unbuckle themselves and I collapse on the ground, panting. How is that possible? The girl looks at us frantically and, though I know she meant to kill me only moments ago, there's yet so much more I need to ask of her. Scythe in hand, I sprint past Casey, who has distracted the demon enough that it no longer holds me in its spell. Grabbing the girl's hand in my own before Thrabr can stop me, I press the scythe into her grip.

"Go."

Without a word, she vanishes.

Thrabr roars, swatting me like a fly, sending me soaring. The force with which he throws me means I crash into a building, its architecture shuddering beneath the force. When he touches me, his form becomes opaque, only to grow translucent again when we lose contact. He's incorporeal. How the hell am I going to fight this?

He rounds on Casey.

"Little girl, I have hurt her. What will you do?"

He drops onto all fours and lumbers towards her, eyes blazing. I see the fear in Casey's eyes. I cannot protect her, though I promised to only hours ago. My back aches and I'm certain something, somewhere is broken. Or many somethings.

Let others help you.

That voice warms in my head, the one I know now belongs to a god. Vaerdiexes.

A god's light. Pritovis.

"Casey! Pritovis' light," I shout, though the words have no meaning to me.

"Pritovis' light?" she asks.

There's a sudden flash, a tear in the fabric of darkness as a ripple of golden light bursts from Casey. The beast howls, falling back. The light expands into a ball, surrounding him. Swirling around, it draws him as if into a vortex before disappearing into a pinprick. Again, there is the darkness of the street, as if nothing has happened. We both stare at where he was a second ago, waiting for him to reappear with bated breath.

"Keep quiet out there!" someone yells from a nearby window.

I stagger to my feet, limping over to Casey who stands, unmoving.

"Did I do that?" she asks, staring in awe at the place the light disappeared.

"I'm guessing that would be one of your powers," I answer, panting.

"How did you know? I thought you didn't know about caeletai umea?" Before I can explain, she reaches out and grips my forearm. "I don't…I don't feel so good," she groans.

I catch her as she collapses.

"We've all been there," I sigh, slinging her over my shoulder.

Chapter XIV.

"I'm sorry, what happened?" Kyle asks again as I lower Casey onto the bed. We're in the upstairs bedroom, Robyn having refused to have either me or Casey on the same floor as her room. Early morning light is beginning to come through the windows, so I draw the curtains shut to give Casey the chance to rest. Not that I think she'll need much help given she's been unconscious since fighting Thrabr. Clearly that spell, or whatever it was, really took it out of her. Commanding a god's power, or channelling it rather, must be exhausting.

"Little girl. Big demon. Both trying to kill us," I grumble, following Kyle back to the living room where I collapse into a chair. "I am utterly defeated. Wake me in a year."

"And you helped the girl get away," Aaron says.

He's trailed wordlessly behind us since I got back to Kyle's. The look of shock when he opened the door to me cradling Casey was amusing and almost made the whole thing worth it. Almost.

"Yes."

"You have got to stop sparing the lives of murderers."

"Potential murderers. She didn't actually kill me. Also, she's like a thousand plus years old. It just feels icky to end a life like that. She's still such a child in so many ways. Plus, there are so many questions I still need to ask her. She knows so much, she may even know something about the jaeitsi, if I can just convince her to work with us rather than trying to kill me."

"That would be helpful on multiple accounts, especially given you claim she has a gods' weapon."

"No claim, I have the solid proof of my ass getting kicked. That doesn't happen too often these days."

"I know, but I've never heard of the scythe before," Kyle says, "I didn't even know Shigami had blessed one of the weapons. I've not seen it in any of my books."

"Have you looked under 'her dad was the smith who made the damn things so he probably gave her it from the get go'?"

They both blink at me.

"Her father is Cassian Cadmus?" Kyle asks.

"Only if that's the guy who made the weapons."

"Okay, say we go along with what she says. Who gives their daughter the scythe of a god of death?" Aaron asks, wrinkling his nose.

"I don't know, the same guy who raised a daughter that pick-pocketed a god?"

"What?" they both ask.

"She stole a stone from Vaerdiexes."

"I'm sorry, you're saying there's a girl out there armed with a Vaerdiexes stone and a gods' weapon, and she believes it's prophesised that she'll kill you? You're fucked."

"I pretty much came to the same conclusion," I sigh, kicking off my shoes and tucking my feet beneath me. I fall back against the armchair. I could so easily close my eyes and fall asleep right here, but I know that I can't do that, not while Kyle and Aaron still have questions for me.

"But why did she wait three years after introducing herself in Aplin Hollow to come find you? And why hasn't she come for you since Casey fought off Thrabr? It doesn't make sense if she's hell-bent on killing you," Aaron asks.

"Maybe because you saved her life?" Kyle says hopefully.

"Or she knows I have a gods' weapon and a Vaerdiexes stone of my own," I reply, though I don't feel the faintest hint of smugness saying it. So comfy. Could so easily close my eyes…

"You have got to stop dropping bombs like this on us. When did you get one of those bad boys?" Aaron demands.

"They're not bad boys, Aaron," Kyle sighs, "they're ancient relics of a god, containing power that this world would otherwise be too fragile to sustain."

"What he said. And about the time I got the katana. It's the emerald in the blade."

"That makes sense," Kyle says, nodding. "Vaerdiexes created the stones before he lost his foothold on Earth and Sundalev. It adds up that he'd want the person he entrusts the Vaerdiexes sword with to have one of them."

"Do you know which one it is?" I ask.

"No, but I'd like to find out. I'd also like to know more about the one she had. Do you know what the one the girl had looked like? Is it weird to call her a girl if she's several thousand years old?"

"Yes to both."

"Let's hit the books."

Aaron groans. "I'll give that a miss if you don't mind. I need some sleep."

"You need sleep? I've been up for three days straight!" I say.

"Well maybe you should consider not partying so hard."

"Both of you, rest. I'll handle the research bit," Kyle sighs. I being to protest, but he shakes his head. "I got a little sleep while you were out. You need it more than I do."

He gets up and heads to the other end of the living room, through a door, into the library.

"He's so self-flagellating, now I feel bad," Aaron grumbles.

"Make up your mind," I yawn, stretching. "I'm honestly too exhausted to fight him on this one. Where's a girl gonna catch some shut eye?"

"You can always come sleep in my bed?"

I know he expects me to refuse, but I just shrug.

"Why the hell not. If there's nowhere else up for grabs."

He raises his eyebrows, but says nothing, leading me back up to the top floor and into the room opposite Casey's. He gropes along the wall for the light switch, illuminating a sparsely decorated room. I suspect the ornamental glass bird on the dresser is the Caverly's doing, out of sync as it is with Aaron's tastes.

"Wow you have such cute taste," I say, picking it up. He swipes it from me.

"Don't touch Reginald."

"You just made that name up, didn't you?"

"Let's go with yes."

He sets it back on the dresser. Other than the aforementioned Reginald, there's nothing personal in here. Yet he called it his room.

"So, you have a permanent room at the Caverly's?"

"Pretty permanent, my parents left me here a lot growing up while they were on missions."

"I can't imagine you with parents," I admit, as I watch him slip beneath the sheets of the king size bed.

"No? How do you imagine me?" he asks, propping himself up

on his elbow to watch me climb in beside him.

"A little pervert wolf being raised in a cave," I reply, and he rumbles with laughter.

"Maybe I was."

"Seems likely. It's strange, I hardly know anything about you," I say, tilting my head to the left to look at him.

"Sure you do."

"Not really. I mean I know you're an arrogant ass who can fight a deabrueon, but that's it."

"What do you want to know?" he asks.

I'm surprised he's offering himself up to me like this, his past suddenly available. Aaron seems the type to play things close to the chest, keeping his true self reserved from people while playing up his persona. But maybe it's not a persona. Maybe this is really, truly who he is.

"Why did your parents leave you here a lot?"

"They both ran missions for the Onyevaras. I stayed with Kyle, Robyn, and their alcoholic of an aunt while their parents were off too. My mum and their mum were on the same squad. I've known Kyle since we were in diapers or, rather, since we were little wolves in a cave."

I laugh, closing my eyes for a moment. I want so badly to sleep, but can't pass up the opportunity to learn more about one of the people who has saved my life so many times. My eyes open again.

"Are you close to them?"

"As close as any dragovik with working parents can be. They've both retired now, moved out of the city, but I see them often enough. Yeah, we're close."

"Any siblings?"

"Do I have the ego of a man with siblings?"

"No, I suppose you don't. What made you," I pause, yawning, "what made you follow in their footsteps?"

"You mean as a soldier for the Onyevaras?" I nod. "I saw the good it did. I saw how they helped people. Plus, it gets you all the glory and the women."

"Is that all you care about?"

"Honestly," he says, falling back onto his pillow and staring up at the ceiling. "Sometimes I wonder if I really care about anything at all."

My eyes widen. How can he possibly say that? His care for his friends is so evident. The way he reacted when Kyle returned from Miesarinda, it's obvious how important they are to him.

"I don't think that's true. You care about your friends. You care about me. What makes you think that?"

"That's true. I do care about all of you." He folds his arms behind his head. "Do you ever feel like you've been offered so much of the world that you go numb to it? The good, the bad. Your world is oversaturated so you forget what it's like to not have it all, you forget what it's like to take pleasure in the small things?"

"I can honestly say I've never felt that way. But, I can understand it."

"I'm not complaining. I'm extremely fortunate. I look at what Robyn has been through or what you suffered and know I'm lucky. But it's as if the world is diminishing and it's hard for me to appreciate things anymore."

"I think you need to make the time to do that then. You'll forget what matters if you don't."

He turns to look at me.

"Who are you who is so wise in the ways of life? What happened to my naïve, inexperienced Thiel?"

"She spent three amazing years enjoying life. And she appreciated every moment of it."

"You're scared of losing your life at NYU?"

"Terrified," I reply.

"I'll fight for that for you. I won't let you lose what's important."

"That right there," I whisper, "that's how I can tell you care."

He offers me a lopsided grin.

"Thanks Thiel."

"No problem."

I blink a few times before reality folds itself up behind my eyelids.

* * *

When I wake, Aaron is gone. I wonder how telling this would be of an encounter in which I actually slept with him. He doesn't seem the type to stick around the morning after. Why am I even thinking about this? I'm not, nor have I ever been, interested in Aaron that way. I yawn, still exhausted from the night before. My back is sore from when Thrabr struck me, but, other than that, I feel incredibly grateful for the lack of injuries. I need to thank Casey for saving my sorry ass when she wakes.

I trot out onto the landing, only to bump into Robyn, who is carrying a tray with soup and some water on it.

"Is that for Casey?" I ask, stretching my arms above my head.

"Yes," she replies in a clipped tone. She sees Aaron's door ajar and her eyes narrow. Her face is imbued with the same rage as when she got home last night. What over? Me sleeping in Aaron's room? There's no way she's still pining for him. Is there? "That didn't take long."

Apparently so.

"I did not have sex with Aaron, Robyn. Just never going to happen. Now if you don't mind," I say, taking the tray from her, "it's probably best Casey wakes up to a friendly face."

"Fine," she snaps, glaring furiously. "By the way, Kyle wants to see your slut-self downstairs."

"Charming," I reply coolly.

Gone are the days of Robyn putting me ill at ease or upsetting my delicately balanced psyche. And, after that comment, I'll have no problem putting her in her place in the future. She whirls around and heads back downstairs.

Following a knock, I nudge open Casey's door, sidling in, to find her slowly sitting upright. She looks groggy and her hair is a dishevelled mess. I can't imagine I look much better at the moment to be fair.

"Well, that sounded unpleasant," Casey says, raising her eyebrows at me as I enter the room.

"Don't mind Robyn, she can't help being bitter and angry," I sigh, setting the tray in her lap. She snorts a laugh.

"You guys have a history, huh."

"Unfortunately, yes. I would have preferred it remained history, but present circumstances demand otherwise. You should eat something."

"I could eat a whale right now," she answers, looking at the soup gratefully before shovelling it down. I sit on the edge of the bed.

"Unfortunately, I haven't got any whale. How does soup sound?"

"It'll do," she says between mouthfuls.

"Thank you for saving me last night," I say. "After I promised to protect you, I've already failed you."

Casey dunks a piece of bread in the soup, soaking it a few seconds. She chews her lip thoughtfully, then shakes her head.

"I wouldn't have known what to do if you hadn't told me. How did you know by the way?"

"Turns out I've kind of got a god taking up residence in my head."

She takes a bite of the bread.

"That sucks."

I shrug.

"It has its pros and cons I guess."

He's chosen you for what Thaddeus couldn't do. That's what the girl had said. So Vaerdiexes was the god that drove Thaddeus to madness. I shudder. Already our lives had seemed such parallels and, even after all this time, it seems the universe is determined to draw us closer together. There's Vaerdiexes, but we were also both tormented by Diane and betrayed by my mother. Him worse than me. All she did was leave me to the Academy, but what she did to Thaddeus I cannot overcome. I cannot reconcile it with the image of maternity a mother should imbue her child with.

"Are you okay?" she asks.

"It's nothing. I should go talk to Kyle, there's some stuff to catch up on. Do you need anything else?"

"Just more sleep. Kyle said Pritovis' light is the most powerful spell a caeletai umea can cast. It rips apart the fabric of the universe with heavenly light to snatch demons back into oblivion."

"Damn. Stay away from your bad side." She laughs, setting the tray aside and slouching back against the pillows.

"That depends, are you a demon?"

"Only of my own making. Sleep well."

Putting the tray on the bedside table, I shut the door behind me before heading downstairs. I don't run into anyone on my way. I wonder where Aaron got to. Perhaps he's already gone ahead to meet with Kyle. But, in the library, I find only Kyle curled up in a massive armchair, facing out towards a window that overlooks the garden. He hears me enter, loud as I am with my poorly stifled yawn, but does not look back. Even after a few hours rest I still feel like I could fall right to sleep.

"I remember reading in here as a kid. The whole world seemed a myth to me still, dragoviks, angeleru. I read about them in books, studied the illustrations. I conjured up stories about them, fairy-tales that I illustrated with crayons and wrote myself. My parents kept me from it all for a time. Not that I didn't know what I was, but I wasn't exposed to that part of our lives. I hardly met any other dragoviks aside from Aaron and Leo. Until Robyn came, I hadn't seen the destruction being a dragovik could result in. But then there she was, covered in her parents' blood, all because of what she was born to be. Like that, all the magic of these creatures was stripped away. They were just monsters. I was a monster."

I sit in the chair beside him and take his hand. He gives mine a weak squeeze, his eyes still turned away from me. My heart sinks, hearing this about Robyn, but I don't push the subject. I don't have a right to her past, that much is clear from the evident disdain with which she treats me.

"You're as far from a monster as can be. I think you might be more of an angel than Casey, but don't tell her I said that." He laughs then, squeezing my hand a little harder in return. "What's got you thinking this way?"

"I don't know. Just being back here, I guess. I don't visit as often as I should perhaps. My parents are away most of the time anyway. They've seldom if ever taken interest in anything Robyn or I have done. They didn't even try to visit while I was in prison, you know? We're not that close. It got worse during those three years after you left; I sort of fell out with everyone other than Aaron. I didn't know how to trust anymore."

My heart constricts when he says this. I did that to him. I took away his ability to trust, his ability to have faith in the people who could have healed the wounds I dealt.

"Aaron was patient with me though. No matter how I lashed out, he didn't let it come between us. Eventually he was the only person who could stand to be around me. Looking back at how I behaved, I feel like a monster. Robyn said some awful things last night that sort of brought all these feelings back."

"She was angry and, to her credit, she had some right to be," I murmur. "Why didn't you tell her you were in prison? Did they not allow you to? But then, why not tell her when you left?"

"No, they would have let me get in contact with her. But why bother her? I hadn't wanted to tell you about this, but, after you left, I wasn't in the best shape. I had lost my arm, then you. I was depressed. People only stick around for so long once you fall down that rabbit hole. They're expecting something of an other side to all the darkness, but, usually, there isn't one. Aaron was the only person who stuck by me through it all. Say what you will about him, but he's a good friend."

"I remember." I remember how strongly he felt for me after I lost Inerea, how he blamed himself though he shouldn't have. How he promised to fight for my life back at NYU only hours ago. Even after I left them, he's still on my side. "I'm so sorry I caused you all that pain Kyle."

He takes my hand in his, turning it over and studying the lines on it. Does he see my future in those lines, how inextricably linked with his it is?

"I understand why you did it, Mallory. Even back then, I understood. But I was still angry and hurt. I forgive you now, don't misunderstand me. I'm not bringing this up to make you feel guilty."

"I know you'd never do that."

"But it was bad, really bad. I slept all day, scarcely did anything for two years. Robyn went to study weapons forging in Miesarinda and we lost touch. Finally, that last year, I threw myself into my work, trying to find something to pour myself into. I was back and forth between Earth and Miesarinda, where Robyn was living, and all that time, I never once tried to contact her. Even before we met you, we were drifting apart. No wonder she had so many awful things to say. I'm a terrible brother."

"You are not. You're amazing, kind, endlessly generous. She's lucky it was you who put her back together after she lost her parents. Besides, I'm guessing not all of the bad things she said were about you," I say.

"No, most of them were about you."

I shrug, leaning back against the soft and worn green leather. Kyle watches me, looking for the signs of breakage I would have displayed back in Aplin Hollow. But I'm stronger now. I'm not as fragile as I once was. I know Robyn's hostility is bred from its own apocalypse of self-loathing, one she extends to me likely because of how similar we actually are.

"It doesn't bother me. I've toughened my hide quite a bit in the past three years. Humans can be just as bitchy as dragoviks."

"Yes, but far worse aim when they throw a teacup at you no doubt."

"Probably. Luckily I haven't enraged anyone that much since Robyn."

"Hm, I don't know, I think there were days I could have lobbed a teacup at you," he teases.

"Well then, I, Mallory Thiel, promise you one good teacup chucking at some point."

He laughs, all traces of the misery this conversation had engendered washing from his face.

"Thanks for cheering me up."

"It's the least I can do. Now, what did you want to talk to me about?"

"Right. I did some research about your sword and the stones. The one set in your sword is not actually recorded as being a Vaerdiexes stone in any of the books about the weapons. It must have been a secret the original smith kept to himself. There's also no history of the sword being paired with anyone before, which is unheard of for a gods' weapon. It means we don't know much about its powers and is probably why no one identified the stone. It's weird though, that it chose you as its first partner."

"No, it makes sense."

"You mean because everything simultaneously terrifying and special seems to always happen to you." I raise my eyebrows. "Not jealous, absolutely not jealous, just saying. So, why's it make sense?"

"The girl said something else to me. She said I had a god in my head." He frowns so I elaborate. "That voice I heard that told me I could heal you, I've heard it before. Do you remember when I asked Illarion about it? The voice I heard during battle with the deabrueon he pitted me against? He said that voice was both a blessing and a curse. And in my visions of Thaddeus' past, he called the god's voice he could hear in his head the first and last principle."

Kyle's jaw drops open. He springs up and rushes to the bookshelf. Scanning quickly, he selects a text and flips through its pages.

"The First Principle. That was what Vaerdiexes' group of followers back in Sundalev called themselves." He balances the book in his hand. "He's who's been speaking to you."

"I think so, yes. It makes sense, then, why he would choose me to pair the sword with. He's already singled me out."

"But why?"

"Because he's chosen me for what Thaddeus couldn't do."

It takes him a moment to wrap his head around the enormity of what I'm suggesting. When he does, he lets the book fall to the ground and begins to shake his head, backing away until he's up against the book case. His eyes are a wildfire of fear and panic. Is it of me or for me?

"No Mallory," he whispers firmly, "it can't be."

"But think about it. I'm the last daughter of the Thiels and the Oviras. His weapon paired with me when it hadn't paired with anyone before. I survived the blow from the sword imbued with the power of the second Vaerdiexes stone when it shouldn't have been possible. I hear him in my head. He's chosen me."

I know how insane I must sound, how much like Thaddeus when he first told people. But I know it's true and it makes perfect sense when I look at all the evidence before me. I just needed that girl to lead me to the conclusion I've drawn: he's chosen me to take the dragoviks back to Sundalev. That's why he was eager to have me agree with Diane's plan to work with the jaeitsi, because it would get us back to Sundalev. He's not concerned with the means, only the end goal.

"Mallory what you're saying is insane. A god has chosen you to be queen of a city our people haven't been to in millennia?" he hisses.

Kyle has never looked at me like this before. Not when he found me in my room at the Academy, drawers strewn about. Not after I broke down following Inerea's death and he had to draw me back to myself. Then he saw me only as someone damaged, in need of help, but mendable. But now, he looks at me as if he does not know me. He can't see the path by which to guide me back to myself.

"Oh, I'm well aware of how it sounds. Don't misunderstand me, I'm not saying I want this. I'm saying simply that it is."

Still Kyle shakes his head in disbelief.

"You're taking this on the basis of what Thaddeus and a mad girl told you? I'm sure they must both be persuasive, but remember Thaddeus was criminally insane. He wanted to tear down an entire government and commit genocide."

"No, he didn't. That's what I was trying to tell you the other day, when I said he was innocent. When I was in the Library Between, three years ago, I came across a record of his time in prison, in which he'd imbued his memories. I saw what he saw, felt what he felt. He was innocent until the Hirutere made a monster of him. Vaerdiexes called on him to restore us to Sundalev and he failed, so Vaerdiexes left him. That's why he went mad."

"Mallory, he could have manipulated those memories."

"Yes, but when I asked Alistair, he said it was all true. He said Thaddeus was innocent. I'm not saying he didn't commit crimes after he escaped, but he wasn't guilty of what they accused him of."

Kyle has no point to rebut this argument. What benefit would Alistair gain from lying to me about this, right before he intended to kill me as well?

"I know it sounds crazy, that I'm as deluded as Thaddeus. But I also know it's true. Don't you trust me?"

He worries his lip between his teeth, trying to reconcile what sounds like madness to the trust I know he has. But I have invoked our friendship, the deepest tie between us that cannot be undone. Not by our separation, not by loss. Even in death it would hold. He closes his eyes and sighs deeply.

"I – I believe you. If you think it's true then I believe you."

I breathe out a sigh of relief, sinking back into the chair. He comes to join me, reluctantly, as though he's afraid to come near me, staring distantly out the window. He touches his hand to the glass before sitting back in his chair.

"Queen of Dragovicia, huh?"

"It sounds stupid. Diane wanted me to call myself the Phoenix Queen."

"Diane did?"

"It's what she wanted from me. To lead the dragoviks in the jaeitsi's cause."

"You haven't told me how you're feeling about seeing her again."

No, I haven't. I've scarcely thought about it myself to be honest. There's so much else that's come to pass since then, so much else to be preoccupied with.

"At first it was like putting on an old skin only to find it still fit perfectly. I couldn't resist leaning into her words, wanting to believe her. I almost let myself be swept up by everything she was saying, everything she was offering me. An opportunity to change the world for the better. She was irresistible to me in those moments. She was the closest person I ever had to a mother."

"That's horrible."

"Given the choice, I don't think I could make one between her and Regan. They're both so horrible."

He nods, but doesn't comment on this.

"The Phoenix Queen. I think it suits you. You've always been sort of regal," he teases, trying to lighten the mood. I can't help but laugh.

"I'm a bumble fucking mess."

"What monarch isn't?"

"Illarion seemed to have his shit together."

"You mean aside from almost losing his kingdom to a witch, stealing basilisk eggs from a god, and creating dragons which almost decimated his city? Oh yeah, he knew what he was doing."

"At least he was born to do this. He knew it was his destiny from the beginning."

"Maybe it was yours, you just didn't know it."

I don't like the thought of destiny. That inescapable future drawing closer and closer, me unable to do anything about it. If it does exist, then it seems all the more likely that I will be forced into the world of dragoviks forever.

"Promise me something?" I say suddenly, turning to him. He holds my gaze steadily and reaches for my hand.

"Anything."

"Don't tell anyone. I don't know what I'm going to do about it, I just know that it's something I'm going to have to deal with eventually."

And there will come a time that I must face this new reality I've been thrown into. Thaddeus failed Vaerdiexes, so the god left him. It's what drove him mad. I wonder if that will be my fate too if I fail him.

"I promise."

There's a long silence unlike any other of our friendship, in which I feel our dynamic is shifting, though I cannot say how. Does he fear me now or just what I'll become? Or maybe he's simply humouring me, aware of what this belief did to Thaddeus. Either way, I know he will stay by my side.

"On to an equally disturbing subject. I found what we were looking for on the Vaerdiexes stones," he says after some time.

"Good news, bad news?"

"You tell me. Which of these is our bad boy, as Aaron put it?"

He passes me the book and I flick through the few pages he's marked.

"Well, this is the one in the katana," I say, recognising the cushion cut stone almost immediately. I clear my throat. "Morvedae is the stone of death. Oh great. That's really cheery."

"Fitting I guess, given it's in a weapon."

"And that it's the weapon of an assassin."

"Former assassin. You're reformed."

"On the straight and narrow," I say, before returning to the book. "Morvedae has been lost since before Illarion's time. Little to nothing is known of its power. Well, that's helpful."

"Yeah, I guess this will be a learning curve situation. Illarion only ever had the second, third, fourth, and seventh stones. The others' names are known but not much else about them. How about the girl's?"

I scan the pages before spotting the rectangular mirror.

"Miro. That's fitting. It means forever. Miro, however was, oh what a shock, lost since before Illarion's time. Little to nothing is known of its power. Makes sense given she pickpocketed Vaerdiexes thousands of years ago for the bloody thing. This is useless."

"About four thousand odd years ago. And she didn't tell you anything about it?"

"Chatty as she was no," I sigh. "Thrabr, the demon, said something though. He said it would make him a god."

Kyle looks worried.

"It's a wonder then the girl hasn't made herself one," he says finally. "That sort of power, you'd think she'd have cropped up before now."

"She has, in a dream I had back in Aplin Hollow."

"You and your dreams. Did she mention the stone back then?"

"No. Could it be the source of her longevity then?"

"Probably. It is the forever stone."

"So, immortality and death. Two sides of the same coin," I say, shutting the book. "No wonder she's a little obsessed with me. I'm her foil."

"It must be lonely, living forever. She probably sees you as the closest thing she has to a friend if you're bound by a prophecy," Kyle murmurs.

"Maybe. All I know is we need to get that sword before she comes after me with Shigami's scythe again."

"Why, what can the scythe do?"

"It phases her between this realm and that of the dead. She can disappear then reappear wherever she wants. Makes fighting her difficult."

"That all fits."

"Does it? Seems a little crazy, even to me."

"Like I've told you before, the realm of the dead exists as if on the other side of a veil. They can see us, but can't interact with us. She can probably move through this world in the land of the dead, but has to return to our realm to attack, as people in the land of the dead can't touch those who are still living. What about this Thrabr?"

"Tall as a three-storey building and can apparently emerge from shadows wherever he chooses. She said he was her other half. She uses the scythe to evade him by slipping into the realm of the dead."

"Hm not too sure about that bit. And she said only you could have fought him with the Vaerdiexes sword?"

"Yes, but I don't know how, he was incorporeal."

"Who's incorporeal?"

My heart drops. Kyle turns around, but I don't need to to know who that voice belongs to. Do I dare look at him after the promise I've broken?

"I heard you got out of prison, so I thought I'd drop by between missions and check in. Heard about the arm too. Congratulations are in order all around it seems."

"All thanks to Mallory," Kyle says, glancing at me. Can he read my shame in the flush of my cheeks?

"The golden girl. Saved your life at the trial. Didn't you, Mallory?"

I rise slowly, turning around. There he is, exactly as I last saw him. I'm surprised by how my heart and mind react to seeing Leo after all these years. Gone is the nervous flutter of affection that tickled my stomach before. Now all I feel is embarrassment. As usual, he gives nothing away with his leonine eyes. They betray no sense of anger or delight at my having returned, despite telling him I never would. No, he's not entirely as he once was. His hair is cropped short now, showing off his sharp cheekbones and jawline.

"I did what was owed," I reply.

"Well, I wouldn't mind if you made me dinner now and again as well," Kyle jokes uncharacteristically, clearly sensing the tension in the room. "It's good to see you again. It's been, what, two years?"

"You too. I've been busy."

"The Onyevaras' top guy I hear," Kyle replies, nodding.

These are not the interactions I'd expect of someone who cared enough for Kyle to send me away. They're utterly devoid of sincerity. Why, then, did Leo come? Surely not to see me?

"Hey Kyle, come here a second," Aaron calls from out in the hall.

I watch miserably as Kyle walks out of the library, leaving me and Leo alone. He studies me impassively before crossing the room.

"You broke your promise."

"I didn't have a choice," I reply quickly. I knew it wouldn't be long before he took the opportunity to bring that up. But he doesn't look angry.

"No, you didn't," he agrees. I'm washed with relief. I have already faced one angry member of our former crew, I'm not ready to face another. And I think Leo could be far more lethal than Robyn if he chose. "Thank you for saving Kyle."

"It's what I'll always do."

"That's what you were promising me you'd do by leaving and it's what you did by returning. That's the only reason you came back, right?"

Do I read something more in his eyes when he says this? A flicker of rage or perhaps it's something else. Surely he doesn't think I came back for him? Those feelings are long gone. They had barely begun to blossom when we parted ways.

"That's the only reason," I assure him.

He nods, reaching into the satchel he has slung across his body. I half think, for a moment, he's going to pull out a weapon. Instead, out comes the wooden box I had given him to keep for me. It stirs something within me to see it. Nostalgia, clouding my judgement, and anger when I think of my mother. Diane said she handed me over to the Academy. If she wanted me gone so badly, why leave me with something to remember her by?

"So, you didn't want this then?"

Oh. So that's what he'd meant when he asked if I'd come back for another reason. I flush pink again. Unsure of what to do with myself, I take the box, though I don't want it in the least.

"Thanks," I murmur, as Kyle returns to the room.

"It's good to see you," he says again to Leo, uncertain of what else there might be to say after all this time. He claps Leo on the back.

"What did Aaron want?" I ask.

"Oh, just wanted to know whether I thought now was an appropriate time to get your neighbour's number off of you. I said no."

Leo clears his throat and we both turn to him. Aaron strides into the room just then, his hand stuffed into his pockets.

"I didn't just come for a social call unfortunately."

"Oh? I'm shocked," Aaron scoffs, rolling his eyes.

It seems the animosity between these two has only grown in my absence. Neither even pauses to greet the other.

"I'm actually here to do you a favour, Aaron."

"Well maybe I should just lick your feet in gratitude then."

"That's enough," Kyle says sternly. "What is it?"

"I came to warn you about something," Leo answers.

"What's the matter?" Kyle asks, exhaustion clouding his face.

I don't think any of us can bear more bad news. Leo's gaze falters for the first time, and I know immediately that it must be very, very bad.

"The Hirutere have made an announcement. They're arresting Mallory Thiel in connection with the death of Captain Alistair Belmont."

Chapter XV.

"What?!" Kyle cries. All eyes in the room fall on me and my idiotic stunned expression. "They're kidding. On what grounds?"

"Apparently they have new evidence, but I've heard from my sources that they don't actually have anything on her."

"That's fine then, we'll just clear her in court," Kyle says, sighing with relief.

"Oh yeah, because the Hirutere are really known for their fair justice system," Aaron scoffs. "You of all people should know not to pin your hopes on their sense of justice. If the Hirutere are out to get Mallory, they'll find a way. No doubt they're still pissed she got you off of your charges."

"He's right. The truth is they don't really need any evidence to charge her. If they can convince the court she was there, that will be enough. Evidence or no evidence," Leo agrees with Aaron.

"Why now though? It's been three years."

"My guess? They're pissed she got you acquitted and want revenge as well as the Vaerdiexes sword. If she's charged, which she will be, the sentence is," Leo falters, avoiding eye contact with me.

"Death."

The room is quiet.

"Which means the Vaerdiexes sword will unpair with her and the Hirutere will have yet another gods' weapon to hoard away," Aaron says.

"But how would they know I was there? Only the people in this house know that. I know Robyn hates me, but she wouldn't go that far, would she?"

"That's not strictly true," Aaron murmurs. I see anger begin to glow in his eyes. "Not everyone who knows is here."

Oh shit.

"You don't think Killian said something, do you?" Kyle asks me anxiously.

"That fucking bellatoja," Aaron growls. For once, I'm with him.

"Seems likely doesn't it," I say bitterly.

I feel numb as the words leave my mouth. I had trusted him. Everything he'd done seemed insurmountable evidence he was on our side, but he must have been playing along to help the Hirutere all along. How could he, after what we've been through, knowing I still need to save Dominic, how could he betray me like this? He had stood up to Algard for me, but was that only because he knew he'd be pardoned once he turned me in? Still, it doesn't make sense. He's known for three years that I was at the Academy that day; why tell someone now?

"So, what, you're here to take her in? Because like hell is that happening," Aaron says to Leo, standing between the two of us.

"Like I said, I'm just here to warn you. I'm not going to help or hinder whatever plans you make to protect yourselves. If the Hirutere question me in connection with this, I'll tell them what I know."

"Which is?"

"Mallory didn't kill those people."

"Thank you," Kyle breathes. Where once there was trust, now he needs assurance of his friend's loyalty. It is good to know, though, that time apart has not made Leo falter. He will defend me, if only to protect his friends as well.

Leo nods and, like that, he's headed out the door and back downstairs. The three of us turn to each other in awe.

"Well, it goes without saying, we're not letting this happen," Kyle says.

"I'm not letting you endanger yourself for me again," I say to him, before looking to Aaron. "Either of you."

"What, you'll just hand yourself over to the Hirutere and let them execute you? That's no plan," Kyle argues.

"He's right. It's not even a question Mallory. We're with you one hundred percent," Aaron assures me, giving my shoulder a squeeze. "Where do we go?"

"Aplin Hollow," Kyle suggests.

I can see him gauging my response, aware I haven't been back there since Inerea's death, since that night Dominic found me. I promised myself I'd never to go back there, but right now, it seems the only place left to go.

"I'll need to go to my apartment and get the sword as well as some clothes."

"We'll need to pack too," Kyle says. "Casey as well. We can't leave her behind. If anything, it will be safer for her being further from the jaeitsi and the Hirutere. Text when you're ready and we'll come for you."

"Are you okay to go on your own?" Aaron asks.

"Who me? I've a got a gods' weapon on my sofa at home and the magic of two supernatural creatures. I can hold my own. If the Hirutere find me, it's better you two aren't with me. Besides, if that girl comes, I stand the best chance of fighting her. If you're there we'll just run the risk of more blood being spilt. And someone needs to stay to protect Casey while I'm gone."

He looks like he wants to argue, but purses his lips instead.

"I know it sounds stupid, but take a cab," Kyle says. "You're less likely to be followed that way."

I nod, taking my sword from Aaron when he offers it to me. Some small protection this will be if any of the many beasts looking for me actually comes. I don't know which of them scares me more at present: that girl, Thrabr, the Hirutere, the jaeitsi, or Diane. Attaching the scabbard to my belt I glance around, but there's nothing left for me to do.

"I'll see you in a bit I guess."

Kyle comes outside with me to hail a cab. The sun is dipping in the sky, indicating I slept in quite late. Not surprising given how tired I was. How tired I still am. Once this is all over, I'm sleeping for a month. I hold out my arm and a taxi pulls up to the sidewalk, idling, waiting for me to get in.

"Stay safe," Kyle says, squeezing my hand. I nod and watch him disappear back into the house.

Climbing into the taxi, I give the driver my address and we set off. It's only a few blocks away thankfully, but, even so, by the time we get there, the sky is dark and MacDougal street is bustling with students and tourists. There's something comforting about this, though I know it's false. A crowd won't stop someone from attacking me. I suspect any one of these creatures would have no trouble dispatching hundreds of people just to get at me. I open my building door and head to the third floor. I let out a sigh of relief as I step into my apartment, as if it changes the state of affairs and suddenly I am no longer being accused of murder. Tossing the box on to the sofa, which I have been holding since Leo gave it to me, I sigh and look around for what will probably be the last time.

Then, a horrible realisation comes over me.

"No."

Dropping to my knees, I tear off the couch cushions, even though I know I left it on the couch. There's no way it could have just slipped into the cushions. The sword is gone.

"Fuck, fuck, fuck," I groan. I pull out my phone and text Kyle.

Sword's stolen. Jaeitsi's people must have been here.

Hadn't the girl warned me that it was gone? Amongst everything that was happening during our fight, it didn't seem the most important detail, but now I realise she had mentioned the sword's absence numerous times. Was she warning me or just taunting me? Either way, I'm lucky I wasn't here when they came to get it. For all I know, they could be watching the apartment right now, waiting for me to return. If not them, then the Hirutere will be on their way soon. I have to move fast.

Grabbing a suitcase from my room, I toss in the sword I have on my side and the dagger sheath strapped to my thigh. In my bedroom, I pull down another suitcase and lay it on the bed to fill with clothes. I open my closet and, on the topmost shelf, I spot my books from the Academy. The ones Kyle had saved for me. I know I don't have much time, but I also know I can't leave this piece of my past behind. Selecting a few favourites from the shelf, I return to the living room and pack them away with the weapons. I pick up the box and turn it in my hands, considering whether to leave it or not. I don't really want this piece of my past, anything that my mother left for me. Even if Diane was lying and my mother didn't hand me over to her, she was by no means a good person. I stare at the engraving on the box.

The Phoenix fears the moon. The box is the key.

Those were the words from that note in Inerea's book, the one I had found just before Thaddeus took me. They hadn't made any sense at the time, but now, looking at the box, they begin to. The phoenix looks up, all courage even in the face of the cold, blistered moon. Why don't you fear it? And what was the rest of the note? I'm certain there was another sentence to it.

I don't hear the door open.

I don't hear the young man, who knows me so much better than I know him, enter.

All I feel is a sudden sense of both danger and security, my heart pounding. My whole world feels as if it is coming to life, a secret part of a garden in bloom at long last, and I know there is someone watching my every movement.

I spin around and come face to face with a tall, gaunt young man with white hair. He has sharp blue eyes and I know them to be my own. His shaggy hair, the inwards draw of his cheekbones, those are all his father's. I don't recall him, but I know him instantly.

"Isabrand," I say.

Whatever he had been expecting, it was not that. For me to know him had been a complete improbability, having no memories of my own of him. But Thaddeus told me of my brother, the result of my mother's cruelty, and I know this is him, standing in my living room. His eyes widen, shock stirring his angelic features and I know it is not a look that often crosses his face. He is unaccustomed to being caught off guard, usually catching others off guard instead. Studying me, he frowns, as if trying to fill the space years have left between us with false memories he makes of me. Then he takes a step forward before pausing. His eyes flicker first to the blood on my clothes, then to the box in my hand, and lastly to the half-packed suitcase on the sofa.

"Who the fuck are you and where is my sister?"

I'm startled by his hostility, but not surprised. He's right, I should not know him, separated as we were at such a young age. I wonder why he too was not at the Academy. At least he was spared that fate. I smile at him grimly before putting my hands up slowly in a gesture of surrender.

"Isabrand, it's me, Mallory," I assure him.

I don't see it happen, but suddenly he's drawn a knife from his pocket. *If you think you or I have become a monster you should see him.* That's what Thaddeus had said. But instead of fear, I feel only pity pouring out of my heart. Whatever's been done to him, it must have been worse than what Diane put me through. And though he's holding a dagger, believing me an apparition of the person he most wants to see, I do not feel a threat in the gesture. He doesn't want to hurt me. He wants me to talk him out of what he thinks he has to do. So, I begin to speak. I unwind from my memory a past best forgotten. With my words I reach out and say *we're not so different.* I will understand the darkest places he has been to and, where I cannot go with him, I will wait on the other side.

Isabrand is still poised to attack when I finish speaking. There are moments, when I speak of the dragoviks or the Academy, that I think he might try to slit my neck, clip the throat of elucidation. As much as I can hardly bear to tell of it, he cannot stand to hear of the life I was left to when we were separated. As if I drew the short straw. Who left those scars on your cheek, brother, the two curls of whiteness that underline the corner of your eye?

Of course, he makes no such threatening move towards me. The fear he pretends not to notice stays his hand. When he thought me an illusion there was no betrayal of panic on his face; he was ready to kill me because we're used to people trying to kill us. Survival instincts overtake morals more often than we care to admit. The prospect of me being exactly who he came looking for, however, has terrified him. Am I not what he hoped to find? Or is it that, against better judgement, he had hoped he'd find a happier picture than the one I've just unfolded?

He's heard of the Academy, no doubt. It's notorious and some of the monsters it created even more so. Does he see that when he looks at me? As if I would lay a hand on him.

The past sits, stuffed into the gap years apart has left between us. I have been calculating in what I've divulged. There's a great deal he doesn't need to know and even more that I am not ready to tell. But underneath all these stories lies the call made unanimously by my words: I am your sister and the hundred other things that have happened to me since that last day we spent together.

He rocks back and forth slightly on his feet, inclining towards me only to pull away. I want to catch him, hold him steady, but that knife in his hand gets between thoughts of comfort and my ability to act on them. His eyes are fixed on the box I'm holding.

"It's different," he says, gesturing to it. Then he inhales deeply, as if that first act of speech, disconnected from all I've said, has enabled him to gather the energy to say more. "How did you end up at the Academy after I left?"

"Our mother," I reply. The relief brought by answering a question, comparatively so much simpler than all those he could ask, is welcome. But of course, families are never that simple.

"That bitch."

Our mother, that bitch. Those would be synonymous to Isabrand after she chose me over him. In fact, she never chose him at all. Not even in those years before she could imagine me.

"Isabrand," I say.

His name has more of an effect on him than any spell I could cast. His eyes widen, are able to meet mine without fear. Then the clarity of our familial connection dissolves back into the overwhelming confusion of our reunion, and he shakes his head. The dagger disappears back into his coat and he puts his hands in his pockets.

"Let's not talk about her. I'm starving, is the Thai place down the street any good?"

"The best."

Without turning from him, I set the box on the sofa and grab my coat off the back of one of the dining table chairs. I move toward the door, but he comes between me and it, all while maintaining a safe distance. Perhaps he's changed his mind. But he makes no movement to take his knife from his pocket again.

"Um Mallory, you might want to change."

I glance down at myself, but already I know he's referring to the blood on my sweater. In my rush to pack I have completely forgotten about it. No wonder he pulled a knife when he first came in. But this draws my mind to another pressing matter. The suitcase in my bedroom isn't packed yet and the others will be here to meet me in an hour. How will I begin to explain Isabrand to them? I haven't told anyone about him yet, not even Kyle. Worse yet, how will I explain them to Isabrand? If I tell him too much too fast, the existing fault lines of our relationship will give way. And I'm not willing to lose him so soon.

"I'll be right back."

My bedroom is small, mostly occupied by a mattress on which lies the completely empty second suitcase. I open my cupboard and the first thing I see is the camel-coloured turtleneck Inerea gave me. It's swinging gently on its hanger as if to beckon me, despite the stillness of everything else, including my heart. After that summer, there were so many things I had to shelve to survive. I finger the hem, the loose thread that I use as an excuse not to wear it. It's warm in my hand and I feel that unwelcome sting in my eyes. Did Isabrand ever meet Inerea before he was sent away? I doubt it. Inerea would never have stopped looking for him if she had known about him. Just one of the many things our mother lied about to Inerea, just another of the many people she lied to. It was usually Isabrand and me on both accounts, so this isn't surprising. No wonder Isabrand calls her a bitch. I pull the sweater over my head.

I take this moment, sheltered from his gaze by the open cupboard door, to slip my phone from my back pocket. I need time, though I know asking the others for an hour was already more than we can afford. Any more might cost my life, especially given my present company. The screen lights up, three texts unanswered. My thumb hovers over the second down. It's from Killian. I know I shouldn't reply to him, but the desire to do so is almost impossible to resist. I busy myself texting Kyle instead.

Need two hours, something's come up. All's well.

I put the phone back in my pocket and close the doors on the clothes I should be cramming into that suitcase as fast as I can.

From the doorway I observe Isabrand. He's guarded even when he thinks he's alone, hiding from himself. Still, he gives his curiosity away by letting his eyes rove over the entire room. What he makes of what he sees I cannot tell. I will have to be an open book to him before he'll give even the smallest part of himself away. When he hears me enter the room, he starts towards the door without looking up. I lock up slowly, trying to keep my hand steady by tightening my grip on the keys until they dig into my palm. I can hear Ellie's two dogs barking, waiting for her to return. Usually, I take care of them when she's away. I'll miss them when I leave.

It's warmer outside than when I was out earlier, but that could have been the chill of knowing that it would be the last time I returned to my apartment. I leave my coat draped over my arm; the restaurant is only a few doors down and it's always stuffy in the small, overcrowded space. Luckily, it's late enough that we've missed the dinner time rush. I'm not sure what two estranged siblings waiting in line for a table would talk about. My limited social experiences haven't exactly prepared me for this. I do, however, know that every conversation is made easier by food. Kyle taught me that. I glance at my phone screen, but he hasn't texted me back. Still that second notification nags me.

We're seated by the window, far from the counter behind which all three of the waiters have crammed themselves. They pay no attention to us and I'm thankful for the anonymity appearing to be a young couple affords us. Isabrand unfolds the laminate flaps of the menu, slouching into his seat as if to be absorbed by it. He doesn't seem to have any intention of speaking first this time.

"How did you know where I live?" I ask.

"I looked up your address through your university's student database when I found out you were…are alive. They don't protect their student data very well."

"I think their locks are to guard against run of the mill breaking and entering, not that of the supernatural." He shrugs off my comment.

"Anyway, I didn't really have a good reason to drop by until my bosses put a hit out on you."

"I get that a lot. Duck Pad Thai, please."

Isabrand is temporarily confused by the latter statement until he spots the waiter who's just appeared by his elbow. It's not like someone such as Isabrand to be caught off guard like that. Whatever composure he's regained since we left the apartment is clearly only surface deep and it's taking so much of his focus that he's distracted.

I glance out the window as Isabrand looks through the menu hastily. By now all manner of creatures will know we're together and I can think of plenty off the top of my head who won't like it. Any one of the people out on the streets, seen and unseen, might have been sent to keep us apart. If Isabrand's not on his guard, he might get hurt. I tap my leg where I had a holster strapped only thirty minutes before. I left it in my suitcase, but that doesn't matter. I won't let anyone near Isabrand, even if I have to expose us. Human memories are erased easily enough, I tell myself, but the hardening lump in my throat tells me I won't be able to do that to the wait staff.

"I'll have the same as her," Isabrand says to the waiter, passing our menus over his shoulder. He waits until the man scratches our order onto his notepad and leaves before speaking again. "You don't seem concerned that someone sent me to kill you."

"Like I said, I get that a lot." I shrug, feigning insouciance as he does. Is this what family resemblance looks like? Two people with the same colour eyes unable to look at one another, slouched in chairs. How underwhelming.

"So much in common." For a moment I think he's read my mind, but am soothed by the thought that we're not the kind of beasts that can do that. "You like Thai food, I like Thai food. You have people trying to kill you, I've been asked to kill you."

"I don't think that would fit on a tote bag. Maybe we can get t-shirts," I suggest.

"I'm pretty sure there's a store in Soho that already prints those."

"No, it's in Brooklyn, haven of the graphic tee." He snorts, staring down at his hands intertwined in his lap.

"And here I thought all they taught you at the Academy was misery 101."

"Common misconception. We took the advanced course as well," I say. He smiles, a mirror image of mine were it not for the single dimple on his left cheek. Like that, he looks so very like his father. That recognition grips me and twists my stomach until I have to look away. "Do you have any intention of following orders?"

I thought I knew the answer was no, but, as the words leave my lips, I know it's a genuine question. One he's still asking himself.

"Not sure yet."

"It's a big decision to make on an empty stomach."

"That's the truth. Why don't you tell me the rest then, to pass the time," he suggests, just as our food arrives.

"The rest of what?"

"Of the touching tale you started in the apartment. How you ended up in New York. Tell me what I missed little sis."

His glibness cuts through the sense of security that familiarity had lulled me into. There's mockery saturating each syllable. *Little sis*. I dig my finger nails into my leg. I tell myself he's only being like this to reassert the predatory dominance that he's used to and that it will put him at ease. This must be how he toys with his victims. His eyes are so full of hunger, ready to devour me. He reminds me so much of his father and it terrifies me.

"Okay, I'll tell you."

He grins, an unsettling act of expressiveness on his closed off face, and turns his attention to his plate.

"Noutsumar letai kokku ni saviski isuazko'caz makun," I whisper beneath the roar of a passing truck. I feel the hilt of my dagger shimmer into existence within my grip as the spell unravels itself from my tongue, my blood. I would die for my brother. But right now, that's not who Isabrand is. He is as much what his employers made him as I am what Diane made me.

He begins to pick at his food. I hardly touch my own, hardly breathe, between telling him about being taken to Aplin Hollow. I manage to tell him about learning I was a Dragovik and Inerea's spell before he interrupts me.

"That's why you didn't remember you were a dragovik and why you could function so well outside of the Academy? Inerea cast a spell on you." Isabrand has paused with his chopsticks mid-air.

"She wanted to take away the pain. I would never have stood a chance of living a normal life in Aplin Hollow if I remembered the things they made me – the things I did there," I correct myself. My blade has warmed in my hand and I press it flat to my thigh.

"She fucked with your head Mallory. Whatever her reason, that doesn't make her a good person."

"I know," I whisper, "but it's so difficult to speak ill of her now. She loved me."

"A lot of people love you, but that's not how you show it," he murmurs. He reaches out a hand and, before I have the chance to flinch, he gently tucks a strand of hair behind my ear. "You can put the knife away, I'm not going to hurt you."

"You saw right through me didn't you," I say, putting the blade down beside me on the bench and reaching over to squeeze his hand.

"It hurts," he whispers, lowering his gaze. "I want to restore something we've lost over the years and I'm not sure how to navigate this situation. But it feels like I've waited forever for this moment, for you to know me and want me near you. That's all I've ever wanted."

"Of course I want you here Isabrand. And not just because you're the only family I have left," I say, reading his thoughts. "I've built myself a family and I know there are people who love and protect me. I want you here because, whatever happened in those years apart, I know you're the first person I loved."

What's come to pass that's left him so incapable of believing those words? Because I see him struggle to process them, struggle to accept my affection as part of the world he's grown up in. I touch my thumb to the scar on his cheek.

"Perova tai ne, perova tai ne noventa, recritar letai laje, remaror tais vuzels." His skin tingles beneath my touch, warming to a heat that should burn us both were we not beyond the pain of fire. Slowly, the scar beneath his eye fades. "You want to protect me from the past as I do you, but neither of us can really do that now. Just let me be part of your future."

"You were always welcome in it, little sis. Now, where were we?"

"I was about to tell you about how I met your father for the second time."

I swallow hard at the mention of Thaddeus. Oh god, this is the part I'd hoped to avoid. How to tell him what transpired between me and Thaddeus. It makes me sick to think on it, especially now that I see Isabrand, the result of Thaddeus and Regan, sitting before me. But I know in order to gain his trust, I must tell him everything. Even that which I have never told Kyle. So once more I start my story, right up until I left Aplin Hollow. I finish and we pay the bill. I wonder how he comes by his money? I know my way certainly isn't conventional. What means are there for a creature such as himself?

Isabrand is silent on the walk back from the restaurant. We hardly touched our food in the end, though the wait staff scarcely seemed bothered. It's not long before we arrive back at my apartment. The dogs have gone quiet downstairs and even the street seems silent.

When we get upstairs, he sinks onto the sofa, clearly bothered by the story, his eyes fixed on to a point in the distance. In his mental absence, I take the opportunity to make a cup of tea. I'm exhausted from the day. Even before Isabrand showed up. I close my eyes. How many more people will have to die for me to survive?

"But that still doesn't take us to the present," he says thoughtfully.

I feel his eyes on my back as I pour the hot water over a tea bag.

"No," I sigh, "but hopefully it helps you understand how I came to be here."

"So, you…you and my father," he begins, his face wrinkling in disgust. My heart sinks. I had so desperately hoped he wouldn't bring that up.

"I had no idea who he was."

"It's sick."

I flinch at the vehemence in his voice. Of all the things the two of us have done, that perturbs him most?

"I suppose it is."

"And you, you're no better than I am. One of the Academy's assassin dogs."

I narrow my eyes at him.

"That's rich coming from the man who showed up to kill me tonight. I didn't choose that life and I left it as soon as I had the chance."

He hesitates.

"You're right. I did come here to kill you."

Before I can move, he's sprung to his feet and sent me spilling across the small table. He presses his forearm against my windpipe and a dagger to my throat.

"Isabrand," I say calmly. But my heart is pounding. If I don't leave here tonight, so many people will die. Dominic needs me. Kyle too.

"I'm sorry sis, but see Regan stole something from me and gave it to you. I want it back."

"What? What are you talking about?"

"You still don't remember?" Grabbing me by the hair, he drags me across the room to where the box Regan left me lies on the sofa. "Maybe this will help."

He presses his thumb against the moon and small triangles

pop up around it, transforming it suddenly into the sun. He turns it like a combination lock and I hear it click each time it stops. On the final turn, the box emits a small popping sound and I see a crevice appear, the place where the lid can be removed from the top.

"Time to remember sis," he says. He pulls the lid off.

Several things happen at once.

The door bursts open and whoever bounds in throws Isabrand's body from atop me.

There's a rush as at last I remember everything. What happened before I came to the Academy. How I died.

Someone extends a hand to help me to my feet.

"Are you okay?" Killian asks, pulling me up before decking my staggering brother clean on the nose. There's a dull thud as he hits his head on the corner of the table before he slumps to the floor.

"Isabrand!"

Part IV

Chapter XVI.

It didn't start with fire and blood.

It started with a corpse, cooling and whitening on the lawn.

It started with knowing I could love him anywhere, even in the land without memory.

***

"Jump! What are you afraid of."

The second part of the statement is phrased like a question and intoned as a taunt. I have heard this call before, in the voices that have spoken to me since my sanity began to slip through the cracks made by all that's been done to me. But in this time in which my dream takes place, those voices have not started speaking yet. I am still too young to know that madness' claws are dug deep in my mind, sharp as the hooks of mortality.

I lean back on my heels and cast my gaze across the river, which is rushing high and fast now it's glutted on the spring melted snow. The water torrents through a bottle neck between two massive rocks into a vast pool that we like to swim in through the summer and even into the cooler early autumn months. On one side, the boy stands, not yet wet from the water, having swung across from the riverbank on the rope that is knotted on the branch above me. There is a patch of snow on the hill behind him. It is the last to melt.

"Jump!" he calls again.

I take a few steps back then run, hurling my body into the air. Flailing my arms, I reach out. My hands meet the rope knotted above me to a tree's branch, allowing me to swing from the shore to the rock, and I hoist myself up. But my upper body is shocked by the heft of my small frame. I scramble to keep a hold of the rope, swinging like a pendulum, back and forth. The boy is shouting at me to drop myself onto the rock he stands on, but I can't think clearly through my shock. Eventually I slip and plummet into the hungry mouth of the river.

If the water level hadn't been so high, the snowfall so great that year, I would have died then. Split open like a too ripe fruit on the rocks. My blood would have run red, then turned to nothing, diluted by the river. I would have dissipated faster than the snow in the budding spring's warmth.

Instead, I am swept along into the churning water, pulled into the pool a little ways down. This is the one we swim in in summer months, when the sun dashes through the trees to warm the pool all the way to its depths. But instead of the warm, still waters I am used to, I find only currents. Like a vacuum, they draw me down. The water slips over my head like a suffocating blanket and I can only make out the cavernous dark blue around me. My body is sucked towards the bottom of the pool, then is pushed up along the edge, only to be dragged back down. It won't spit me out. I claw at the soft riverbed, at the hard rocks, but nothing gives way to my grasp.

Again and again the river forces me to do this dance, spiralling my body with more grace than I inherently possess. I move like an angel on the back of the wind, move like a ballerina caught up in her dance. Only I don't want this, this violent show of water's mastery over my body. I don't want to be swept away into the current, forced to dance for whatever might be watching me from the water's depths. I can only distinguish the bottom of the pool from the top by how much light filters down to me.

My head begins to spin. The water begins to fade to black all the way through as my eyes shut, growing heavy from the lack of oxygen. I have been beating against the water with my arms until now, but they've begun to feel leaden and tired. There is no use fighting; there never is.

Somewhere out there, I know he's screaming. The boy whose name I can't remember.

Somewhere out there, they are rushing from the house to dredge my cold body up from the river. My lips will be blue before they reach me.

There is a single patch of snow.

It is still melting.

* * *

Next thing I know I am dead. Not CPR can resuscitate dead.

Dead dead. I am in heaven, the place Illarion would show me many years later. I am only a child after all. My wrongdoings have not yet amounted to the right to a place in hell. Or at least, I think I am in heaven. Perhaps I was only ever in the go-between realm that sits between the afterlife and the world of the living. I sit on the banks of a phantom river, watching the smoke-like figures of my mother, father, and brother crowd around my body, an empty vessel. Every second it lies there without my soul in it, it cools, drawn back to the earth from whence we all came. Soon, I will be in a coffin. Soon, I will be worm food. Soon, I will be earth. So it goes.

"And who might you be?" a voice asks.

I blink up into the blinding light, shielding my eyes before I make out a towering figure. He's dressed in a rich red cloak, which hides everything except for the brown boots that peek out beneath it. He's larger than anyone I've ever seen before, leaving cavernous footprints in the grass he tramples. His face is hidden by his cloak, though there is sleek pale gold hair that emerges from either side of the hood. It reaches all the way down to his belt and is bound by rings of gold.

"Mallory Thiel," I answer.

My mother tells me not to answer the door. When we go out, she tells me not to speak to anyone. She holds my hand and keeps me close to her side at all times. All strangers are the enemy and I must constantly be shielded. Even when we go to the summer festival, I mustn't stray from her side. When the man at the stand with the scones asks what kind of jam I want, she answers for me. I have no voice of my own. I have been conditioned to fear the unknown. But this cloaked man piques my child's curiosity.

"Who are you?" I ask in turn.

"Vaerdiexes," he answers, before lowering himself to the ground beside me. He says no more, surveying the scene of my family kneeling beside my body where my father has dragged it from the river. My lips are blue already, kissed as they are by Death herself. He's trying to give me CPR, get the water out of my lungs, but it's too late for that. The house was too far from the river. By the time Isabrand had run up to the house to get them and returned, I was already dead. "They're going to miss you."

"Mother will. She tells me I'm all she's ever loved. And I think

Isabrand will too," I say, watching my brother as he falls to his knees and sobs. My bottom lip quivers. "I don't want him to be lonely."

"Is that why you're still here? You want to go back to be with him." I nod. "There aren't many people who have the strength to stay in this plane between the mortal realm and the afterlife. Usually Shigami or one of the other gods of death have ushered people along by now. I wonder why they let you stay."

"I don't know Shigami, but no one's asked me to leave yet."

"It must be a busy day for them," Vaerdiexes sighs. "There have been a lot of those recently."

He looks to the sky as if waiting for it to cloud with the signs of a storm. Yet nothing obscures the blazing sun. It splashes across his face and obscures its details from me, as if it were his face that is radiating light. The warmth of the sun's rays basking me are soporific. It would be so easy to close my eyes and let go of this world.

"You're not afraid to be here, are you?" he asks, rousing me.

"No," I answer.

How could someone fear this place? It is safe and warm. I think that, even if I went to swim in the river, I would not feel its cold anymore. I would not feel its currents battering my small body. Everything will be warm, like the perfect summer day eternally basking my skin. I look out behind us, into the field of wildflowers I know I must soon enter, leaving behind my old world forever. Leaving behind Isabrand. That is all that keeps me here, feet tucked beneath me, on the shore of the river I died in. The thought of my brother alone on Earth breaks my young heart.

"I'll tell you what Mallory Thiel, I'll make you a deal."

"What's that?" I ask suspiciously.

"I will send you back to your brother if, when you grow up, you will be my prophet in the mortal realm. You will be my eyes and ears on Earth and Sundalev, where I can no longer go. You will secure my legacy for me as I cannot hope to do from here."

"Why not, are you dead too?" I ask.

"No. I'm a god," he sighs, picking a nearby buttercup and offering it to me. I pluck it from his fingers and twirl it between mine. Light dances off of its warm yellow petals.

"That sounds better than being dead."

"It has its perks, though it's not dissimilar," he laughs, a low warm rumble from deep within his belly. I find the sound soothing, like more sunlight washing over me. "So, what do you think?"

"What do I have to do as a prophet?"

"You'll have to save your kind. You'll have to be a queen. I don't meet many mortal girls, so I'm not sure if that's something that interests you."

"I think they usually want to be princesses. That's what the storybooks say."

"What do you want to be?"

I stare at Isabrand, doubled over and sobbing as my mother screams at him. *It's your fault,* I know she's saying. She has never been kind to my brother. I have wondered why many times, why she dotes on me and not him. I have never been brave enough to ask why, to step in when she yells at him. I have only ever wrapped my arms around him in the aftermath, held him as he weeps and shakes.

"Safe and loved. I want to know the people I care about are too."

"You can ensure that by returning to Earth as my emissary."

"How will you do it?"

"It starts, as all things great and powerful do, with fire." He holds out his arm and his cloak falls back to reveal he is wearing a falconer's glove. Whistling once, he waits until, from the sky, descends a beautiful red bird with some golden plumage in its tail. It's also streaked with orange and purple, a molten sunset contained in its feathers. It beats its wings, hovering, before perching gracefully on his arm. "Hello."

"That's the phoenix," I gasp.

It chirps twice at me before picking at its feathers. It is so much more exquisite than any of the depictions I have seen in the books in our library. No pen can do her justice. No paint has ever captured the colours of her feathers so beautifully.

"Yes, she is. She is my familiar. I want you to take part of her with you to Earth. With it, you will have the strength and power you need to be my emissary and it will form an unbreakable connection between us. Do you accept?"

I hesitate. I am too young to realise what I am getting myself into, yet I know there is weight to this promise, even if I have not felt its burden yet. I glance at my family. My mother's hand strikes Isabrand's cheek. He grips it, eyes wide with tears. Who will hold him when he cries himself to sleep tonight if not me?

"Yes."

Vaerdiexes takes the buttercup from me and offers it to the phoenix. Tilting its head left and right, the bird clicks its beak twice before coughing up a single spark of golden fire. The flower ignites, but does not burn. Instead, it shimmers, its natural golden hue augmented by the eerie golden flame. Stroking the bird, Vaerdiexes hands me the flower. I accept it carefully, feeling the immensity of the flame's heat emanating down to my hand. It could eat me whole if it wanted to. And this, only a small piece of their power.

"When you reach Earth, this flame will become part of you, as it once did with the dragons. We will be eternally bound and there will be no going back on your word."

"How do I get back?" I ask, watching the small dancing blaze. I think it is one of the most beautiful things I have ever seen. Small and soft. I want to put it in my mouth to keep it safe, else annihilate it.

"You must take the path across the field down into the gardens of Yima. She will guide you home from there. Be wary of anyone that may approach you, for they will seek to send you into the eternal realms."

He rises and begins to walk away. The bird turns to look at me, it's flaming eyes full of trust. She expects me to do what Vaerdiexes has asked and believes I will not waver.

"She likes you," he says, pausing to stroke her beneath the chin.

"How can you tell?"

"Because the phoenix, while a familiar, is no slave. She would not have given her fire to just anyone."

He starts off again.

"Wait!" I cry out, scrambling to my feet.

"Yes?"

"How will I know what you want me to do?"

"When the time is right, I will tell you," he says. "Until then, guard yourself, Mallory Thiel."

He turns away once more and, like that, he and the bird vanish into the blinding light of the sun. When I shade my vision, they are nowhere to be seen. All around me the field is contained within its own riot, the wind corralling it. I'm filled with a sense of dread at entering its endless expanse. I look once more at Isabrand as my mother screams at him, striking him again. He cowers, pleading with her to stop. I will not leave him to her wrath. Grabbing him by his hair, she drags him to my corpse and sets a hand on either of us. This is it. Already I know Vaerdiexes' plan to resurrect me is in motion and I must hurry. I find the cobblestone path that cuts through the grass and run along it.

My legs grow tired and there is sweat on my brow, as I am certain hours have passed since I started running. But when I look up, the sun still sits at its peak, beating down on me. No more than a minute has passed where my mother and brother are. I am certain of this somehow. But when I look over my shoulder, they are nowhere to be seen. There is only the field.

I see a shadow in the distance. Then I blink and it is right before me. A beautiful woman, her face painted with a myriad of colours. She has gossamer white hair that hangs to her waist and wears a diaphanous gown of gold. It's all but transparent and I can see the broad strokes of colour across her body beneath it. The flower's beauty diminishes in her presence. I have never seen anyone or anything so full of life. She pulses with vitality, as if ripples of energy roll off of her, and, though Vaerdiexes warned me to stay away from anyone I might meet, I cannot help but stop when she appears.

"Who might you be?" she asks.

"Mallory Thiel."

She cocks her head to the left and looks from my face to the flower.

"What's a little girl doing carrying the power of the god of sun and flame?"

"He asked me to be his emissary."

She frowns, concern creasing her brow. I reach out to her, but she flinches away.

"Sorry, I didn't mean to," I whisper.

"No, precious. You did nothing to upset me. But if you touch me, I'll have to take you," she says. "And whatever Vaerdiexes' plan, I don't think he'd be very happy with me if I did that."

"Who are you?"

"Shigami, a goddess of death."

This, this is death incarnate? She is too beautiful, too full of life to be death. I'm mesmerised by her eyes, which seem to constantly change colour. They're like a rippling pool of oil.

"Where are you going little one?"

"To find Yima."

"Then I will escort you. There are other gods out here that would take you for their own."

She turns and begins to walk, so I follow. My pace is quicker than before, matching her adult strides. Her hips sway as she walks, the curve of them rolling in at her waist and out at her pelvis. Her legs are thick, sturdy like something rooted, which seems poorly suited to death which uproots us. We walk in silence until we finally come to the edge of the world and a steep set of stairs made of packed earth. Grass is beginning to seed on them. Though Vaerdiexes had not mentioned them, I know they lead to the garden, so begin to follow their winding path down a sheer cliff side. Shigami stops though, so I pause on the stairs, looking back up at her beautiful face, which has now turned blue.

"I'll go no further. The other gods don't like us entering their domains."

"Why not?"

"To be a god of death is to be nothing. We're not looked upon well. Be safe, Mallory Thiel."

She's gone in another blink of an eye. I search the horizon for her all the same, but it's all wildflowers. In that moment, I fear I will never see her again. But I will. We will all meet her eventually.

Turning, I start down the stairs. Another age passes. It takes a great deal of care not to stumble and fall on the way down. When I finally reach the bottom, I am exhausted, ready to collapse in the silk grass. Did I really think coming back from the dead was going to be easy? I fumble for something to prop myself up on, closing my eyes. Eventually I find a thin tree and lean against it. My breaths are ragged, but the air is pure here. It clears out my lungs and restores my senses.

I open my eyes to find myself in a small, but beautiful garden.

To my right is a pagoda style house painted brilliant red. It's very little, just enough space for one. On my left is the clearest pool of water I have ever seen. It cuts perfect reflections of the branches of the trees surrounding it, as no painter could do. There is no breeze to stir it from clarity. Beside it is recently dug earth and a clutch of pink petalled flowers, ready to be planted. I hear a gentle tapping behind me and spin around, expecting to see someone. Instead, I spy a fountain beside the pagoda. The spout is a hollowed out bamboo shoot that pours out water, before tipping backwards, making the tapping sound and refilling. I draw closer to it.

"It's a shishi-odoshi."

I halt my advance, looking behind me. I had not realised there was someone else here and I didn't hear anyone emerge from the pagoda. But it seems the gods are capable of moving without me even noticing. A woman of indeterminable age kneels by the pond, dipping a bucket in. I am certain she had not been there moments before. She wears a long flowing white gown and has pale, ghostly blonde hair. Her feet are bare and her soles are dirtied with earth. She turns to me to reveal the milky eyes of blindness.

"I could tell you were looking at it," she explains, pointing to the fountain. I walk over to her, hand still clutched around the flaming buttercup. She tilts her head up as if to gaze on me. She pats the ground beside her.

"Please, sit. It's rare mortals come to my garden."

I lower myself beside her and can feel the wet dew of the grass seeping through my dress. I'm surprised then to realise that the dress was not already soaked from my plunge into the river.

"Are you Yima?" I ask.

"Yes," she replies, lifting the bucket from the water. The movement creates no ripple across its surface.

"I'm Mallory," I say.

She makes no reply, only peers into the water in her bucket and frowns. Turning the bucket this way then that, she tilts her head to the side and sighs.

"There's nothing much to this one I'm afraid," she says over her shoulder. I look behind us, but there's no one there. I'm about to turn back to Yima when suddenly the air by the pagoda shimmers golden, the faint shape of a woman appearing. Is she a ghost too?

"Who is that?" I ask.

"That's Kora. She likes being here as only I can see her since she fell. But now you've made something of the shape of her too. That's a rare gift for a mortal: to perceive what the universe wishes you not to."

She dumps out the contents of her bucket and takes another scoop of water.

"That's better," she murmurs, studying it intently. I look for Kora again, but she's vanished. Turning impatiently to Yima, I wait for her to say something more, but it's as if she's forgotten I'm here. All she does is examine the water in the bucket, which does not reflect her. It does not reflect anything.

"Vaerdiexes sent me," I say. "He said coming to the garden was how I would get home."

While not removing her clouded gaze from the water, her attention is now mine. Reaching out a hand, she runs it gently over the contours of my face, determining the shape of me.

"Are you a god too?" I ask, though she scarcely looks like one. She is not large as Vaerdiexes was, nor is she inhumanly beautiful as Shigami was, but appears as a normal woman.

"Yes."

"Can you help me get home?"

"I am wondering why Vaerdiexes has sent you to me. He's never asked for me to help a mortal pass from this realm into the other, though the garden could certainly be used as a gateway. What did you say your name was?"

"Mallory Thiel," I answer, though now it is with mild irritation. I need to get back to Isabrand before it's too late, before my mother hurts him even more. Yima smiles as if she can sense what's on my mind. Perhaps she feels my displeasure in the contours of my face. She removes her hand from my cheek and pours out the contents of her bucket, before taking another scoop. Examining it, she says nothing for some time. "What are you doing?"

"Finding the shape of things to come," she tells me, "You think you know, what you are, what's to come. You think this will be the greatest obstacle you'll have to face, but, with it, you have only just begun. Yours is a dark path and all because Vaerdiexes has seen to light it with his fire."

"Yes, I'm to be his emissary. The flame will be a part of me."

She shakes her head.

"It will consume you. A mortal body cannot withstand its power. Even immortal ones are susceptible to its wrath."

Here she gestures to her eyes.

"Vaerdiexes did that?" I ask, suddenly shivering despite the sun on my back. Is his wrath so great?

"Unintentionally. Gods can be so careless with their toys. He and Alastor were squabbling. They wanted to build the universe, you see. But the fires kept growing and growing. So, I put a ceiling on all things, keeping us from the mortal realm. In doing so, I got injured. It was the price of creation. Fire is not a kind friend, but it is a great ally."

"If it will kill me, does that mean I can't go back?"

"You can. At a price."

I hunch over. I am weary of gods and their prices. I do not yet know how much my deal with Vaerdiexes will cost me.

"Don't worry, I ask nothing of you in return. I offer only a solution, which will come with its own set of problems."

"I don't think I have a choice."

"No, you don't. I've read it in you," she says, tapping the side of the bucket. "I see what you cannot."

"You read the future."

"Yes. After I was blinded, my Vaerdiexes made this garden for me where the sun always shines and the flowers bloom all year. Kyeres drew the earth to the sky and Alastor poured his healing waters into a pond. I drank them and they returned my sight in a new form. Now I can see the future of everything and everyone, the clearest glass through which to see."

"What does that have to do with me?" I ask. She laughs.

"Ah yes, you're still a child. I forget these things, now I've seen you all grown up. So impatient. You'll lose that with time. You'll lose a lot. But the water. When Vaerdiexes first made the dragons, he told Illarion to steal three basilisk eggs from Alastor. He knew if he put the fire in basilisk eggs, the water would temper the fire," she explains.

"So, I have to become a snake?"

She laughs, again tilting her head back so the sun catches in her ghostly white hair and renders it silver. She is beautiful in her own way, a manifestation of peace where Shigami was vibrance incarnate.

"No but you will need some of this." She passes me the bucket. "Drink it and you will have the strength to withstand the fire. But the price is high. You will always be torn by the duality of what fights to consume you: fire and water."

"But I'll die if I don't," I say.

"It is true. And it comes with gifts too, as most curses do. Much as I do, you will be able to determine the future. It may not appear to you with such clarity as my own visions, but it will come all the same."

For Isabrand I will do this. Reluctantly, I entrust her with the flower. I lift the bucket to my lips and drink deeply. The water tastes sweet, but not cloyingly so, coating my tongue in its sugariness. When I have downed my future, I set the bucket down beside me and turn back to Yima.

"What now?" I ask.

"Now? You go home."

She takes me by the hand and leads me past the pagoda to the edge of the garden. I see Kora again, shimmering beside us.

"She likes you, you know," Yima says. "She likes being seen."

That's two of the heavenly ancients I'm favoured by now. I look back at Kora, who I think is reaching towards me. Is she warning me not to go back? But I have no choice. I have made my deals and my brother needs me. Peering below, I cannot make anything out other than clouds.

"Off you go."

"You want me to jump?" I ask, panicked. Again, she chuckles.

"You've just pledged yourself to the god of sun and flame and you fear falling? Don't fear the air, but the ground. It'll be okay, I've sent word to Kyeres to catch you."

Yima places her hands on my back and gives me a push. I fall, clutching the burning flower to my chest. The wind eats at its flame, trying to extinguish it.

I fall and fall, but don't land.

The flame flickers and flickers, but does not go out.

So we burn.

Chapter XVII.

The memory comes as a torrent, restored to its rightful place in my mind. It brings with it countless others, all of which begin to rearrange what I knew to be true of myself and my family. Regan, so cruel to Isabrand, yet she loved me so. She whispered it to me over and over again while she plaited my hair in bed at night. The sheer force of these memories causes me to fall back slightly, catching myself on my elbows as I do so. I take a deep breath, as if it is the first I have ever taken in my life. My heart is hammering, shuddering from the intensity of these recollections. How is this possible? How could I have forgotten my entire childhood before I came to the Academy?

Killian is still holding my hand when I blink my way back into the present. Suddenly, the man on the floor, my brother, is illuminated by the hundred memories of him I had not known I'd had. It was him who kept me safe when no one else did. He was my only companion during a childhood of isolation at my mother's command. He told me stories and I told him some too in the late-night hours when I could not sleep because of my nightmares.

I rush to his side, kneeling and gently shaking his shoulders. He does not stir, his lips slightly parted. He looks just as I did by the riverside, though I know he is not dead. It's as if there's a bond strung between us, one that's always been there, I had just forgotten about it. Through it I can sense that he is alive, but in pain. When I lift his head into my lap, my hand comes up red. I try to wipe it on my jeans, as if ridding myself of it will mean the wound of its source will no longer exist.

"No, no, no," I mutter to myself, shaking for fear of what's been done.

I can't lose Isabrand just when I've got him back. My beloved Isabrand. I look over my shoulder at Killian in horror. He has risen and now stands there, hand outstretched as it had been to help me up, utterly perplexed.

"He was trying to kill you," he manages, as if he needs to explain his perfectly rational assumption that he was doing me a favour by protecting me.

But he does. In this moment, I feel only a swelling fury at the sight of his face. Were it not for him, I wouldn't have been back here packing my bag, ready to go on the run from the Hirutere. Were it not for him, I wouldn't be sitting here in my brother's blood. There's going to be hell to pay once I've healed my brother.

I press my hand to Isabrand's head, praying I'm not too late. I can still see the slight, sharp rise and fall of his chest. There's time yet.

"Lueicht, nandirava letai nevorso ni isuazko etev udiyat," I say.

My hand glows, illuminating his white hair golden but, when the light fades, I still see the gash made by the corner of the table. This spell has never failed me before. No, there's no reason it shouldn't work. I look at Killian in panic. Gone is my anger, replaced only by the fear that my brother will die in my arms. Killian hesitates, assessing the situation for a moment before rushing to my side. Crouching beside me, he tries to take Isabrand's weight into his own lap. I hiss at him, drawing my brother closer.

"Mallory, who is this?" he asks, trying to inspect the wound from his poor point of vantage.

"He's my half-brother and I swear to Vaerdiexes if he dies because of you, I won't even give you the chance to explain why you turned me in to the Hirutere," I snarl. Invoking the god's name sends a shiver of power through me. All along there has been something within me, a god's fire burning. Saying his name dredges up that primal power, brings it to my fingertips. It tells me to burn.

"What?" Killian demands, confused by my statement on multiple levels. He shakes his head. "Time for that riddle later. If what you say is true about him being your brother, then there's another spell we could try. In the ancient language say: my blood is yours and by it let this wound be undone."

"I don't know the ancient language," I say, panic rising in my voice. Isabrand groans before his head goes limp in the cradle of my arms.

"Okay, okay it's something like… saviski…. saviski isuazko ne siexata etev tsi tai destoyar lera kour darava pritaiy."

"Saviski isuazko ne siezata etev tsi tai destoyar lera kour darava pritaiy," I repeat, my shaking hand pressed to Isabrand's scalp.

I let out a sharp cry as a small laceration opens itself on my hand. I watch as my blood slips out in a slender ribbon, rising into the air, before plunging down and stitching together Isabrand's wound. This is blood magic. The skin closes itself up, though the blood does not disappear from his hair. Its work done, my blood congeals over my palm, sealing the wound shut. Though he doesn't stir, Isabrand's breaths begin to steady. I breathe a sigh of relief, kissing his forehead and pulling him into my lap from which he's begun to slip. I stay like that for a few moments, our foreheads pressed together. My precious Isabrand. I have only just got him back and already almost lost him. I must be more careful, must be sure to protect him now as I could not do when we were children.

"So, this is your brother?" Killian asks, reawakening me to his presence, which was forgotten in my momentary assurance of Isabrand's safety. I start and pull Isabrand away from him. Snatching up Isabrand's fallen dagger, I hold it between me and the man who has betrayed my trust.

"You first. Why'd you turn me into the Hirutere?" I say, narrowing my eyes at him. A look of shock flashes across his face before hurt settles in its place.

"You think I did that?" he demands.

"Didn't you?"

"After everything I've done to keep you and your friends safe, you really think so low of me? You think that I would wait three years just to betray you?" he murmurs, before turning away. "And dragoviks think the bellatoja are prejudiced."

Studying his face, I find my heart sinks. He's right. How could I have so readily jumped to such a conclusion when all the evidence overwhelmingly pointed to the contrary? I lower the dagger back to my side.

"I'm sorry, I didn't mean to assume. But you have to admit, things look bad. No one other than you and my friends knew."

"I know, why do you think I came? I was trying to get in touch with you, but you didn't reply to my texts."

"If not you then who? And where have you been?"

"I was back in Miesarinda. Remember that crash that comes over me after the adrenaline high? Well, it kicked in. I needed to rest. But while I was there, I heard from one of my housemates that Algard had decided to press charges. He has no evidence, he's just furious about what happened at Kyle's trial. He's humiliated so wants a big win. Bringing in Alistair's killer would be exactly that. Bringing in a Thiel who is considered a threat to the Onyevaras' power is an even bigger bonus. Not to mention it would get them the Vaerdiexes sword, which cost him a lot of points with the Hirutere when you got it."

"We pretty much assumed that's why he was doing it. Figures it's Algard. He was making all those cryptic comments last time we saw him."

"Mallory, I swear I didn't tell him anything. When I found out, I knew I had to warn you, but it seems someone beat me to it."

"I've got my sources. So, you're not here to take me in?" I ask.

"How many times do I have to kill a deabrueon, protect one of your friends, or take you for chilli cheese fries before you get the point? I'm on your side Thiel."

"Why? We hardly know each other?"

"Trust really doesn't come easy to you, does it? I'm here because we want the same thing. To win this war without corrupting ourselves or losing anyone we care about. I don't think the Hirutere are shy about morally compromising themselves or their soldiers in order to retain power. That much is obvious from this case against you. I want to avoid doing that if I can and I think fighting by your side is the best way forwards."

Finally, I set the dagger on the floor, hanging my head. Isabrand is breathing softly in my lap.

"I'm- I'm sorry I doubted you. And after you just helped me save Isabrand's life as well. I'm just so on edge since Leo told me about the Hirutere's arrest warrant," I sigh, rubbing my forehead.

"You saw Leo?" he asks.

"Yes."

"Oh. I didn't know you were still in contact."

"We weren't, or aren't. He just came to warn me and give me that," I say, nodding to the box, which has slid under the sofa in all the kerfuffle. "I'm sorry I blamed you. You're right, you've gone above and beyond helping me. I don't know what I would have done without you the past few days."

"Died in Brooklyn for starters. That's a grim way to go." He pauses, casting a glance at Isabrand. "So, you have a brother?"

I look back down at Isabrand, the man who tried to kill me moments ago. But he's also the boy who secreted away all manner of treats from the kitchen for me and took the blame when our mother came down on us. He's the boy who indulged my late-night stories of warriors and queens. The boy I lost when my mother's resentment for him finally made her send him to boarding school after my death. I brush his floppy hair from his eyes, which are still closed tight.

"Yeah. Half-brother."

"Thaddeus'." I nod. "That's why Thaddeus let him live when he killed the rest of—sorry."

"It's okay, we can say it. When he killed the rest of my family."

I can't say my mother didn't have it coming. Memories of her cruelty towards the son born of Thaddeus' rape make me sick. And all the while she was considered a saint by my father and his family for raising Isabrand, believing it was Thaddeus who had attacked her. My father had worshipped her and, though he didn't outright mistreat Isabrand, he never stopped my mother from yelling at or striking him. None of us did. My eyes cloud with tears. Had I been so weak as a child? But, of course, I already knew that from the night I betrayed Lilith.

"Looks like murderous intent runs in the family. Why was he trying to kill you though?"

"Apparently his bosses sent him, whoever they are," I sigh. "Just add them to the ever-growing list of people I need to run from."

"Is that what you're doing?" he asks, nodding to the suitcase.

I study him. Just how much should I reveal? He may not have turned me in, but a large part of me is warning me not to trust him all the same. Yet the look of hurt that commanded his expression moments ago reminds me that, despite the innate distrust I have for bellatoja, Killian is different. He's fought by our side, worried over me and my friends, proven his loyalty again and again. I can trust him.

"We're going to Kyle's place in Aplin Hollow," I tell him, only to illicit a head shake from him.

"Algard has already thought to send people to Aplin Hollow. He knows you have a history there and, besides, it's obvious Kyle will be helping you escape."

"So where to now?"

"Is there anyone else you can think of who might help?"

I stare at him blankly before it dawns on me.

"Yeah, but I don't think she'll be happy to see me."

Just then, the door bursts open. Killian springs to his feet, sword drawn, but lowers it when he sees Kyle and Aaron.

"You," Aaron snarls, lunging for Killian.

"Aaron, stop!" I cry out, but Killian is already sailing across the room. He bounces off the doorframe leading into my bedroom and stumbles to his feet. Before Aaron can make another move, Isabrand lets out a loud moan and his eyelids flutter open. Suddenly, the other two spot all the blood on my jeans.

"What happened, who is that?" Kyle asks.

"My half-brother and he almost died. Long story," I add when both of their mouths fall open.

"Your brother?" Aaron demands, looking at Isabrand in disbelief. If he saw those eyes, mirrors of my own, he would believe me.

"I'll explain later. Where's Casey? Why are you here so soon?"

"After the texts you sent? I was worried! I came as fast as I could. Don't worry about Casey, she'll be safe with Robyn," he assures me. He gives Isabrand a peculiar look. "Another Thiel."

I shake my head.

"Velemir," Killian says.

Kyle's eyes widen. He knows as well as I do what this means about the strange prophetic girl's belief that my destiny is to rule Dragovicia. Isabrand has nearly as good a claim as I, or would were it not for the fact that I was chosen in death by Vaerdiexes. I make a mental note to fill Kyle in on what I have learned later. It seems everything I had assumed about Vaerdiexes was correct.

"Remind me why I'm not killing this guy?" Aaron asks, glaring furiously at Killian.

"It wasn't him who turned us in, Aaron. No one did. It's just this guy named Algard's vendetta for helping Kyle get off his charges. Killian's here to help."

Aaron doesn't believe me, though whether it's down to his loathing of the bellatoja or genuine disbelief I can't tell. He keeps glaring at Killian while Kyle stares in shock at Isabrand, lying on the floor.

"Listen, I'll tell you guys everything later, but right now we need to get going. And not to Aplin Hollow," I say.

"Why not?"

"Algard's already sent men there according to Killian. He'll find this place too, soon enough, if he hasn't already. Luckily Dominic was thorough in his protection. He kept the apartment's registration details in another name, but the address is registered to my school's database, which I'm sure they can get access to."

"Where do we go then? If they think to look at Kyle's place in Aplin Hollow, surely they'll think of any other properties the Caverlys own. Not to mention they're undoubtedly going to be here soon," Aaron says.

"I have an old friend," I offer.

"Who?" Aaron asks.

I exchange a look with Kyle and he must read my thoughts. He rubs his face, thinking that perhaps this is not the best idea but that we don't really have an alternative at this point. She sure as hell is not going to be happy to hear that I might be dropping out of university, if she doesn't already know about our exploits from the past few days. She doesn't actively keep tabs on me, but I know she's tuned in enough with the supernatural world to hear about Kyle's trial and my appearance at it.

"Doctor Lindberg," Kyle and I say in unison.

Chapter XVIII.

It takes a while to navigate the wards obscuring Doctor Lindberg's address from my tracking spell, but eventually I manage to find it. Aaron texts Robyn the address at which to meet us with Casey. By the time we arrive at the apartment building, a still unconscious Isabrand slung over Aaron's shoulder—'drunk' we say to the cab driver, who doesn't seem to care much—Robyn and Casey are already waiting for us. Robyn has her arms crossed over her chest and she looks irritated, as if they've been there a long time. In reality, it may have only been seconds and Robyn would still be irritated. That girl needs a serious spa day or something.

"About bloody time. Who's that?" Robyn asks, spotting Isabrand.

We all grumble unintelligible responses, tired from the cramped cab ride to Lenox Hill and she shrugs. Just another unconscious person to deal with. Nothing new to see here folks.

"Working for the Academy clearly pays well," Aaron comments, glancing up at the large pale stone building. "First Diane at Bleecker Street, now Lindberg here. Just saying," he adds when Kyle gives him a pointed look. Then he narrows his eyes at Kyle. "How much did you make working for them?"

"Your insensitivity knows no bounds," Kyle says.

"That much, huh?" Aaron shifts Isabrand's weight on his shoulder before turning to me. "I can't believe you went and had dinner without us. What did you guys eat anyway, he weighs a ton."

"Just some Pad Thai. Besides, we hardly ate any of it," I insist, leading them into the lobby. The glamour I've cast over us means the man at the reception pays us no heed. We crowd into the elevator, closely packed together. Aaron whirls around, facing the doors, bonking me on the head with Isabrand's forehead. "Could you stop spinning around? I just got headbutted by my unconscious brother."

I swat at Aaron's shoulder, hoping to still him. He picks up Isabrand's limp hand and makes it wave at me.

"Fourth ring of hell, one junior sweet with a hot tub," I say, but can't resist high-fiving the hand.

"I'm sorry, your brother?" Robyn demands.

"Half-brother," we all reply in unison.

"Oh great, as if one moron sprog wasn't enough, one of your parents had to procreate more," Robyn says. "How'd we not know about this?"

"It's a long story we've yet to be told," Aaron says, reassuring her with a pat on the back from Isabrand.

"Stop, please."

Isabrand lets out a grunt, but doesn't stir.

The elevator doors glide open and we exit into the hall. There are two doors to choose from, but, luckily, I know which we're headed to. I rap on the door before stepping back and crossing my arms. It's been years since I've seen Doctor Lindberg, our rare exchanges regarding tuition and rent occurring over email perhaps bi-annually. We met once when I first arrived in New York to discuss the terms of our arrangement and because, despite her cool exterior, she was worried about me. I could tell the moment she walked into that rundown café we chose as the venue for our reunion. She had looked so anxious until she set her sights on me. Then relief broke across her face. Then sorrow. Then came the torrent of apologies, the sympathy for my loss. I hadn't wanted to hear it, knowing Inerea's death was my fault, but I didn't know how to tell Lindberg to stop, to please stop saying my grandmother's name. After that I decided all contact would be via the phone or email. After all this time, I don't expect she'll be glad to see me in the flesh, especially given what trouble I bring with me. We wait and, when there's no answer, I glance at the others.

"It is pretty late," Kyle sighs.

"That's not why she isn't answering. This woman worked at a place that saw a massacre when someone came looking for her. She's probably terrified every time the pizza delivery man comes to the door," Aaron says.

"Doctor Lindberg?" I call from the other side of the door. "It's Mallory. Mallory Thiel."

Like that, the door swings open to reveal a slightly dishevelled Doctor Lindberg as I've never seen her before. Her hair is out of its customary bun in long tresses that reach past her shoulders. I can see it's become streaked with grey since we last saw each other almost three years ago. Her eyes are lined with exhaustion and newly emerging wrinkles, but her eyes themselves are lit with curiosity. She looks at me before glancing over my shoulder, one exquisitely manicured eyebrow arched in bemusement at the sight before her. Aaron waves at her with Isabrand's hand and I sigh, burying my face in my palm for a moment. Does he have no sense of decorum?

"Well, I suppose you should come in," she says, stepping back and holding the door open for us.

We file past her into a spacious and decadent octagonal entrance room I wouldn't have expected to be to her tastes. The ceiling is decorated in gold foil and there are four mirrored doors which lead into the rest of the apartment. There are plush white velvet sofas and chairs centred around a marble table with a beautiful Rothschild slipper orchid sitting in a gold pot and several linen bound coffee table books.

"No seriously, how much did you make?" Aaron asks Kyle again, looking around in wonder. Kyle swats him before turning to Lindberg.

"It's good to see you again Felicia," he says, shaking her hand. I've never heard anyone call her by her first name before. Even her guards and colleagues called her Doctor Lindberg, at least in front of us. But Kyle softens everyone, so it's no surprise that even Lindberg allows him to use her first name.

"You too," she replies, smiling more than I have ever seen her do so before. "Though undoubtedly not under great circumstances?"

Her eyes rove from Isabrand to my jeans, newly bathed in his blood, and the suitcases we all have.

"Unfortunately not, we're in a bit of a bind."

"Mallory's arrest warrant," she says, rubbing her wrists and nodding.

"You heard?" I ask, shocked.

"They got in touch with me right away after the Academy was attacked all those years ago. They were suspicious as to why I wasn't there and wanted to know who I thought might have done this. Not you, of course," she adds, studying my face, "this is beyond your capabilities. Not as a witch, but as a person. Then I heard about the warrant from a friend of mine in Miesarinda. She doesn't know I've been helping you, of course. No one does."

There's a moment between us, when she stops speaking, where our relationship re-establishes itself, that old respect and familiarity flooding back to us. In all the years since I left the Academy, in our brief exchanges, I have not once said thank you for all she has done to help me get back on my feet. I flush furiously, embarrassed by my selfishness. How have I not thought to say thank you until now? She smiles, seeming to read my mind.

"Come and have some tea, I find these sorts of exchanges are less uncomfortable when there are things to hold and biscuits to eat."

"Got any coffee?" Kyle yawns.

"Absolutely not," Robyn and I say at the same time.

"Fine, fine," he scowls.

We follow Doctor Lindberg through a mirrored door to the right, which opens into a spacious kitchen in which everything is made of flawless white marble. She gestures to the breakfast nook by the window, before setting about making some tea.

"Not to make things awkward, but do you have somewhere I can tie this guy up?" Aaron asks, nodding to Isabrand. "He seems like a top lad, what having just tried to murder my friend, but I'd feel more comfortable with ropes around his wrists."

"Likewise," Killian agrees, though Aaron seems mildly displeased with his assent. Clearly he's not forgiven Killian, though the latter has not done anything wrong in the end. Aaron can be stubborn like that I've realised.

There's a sound from the entrance room and Lindberg suddenly looks anxious, glancing back at the door. The others draw themselves back upright from their chairs, reaching for their weapons. But when a little girl appears in the door, they quickly let their hands fall away. Who is she?

"Mommy?" the girl yawns, rubbing her eyes. She takes us all in, uncertain of what to make of us with our swords and suitcases. Mommy? My jaw drops.

"Hi sweetie, what are you doing up?" Lindberg coos. She swoops down and scoops the girl into her arms. Turning her body, she puts herself between us and the girl. She might trust us, but protecting her daughter is instinct. She'll put herself between her daughter and the world if she has to. Her kindness suddenly seems so obviously born of maternal instinct now. How had I not realised? Perhaps because I never knew a mother figure of my own and, by the time I met Lindberg, it was too late for me to know what one was.

"I heard people outside my room." Still she doesn't look at her mother, eyes trained on the seven of us instead. She presses her thumb to her lower lip, which she juts out. "Who are they?"

"Old friends from work. Come on, I'll take you back to bed."

"Okay."

"And follow me. I'll show you a place," she adds to Aaron and Killian, her voice suddenly dropping back to a stern register. They exit the room, leaving Kyle, Casey, Robyn, and me sitting around the table.

"Your brother tried to kill someone?" Casey asks, a look of panic striking her face. She's still not used to what a regular occurrence that is around here.

"Me," I sigh, going to pour the boiling water from the kettle into the teapot. Lindberg has already dropped two teabags in.

"Who can blame him," Robyn mutters, ignoring Kyle's dirty look.

I don't heed Robyn's comment, my thoughts currently occupied. Who would have thought Lindberg was a family woman? The girl looks old enough to have been around since I was at the Academy. How is it Lindberg managed to balance an ordinary life with what she did there? It's always struck me that you must choose one or the other: the supernatural or the ordinary. I bring the teapot and tray of teacups to the table, filling them and passing them out to everyone.

"Why would he do that?" Casey asks, drawing the cup towards her. "Are we safe from him?"

"Well, that's a dumb question," Robyn says to her. "We're never safe."

"Shut up Robyn. It's sort of a long, very, very weird story. Basically, someone hired him to kill me. But he didn't," I reply.

"Because Killian stopped him," Kyle reminds me.

He's half right. But the moment before Killian had come in, Isabrand hadn't been trying to kill me. His last act was to open the box and reopen our history. He wanted me to remember our childhood. I hope that's because he wanted me to remember him and the love I held for him as a child. It seems part of him isn't ready to let go of that yet. Yet how had he known the box contained my memories? What had made him realise that? There are so many questions I need to ask, so much of our time apart that I need to know about. Doctor Lindberg re-enters the room.

"Apologies," she sighs, coming to sit at the table.

"No apology necessary, we've barged in on you in the middle of the night."

"With an attempted murderer no less. How did you manage to find me through the wards by the way?"

"Mallory."

Lindberg frowns.

"I know you're powerful, but I wouldn't have expected even you to get around my wards. The artari have granted me the highest protection after what happened at the Academy."

"That's artari magic for you," Robyn says, shrugging and sipping her tea. She's clearly said something very rude because Kyle gives her an absolutely foul look. "What?"

"I'm artari," Doctor Lindberg says sternly. She gives Robyn an appraising look and comes up unimpressed. That makes two of us. Then she turns back to me. "Did you have a second for the locator spell?"

I look to Kyle for some help, but know it's my duty to explain what happened with Diane.

"I took someone else's isuazko recently."

Her eyes widen, and I know instantly something is wrong. Robyn coughs, choking on the biscuit she's eating.

"You did what?" Robyn demands, spewing a few crumbs from her mouth. I look to Kyle again, but he just shrinks back.

"I had to!" I say, though I'm unsure why I suddenly feel a need to defend myself. Wasn't I saving our lives? Kyle, Aaron, Killian, Casey, and my own? Not to mention the hundreds of others Diane has hurt with her power over her life time. Kyle said there was no other way to stop her. I was only doing what was necessary.

"Mallory," Lindberg starts, shaking her head as she goes on. "Taking another creature's isuazko is a serious matter, taboo even.

It's on par with blood magic. Not to mention the fact that with the power comes other things."

My blood goes cold. Other things? I distinctly recall no mention of such consequences being made by Kyle. He won't even look at me now.

"Like what?"

"It can vary, but usually it manifests as aspects of the person from whom the isuazko has been taken."

It is as I had feared. I needle Kyle with a furious look.

"Why didn't you tell me?" I whisper, unable to raise my voice for fear I'll lose control of it if I do. I have no doubt, as thorough as he is with his research, that he knew this when he told me to cast the spell. Yet he told me to do it all the same. He hadn't known it was Diane when he told me to cast the spell, but he still knew it was an avika working for the jaeitsi. That should have been enough for him to decide this wasn't the right decision or, at the very least, a decision he should be making for me.

"It was the only way to stop her Mallory, we had to. For Casey, for you, and all the other people she's hurt. I didn't know it was her when I told you to use the spell."

I feel tears prick my eyes. He knew the last person I would want to be like in this world is Diane, the woman who robbed me and Dominic of our childhoods and, in some ways, our futures. A normal one at least. He knew that and yet he sacrificed me for the greater good. No, that is not the part that stings my heart so badly that tears begin to track down my cheeks. I know he was right in doing so, but it hurts knowing he didn't trust me to make the same choice myself if given all the pertinent information.

"Who was it?" Robyn asks.

"Diane."

I hear Lindberg's sharp intake of breath. I know what she's thinking. It is undoubtedly what I am thinking. I have destroyed my maker and, in doing so, may now have become her. I try to think on the past day, whether I've felt a change. In my power, yes, but in my demeanour? I'd like to think I haven't changed, but there is evidence to the contrary. Did I not tell Kyle of my destiny as if it was my right, with a sense of entitlement I had never known before? And the way I sprang on Killian with such rage, it was so unlike me. I feel sick. Pushing my teacup away, I stare down at my hands.

"I'm so sorry Mallory, but I had to protect those people she would have hurt," he says, reaching for my hand. I snatch it away.

"Don't you think I would have done that anyway? I, who knows better than anyone what she's capable of? You think I would have let her hurt anyone else given the choice?"

"I don't know what you would have done. I can't know where your head is at. I couldn't leave the choice up to you."

"But that's just the problem, it was my choice to make and you took it away. You think so low of me that I would choose myself above others?"

"But you did," Robyn interjects. Even she looks uncomfortable now. "When you left us three years ago, that's exactly what you did."

I look from her to Kyle and can tell by the way he bites his lip and can look anywhere but at me, he agrees.

"You still think that of me?" I ask him. "You still think I left for myself? After I told you I left to protect you."

"You left to protect me, but you also left to make yourself happy. Didn't you say as much?"

"I left for you! I left to protect you from what inevitably follows me: death and destruction. I chose you and, when I walked out the door of your home in Aplin Hollow, I had no clue where I was going to go, what my future was going to be. I gave myself over to the unknown entirely so that you would be safe from whatever might hunt me next."

Just then, Killian and Aaron re-enter. The tenseness between them seems to have eased, but they freeze up when they spot the five of us.

"Woah, what did we miss?" Aaron asks.

"Nothing," I bite back, glaring at Kyle.

"Not to break up the party, but he's awake. He's asking for you," Killian starts, but slowly peters out when I don't look away from Kyle.

"It's going to take time Mallory," he sighs, finally meeting my eyes. "Please understand I want to forgive you, but we're up against three years of hurt."

"You said that you forgave me. So what, you're lying to me now? And what about what I have to forgive? Are your wrongs null and void because I fucked up three years ago? You can just endlessly hurt me now, is that it?"

"No, that's not what I'm saying," he starts, but I cut him off by raising my hand and standing up.

"Whatever. I'm going to speak to Isabrand."

"I'll show you where he is," Killian says quietly.

He waits, but, when I don't start towards him, he clears his throat. I finally look away from Kyle, my heart pounding with his betrayal. Following Killian back into the entrance room, I feel myself crack. The tears spill down my cheeks. I take a shaky sob and Killian glances over his shoulder.

"Shit," he murmurs, pulling me into his arms. There, in that place of safety, I am wracked with sobs. They rattle the architecture of my being until I can all but feel my bones shaking. Killian holds me steady, but he cannot still me.

"I can't," I whisper. "I can't become her."

"Who?" he asks, sweeping my hair from my face before it can be matted to my skin by tears.

"Diane. I can't be like her. I'd ra– rather be dea– dead," I manage through sobs, before I choke on my tears. Coughing, I press my face back to his chest, but he draws away. He takes my hands in his own and looks me dead in the eye.

"I can't speak from experience as you can, but I know enough of Diane to say with certainty that you are not her. Whatever part of her flows through you now is magic, nothing more. You won't become her Mallory, there's too much good anchoring you to be swept up in her darkness," he assures me.

I shake my head.

"But Kyle's right. I'm selfish. I don't know that I would have chosen to take her magic away if I'd known the potential consequences."

"I like Kyle as much as someone can without it becoming romantic, but don't let that asshat make you doubt yourself. You would have chosen to stop her even if you had known the risk you were putting yourself at. For the same reason you saved the life of someone who tried to kill you only an hour ago. For the same reason you helped that raika escape. You are a good person who is willing to endanger herself to do what she believes is the right thing."

All while he is speaking, he doesn't lose eye contact. I am lost in the forest of his eyes that beam only kindness and reassurance. They don't know how to be mistrustful, how to see the worst in people. He squeezes my hands, then wipes the tears from my cheeks. In the time he has been speaking, my sobs have silenced themselves to hiccups that draw my chest up in sharp gasps.

"You might be like that, helping a near complete stranger. I saved Isabrand because I couldn't watch him die. The same goes for the raika. It's fear, not goodness."

"You tell yourself what you need to to make a monster of yourself. You deserve better than the darkness so many have tried to pull you into."

He doesn't say anymore, turning away and walking across the foyer to another door. But he doesn't drop my hand either. I want him to hold it forever, want to feel the warmth he radiates, both physically and emotionally, stilling my frantic soul. We make our way silently through the door and down the hallway before turning into an office. There, on the floor in the corner, is Isabrand.

Chapter XIX.

Isabrand's hands are bound behind his back and his legs are tied together with lengths of rope. I don't really want to imagine why Doctor Lindberg had those handy. They look incredibly tight, scrunching up the hem of his trousers. I'm tempted to undo them, worrying, as I do, that they must be hurting his wrists and ankles. But then I remind myself that, just because he didn't kill me, doesn't mean he hadn't come to my apartment with the intent of doing so. That thought might still be there. And my heart breaks against the shores of my ribcage, hammering away to look upon my brother and not know him, not anymore. Not for all the years we've spent apart. What can I make of him in this moment?

He stares, melancholy, out the window onto the noisy street below, though his eyes are glazed over. He's not really looking, but waiting instead. For me? For his opportunity to escape? Or for death? His shoulders are hunched forward as if he is bracing himself for whatever blow may come down next. As if he's used to them falling repeatedly on his shoulders. From what I've seen of him so far, I don't doubt he is. Again the urge to untie him sweeps over me and I step towards him.

My movement alerts him to our presence and he spots us entering. Squirming, he tries to stand.

"Oh no you don't pal," Killian says, swaggering forward and pushing him roughly back to the floor.

I bite my lip, wanting to stop Killian, but also fearing he's right to protect me. Seeing Isabrand awake, I remember the wild-eyed look on his face when he said he'd take back what Regan had stolen from him. When he held me down, a knife to my neck and no reservations about slitting my throat. I shiver. He was going to take back the lifeforce my mother had taken from him to bring me back to life. She hadn't needed to. Vaerdiexes would have brought me back all the same. Isabrand ignores Killian, looking only at me.

"Mallory please," he starts, struggling before going limp. His face is made up of a look of resignation and bitterness. "Please. You don't have to untie me, just hear me out. I promise I can explain."

Killian looks back at me and I nod. I am desperate for an explanation, some reason to untie Isabrand and pull him into my arms other than the ache in my chest.

"I'll be just outside. If he tries anything, call me."

Killian glances once more over his shoulder before he shuts the door behind him, leaving us to our silence.

Though he said he wanted to speak, Isabrand seems suddenly devoid of speech. His mouth is agape for a moment before he shuts it and simply looks at the floor. Unable to just stare at him tied up, I pace back and forth, looking around the room. There is none of the archaic décor as was in Diane's study. Instead, the room is done up in a pristine, ultra-modern style, much as the kitchen and entrance are. There's a vast glass desk, polished so well I can see my reflection in it. A pencil pot with ten identical, neatly arranged pens sits on the top right corner and a closed laptop rests in the middle of the desk. I wonder what secrets it contains. Does it hold my past? I walk over to the desk and press my thumb to the glass. Pulling it away, I find reassurance in the smudge it leaves. Something passingly human has been here.

"You wanted to talk," I say, finally, looking at my brother.

He catches my gaze. Those eyes are so like my own, so inhuman and cold when they want to be. But, for now, he has imbued them with warmth. He is trying to reach out to me as he has not had to do with someone in so long. This is a good sign, I think. Unless he's trying to lull me into a false sense of security. I wait but, still, he makes no reply. I clear my throat.

"You were going to kill me."

"No, I," he starts, before hanging his head. "Yes. Maybe, for a moment. You told me your story and I wanted to so badly. It would have made everything easier. Then I wouldn't have had to accept all the horrible things you said had happened to you were true. I could have put your past to rest with you. All I wanted in that moment was for it to be over, for your pain to be over. And I thought death was the answer."

"But instead you opened the box. Did you know what that would do, that it contained my memories? Did you know– "

"What Regan had done? I had guessed. The day she sent me away, I saw you in the entrance hall of our home. They were hauling me out and you came down. I tried to run to you, tried to fend them off. I managed to reach you, only you looked as though you didn't know me. I expected fear, after what had happened at the river, or hurt. But not that look of an absolute absence of recognition. That was when I stopped fighting and let them drag me away. I realised Regan must have cast a spell."

"But she's dead. How could her spell still hold?"

"If anyone could have cast a memory spell that held after her own death it would have been Regan. She must have bound it to the box so it would outlive her," he says bitterly.

How could he not spit acid into the words surrounding our mother's name, after how readily her hand came down upon him? I remember her striking him by the river and my heart roars to flame. Would that she were alive only so that I could kill her again. I want her to know, that woman who loved me so, how much I despise her, if only to hurt her.

"She was a bitch," I finally say, agreeing with his earlier statement from back at my apartment. He chuckles, smiling to himself.

"And I a bastard. Or so everyone tells me."

"What is it Byron said? 'I love being called a bastard. It somehow implies that the most heinous thing I've done is exist'."

He looks up from the floor, catching me in those glacial eyes. I freeze, ceasing my nervous pacing. I feel like a fly in amber; I could be held by his gaze for millions of years, perfectly preserved in his eyes.

"Do you feel that way too?" he asks.

"All the time."

There is a cord that stretches from my heart to his. There are parallels in our lives that span the distance between us and make passable roads by which we can traverse the years gone by and reach one another. We are not so far apart as I had imagined.

"Well, our mother didn't think so. She adored you. Me, on the other hand."

"You were a reminder of what she had done wrong. She feared you because she feared others may see the truth of what had happened in you," I assure him.

"She feared me enough to send me to boarding school so I wouldn't hurt you again after that day."

"So, tell me about it," I say, sitting beside him. "All I need to know. Tell me everything, just as it was, from the beginning."

He lowers his head, the past heavy upon him. I know its Atlas burden, have held it every day. I am trying to shoulder his now, trying to help him lift it off his back. His mouth opens as he tries to fit the past on his tongue, find a way to bring it into the present without hurting himself. Just as I had done for him hours before.

"The boarding school was run by Vaerdiexes' acolytes: The First Principle. It was fine. They were a bit nutty, but they took care of me. Taught me to be an upstanding believer in the faith. But after Regan died, there was no one to foot the bill. They brought me to New York. Left me here."

"Alone?" I ask.

He nods. That loneliness was exactly what I had been fighting against when I made my deal with Vaerdiexes. Yet I failed Isabrand. I try not to picture my brother, young and vulnerable, alone in the streets of New York, but the image comes all the same. He is small and shivering. He is susceptible to whatever demands are made of him in exchange of food or a place to stay. I place my hand on his knee and do my best to hold in the tears that seem to keep coming tonight.

"I slept on benches in parks for a while, before they found me. They said they were like me, not of this world, and could give me a place to stay."

"But you had to do something for them," I say.

That's what this world is made up of after all. People take advantage of our weaknesses for personal gain and we think we're getting a good deal out of it. Isn't that what Vaerdiexes did with me? He saw my love for my brother and took advantage of it to have me pledge myself to him.

"They trained me, taught me how to kill and how to go unseen. Not unlike what you learned at the Academy. I must have been about fifteen when I started actually completing assignments though. I heard it was a lot earlier for you. It wasn't long before I was the best. Never failed, not until tonight," he sighs. "It's times like these I could really go for a shot of tequila."

"You and me both," I agree.

We don't say anymore for a time. Hours ago, I knew I had a brother, but I didn't know him. Now it feels as if we're as close as we could possibly get given the circumstances. To think I had lived without him so long and all because I hadn't tried to open that box sooner. Kicking myself at not putting it together earlier, I suddenly realise the meaning of Inerea's note, found tucked away in that book all those years ago.

"The box is the key," I murmur again. "He doesn't know about her. So, it was you, all along."

"What do you mean?" he asks, his brows knitting together in confusion.

"It's nothing now."

It's not worth telling him and hurting him with what I now know to be true. Inerea had known about him then, if that note is to believed. *He doesn't know about her*. It was talking about me and Isabrand. She had known and she had chosen not to go looking for Isabrand. Was it because she believed he was a product of her daughter's rape? I can't believe my grandmother could be so cold as to hold his father's perceived act of malice against Isabrand. Again, I find my heart harden towards my mother and the cruelty she brought down upon Isabrand in order to maintain her lie. She must have been some liar to convince Inerea that Isabrand was so bad. But then, Inerea hadn't known about me until the Academy contacted her. She must have only thought to look for Isabrand then, with the help of Mr Bowen. She had taken me in, knowing what I was, but Isabrand she'd left to fend for himself. Could he really be so bad? Even Thaddeus seemed to think so in comparison to himself and that's a generous measuring stick for evil being used there. But I look at my brother and I cannot know him as evil, only the kind little boy who held me through my night terrors.

"Why would Regan want me to forget you?" I ask, changing the subject.

He gives me a grin, but only lifts half his mouth, so it seems more a grimace.

"Mother dearest wasn't too fond of me and, given how I came into being, I'm not all too surprised."

"Your father didn't rape her, Isabrand. It was the other way around," I murmur, leaning back against the bookcase behind us.

His eyes widen before flattening back out until there's no warmth left in his eyes. So, this is how it will be when we speak of our parents: divesting ourselves of emotion to survive the turmoil that threatens the foundation of the fragile lives we've constructed for ourselves.

"Go figures that bitch would do something like that. Poor father. Guess you made up for that, huh?"

I flinch away, the coldness with which he refers to our mother now extended to me. He shakes his head suddenly.

"I'm sorry, that was cruel. I'm just not used to," he starts, pausing.

"Talking to someone?" I ask.

"Loving someone."

I take in a sharp breath. I hadn't expected him to say it, this man of reservation and death. He's trying to be honest now, at whatever cost to himself. He's trying to strengthen the cords between us.

"It gets easier," I lie. To love someone in a world of death such as ours is the hardest thing. "So, Regan didn't want me to remember you because she didn't like you?"

"She probably thought I'd be a bad influence on you, which is why she sent me away. After that day by the river, she never trusted me with you again. We were kept in separate wings of the house until I was sent away, which wasn't long after."

"But that wasn't your fault," I say, reaching again for his knee.

He doesn't stir, in fact stills all the more, in my proximity. Does he fear me or worry he'll scare me if he moves? Do I seem so fragile to him? His chest hardly rises with every quiet breath he takes. I am overwhelmed with the urge to reach out, press my hand to his chest and feel his heartbeat. So, I do. I feel the warmth within him and his heart as it thuds away, a hurried pace. So, I have the same effect on you as you do me, brother.

"It was," he whispers, hanging his head. "If I hadn't urged you, you never would have jumped. For all my hatred of Regan, were it not for her, you'd be dead."

I shake my head before telling him about my death.

"Vaerdiexes brought me back, not Regan. If she was able to, it was only because he let her," I finish.

"That makes sense. I'd never heard of the spell she cast to bring you back, nor have I heard of it working since," he says. "To bring back the dead is supposed to be impossible. Vaerdiexes must have temporarily given her the power to do it."

"How did it work?"

"She transferred my fire to you, reigniting your life. It's why you're so powerful; the magic of two dragoviks in one. Two flames. Or three, if you count Vaerdiexes'."

Four if you count Diane's. How many people's magic will my power demand? I swallow hard.

"That's what you wanted back from me, the thing she took."

"Yes. I thought, maybe, if I could get it, I could somehow escape my bosses' command. I could be restored to our childhood. But I see now that's not what could awake the fire in me again. Only you can do that."

I shiver. I cannot imagine the absence of what it is that warms my blood, what fuels my magic.

"She wanted to put more space between you and her, you and me, by blanching you of everything that made you one of us," I whisper, running my hand through his hair. I remember now, it had been black as mine before that day, before she drew the colour from his cheeks and the fire from his veins. No wonder he had no trouble falling to darkness without the light of the phoenix to guide him.

"She adored you," he continues. "You were the only thing she cared about. Even your father didn't matter to her. And she left her family behind so readily to raise us in secret. To raise you in secret, for fear of what Thaddeus would do if he got out and ever found you. She did everything to protect you."

"But in the end, she abandoned us to the same fate. Her love didn't spare me any more than her hatred cost you. Two assassins, one asked to kill the other."

"I don't want to kill you Mallory," he says suddenly, a miserable expression crossing his face.

"I'd kind of prefer if you didn't myself," I tease, but he does not smile. I know why. Refusing to kill me is effectively him giving notice to his bosses. My guess is they don't take kindly to that. Termination of contract usually ends in termination of life in our line of business. "I'll keep you safe."

"Isn't that what big brothers are supposed to do?" he asks, and now his eyes are laced with mirth.

"I'm all about subverting gender roles. I'm way stronger than any of those guys out there. Don't tell them though, it will hurt their delicate male egos," I joke. He laughs and it reminds me so much of Dominic in its ill at ease sound. But his smile is soft and genuine. I look at the ropes, tied so tightly around his wrists. "You mind if I take those off?"

"I wouldn't mind getting the feeling back in my hands," he says, nodding at the ropes.

Reaching around his torso as if to hug him, I pull the ropes loose from around his wrists before undoing the ones around his ankles. He doesn't move, doesn't even breathe, as I work the knots free. Finally, I draw back and meet his gaze as equals. I have no fear that he will hurt me.

"Can I?" he starts, reaching a hand out to me. I nod, and he places it on my cheek. He makes a strange coughing sound and I realise he's holding back tears. "Hey lil sis," he whispers.

"Hey."

It seems too much to reach out and hug him, so we just sit, staring at each other and relearning the shapes of one another's features. His sharp cheekbones and hollowed out cheeks, so like my own. The deep dip of his cupid's bow lips, strung with a smile. He sweeps his thumb across my cheek and swallows hard. Is this how it was between us as children? So much love and so easily transmitted even without words? I feel as if I can read the same thoughts on his mind and he grins.

"You sort of can," he says and I'm startled.

"Read your mind?"

"How do you think I realised you were alive? I knew before my bosses told me, but I didn't dare come looking for you in case it led them to you. On Friday, I just woke up and it felt as if part of me was coming to life again. I knew it was a part that had died the day you did. Suddenly, I could sense you from miles away."

"How is that possible?"

"It's not direct telepathy, we can't speak to one another, but after Regan's spell we were always in tune with each other's thoughts. I could sense where you were and how you were feeling. It's how I knew when you'd swiped my last cookie from my plate when I wasn't looking that day when they brought us back up to the house, before they separated us. You felt so guilty."

"I sound like a right brat," I laugh. "I'm amazed you put up with me. But how come you couldn't find me sooner then?"

"I lost sight of you at the Academy where you were obscured by Diane. Then, in Aplin Hollow, Inerea must have cast spells to keep you from the Onyevaras and Hirutere, but they hid you from me too. Then, in New York, Dominic's witch kept you safe. None of them meant to keep you from me, but they all did inadvertently. But after Dominic's witch's spell slipped, suddenly I could see you clearly again."

That's why he could sense me on Friday. It was the day Alice died. I frown, suddenly confused by something else.

"How did you know about Alice?"

"The witch? My bosses told me about her."

There's a sudden knock at the door, but, spun in the myriad of thoughts that fill my head, I can't respond. The door creaks open and in step Kyle, Aaron, Killian, and Robyn.

"Hey, is everything okay in—oh for heaven's sake Mallory. You untied him?" Aaron demands.

"It's alright, he's not going to hurt me," I assure them.

Isabrand shrinks back in their presence, snatching his hand from my face. It's not them he fears, but them seeing the display of affection he's exhibited. Sentimentality is a weakness in our business and not something we readily give into.

"And you believe him? For all we know he's working for Diane or the jaeitsi."

I look to Isabrand, awaiting confirmation that this is not the case. He merely shrugs at me before looking back at Aaron.

"I actually have no clue who's top of the food chain," Isabrand sighs, his insouciance returning by way of an indifferent tone. "Orders come, I follow them."

"Like the one to kill Mallory?"

Isabrand's eyes flash dangerously and I suddenly doubt any of them could take him, even unarmed as he is.

"I wouldn't."

"You mean aside from a few hours ago when you almost did?"

"You have no idea what you're talking about. Mallory's my sister and I have no intention of hurting her."

"I'll believe it if you subject yourself to a truth spell."

"By all means," Isabrand replies, unwavering in his piercing stare.

This is not the response they had expected. Aaron glares at him, waiting for Isabrand to change his mind. When he doesn't, Aaron turns to me.

"What?"

"Well, you'll need to cast it," Killian says. Kyle nods, seemingly unwilling to speak after our earlier argument. I'm still mad at him, though that has somewhat diminished in the face of my reunion with my brother. My heart feels softened to all things.

"I told you, there's no need. I trust him," I reply, taking my brother's hand. Isabrand shakes his head.

"I appreciate the show of confidence, sis, but it's better this way. No shadow of a doubt, right?" he says, squeezing my hand.

Despite his assent, I still feel uncomfortable tapping into his mind like that. I can intuit his feelings and I know he is telling the truth when he says he won't hurt me. I spot Robyn leaning on the doorframe.

"Fine we can cast the spell, but only if Robyn does it."

She grins wickedly, delighted to finally be in on the action.

"My pleasure."

In a few strides, she crosses the room. She kneels beside us and rests her hands on either side of his face.

"This will probably hurt," she replies, though not apologetically.

"I can take it."

She grins, holding his gaze as none of the others have done.

"I think I may prefer you to your sister," she says. I look on in horror. Is Robyn flirting with my brother? "Valja hetika hendarava kour akel, perova letai derika darava feti."

Isabrand scrunches his eyes shut in pain as Robyn's fingertips glow silver. Tendrils of light snake free of her fingers, permeating his head to loosen his thoughts and his tongue. Suddenly, his spine snaps straight and he's sitting completely upright. His mouth opens, his eyelids following suit. His eyes fix themselves upon Robyn. They have a peculiar silvery glow to them.

"Didn't know you could do a truth spell," Aaron says, impressed.

"I've been practicing," she replies smugly, before turning back to Isabrand. "Do you intend to hurt this moron?"

His tongue twitches wordlessly in his mouth, ready to answer. Then, there's a flurry of motion. Aaron crashes through the glass desk. It shatters, shards flying across the room. Killian whirls around, but is knocked across the room by a single blow. Into the room have crept five men. One of them drags Doctor Lindberg and her daughter in in headlocks. The little girl wails and wails until the man throws her to the ground and kicks her in the gut. She falls to quiet whimpers, nursing the place he has struck.

"Let her go!" Lindberg shrieks, struggling against her oppressor.

A swirling golden pattern ignites her skin and bursts from her fingers. Her eyes blaze gold. She throws the man clear across the room in a display of strength I would not have expected of her. She makes a move towards her daughter, only to be grabbed by another of the men. He wallops her over the head with the pommel of the sword and she drops to the floor. The gold pattern recedes and she lies motionless.

"Artari bitch," he snarls, kicking her for good measure.

Aaron struggles to his feet, his skin marked by small lacerations where the glass has cut him, but one of the men has already snatched him up and thrown him against the wall. Robyn recoils from Isabrand's face. Her magic leaves him and he slumps forward. His eyes shift around and he's clearly been disoriented by Robyn's spell. Her hands are up in an instant, but, before she can work any magic, one of the men tosses her out of the way.

Rise, I call.

Shards of glass draw themselves up from the ground and shoot through the air. The man closest to us cries out as they prick his body like thorns. He stumbles back. I flick my wrist and one shard impales him in his throat. He frowns, licking his lips. I see the blood in his teeth. He coughs once, as if to clear them, but soon more follows. His head lolls forwards and he collapses, dead.

"Bellatoja," I murmur, but this only stirs a mirthless laugh from one of the men.

"Wrong sweetheart. You have no idea what we are. But we know who you are. And the boss wants you and your traitorous brother."

"Not going to happen," I assure him.

As two more close in on me, I pull Isabrand's body to mine. *Protect us.* A burst of light emanates from us, Robyn, Kyle, Aaron, Killian, Lindberg, and her daughter. Surrounded by our bubbles, I draw my hands tightly into fists before thrusting my palms towards the men. The windows behind me shatter, spraying them with glass. They all stagger back, but none of them are inflicted with fatal wounds. My hands are shaking and I have no time to cast another spell before one lunges at me, grabbing me by the wrists and pinning me down. Another pulls out a set of handcuffs that glow blue and quickly attaches them around my wrists. I feel my magic mute itself in my fingers, my fire yawning into ash. I've seen these before, the night Lilith and I tried to escape. They kept me from casting any spells until Diane arrived. Once she was there, she only needed fear to keep me from casting.

"You're from the Academy," I breathe.

"That's right. Time for a school reunion," the man says, knocking me across the head. The world goes blank.

Chapter XX.

I don't dream while I'm unconscious, though this should come as no surprise. My brain functions have been physically disrupted and nothing, aside from the bare minimum, goes on. But the world tilts, groaning back to life around me. There's feeling first. I'm lying on a cold floor again, which I can feel even through my clothes. The air around me is set with a chill I would not expect this late in spring. I open my eyes, not worrying whether someone else will notice. I need to find Isabrand. I look up at a rocky formation above. Surely this isn't the same place I was in before? They wouldn't bring me back there yet again. The others would know how to find us. The others. That's if they left them alive. I moan, tilting my head to the right. My vision goes blurry, but, when it comes back, I make out Isabrand's white hair, sweeping across his face. I try to reach out for him, but my hand comes up against cage bars.

"Why does this keep happening to me?" I grumble. I roll onto my side, my head pounding with the weight of my recent unconsciousness. I hear Isabrand still breathing and am swept with relief. My suspicions that they only took the two of us were correct. None of the others are here. "Isabrand."

Nothing.

I grab a small rock from the floor of my cage and toss it at him. He winces, blinking a few times before he realises it's me. He shifts his arm but doesn't sit up.

"Mallory? What happened."

"You don't remember?" I ask, slowly using my arms to heave myself into a sitting position. The world keeps swimming in my eyes until there are two Isabrands in front of me. Now that's a scary notion.

"It's a side effect of a truth spell. Your conscious goes to sleep so the unconscious can speak for itself. I've seen it done a few times." He rubs his head and sits upright. "Fuck."

Gagging, he spews some vomit across his cage floor. He wipes his mouth with the back of his hand and leans back on his hands, panting.

"Are you okay?" I ask, darting to the bars.

"I'll be fine, must just be a side effect of the spell. So, what happened?"

"Well, after Robyn cast the spell, some men broke in. They incapacitated us before we could even rally ourselves. We got kidnapped by—"

"My bosses," he interrupts, taking in his surroundings. I frown.

"No, they said they were from the Academy."

He shakes his head at me.

"Mallory, I know this place. It's where we bring prisoners to..." he falters, but I know enough of the world of assassins to finish his sentence for him. It's where they bring prisoners to torture and kill them.

"But if you work for them and they work for the Academy—"

"Then it's almost like you two worked for the same person. Hello darling," Diane says from the recently opened door. She sweeps into the room, followed by two of the men who had taken us. One of them grins, all teeth, at me. He said he isn't bellatoja, that I couldn't even imagine what he is. I shiver. Surveying the room with mild disgust, Diane turns to one of them. "Don't we have a better room for our esteemed guest? She's a queen after all. Or will be."

She smiles at me, perfect white teeth on display. How is she so calm after our last encounter? I expected rage, vindictiveness. But here she is, still speaking as though she wants me on her side, a smile on her face.

"All the cells are occupied, ma'am."

"That's the problem with waging war. So many prisoners. Well, one of the problems. The relocation from Bleecker is a bit of a letdown to be honest. I quite liked that apartment. But we all must make sacrifices, mustn't we?"

On this note, she stares at me. I know more of sacrifice than she can imagine, more than just what she made me give up in order to survive. I parcelled out pieces of my heart in the years after she left me and had to leave them behind. Without looking away, she clears her throat. One of the men draws forward a chair for her, his head bowed, before backing away. They stand either side of the door, identical statue sentries. Were they at the Academy too? If so, she broke them completely. She doesn't sit, a look of mild irritation flickering across her face and I flinch. Time was, a single look like that to a guard could mean a beating for me. Then again,

I'm sure these men would be more than willing to oblige. The man comes forward again and dusts the unseen dirt from the chair before returning to his post.

"That's better," she sighs, seating herself and crossing her legs. She's dressed in a vibrant red wrap dress that is ill-suited to the dank cave venue our reunion will take place in. Leaning forward, she rests her elbows on her legs. Her red curls fall forward around her face. "I hear you've been disobedient."

She's addressing Isabrand when she says this, her sharp eyes trained on him. I see a tremor run through his body and know he has known her cruelty as I have. My hatred for her doubles over and over, a roar for revenge rising with blood to scream in my ears. Did she use magic to leave that scar on his cheek, as she'd done to me? This and so many other marks of her cruelty left on his body and his mind. I cannot take those away from him so easily as I did that scar. These are the breakings that cannot be unbroken. How I wish I had slit her throat back at the apartment.

"You were told to kill your sister. The command came from the top I hear. Well, near the top, it wasn't me who issued it. So why did you disobey?"

"I won't hurt Mallory. No matter what you do to me," he answers through gritted teeth. It is a display of courage, I know, for him to speak back to her like this.

"Don't misunderstand me, I'm pleased you didn't. Not that I think you could manage to kill her, but if she'd let anyone get close enough to do it, it would be you. But I'd never do that to either of you. I don't want Mallory dead," she assures us both with a kind smile. "So I suppose it's a good thing you didn't comply."

"So, you won't punish him?" I whisper. She sighs.

"That's the problem sweetie. While I'm so happy to see you alive, Isabrand still disobeyed his superiors. I can't stand for that in my ranks."

She stretches out her hand behind her. One of the guards steps forward and hands her a whip. My stomach lurches and I curve away from her, pressing my back to the bars of the cage. She gets to her feet and opens Isabrand's cage. I silently urge him to run, hoping he'll hear me through the connection he spoke of. But he is struck by the same fear as I was when I first saw her. It overwhelms his senses. He scuttles to the back of his cage, but, when there's nowhere left to go, all he can do is cower beneath the oncoming whip. We cry out at the same time when the whip comes down on his shoulder, his pain mine. I feel it as if my skin were on fire. I lunge, grabbing the cage bars as if I could wrench them from their place, but those handcuffs are still on, keeping my magic from me. Again, the whip comes down, splitting the skin on his arm. I cannot look away as blood rushes fast and thick to the split lip of his skin.

"Stop!" I scream, reaching frantically through the bars. "Please."

Diane hesitates, studying me before sealing him in the cell once more. He falls to the ground, whimpering. I try to reach out to him, but he doesn't even seem to notice I'm there. If he'd just hold my hand, I could heal him. Or perhaps not. Perhaps even that I could not manage with these handcuffs on. I turn to Diane, who is still studying me. My eyes flicker to the whip. Is it the very same one?

"Oh, don't worry, I won't do this to you. We can't go marring the face of a ruler. It's so much easier to follow the beautiful," she reassures me, sitting back down. The whip falls to the floor with a clatter, the sound bringing with it a sickening onslaught of memories.

Tell me what you see.

Me.

Yes. What are you?

Nothing.

Only now I am not. I am an accumulation of life that has blossomed despite the darkness she planted me in. I am the good as well as the bad, the kindness I have been offered and the love I have given as well as have been given.

"You told me I was nothing, but now you'd crown me a queen," I say.

"Yes. But now it would be in name only. Our previous arrangement doesn't stand. Not after you misbehaved. You'll be a puppet, my darling, completely under my command. What I say you shall do. You're almost as unreliable as Thaddeus. It's a shame your brother doesn't have as strong a claim as you. I could break him so much more easily," she sighs.

"Don't you dare touch him," I hiss.

She laughs, eyes glinting. She licks her lips.

"You can't stop me sweetie, strong as you are. Not with those around your wrists. I invented them myself, you know? Wrote the spell and everything. Of course, I had to use blood magic to enchant them, but, after your mother died, I had some handy."

My mother, keeping me from the truth of myself even in death. I glower at Diane, who keeps smiling at me.

"I wouldn't help you before, what makes you think I'll do it now?"

She raises her eyebrows and looks to Isabrand.

"Not to mention dear, dear Dominic. He called out for you, you know? Said you'd come for him. But even after you left me you didn't. I was a bit surprised by that to be honest. Not your modus operandi to abandon a friend in need. I told him that and he finally stopped calling for you. He must have lost his faith at last. How sad," she muses. "It's simple really. You'll do as I say because, if you don't, they get the whip or whatever other form of torture I deem appropriate. See, Mallory darling, I learned a couple very valuable lessons that night you tried to leave me. One, to never underestimate you. Two, that the way to you is through the ones you love."

She rises once more, but doesn't reach for the whip. Instead, she crosses the room, in a slow easy walk, to my cage. Crouching beside it, she wraps her manicured nails around one of the bars. They're just as they were in my childhood, stilettoed and painted deep red. Wasn't there always enough of that? Isn't there enough of it now, seeping across the floor of Isabrand's cage?

"You underestimated me when we last met," I remind her.

She smiles, no trace of anger on her face despite the humiliating loss she suffered that night. I had so easily tricked her when I managed to steal her magic, but she won't make that mistake again.

"When will you learn that I am only ever proud of the actions you take to make yourself more powerful? Of course, we'll have to undo that spell, I can't have you running around with my magic. But still, very impressive. I didn't understand how you managed to pull off such a powerful spell without a second until my men overheard your conversation with your brother. Blessed back to life by a god. Isn't someone the chosen one all around? Doesn't it make you wonder?"

"Make me wonder what?" I ask, when she doesn't continue.

"The fact that Vaerdiexes and I have the same plan for you, to crown you a queen. Doesn't it make you wonder whether I'm doing a god's will?" she asks, glancing to the ground then back up at me through her eyelashes.

"This isn't how he'd want it done."

But I know that's a lie. He has already shown me he would happily have me go along with Diane's plan.

"You still think your god is good. But sweetheart if you only knew the destruction he wrought before disbelief banished him from Earth. He doesn't care how his will is fulfilled, only that he gets what he wants. He drove Thaddeus mad for it without a second thought. And we all saw what happened there."

"I suspect you had your hand in that too," I say.

I mustn't listen to what she says about Vaerdiexes. I won't let her twisted logic poison my thoughts.

"Oh yes, dear Thaddeus confessed everything to you, didn't he? About his time in prison and what Regan did to him. I understood why when I met him of course. He was beautiful and so innocent. Even hardened by that experience as he was, he still wanted to see the best in the world. It was delicious. And that softness persisted long enough for him to fall in love with you, to try and take you in Aplin Hollow. He told you he was working to take me down, but here's the funny thing," she starts, righting herself, "here he is, with that dear jaeitsi, Clara, working with me. See, I revealed myself to them, after our last encounter. And they're both still here. Men will say anything to get what they want it seems. And what he wants is you."

My body goes still as she speaks until I find I'm hardly breathing.

"The jaeitsi are here," I breathe. "Thaddeus, too?"

"Mm, welcome to headquarters sweetheart. This is where we've all been staying since that moronic raika brought you to our old hideout. It's not the nicest, I'll admit, but don't worry, your room will be much cleaner than this. We'll let you out as soon as

I've got my magic back. You're room's right next door to mine. After all, who else is going to keep you in line if not me?"

"Thaddeus wouldn't help you nor would Clara. Not after all what you did you us as children."

Like lightening, she reaches between the bars and cracks her hand across my face. My vision is showered with black spots before clearing.

"Don't think like an emotional girl. Think like a warrior," she says, her voice icy. My hand jumps to my cheek, the skin warming where she's struck me.

"The enemy of my enemy is my friend," I say numbly, and she nods. "The Hirutere and the Onyevaras."

"Bingo. Thaddeus has hated the Hirutere longer than even me. And for a jaeitsi, it's just instinct to despise them. Especially given they sent a team to kill Clara at the Academy. You have no idea what a nightmare it was to protect her from them back at the Academy."

"Why did you turn on your own people?" I ask.

"Hm, I suppose I could bore you with the details of my past. It's so rare I'm speaking to an equal after all. I disagree with their politics, plain and simple. They guard the portal to Sundalev, but why? Because the angels or Pritovis decreed it. But the angels do nothing for us, just force us into this futile existence of protecting something that doesn't need protecting. We deserve better. So do the dragoviks."

"That's all it took for Thaddeus to overcome you torturing him? An agreement over politics."

"Well, it is said to be a very divisive subject. It can also bring people together. And boy was he mad when he found out the Hirutere wanted you for those murders at the Academy three years ago. Especially when it's so obvious Clara committed them. Now there's a terrifying girl and no mistake."

"If you don't want me dead and I know Clara and Thaddeus don't, who ordered Isabrand to kill me?" I demand.

She sighs, running a hand through her red curls. They splay across her collarbone, like rivulets of blood running from her throat. If only I had followed through and killed her the last time we saw her, maybe we wouldn't be here.

"Honestly when I found out I was quite surprised, given, of all of us, he has no history with you really. I think he's a little jealous of you, what with you being my favourite and all. He's a bit of a momma's boy." She taps her chin.

"Who?" I ask again.

"You've met and I don't doubt you will again. Not before I have a serious talk with him though. I can't risk you two interacting before I quell this murderous impulse of his."

There's a knock at the door and one of the guards opens it. He confers with another man before turning to Diane and clearing his throat. She nods to him.

"Speaking of, looks like he's back. Best go have a chat now before he finds out you're here. He'll be very upset Isabrand's failed and I don't fancy having to restrain him from killing you himself. I'll be back in a bit to get what's mine," she says, winking at me. "Until then, rest a bit dear."

She saunters out, flanked by her two guards. In exchange, the man who came to inform them of this mysterious person's return steps in. He shuts the door behind him before turning around and holding a finger to his lips, urging me not to speak. Carlisle. I open my mouth but don't say a word. We wait in silence until the clack of her heels can no longer be heard.

"What are you doing here?" I hiss. "I thought you said they'd kill you if they found you."

"They didn't. Obviously, seeing as I'm alive. Given it was me against the four of you, they realised I never really stood a chance. But they didn't give me a choice about coming back either," he replies, crossing hastily to my cage. "Works out for you though. Know any other servants of the jaeitsi who owe you their lives?"

He crouches down, inserting a key into the lock and fiddling with it until we hear the click of it popping open. He opens Isabrand's as well, but the latter doesn't seem to notice in his pain.

"How about these?" I ask, offering my manacles up to him.

"Diane keeps the keys for those," he says apologetically.

Damn. With them still on I won't be much help trying to escape nor will I be able to heal Isabrand. If anyone catches us, we won't stand much of a chance, what with both of us incapacitated.

"I'll get you out," Carlisle says.

"Why risk your life?"

"You risked yours," he reminds me, "and I'm assuming if I do this, you and yours will keep me safe. They may have brought me back here, but I know my time's running out. They're not big on forgiveness."

"Figures," I sigh. "Fine. Help Isabrand up."

He slings Isabrand's uninjured arm around his shoulder and hoists him to his feet. Adjusting his weight, Carlisle moves him slowly out of the cage where I'm waiting.

"I'll manage him as best as I can. You'll need to be on guard if someone sees us," I say, nodding at his sword. He wraps Isabrand's arm around me and lets me shoulder the bulk of his weight. Without the use of my hands, it's quite the chore to keep us both upright. His arm is slung over my shoulder and I lift both hands up to hold it there. We start down the hall at a snail's pace. "Where are we?"

"Jaeitsi's headquarters. I'm not sure where exactly. They put a bag over my head when they brought me in; I'm guessing they don't trust me much. Still, it took longer than I expected for them to find me thanks to your wards."

"It just doesn't make any sense; they don't seem like the type to forgive?" I ask, squirming uncomfortably beneath Isabrand's weight.

"I'm sorry, are you disappointed that I'm alive to save you or something?"

"That's not what I meant."

"You think I'm setting you up?"

"It seems within the realm of possibility."

"Listen, the jaeitsi are powerful, but, beyond brainless deabrueon, they don't come by many followers. They can't just be casting us aside. Besides, Diane didn't want you dead. If she had and I'd failed it would have been a whole different story."

"So, who told you to kill me?" I ask.

"Hey, you!" a voice calls from down the hall.

There's the sound of heavy footsteps as the two men who had been with Diane charge towards us. Carlisle catches the first's sword on his and, with deft movements, slits his stomach open. The man spills forward, his guts spewing across the floor. Carlisle's not so lucky with the second one. He manages to catch his blow just in time, losing some ground between us and them in the process. Stumbling back, he parries, before pushing forward. But the second man is just as swift with his blade. The two duel, going back and forth while I frantically try to keep Isabrand from slipping.

"Now would be a great time for you to feel better," I plead. He groans in response, blinking at me as he finally comes back to himself. "Thank heavens."

Alert, he glances around and spots the fight. He stands upright then grimaces at the pain of his wounds.

"Who's on our side?"

"Slightly green dude," I say.

Springing into action without a weapon, Isabrand weaves skilfully between them. His wounds do nothing to hinder him. He snatches a dagger from the man's sheath and slits his throat. My eyes widen. I killed a man only hours ago in Isabrand's defence, but to see him do the same for me is startling. The man coughs up blood, dropping to his knees before falling forward.

"Thanks," Carlisle pants.

"I'm guessing you freed us, so consider it a debt repaid." Isabrand stoops to grab the man's sword. He offers me the dagger only to see my wrists bound. "Nasty little contraption those."

"Any way to get them off?" I ask. He shakes his head. "I guess we've got to find Diane then."

Carlisle begins to shake his head, backing away.

"I said I'd get you out of here. I am not going back in there. The door's only a few feet away," he says, nodding forwards. Ahead of us, I see early morning sunlight plastering a strip of light down the hallway. "A witch with a second and a third should be able to remove those."

"No can do. Even if I didn't need the key, Dominic is here."

"Well, I'm out of here."

Like that Carlisle dashes to the door, disappearing into the dazzling sunlight.

"Brave man," Isabrand remarks. I look to him.

"You can go too if you want," I say.

"And leave you defenceless and handcuffed? Not going to happen," he assures me. He raises the sword. "Besides, where's the fun in running away?"

I smile at him, laughing.

"We should go the way those two came from. They must have been coming from Diane," I say.

"I'll go first."

Our footsteps fall just out of sync like a heartbeat, one echoing off the cave walls after another. Our steady rhythm follows us down the corridor to the right, until we reach a large corrugated metal door. Above it drips slow, steady drops of water and the metal has begun to rust over time. This must be it. Exchanging a look, we push ahead. Isabrand opens the door and I follow him in.

The room is completely dark, save for the small illumination provided by the light from the hallway. I assume it's a large room because the hall light does little but make clear a several foot radius around the door. I grope at the wall in search of a light switch, but only come upon rock. There's no sound at first, but, slowly, from the darkness, emerges a low groan. Isabrand raises his sword, but I stop him from moving forward with my outstretched arm.

The groan comes again, followed by a cough. It's not the sound of a deabrueon or other beast, but a creature in pain. And, even through the anguish, I recognise the voice.

"Dominic," I breathe.

Like that, lights come to life all around the room. We're in a cavernous hall, its ceiling hung with chandeliers. It's empty save for four chairs carved from stone on the opposite end of the room and the figure curled up in the middle of the floor. I rush to his side, ignoring Isabrand's warning call.

"Mallory stop, it could be a trap!" he says.

It almost certainly is a trap, but I ignore him, dropping to my knees. Gasping, I take in what is before me.

Dominic's face is purpled with bruises and bloodied by cuts. His skin is so swollen I'm not sure I'd recognise him if I hadn't already realised it was him from his voice. He's wearing the same clothes as when I last saw him, but now they're dirtied by blood and grime. I pull him into my lap and he moans in pain. I try to will magic back into my hands to heal him, but it does not come.

"Ma-Mallory," he manages through he swollen, rouged lips.

"It's okay, I'm here now. I'm so sorry I left you for so long," I whisper, pressing furious kisses to his head. I try and pull him to his feet, but he sags. "Help me," I call to Isabrand.

No response.

"Isabrand?"

There's a slight scuffle, followed by a clatter.

I spin around.

Isabrand's back is drawn straight, his arms pulled behind him. His sword lies on the floor by his feet, but his assailant is quick to kick it away. Isabrand's eyes widen as the man behind him presses a curved blade to his throat. I cannot make out the doorway for the massive pair of grey wings which extend from his back. I recognise him almost instantly, though we've met but once. So, this is who ordered Isabrand to kill me. The angel whose life I had saved at the expense of Lilith's, the night we tried to escape the Academy.

"Elias," I say.

"Long time no see," he says, his face giving away none of the delight implied in his statement.

Chapter XXI.

"This is a really diabolical plan you've got here: coming into my home, with no weapons, no magic. Whatever am I to do?" Elias asks in a sing-song, mocking voice. He kicks Isabrand in the back of the legs so my brother falls to his knees with a groan and a hiss. "Down dog."

I rise, coming between Elias and Dominic.

"Did you do this?" I ask, nodding to my friend.

"Not directly, I don't waste my breath on scum like him. You on the other hand. I had thought to send your brother after you, but you'll make a worthwhile sparring partner. For a little while at least."

He doesn't break eye contact with me as he places his foot on Isabrand's back and pushes his stomach to the floor. He grinds his heel into Isabrand's lower back, taking no pleasure in doing it. All he believes is that this is his rightful place: on top.

"Why don't you take these cuffs off then and deal with me yourself." He doesn't reply, staring at me blankly. "Maybe it's because to do so you'd have to get the keys from Diane and you know she doesn't want you laying a hand on me. It was you who ordered the attack, wasn't it?"

He doesn't answer the question, merely curling his lip back in a snarl.

"Diane's deluded. She thinks we need you to complete our plan. I keep telling her this one will do just as well. Better even. He's usually so obedient," he says, looking down at Isabrand. He moves his foot to Isabrand's shoulder, the one the whip had come down on, and digs his heel in. I see the dirt he rubs into the wound, caked as it is on the bottom of his shoe.

"Let my brother go." I don't know where the assertiveness comes from. Right now, the only thing standing between Isabrand and Dominic and this lunatic is me, with no way to defend us.

"What will you do if I refuse? Beg? I bet you're good at that. I bet Diane taught you well. Alright then dog, beg, just as Diane taught you."

He lifts his foot off of Isabrand and draws his wings back to himself so they rise tall and narrow behind his shoulders.

"I've had a fair few years to forget what she's taught me, unlike you. I don't beg so well these days."

He laughs, the sound cold. The cavern walls snatch the sound and double it back until it echoes all around us, stopping only moments after he does.

"Let's fix that."

Out of nowhere appears a graemar. It lumbers forth from the shadows, resting its weight on its muscular forepaws. It opens its mouth, yawning as though it's just been roused from a deep slumber.

"You, you called that. You're a jaeitsi," I say breathlessly.

"You didn't know? I thought the wings were a dead giveaway, but I guess this is what you get for living in the human world. One of the four," he answers before beckoning the deabrueon.

It bounds forward and I expect it to spring on me, but instead it halts by Dominic. Grabbing him in its massive maw, it shakes him about like a ragdoll before flinging him across the room. He crashes at the feet of the chairs, utterly silent.

"No!" I scream. I start to run towards him, but the deabrueon comes between us. Dropping low to the ground, it growls at me, its blood red eyes locked onto my face.

"Now, want to try that begging?"

"Go fuck yourself," I snarl.

"Mallory," Isabrand groans, "do what he says."

"Listen to your brother Mallory. He knows how to be a good boy. You don't stand a chance if you don't play by my rules. After all, I've got this," he taunts. I dart a glance at him. From behind him he draws a sword, still sheathed. The Vaerdiexes sword. "Really careless of you to leave this lying about. I'd love to see what it does, but to do that I'd have to give it to you. Shame only the wielder can know it's power."

"Why don't you give it to me then, unless you're scared I'd beat you with it."

His eyes flash in anger.

"Girl, you may be powerful, but you are nothing in the face of the four of us. I will command armies, I will rain despair on your people and all the creatures of Earth until I get what I want."

"And what exactly is it that you want, mommy's approval? Diane will never love you. Besides, to do those things you'd need all four of the jaeitsi and, right now, it's just you."

"That's still enough to kill you," he hisses.

I feel the rush of air just before the graemar bats me aside with its paw. I skid across the floor, unable to use my hands to catch myself. Rolling onto my side, I look up to see Elias watching me, his face now devoid of emotion once more.

"See I figured you'd talk big, but, when it came to the fight, you'd be weak and pathetic," he says.

"Easy to say when you've got me in handcuffs," I reiterate, groaning from the pain lancing through my back.

"I suppose. But then, I'm not one to give up an advantage over your weak taunts. Make your move, Thiel."

I stare at him, grinding my teeth together. If I can distract him, maybe I can buy Isabrand the moment he needs to attack Elias.

"Why are you doing this? I saved your life," I remind him. He starts walking towards me slowly.

"True. Without you, my wings would still be broken. A pathetic shell of the powerful creature I was destined to be. But see, it's a simple matter of not liking you."

"Because of Diane? But she broke your wings in the first place."

"She taught me to be more than my innate power. She taught me to be strong when all I was born with was stripped from me. What would you know? She never loved you. You were a means to an end. A way for her to lay claim to the power of the dragoviks."

She never loved you. Is that what he wants then, Diane's love? Can't he see that that is reserved only for herself?

"No Elias, she never loved you. If there's anyone she loves, it's me. Why do you think she keeps pushing you to form an alliance with me, despite the fact neither of us wants one? Because you know she cares about me, as she'll never care about you."

He freezes in place, his eyes widening.

"Let's see how much she loves a heap of flesh when there's no life to breathe through it. Kill her," he orders the graemar.

"Mallory!" Isabrand screams, scrambling to his feet. The graemar races towards me. This is it.

You made me a promise. I will ensure you uphold it.

Vaerdiexes.

His power lights within me, the fire dormant until now burning like the mouth of a forge. My wrists burn hot and the handcuffs glow red, before shattering from my wrists. I raise my palm, unsure of what power I will unleash in doing so. A torrent of flame pours from me.

I have seen my flames burn before, but never so brightly or with such violence. This is not my power: it's a god's. It nearly overwhelms me, consuming me as it does the graemar, which is released to ash in an instant, before it can even cry out. I scream with the force of it, doubling over when it stops. Stumbling backwards, I catch myself on the wall. The world spins, but doesn't drop from sight.

"How," Elias breathes, looking on in a mix of fear and awe.

"Try 'I'm blessed by a mother fucking god'. And you, sir, are an idiot."

I dart for him, my hand extended for my katana which he still holds. He manages to evade, drawing his curved sword from his scabbard. He tosses the katana clear across the room, where it clatters to the floor, and lunges at me. I fall back. I know I don't have the strength to sustain Vaerdiexes' power again. I'll have to rely on my own magic for this. I glance around the room for something to weaponise.

Swiping my hand through the air, I raise one of the stone chairs from the floor. I hurtle it towards him, but he ducks. It crashes against the far wall, the sound shuddering through the room. Still, I have put distance between him and Isabrand. The latter grabs his sword from the floor and rushes to my side.

"Get Dominic," I order. He nods and starts toward my friend only for more deabrueon to spring up between them.

"Impressive," Elias calls out, "but we both know you can't call upon that power again so soon."

"I don't need it to fight you."

I try to circle around him to my sword, but he blocks me every time. Yanking the door from its hinges with my magic, I send it soaring towards him. He ducks, but it manages to decapitate one of the deabrueon creeping up on Isabrand. He takes out two of them with swift blows before a third knocks him to the ground. In my distraction, Elias sneaks up on me. I feel his sword bite my shoulder as I spin out of the way and cry out. *Heal*, I command and the skin closes itself back up.

"Very handy. It will make killing you last all the longer."

He runs for me again and I flatten my hand, drawing it towards my chest. *Let my life be yours*, I will. One of the deabrueon's bodies goes rigid. It tilts its head mechanically before racing towards Elias. This only buys me a few seconds before he skewers it through the chest, but that's enough for me to finally get around him. Racing across the room towards my sword, I can hear him coming up behind me. I'm almost there when my foot catches on something and I go spilling across the floor. The rough stone grazes my arms and legs. I feel that sting of blood rushing to the surface. Rolling to the left, I dodge his oncoming sword and, once again, he's put himself between me and my katana. If I could only get to it.

"Mallory!" Isabrand calls out. The deabrueon have him surrounded.

"Impressive trick, taking my own slaves from me," Elias says, towering over me. "But I can summon them endlessly. You and your brother don't stand a chance."

I pant, looking towards Isabrand as he fends two more off. They're toying with him now, on their master's command no doubt, circling slowly. This show is all for my benefit. I glance to the katana again, but it's too far away. My magic won't work to get my sword, it's impervious. And Elias knows this. He towers over me, savouring the moment before the final blow.

There's a shudder as reality splits open to my left. Out of nothing leaps a lithe figure, clad in black leather armour. She bears down on Elias, who only just manages to match her blow, so strong for one so small.

"You?" I gasp.

"Hello friend," she sings, the girl with Shigami's scythe, before her blade flashes forward once again.

Elias falls on his back, bracing his sword against her blade. She pushes her weight against it before vanishing once more. Friend?

I spring to my feet and grab my katana from the floor. My body begins to pulse with power as I draw it from its sheath. The pattern blossoms across my arm and I roar to life with Vaerdiexes' strength once more. The girl rematerializes and catches Elias off-guard. She slashes a shallow cut across his ribs. Snarling, he falls back. She's more than capable of holding her own against him. I race towards Isabrand and manage to graze the shoulder of a deabrueon before it dodges me.

It hisses, ready to attack before its body goes stiff, unyielding to Elias' command to kill me. The lights flicker and there's a hush before I hear a whisper in Vaerdiexes' voice, speaking into the room.

Sa mesit siezaeta morvedae.

I know only the last word, the name of the Vaerdiexes stone that now radiates an eerie light. Morvedae. Death.

The curse unfurls itself from the non-fatal wound, illuminating the deabrueon's veins the same dark green as the stone. It pervades the creature's body before it bursts into flames, reducing it to ash. The other deabrueon fall into a hush, their mortal fear overriding Elias' command.

"Kill them!" he screams, barely matching the girl blow for blow. She dances out of the way of his sword as he swings at her in a blind rage. Her laughter bubbles up, delighting in toying with him now.

The deabrueon creep forward. All I need is the smallest cut. That's the power of the sword. Death is my gift, as it ever was.

I jump back, landing on my right foot, and spin out of the way of an oncoming claw. Lunging forward, I slice through the deabrueon's forearm. Again, the curse whispers itself into the air and the beast howls as it burns to nothing. The others, now wary, begin to back off. Isabrand pulls Dominic over his shoulder.

"Let's go!" he says.

"You go ahead. I'm not leaving without her," I reply. He starts to protest. "I can't fight if I'm worried about you two. Go!"

As he makes his way out, I dash across the room to where Elias and girl are locked in battle. He sees me coming and leaps into the air, beating his wings. High above the ground, he looks down on us. I come to a halt by her side.

"Come on," I urge her. Between the two of us, we can definitely take him. But she shakes her head.

"The future can't come to be if he dies," she says. She takes my hand and I know I have nothing to fear from her anymore. "Let's go."

The realm of the dead splits open, but, this time, she takes me with her.

It is exactly as I remember it from after I died. Everything seems like blue vapour, smoke brushing against us. I see Elias looking around furiously and pray he doesn't go after the others. Luckily, he seems too concerned with where we might have gone. The girl leads me forward, slinging her scythe over her shoulder and humming to herself. The tune is broken, as if uncertain of coming into being.

"The others," I start, but she silences me with a nod.

"We'll go get them now," she assures me. We walk out into the hall, down which Isabrand stumbles beneath the weight of his charge. "Take hold of his hand."

Sheathing my sword, I reach out and take Isabrand's hand. He starts, spinning around. At first, all he takes in is the new way in which the world appears: the white shimmering of things corporeal made incorporeal. Then he sees me and the girl.

"What's going on?"

"We're in the realm of the dead," I explain, though, realising it's not an explanation, I elaborate. "She has a gods' weapon. That's its power. No one can see or hear us while we're here."

He looks at her, clearly impressed. She smiles and giggles.

"You're cute," she says. The tips of his ears go slightly pink. What is with everyone hitting on my brother?

We make our way back to the exit Carlisle had slipped through and step out into the sunlight. It seems as if a fine mist has settled over the forest we find ourselves in, easy to obscure ourselves in. We pass under an old stone arch, winding our way through the trees in silence. I can scarcely make out the shape of things in the dense fog surrounding us, so I keep letting her guide me. A long time passes before I finally speak.

"Why did you save us?" I ask the girl. She hums again, tilting her head sideways before she casts a glance over her shoulder.

"You were right. I owe my life to you, not in its end, but in its saving. As, now, do you to me."

Suddenly the world flashes back into clarity, forms becoming sharp and clear, and I know we've returned from the other world that is wrapped within our own. The sun beams down, lighting the dewy morning grass like crystal. It's a relief to be back in its warmth, which seems to have dispelled the mist that once took hold of our surroundings. Isabrand looks around anxiously and the girl reads his expression.

"They won't find us," she assures him.

"How do you know?"

"It's not fated."

"A seer. Lovely. You see any pie in my future?"

"Yes. Peach."

His eyes widen, shocked by her sincerity. He kneels down, lowering Dominic to the ground. I join them, placing my hand on Dominic's face.

"Lueicht, nandirava letai nevorso ni isuazko etev udiyat," I murmur, sweeping my thumb across his cheekbone. I hear Isabrand's sharp intake of breath and know he reads my feelings for the man in my arms. We watch as his wounds wither and fade back beneath his skin. There's a gentle sputter of breath that slips his lips before Dominic begins to breathe normally. "The rest will take time."

The girl sits on a rock, her armour melting back into the dress she favours. She rests her scythe across her legs and assumes a studious air as I heal Isabrand before turning to her.

"Thank you," I sigh.

"I told you, I was repaying a debt. Besides," she starts, sweeping towards me. Leaves whisper beneath her skirt. She kneels in the dirt. "That's not all I came for."

"Oh? If not my life, then what?"

"I heard it. When you remembered your fate last night, your future bloomed in my mind. I've seen what you were not born to be, but made to be. Yours is a worthy cause."

She bows her head low, holding her scythe out flat towards me but says nothing. I glance at Isabrand.

"Okay, you need to explain," he says to me, but I shrug.

"I'm in the dark."

"Mallory Thiel, I, Proserpina Cadmus, swear my life and fealty to you and the restoration of dragoviks to Dragovicia."

"What?" Isabrand and I gasp in unison. She doesn't answer, just stays, kneeling before me.

"Permission to rise?" she asks finally.

"Uh, sure," I reply, "permission to do what you want in general."

"You're a benevolent queen," she says, beaming at me. I flush pink, feeling Isabrand's curiosity piquing.

"I'm sorry I'm confused. Why are you swearing fealty to my sister?"

"She's the next queen of Dragovicia. Vaerdiexes has ordained it so."

"Yeah I know that. Don't get me wrong, really proud of her, but why are you pledging yourself to her?"

"She's going to kill Thrabr."

Part V

Chapter XXII.

Kill Thrabr? What, the giant incorporeal demon that came after us the other night? How in the fresh hell am I supposed to do that?

"No, no, no," I say, shaking my head. "That's not on the agenda today. Or any other day for that matter. Consider it permanently off the agenda."

Her expression clouds over.

"Why not? We got your sword back."

"He's literally vapour. I can't fight him."

"Who's Thrabr?" Isabrand asks.

"Some demon thing."

"Not a demon. The demon. The original demon. The reflection of the worst of humanity," Proserpina explains.

"Your other half, you said." She nods, eyes glazing over. There are pieces of this puzzle missing. And, for all my protestations, I do want to help. This girl has clearly been tormented by Thrabr for a long time, lives her life in fear of him. But how can I help if I don't understand what I'm up against? "What is he exactly?"

From beneath her dress' neckline she draws, once again, the forever stone. It glints in the light, but, where it should reflect me and the forest, it winks back an empty expanse.

"Four thousand years ago, I took from Vaerdiexes the mirror stone. See my father and I lived alone together after my mother died. After her death, the gods' weapons became his obsession. He poured himself into them. The gods came one by one to bless the thirteen weapons he made. Shigami was his gift to me," she says, raising the scythe. "Vaerdiexes came last. He was quite unlike any of the others. Friendly and warm. Makes sense from the god of sun and flame. He brought honey cake for me. After he and my father had spoken at length, he pulled from his red traveller's cloak a small velvet pouch and out he poured six stones: one blue, white, red, green, yellow, and black. They were the source of all his power. He gave my father the green stone, Morvedae, and told him to put it in the katana. He did not wish to bear death any more. I asked if he had a stone that could resurrect the dead and he said he did. The black stone, the mortal stone. He put the stones back in his pocket. As he left, I reached into his pocket and plucked out one of the stones. I thought I knew the shape of the mortal stone well enough to fish it out. But, once he was gone and I opened my clenched fist, I found this. The mirror. I had not seen it before."

"You stole from a god?" Isabrand asks, looking at her in awe. She shrugs.

"Gods believe themselves above such pettiness. They'd never expect a little girl to steal from them, so it was easy. Why he did not come back for it though, that I cannot say. That night, I lay in bed, staring into the mirror that did not reflect me, cursing my foolishness in selecting the wrong stone, my weakness, my failure. I poured all my self-loathing into it and, slowly, something appeared in its reflection. It was not my face, but it was. Red eyes and seething hatred. Thrabr."

"You made him with the forever stone?" I say.

"Yes. He is the worst parts of me made manifest. The hatred I bore for the humans that cost my mother her life became a hatred for all humanity. He crawled forth from the mirror and killed my father who tried to defend us with one of his swords, only to find Thrabr became incorporeal when he wished, as a shadow. I watched as he tore my father apart. He came for me next, demanding the forever stone, but I used Shigami to hide from him in the afterlife. I gripped it and willed myself into the world of the dead. I saw my father's soul, still waiting to leave, the tattered pieces of it that remained after my mother's death. For the next four thousand years, Thrabr hunted me, seeking the forever stone so he could will from it his own army. As long as I have Shigami, though, he cannot catch me."

"That's why he came the other night, because I took it from you." She nods.

"But you gave it back, saving my life and the world from the destruction Thrabr would have brought down upon us."

"And I appreciate you returning the favour but, if you can't fight him, how can I?" I ask.

"Vaerdiexes' sword is unlike any other. While the others were blessed by gods, Vaerdiexes put a piece of his godhood within the sword. Morvedae imbues it with a number of powers, one of which you've already seen."

"The curse that killed the deabrueon."

"When willed to, the stone unleashes death itself. All it needs is to touch one drop of the victim's blood. But the more powerful the bond between wielder and sword, the greater Morvedae's power becomes. It can fight the dead, ghosts, phantoms, even– "

"Thrabr," I say at last. She nods.

"Like Shigami's scythe, it exists between the land of the living and the land of the dead. But Shigami can only strike blows on the living. Vaerdiexes' sword can pierce the veil itself. Spirits become flesh beneath its touch."

"But that's only if the bond is strong enough, right?" I say.

"Well, I imagine your bond is pretty damn strong. You're the first person to ever pair with the damn thing and Vaerdiexes' chosen one," Isabrand adds. But Proserpina's face tells me otherwise.

"It's not enough," Proserpina informs him. "Its loyalty demands blood."

"I have to kill with it," I say, swallowing.

"If you do, it will be more than just Thrabr you can stop. Morvedae's final power is its greatest. It can command the spirits of those who have fallen beneath it."

My stomach knots itself.

"You mean those I've killed."

"Yes."

"It's not enough that I've murdered them? Then I call their spirits from the grave to do my bidding?"

"Do you lament the loss of those deabrueon's lives? The ones that would have killed the three of you? You do not kill the innocent Mallory. Remember that."

"I won't do it. I won't rack up a body count for that purpose. I'll fight Thrabr for you, but I won't kill just to gain more power."

Her face lights up when I say this.

"Oh, thank you!" She dashes towards me and pulls me into a hug. I squirm for a moment, taken aback by the affection, but quickly resign myself to her embrace. She's stronger than she looks. She steps back and bows. "Then my life is yours. Command me as you will."

"Uh, okay," I say, looking to Isabrand, but he's just as taken aback as I am. "Well, I guess we should go check on the others?"

She nods, skipping ahead. Isabrand slings Dominic back over his shoulder and starts forward. We fall in step a few paces behind her as we make our way through the woods, over the knots of roots pushing through the earth.

"Don't get me wrong, I'm a fan of the girl, what between her saving our lives and being a holy pickpocket. But why'd you agree to help her?"

"Because, like it or not, Thrabr is dangerous. Anything that wants to use a Vaerdiexes stone to create an army of demons to kill humans equals evil in my book. Besides, Vaerdiexes stone, gods' weapon toting, four thousand year old crazy woman? I want her on my side."

"Sound logic," he says before calling ahead to her. "Hey do you know where we are?"

"Yes. Hoboken."

We both groan.

* * *

I knock on Doctor Lindberg's door, but there's no answer. I look to the others nervously. During the course of our journey, Dominic has managed to get back on his feet. He's still disconcerted though, so leans on Isabrand for support. His head hangs relatively limply forwards and he groans occasionally. I've done all I can to heal his wounds. The rest will take time.

I worry my lip between my teeth. What if those men killed the others after knocking me out? They didn't seem beyond doing so. I turn the handle, but it doesn't give way.

"Who's there?" Lindberg's voice sounds terrified from the other side of the door. It sets a flood of relief through me. If she's alive, the others must be too.

"It's Mallory."

She breathes a sigh of relief. But still the door does not open for us.

"You understand I can't let you in. Not after," she falters.

"Is your daughter okay?" I ask, realising how selfish I'd been in not even thinking about the two of them. I had been so concerned for Kyle, Casey, Killian, Robyn, and Aaron, Lindberg and her daughter hadn't even crossed my mind.

"Is she okay? She's terrified. She was just attacked by five strange men who knocked her mother unconscious and beat her. She's never going to sleep again. Is she okay," she repeats, and I hear the fear and fury that shakes her voice.

I press my hand to the door and draw over the apartment the same veil I had put on Casey's. Doctor Lindberg must see the glimmering traces of the spell inside because I hear her gasp.

"I'm so sorry. I had no idea they'd come for us here. These should keep you safe."

"Thank you."

"And the others?" I ask hopefully.

There's a pause during which my heart lurches. They have to be okay if she is.

"The Hirutere arrived not long after you were taken. We didn't have time to recuperate and put up a fight. The Hirtuere have imprisoned them for helping you evade capture and suspected aiding and abetting the murders of the bellatoja. Except for the girl. Casey. Robyn managed to create a portal to get her to safety before they were apprehended."

I swallow hard. How am I supposed to rescue them from Miesarinda? They have an army of bellatoja and I have only the four of us. No, one thing at a time. Casey's all alone and she's probably terrified, if not in imminent danger.

"Do you know where they sent her?"

"Back to their house. They said to tell you if you came back here."

"Thank you. We'll leave now."

"I'm-I'm glad you're okay," Lindberg says, her voice urgent and full of concern. I know she is a moment from opening the door to me, a moment from hugging me. I can't stand that sort of affection from her, not after how I've failed her.

"Likewise."

We get back in the elevator. As the doors slide shut, Dominic lets out a grunt and rubs his head, the first signs of awareness since we found him. He lifts his head and blinks at me a few times.

"Mallory?"

Despite having regained consciousness on our way here, it's as if he's just coming to. I rush to his side and wrap my arms around him. He pulls me in, burying his head in the crook of my neck.

"Thank heavens, you're okay. I've been so worried."

"You've been worried? I haven't been held hostage for the past few days," I say.

I stare up into his dark eyes, my heart pounding just to be close to him again. I remember what Diane said, about him calling out for me until she told him I had not come for him. Did he give up hope so easily or was that just something she said to torment me?

"For all I knew, you were. When they took me, I thought for sure they'd have found you too. I knew you'd come for me if they hadn't though. And you've made friends I see," he adds, nodding to the other two. "I don't know you two."

"Isabrand. I'm the big brother," he says coolly, narrowing his eyes at Dominic. I sense overprotectiveness emerging. "And this is Proserpina. She's four thousand years old."

"Four thousand and twelve," she corrects, smiling at him.

"Right," Dominc replies, uncertain of what else to say before he looks back at me. "How'd you find me?"

"We got kidnapped. Worked out well though," I answer cheerfully when he looks at me, horrified. "We found you and I got this nifty sword back."

"We should report back to Emmett," he says. "He'll be worried."

"No can do, mate," Isabrand interrupts before I can speak. "I don't know who this Emmett bloke is, but we've got some people to save from the Hirutere. Now we're done saving you of course."

"Sorry, weren't you kidnapped as well?" Dominic asks, sincerely confused. Isabrand doesn't take it well, letting out a huff of air.

"Yeah, but at least we managed to escape."

"Okay, well sorry to break off this testosterone rally, but we've got a caeletai umea to rescue first," I interject.

Both of them look at me, wide eyed, distracted from the previously impending feud.

"You found her?" Dominic demands. "How?"

"After you went missing, I found Emmett, who enlisted me to get her. It's been a while since, but basically she's on her own, unprotected right now."

Actually, it hasn't been that long since we found her. It just feels like months have passed, what with all that has happened.

"We can't let the jaeitsi get her. She's too great of a weapon."

I frown at him.

"We can't let them get her because no one deserves that fate, right?" I correct him. "She's not just a weapon in your war."

"I know that," he says, but looks confused.

We make our way back to the Caverly's house, taking a cab there. Proserpina sits up front, fiddling with the radio. I tip the cab driver extra for the irritation. We head up the steps of the brownstone and I knock on the front door. I'm not expecting Casey to answer after all she's been through and I'm right. All remains quiet in the house. I can only pray that no one else has got to her first. Eventually, I call out her name. The door swings open instantly and there's a flurry of red hair and arms as she throws herself at me.

"Oh, thank heavens," she gasps through sobs. "After Robyn sent me here, I didn't know what to do."

"It's okay. I'm here now," I murmur, stroking her hair in an attempt to soothe her. "Let's get inside."

She looks over my shoulder and frowns as we go into the house. "Where are the others and who are they?"

"The Hirutere took them from Doctor Lindberg's after Robyn portalled you here. And these are some of my friends. This is Dominic, Proserpina, and my brother, Isabrand, who you met already."

"Didn't he try to kill you yesterday?" she asks, eyeing Isabrand warily. I feel her arms wind around me protectively.

"You tried to kill her?" Dominic thunders. He lunges for Isabrand, all brute strength, but my brother dodges with catlike grace, slinking into the house.

"Like she said, that was yesterday," he yawns, shrugging. "You got any food here? I'm starving."

Dominic and Casey stare at him incredulously before looking at me to gauge my reaction. Honestly? I should be more pissed than I am. But between the exhaustion and the sheer delight of seeing him again, I just can't be mad. I shrug at them and head upstairs to the kitchen, which he's managed to find his way to. Rooting around the fridge, I'm greeted by a half empty jar of mustard and a withered lime.

"This is what happens when Kyle moves out. Otherwise, there'd be muffins," I grumble. "I'm ordering pizza."

"Not Joe's, that's so overrated," Isabrand says, dropping into a chair and putting his feet up on the table. I give him a dirty look, but he ignores me.

"Prince street?" Dominic asks.

"Prince street," we all agree. I pull out my phone and place the order.

"Five pizzas? There are only four of us?" Casey says, peering over my shoulder.

"Remember how you felt after fighting Thrabr? Yeah, try channelling a god's power to fight a jaeitsi then wielding a god's weapon. That'll really make you hungry."

"That and not eating for four days. Thanks for healing me by the way," Dominic adds, sitting opposite Isabrand. "So, brother?"

"Boyfriend?" Isabrand asks.

"No!" Dominic and I say hastily, though my heart aches at how readily he denies it. Is the thought of dating me so repulsive? He flushes intensely, not looking at me. Isabrand puts his hands up in the air.

"Okay, we won't be touching that subject with a barge pole."

I sigh, sinking into the chair beside Dominic. Casey takes the head of the table.

"Nice kitchen," Proserpina says, wandering around and opening cupboards. She examines a serving platter with a painted fish on it, tilting it this way and that. I wonder how it is she lives her life after four thousand years of it?

"Hey, what's with the dress?" Isabrand asks. "It's a bit fifteen-hundreds, don't you think?"

Proserpina looks down at herself, genuinely perplexed as to what the problem is.

"My dad bought it for me."

"Try a bit two thousand BC then," I sigh. "It's in remarkably good shape. He's right though. It doesn't exactly blend."

"Oh. How about this?" Her dress phases back to her armour.

"Sexy? Yes. Appropriate? Maybe for the battlefield," Isabrand quips. She flushes, delighted by his compliment. Dominic and I exchange a concerned look. These two seem like just about the most dangerous pair on the planet; I don't really want to imagine them getting together.

"Okay, this?"

Her outfit shifts again and suddenly she's wearing the exact same clothes as me, right down to the blood spatters.

"That's too weird. How do you do that anyway?" I ask. She taps the mirror stone.

"It brings whatever I will into being."

"How about some peach pie?" Isabrand asks. She stares at the table and a peach pie with the most heavenly smell materialises.

"Why did I just spend one hundred dollars on pizza?" I demand, as Proserpina passes Isabrand a fork. She sits beside him and watches as he begins to shovel it down. "Are you going to share that?" I ask.

He wipes his mouth and stares at the pie, his eyes heavy lidded, as if he's just found true love.

"No way. This is the best damn pie I've ever had. You should be a chef," he says between mouthfuls. Proserpina beams.

"What's a chef?" she asks. He stares at her mid mouthful.

"Why doesn't she know what a chef is?" Casey asks quietly.

"She's four thousand years old."

"Of course she is," Casey sighs, rubbing her forehead.

"Okay so the Hirutere have your friends because they were keeping you from being apprehended. Why do they want you?" Dominic asks. He's not reading the cues of the room, jumping instead to the task at hand. I frown at him. We've only just been reunited after days. Surely he wants to take some time to catch up? I don't know, ask how I've ended up using magic again perhaps?

"Mallory's been accused of murdering everyone at the Academy," Isabrand manages, a bit of pie falling on his shirt.

"I didn't do it! Okay, one of them, but he attacked me first," I clarify. "It was three years ago."

"Ironic that you're being charged with murders you didn't commit given all the murders you have committed," Isabrand says between bites of pie. I raise my eyebrows at him, tilting my head. "Just saying."

"The Academy? After all this time?" Dominic asks, ignoring

Isabrand.

"Yeah. Basically, some head honcho of the Hirutere named Algard is really pissed I got my friend off a different charge, so he's accusing me of murder."

"Why are you all so criminally inclined?" Casey asks, snatching a peach from the pie dish and sucking the syrup from it.

"It runs in the isuazko I guess. Or maybe we just get it from our mom," Isabrand says.

"Now that's a terrifying notion."

"Honestly, I'd rather be like my father, and that's saying something."

"Ah to be Freud and studying the two of us," I sigh, and he chuckles.

"Anyway, how are we going to get them out?" Isabrand asks, swatting Dominic's hand away as he reaches for the pie dish. "My magic pie."

"Has anyone ever told you to play nice with others?" I ask.

"Yeah, I usually just kill them." Why do I get the impression he's not kidding? I frown at him.

"As for how we're going to get them out, there's really only one choice," I say. It's not ideal, but it's something I resigned myself to on the way over here. "I've got to offer myself in exchange."

"What?" Casey says.

"Absolutely not," Dominic says at the same time. I look at them incredulously. There's obviously no other solution.

"What do you suggest? Have you seen Miesarinda? There's no way we're breaking them out of there. Besides, we can't fight on two fronts. The jaeitsi will be after us again. With me out of the equation, the Hirutere will protect all of you, and them."

"Mallory that's not even an option," Isabrand says, "you're not thinking straight. Eat some pie."

He brandishes his fork at me.

"It's the only option," I reply.

None of them respond, telling me with silence what I know to be true: I'm right. After everything they've done to keep me alive, here's where the line ends.

"I have an idea," Casey whispers. We all look to her and, based on the sad glint in her eyes, I already know what she's thinking.

“Not happening. I won’t let you do that for me.”

“They want me, right? I’m a caeletai umea. So, I agree to help them if they let the five of you off all charges.”

“No Casey. You made me promise not to let them have you. I’m not going to let you do this for me.”

“Mallory, things are different now. It’s like you said, the people I care about will draw me into this war.” I feel Proserpina’s eyes on me and I wonder if she recognises her own words. I don’t doubt she does. “You’re my friend. Kyle, Aaron, Killian, hell even Robyn. You’ve saved my life. Let me save yours and theirs. Besides, if I go and fight with the Hirutere, it’s not just you I’d be helping, right?”

“She’s right Mallory. With the help of a caeletai umea, we stand a fighting chance against the jaeitsi,” Dominic murmurs, putting his hand on my shoulder. “Why do you think Alice and I were going to find her?”

“Hate to agree with the non-boyfriend entity, but he’s right. You want to help the war effort? Having you, Casey, and Proserpina is the way forward for the Hirutere,” Isabrand says.

His face doesn’t betray for one second what he, Proserpina, and I know. The Hirutere will have to fall for me to claim my throne. They will not let me take it so long as they stand and they certainly won’t be letting me through the portal. But that is a problem for another day. Vaerdiexes said he would tell me what to do when the time came, which means his silence can only mean he’s not ready for us to make our move. For now, we have to fight with the Hirutere.

“Don’t call him the non-boyfriend entity, you’re making them uncomfortable,” Proserpina intones, dabbing at the pie stain on Isabrand’s shirt. Dominic shifts awkwardly in his chair, not daring to look at me. His hand quickly slips from my shoulder.

“Yes and saying that out loud didn’t make things weirder at all,” I sigh. I turn to Casey and take her hands. “Promise me you’re doing this because you want to and not because you feel like you have to. Assure me, as best you can, that you won’t regret this.”

“How could I regret it if it means saving my friends?”

Chapter XXIII.

"How will I know which book it is that opens the portal?" Casey asks, squinting into the dark of the library.

"I don't know exactly how. Killian just said an angeleru would always know when they see it. I'm guessing the same goes for caeletai umea. They still count as angeleru, right?" I reply hopefully.

We're back in the Brooklyn library, huddled together around the light emanating from my palm, in search of the book that will take us to Miesarinda. At least at this library I know which section it's in, even if I can't quite remember what the book looked like. Casey gropes along the bookcase, as if she can feel out which one it is. She taps them, pokes and prods, but nothing comes of it. There's no sudden flash leading us to that sandstone staircase.

"It was green," I say, pausing, "I think."

"Great plan you've got here," Isabrand grumbles, his foot catching on something in the dark. Proserpina catches him, pulling him back upright. I see them exchange a look before he quickly glances away, his pale cheeks flushing. Are they really so quick to react to each other in such a way? They hardly know each other, their experiences as disparate as possible. "Can't you turn the lights on or something?"

"It might draw attention if the whole library suddenly has its lights on. Hold on."

The whisper of light in my hand swells, casting its glow a few feet further ahead of us. I start to turn right amongst the shelves, but Casey pulls on my sleeve.

"Wait, there it is!" Casey declares. I look around, but don't see anything in the grainy darkness. Still, she sounds so certain, so we follow her as she picks up her pace. She comes to stop in front of a bookshelf.

"How can you tell?" Isabrand asks.

"It's got a sort of glow to it."

I hold up my palm and, sure enough, there is the book Killian had used to get us to the Library Between only days before. It looks completely ordinary to me.

"So, how does this work?"

"You mean you've never been?" I ask Isabrand.

"Funny how the Hirutere don't like the jaeitsi's assassins poking around."

"Yeah, former Academy members aren't exactly welcome either," Dominic intones.

"I went once. They had good gelato," Proserpina muses, before turning to Isabrand. "We should go get some."

"Yeah sure," he says, seemingly dazed by the dazzling smile she offers him. He stops short of saying *whatever you want*, though I don't doubt that's what he's willing to give her.

"Okay well we all take hands, forming a chain," I explain, extinguishing the light in my hand to ready myself.

"I've got Isabrand's," Proserpina says, clutching his hand between hers and holding it up like a prize. He ducks his head, unable to hide the scarlet fire beneath the skin of his cheeks. I feel Dominic take my hand in the darkness and that same flush creeps into my face. I'm quick to remember how dismissive he was of Isabrand's boyfriend comment though. Perhaps he sees me only as a sister, as small and scared Mallory who cowered in the corner during our missions at the Academy.

I take Casey's hand in mine and glance back to make sure we're all connected in a chain.

"Now just take hold of the book. I think," I say to Casey, frowning.

Casey reaches out and we're swept up in a golden light that leads us to that familiar landing. It feels peculiar being one of the only two who's been here before. Since when did I become the expert on all things supernatural? I lead the way downstairs, hastily dropping Dominic's hand, but keeping hold of Casey's. I can feel her shaking beneath my grip, anxious, no doubt, about what's to come. She's about to surrender her life to an unknown fate for the people she calls her friends. I understand that better than I'd care to. The Hirutere will treat her well, I hope, given how important she is. The malice that they reserve for dragoviks won't extend to her. I try to smile reassuringly at her, but know the jump from this platform to the next will only serve to exacerbate her stress.

"Follow my lead. Whatever happens, don't let go of my hand."

I leap from the platform, pulling Casey after me. She gasps flailing with her free hand before we summersault. I have to tighten my grip on her hand to keep it from slipping. As our bodies complete the rotation, I extend my legs, stumbling onto the landing with far less grace than I had done with Killian leading me. Again, that burn in my cheeks rises at the memory of his warm, large hand encompassing mine. Things had seemed simpler then. I loved Dominic. Now I can't seem to shake Killian from my thoughts, as though he gets snagged on the edges of my mind. I worry for him as much as any of the others and know he has come to be a dear friend in the past few days. I won't let anything happen to him. I lead Casey up the stairs to the door and the others follow.

This time, when we enter, I am not struck by the beauty of library, but the sheer stupidity of what we're about to do. I've brought Casey, our only bargaining chip, directly to the Hirutere with no backup plan. There's no guarantee they won't just take her and imprison us all anyway. I could be leading Dominic and Isabrand to their deaths, as well as me to my own. At least Proserpina will be able to escape. She will be our only chance of getting out of here, worse comes to worst. I swallow the fast-forming lump in my throat, but it remains lodged in my oesophagus. Even with the small sliver of hope that Proserpina presents, I still feel helpless.

"This place is beautiful," Casey breathes in awe, much as I had on my first visit.

"It gets old," I lie, eyeing up all the beautiful books I will never have the opportunity to read. Not that they'd let me borrow them anyway. I'm sure after I threw up on the library floor three years ago I was permanently blacklisted. "Come on."

"I've seen better," Proserpina sings in her beautiful and clear whistle of a voice. "You should see the library in Udayat."

We all frown at her in confusion.

"It's a city in Sundalev."

"It's easy to forget you're four thousand years old and from Sundalev, you know," I sigh.

"Because I blend in so well?"

I look at her, wearing the exact same clothes as me, but, somehow, even in something so commonplace, she is anything but. She looks too doll like, utterly inhuman.

"Yeah, sure. That's it," I say. She beams at my compliment.

We make our way down a ladder to the ground floor. Dismounting, I turn around and come face to face with none other than Algard. His face is lit with a grin. Behind him are two orderly rows of bellatoja, ready to take us away.

"Oh, I can't wait to hear what you're doing here."

Shit.

***

"The courtroom will be closed to the public at this time," a man announces to the people in the crowd occupying the hallway, all of who are craning their necks trying to get a peek at the five of us on the stand. There's a unanimous outburst of displeasure, but the doors are soon shut, blocking out their murmurs of dissent. I'm sitting on one of two benches, which are occupied by me, Casey, Isabrand, Dominic, and Proserpina. They have not brought the others out for our trial. Though the five of us exchanged brief glances when they brought us from the library, there was no opportunity to speak. No chance for me to apologise for being so stupid. I look to the podium opposite us where Algard stands. His lips are upturned in a smug smile. He's not prepared to lose as he did before. He clears his throat, preparing to address his emerald robed peers occupying the mostly empty benches. The absence of the public gives me some hope. He isn't willing to risk another public spectacle, which means even he has doubts about my guilt.

"My dear colleagues," he begins, with a cold tone of voice that suggests, in fact, that none of them are held dear. "Here sits before you nothing less than the worst sort of criminal. Having evaded our attention for three years, she then enlisted various dragoviks and, I am loathe to say it, even a bellatoja, to aid in her escape when called to face justice for her crime: the murder of innocent bellatoja."

There's a murmur of outrage when he refers to Killian, accompanied by the loud snore of an elderly gentleman who has already gone to sleep. Algard coughs twice, but it does nothing to rouse the man. I twitch anxiously in my seat. What hope I had before alights after his opening statement. He hasn't let the public in because, last time, I managed to sway them. Here now are only his fellow members of the Hirutere, as hateful of dragoviks as he is, no doubt. He's going to paint this as badly as possible, portray me as the indisputable culprit of all those murders. If I want to best him and win our freedom, I'll have to play by his rules, remaining obedient and quiet until called upon. Anything else will look bad to the rest of the Hirutere, who are scrutinising us closely.

"After receiving intel from an unidentified spy planted among us about her impending arrest, she went on the run. She evaded attempts to capture her, though allowed her so-called friends to go to prison for her. They too will be brought to justice. But for the singularly heinous crime of slaughtering innocent bellatoja warriors, Mallory Thiel is hereby charged with murder and, if found guilty, sentenced to death. Are there any objections to the proceedings?"

At this, Isabrand scoffs. The rest of us look to him nervously, silently urging him to bite his tongue. But Isabrand is leaning back and somehow manages to look cocky even with his handcuffs on.

"Something to say, boy?" Algard says loudly.

"Well, there's not exactly someone to object, is there? Unless you don't mind if I do so," he replies, gesturing with his manacled hands at the near empty courtroom. There's a quiet titter throughout.

"Yes, very amusing. Will it amuse the court to hear that, prior to this trial, I did my research on this young man and discovered he is none other than Isabrand Velemir, son of Thaddeus Velemir, half-brother to Mallory Thiel, and an assassin?"

The hush that had accompanied my introduction is nothing compared to the unanimous petrification of the court when these words are spoken. All go still, fearing the presence of the man they're in. I bite my lip. How many of their people must Isabrand have killed in his time? Enough, no doubt, to earn him a place at the guillotine after me. I was so stupid not to think of this when we came here. Our plan was so hastily cobbled together, suddenly all manner of overlooked details are emerging. Even if they set the others free, how can they possibly pardon Isabrand of his crimes, of murder? My desire to rescue the others has clouded my judgement and might cost me my brother once more.

"That's what I thought," Algard continues. "Three years ago, Mallory Thiel was the only known survivor of a massacre occurring at the notorious Academy, having been trained there as an assassin herself. It is the prosecution's belief that Miss Thiel survived because she is the one who killed Captain Alistair and those under his command that day. Do you deny these charges?"

"To some extent," I start, but he cuts me off, feigning shock to the courtroom.

"To some extent? So, murder can be committed in part now, is that what you're saying Miss Thiel?"

Though he intones this humorously, it elicits no laughter from the audience.

"No that's clearly not what I'm saying. I mean I didn't kill all of them."

"Ah so you had an accomplice? Your brother, no doubt."

"I didn't even know Isabrand back then," I reply.

"No matter. Perhaps it was someone else, one of your other friends we have apprehended? Or maybe this young man here," he says, gesturing to Dominic. "Or perhaps you colluded with Thaddeus Velemir himself, you brother's father."

"No, stop! You've got this all wrong!" I declare, shifting in my seat. I turn to the audience, hoping they'll be somewhat more sympathetic, but am met by only cold glances, if they are brave enough to meet my gaze at all.

"Then tell me, what happened. Your 'version' of events," Algard says, his lips curling into a smile. He's been very careful in his wording, using the word version to colour my account with incredulity before I even begin.

"I was kidnapped by the bellatoja. They used me to cast a locator spell in order to find the Academy."

"Already an unlikely story. Many witches have been enlisted to cast locator spells to find the Academy, but none succeeded."

"Mine was different. None of your witches had been there before. I used a memory to find the place. When we got there, the bellatoja that arrived ahead of us had already rounded up the members of the Academy in search of the girl named Clara, the jaeitsi. When they couldn't find her or Doctor Lindberg, they then proceeded to kill innocent people, without permission from the Hirutere I might add."

"When in the pursuit of a jaeitsi, a bellatoja captain need not report to the Hirutere for orders, but instead take any measures necessary to apprehend the creature. From what you're saying, everything Captain Alistair did was for a noble cause."

"How about trying to rape me?" I hiss, narrowing my eyes at him. The woman closest to our stand gasps and there's an exchange of murmurs throughout the crowd. Alistair was a cruel and vicious man. My hope now is that his reputation extends beyond just us. From the looks exchanged amongst the Hirutere, I'm guessing it does. I can only pray that he never succeeded in doing to another what he attempted to do to me.

"Hearsay from his murderer. I'll ask again, did you or did you not kill Captain Alistair?"

There's that moment in which silence opens as a well and my heart drops into it. What can I do but tell the truth?

"Yes. To defend myself."

"And the other bellatoja, did you not kill them too?"

"No, that was Clara," I say.

"Convenient scapegoat, isn't she? A jaeitsi on whom to pin all of your crimes. You're a smart girl, Miss Thiel," he says, his condescending smile reaching his dark eyes. Playing by the rules is getting me nowhere it seems. I need to change my tactic.

"Did you see what was done at the Academy?" I ask him.

"Miss Thiel, I'll kindly remind you that I am the one asking questions."

"But did you?" I demand. All eyes turn to him and I know I've got him caught in an impossible place. He has to answer me.

"Yes."

"And you think an ordinary dragovik witch could have done that? Those people were ripped apart. Perhaps if it were a male of our species in their dragon form it could have been done. But not the witches, not an ordinary witch. Besides, what cause had I to kill those who weren't bellatoja?"

"I suppose you're right. An ordinary dragovik witch could not have done that. But a dragovik with a gods' weapon, the power of two of the original dragovik families, and the training offered at the Academy? I think a beast such as that would be quite capable of the destruction I saw. As to your other point Miss Thiel, I cannot speak to the actions of a troubled woman such as yourself.

Why you undertook to wipe out the remainder of those from the Academy I can only assume. Perhaps a fit of rage, blood lust, much like Thaddeus Velemir. Or, perhaps, you wanted to erase all traces of you past. Did you not run away to New York to evade it? Or was that you hiding from retribution for what you'd done to our men?"

Even my life in New York he manages to use against me. He's manipulated my attempt at a normal life into evidence that I'm a murderer. Bastard. He smiles, knowing he's backed me into a corner. What can I say to these accusations?

"I believe, at this point, the court has heard enough to make its judgement."

"No. They haven't," Casey says, her voice shaking as a result of her anxiousness.

Algard's expression changes in an instant. What he had feared, prompting him to make this a closed courtroom, is about to come into being before his eyes: my get out of jail free card. Or, in this case, get out of death sentence card. Slowly, and almost toppling the entire bench over with all her shaking, Casey rises. I curl my body forwards to steady the bench, not having the use of my hands. She clears her throat, staring out at the audience but at no one in particular. Then her eyes drop down to the floor. *Look up* I want to tell her. *You're not their equal, you're their superior.* Not because you're a caeletai umea, but because you are kind and good, and chose to help us not yet knowing the cost.

"The court has not called upon you to speak Miss…" Algard starts, before looking to the guard. "Who is she?"

"Her name is Casey Astor," I answer on her behalf.

"And I believe in these situations, it's best to defer to your superior when they wish to speak," Isabrand says to Algard, whose chest swells with irritation.

"Neither you nor this dragovik are my superior," he hisses, looking at us in disgust.

"You are very much going to regret that comment," Isabrand replies, laughing to himself.

"It's funny because your arrogance has blinded you to the truth of things," Proserpina explains when Algard merely stands, his mouth opening and closing.

"You tell him," Isabrand says to her, reaching out his manacled hands and patting her on the back.

"I am one of the caeletai umea. I am here to help the Hirutere in their war against the jaeitsi."

The room falls dead silent before us, mouths gaping wide. Casey seems unsure of how to proceed from there. She has just claimed to be their saviour and, what's more, has implied that her very existence means they are in need of saving. That is not something the ego of the Hirutere will handle well. Eventually, Algard sputters out a laugh. The remainder of the courtroom glances from him to Casey, uncertain of whether to believe her or not. From what Kyle has told me of her kind, there hasn't been a caeletai umea born for at least three generations, so, other than Proserpina, no one in this room has seen one before. What to look for? She bears no angelic grace in the forward hunch of her shoulders or downcast eyes. Casey's cheeks flush pink and I see her hands tremble.

"Impossible. There must be two at all times and no second has been heard of," Algard says.

"Not if Diane has kept the other hidden from you, as she did the jaeitsi," I say.

"You're lying. This is another one of your desperate attempts to prevent justice."

"You have tests though, right? So, check. If we're lying, you'll have our heads," Isabrand says, shrugging.

"If not, the Hirutere will extend both its pardon and protection to all of my friends for keeping me alive long enough to reach Mies-Mies," Casey starts.

"Miesarinda," I whisper to her.

"The Hirutere will extend both its pardon and protection to all of my friends for keeping me alive long enough to reach Miesarinda and aid the Hirutere in defeating the jaeitsi," she says, though she intones it more as a question than a demand.

Algard has recovered himself from the shock of our claim for the most part, masking his anxiousness with disbelief.

"Very well then, Casey. Show us your divine power."

"Uh." She looks at me, as if I have some sort of precedent on how to proceed in such situations.

"Pritovis' light?" I whisper the suggestion, but in all honesty have no clue what it will do without a deabrueon to attack.

"Um, okay, Pritovis' light!" Casey commands.

Nothing happens. Algard's eyebrows rise slightly, his disbelief cementing itself further into his features. They wait a moment, but still nothing comes of her spell. Her words drop like stones to the floor.

"Ah yes, such overwhelming power," Algard says, and the courtroom laughs.

They've all eased back into indifference, not caring whether we live or die. I see Casey's knees buckle a little, but she manages to catch herself. She's doubting herself, though she's seen the enormity of her own power. My nostrils flare and my heart pounds, furious at the humiliation Algard is subjecting her to.

"She came here to help you," I snap, rising to my feet and going to stand beside her. "She came here to risk her own life in order to help you win a war you can't possibly fight on your own and you treat her with scorn? These are the great leaders who will wage battles from their ivory towers, letting the bellatoja they care enough about to prosecute an innocent woman die because they can't humble themselves to true power?"

"Miss Thiel, as your friend has just demonstrated, she has no power."

Suddenly, I have an idea. I turn to the others.

"Cover your ears." They oblige without hesitation, ducking their heads to tuck them safely between their knees. I take Casey's hand. "Sing."

"What?" she asks, looking confused.

"You won't remember now, but it's what you did back at Diane's apartment. It's how you put the others to sleep."

"The angel's lullaby."

I nod. She turns towards the audience.

"Stop whatever you're planning. Guards!" Algard calls.

Like that, I'm knocked over the edge of the stand, my face smacking into the courtyard's stone floor. The woman who had been closest to us leaps back as the guard pins my arms behind my back. Casey has been grabbed by another one, but he doesn't know to cover her mouth. She opens it wide and out comes a song I thought I'd never hear again.

"We're so beautifully human, so beautifully pure

unknown to mankind, hidden in their folklore.
They like to tell stories about all their worries
and if they could go back in time, they would unwind
the mistakes they made that led to the future,
cold and unyielding, what's become of your feelings?
Time can't you reverse, take back your wicked curse?
I don't know what we've done that's left us on the run.
But I won't stand for this, no we won't take this.
It's not in our nature to be bound or lost,
it's not in our nature to let ourselves be double crossed.
Beautifully human, so beautifully human we are."

As she sings, an immense fog of exhaustion draws itself over me. Sleep dawns, shaking its feathers as it rouses itself to draw the black sky above our heads. I blink rapidly, resisting the urge to fall asleep. I feel the guard's grip slacken on my arms before he slumps to the ground, snoring beside me. Casey stops before the song can put me to sleep, but, when I right myself, I see most of the audience has dozed off. Algard only just manages to stay awake, though he's leaning heavily on the podium. Slowly, he manages to emerge from this false tiredness. As drowsiness clears itself from his face, he looks at Casey in awe.

One by one, the sleepers rouse. It's as if a curtain has been drawn back. They all look to Casey, respect and wonder on their faces. They rise to their feet before kneeling, their heads bowed, all in her direction. Algard is the last to do so, but, eventually, even he kneels. Casey looks to me, even her eyes wide with shock at her own power. In that moment I know she has sealed her fate, bound herself to the Hirutere. She may never see her father again, or even return to Earth for that matter. She will not get to live out her human life as she should have been able to do. As I should have been able to do. My heart sinks, thinking of the future that has been snatched away from her in order to save us, but I do all I can to muster a smile for her sake, which is returned.

Algard shuffles some papers on the podium and, in a voice of resounding defeat, scarcely manages the words, 'cleared of all charges,' before descending from his podium and disappearing through the opposite door. There's a sudden uproar from the rest of the room, cheers of delight, and even the old man wakes from his sleep, applauding for no reason other than that everyone else is.

Chapter XXIV.

"The blue one. No, wait, that would look best on Mallory. How about the red? No, that would suit Proserpina," Casey murmurs to herself, flicking back and forth between the two options.

Though she has two entire racks of dresses to choose from, she hasn't got past the first five dresses and is now stuck on these two. Proserpina and I are far less interested in the clothes than we are the small buffet that's been served in Casey's new quarters. The room we're in is a sitting room, with splendid cream sofas and pouffes, plush carpeting, and great pastoral paintings hanging on the walls. On a long table abutting the wall are the many plates of food that have been served, from which Proserpina and I have helped ourselves. My plate is loaded with as much food as possible, a precarious balancing act.

The centrepiece is a slice of crepe cake, each layer separating warmed goats cheese infused with honey and orange. Its syrup oozes down along the side of the slice and I pluck free a pistachio and rhubarb macaron that has become lodged in it. Proserpina leans across me and takes the entire plate of fries, her whole face beaming with excitement. What exactly does someone as old yet seemingly naïve as her eat? I can't fathom how she lives, can't imagine her going back to an apartment at the end of the day and sleeping there. Oddly enough, however, I can definitely picture her owning a cat. Or several.

"Casey, it's your day. Wear whichever you want. Besides, I'm pretty sure Proserpina's already got her dress for the occasion."

There's a static sound as Proserpina's clothes phase from the outfit she'd copied from mine to her own floor length gown. She doesn't stop gobbling the fries for a second as she does this. I can't help but giggle at the sight of her in an elegant gown, scarfing fries.

"What?" she asks through a mouthful.

"It's nothing," I say.

"In that case, I guess the red. Or do you think it's too much?" Casey asks, taking it from the rack and holding it up to herself.

"I think nothing celebrating the arrival of a caeletai umea could be deemed too much after they brought ten different flavours of macarons, eight cakes, and an entire roast pig," I laugh, setting my plate down on the table beside me. I come to stand beside her, examining the red gown she's picked. I sweep my gaze over the rest of the rack. I'm careful to wipe my hands clean on a napkin before reaching for the golden gown I spotted moments ago. "I also think this would not go amiss."

She sets the other one aside on an oversized round chair upholstered in cream linen. Holding the gold dress up in front of her, I let the full skirt fall to her feet. The entire dress is decorated in sequins so small and delicate that they seem stars in the distance. The straps are chunky twisted leather cords that are smooth and buttery to the touch. It has a modest neckline, not revealing too much. Casey studies it in the mirror.

"I like it," she says, beaming at me before her expression clouds over.

She lays it down on top of the red one, sighing, and walking past the clothing racks to the balcony. The doors have been left open, letting the warm spring air, perfumed by flowers, flood the room. As soon as the cheers had stopped in the courtroom, we were escorted to the chambers of the last caeletai umea, Casey's new home. A week long festival was announced to be taking place in her honour, starting with a party tonight, at which Casey will be presented to the citizens of Miesarinda. I can't begin to imagine how overwhelming it must be to go from an ordinary girl in Brooklyn to someone who is all but deified by a race of earthbound angels. She's handled it remarkably well, but I think that's the blend of shock and the distraction of the dresses. The sheer enormity of what she's gotten herself into must finally be hitting her. I come to stand beside her, leaning on the railing and overlooking the city, which is clouded by a hazy pink sunset.

"It's beautiful here," I start, but am unsure of where I can go that will reassure her. What can I possibly say?

"Like a fairytale. I'm lucky. Of what I've heard of your past, you didn't come into this world so easily."

"It's not a competition. You've been through a lot in the past few days and that shouldn't be dismissed because you think someone else has had it worse."

"I didn't mean it like that."

I look over my shoulder to where she stands, surveying Miesarinda.

"You meant it like you don't want it, but you feel bad saying it?" She nods and I go to her as soon as I see the first tear spill. Like most things, it does not rush, but goes slowly down her cheek. I don't give it the chance to drop from her chin, brushing it away with the pad of my thumb. "Casey, it's okay for this to not be your dream. It's okay to feel it's a sacrifice. Letting them all but enshrine you here, not knowing how much of your life will be your own now you've pledged yourself to them must be terrifying. But maybe, before we start making judgements on how good or bad it is, we should party a bit first. And try the macarons."

She laughs through her tears, wiping them away. We both look to Proserpina for affirmation, but she's completely absorbed with the contents of my plate.

"Yeah, why not. We're going to save the world, I say we party."

"That's my girl. Now, which dress did you say was perfect for me?"

We go back into the room. I let her distract herself from her anxiety by trying on as many dresses for her as she wants me to. It isn't until we're on the sixth option, an absolute no as Lena would say, that I dare to broach the subject that's been bothering me since the courtroom.

"Hey Casey?"

"Mhm?" She emerges from the racks with two more dresses. Oh dear Vaerdiexes, will this torment ever end? At least Lena always knew exactly what I was going to wear. There was no trying things on.

"That song you sang. What is it?"

"Oh, I don't know. It just kind of popped into my head. Must be one of those songwriter things, you know?"

"Yeah, must be."

Only she can't have written that song if my caretaker sang it to me almost two decades ago. So how did she know it? I accept the first dress she hands me and dart behind the screen to change.

I don't ask her about the song any more after that. It seems she knows nothing of it and I don't want to make her worry. What there is to worry about I'm not sure. But it just seems too peculiar a coincidence not to be concerned.

After a couple hours of reassuring her and gorging on food until we feel beyond the capacity to move from where we lie on the floor, a team of bellatoja sent by the Hirutere come to collect Casey. As the members of the Hirutere in the courtroom had done, they kneel before her, gazing upon her face in wonder. I wouldn't be surprised if a couple of them were checking her out. Casey stuns in her golden gown, which rushes like water made silk from her hips to the floor, spilling around her. They guide her out, creating a tight formation around her, before one of them remembers we exist.

"The festival will take place in the agora, outside city hall. Your friends have been released from custody and will meet you there," he informs us, bowing his head and nodding. It's the most courtesy I've been shown by an angeleru other than Killian, though it does feel slightly forced. Casey must command a lot of respect around here.

"Ugh I need to get dressed," I groan to Proserpina as he closes the door. "I don't think any of these dresses will fit me anymore. Can you do that magic dress phasey thing on me?" I ask her hopefully.

She lets out an unearthly burp and shakes her head.

"I don't use my power for evil."

"You made my brother a peach pie."

"I like the way his ears turn pink when he's embarrassed."

"My ears do that too," I grumble.

There's a sharp knock on the door and, before we can answer, Isabrand and Dominic swagger in. Their faces look equally green, having undoubtedly feasted as we have. I burst out laughing when Isabrand steps forward to reveal Dominic. Proserpina looks up and begins giggling hysterically as well.

"Don't. It was the only thing they had in my size," Dominic says, glancing down miserably at the brown doublet they've dressed him in.

"Okay, two more stipulations Casey must insist upon: this chef needs to marry me and, fashion-wise, they need to move out of the fifteen-hundreds."

"Well, this is alright, isn't it!" Dominic scoffs, inspecting a few of the dresses.

"It's not that bad, mate," Isabrand assures him, walking over to where Proserpina has sat herself and crouching down. He pokes her belly playfully and she groans. "Enjoying the food are we?"

"Easy for you to say. You look like Geralt of Rivia," Dominic mumbles. He has a point. Isabrand is wearing a well fitted black, quilted jacket with buckles and black trousers. As I'd have expected of him, it's the most inconspicuous outfit possible. He doesn't bother replying to Dominic, gazing instead at Proserpina, who lies sprawled across the couch, her eyes closed and arm thrown above her head. He looks utterly enraptured. Dominic glances at me. "And how come you're not dressed yet?"

"We ate too much," I tell him, inching across the floor to the dress rack.

"The party's going to start soon, have you even picked something out? Who needs this many dresses?"

"Excuse me, this is necessary given our level of indecision," I say, clambering to my feet and beginning to sift through the rack.

"If anything, they should temper your indecision by only giving you one option."

The blue one Casey had mentioned is stunning, albeit perhaps a little over the top, what with all the lace. I settle on a diaphanous silver dress and slip behind the screen to change into it. The straps are joined by delicate bronze hoops that rest on my shoulders. Stepping back out, I find the banter that had occurred in my absence falls quiet. They stare at me in silence before Dominic blushes, turning away and clearing his throat.

"What, am I flashing tit?" I ask, glancing down at myself.

"Sis, if that were the case I'd be puking, not sitting in awe," Isabrand assures me.

"You look beautiful is what he's trying to say," Proserpina murmurs, glaring at Isabrand before joining me.

"Oh." My cheeks flush and for a moment I feel as though I am back with Lena, enjoying getting ready for a party, without the enormity of the supernatural world weighing on me. "Thank you. You look amazing too."

"This old thing?" Isabrand says, nodding at Proserpina's dress. She swats at him and he laughs playfully, catching her hand in his. It puts me at ease to see him so happy and open with someone, though again I am awed by the speed with which they've gravitated towards one another. I'm still aware of Dominic staring at me and it makes my cheeks burn all the more. Why does he look at me as though he's seeing me for the first time?

"We should get going," he says, offering me his arm, "m'lady."

"M'lord," I reply, graciously accepting his arm with a curtsey.

We lead the way down the massive spiral staircase of the building, which widens the further down we go, giving it the appearance of cerith shell. The floors are made of a waxy pink marble that glows warmly in the peach sunset's light. Imbedded within it are shimmering gold patches that light up blindingly when touched by sunlight.

Outside, the streets are empty, as they have not been on my previous trips. When Algard took us from the library, it seemed all the world was outside to observe the spectacle. Now a few passers-by rush along the streets towards the Hirutere's headquarters and the agora. Why do I feel nervous all of a sudden? I know I am safe, as are my friends, for the first time in a long time. We have the protection of the entire bellatoja army, not to mention I will always have my own magic to protect me. But leaving Vaerdiexes' sword in the room feels ill-advised after what happened last time I left it alone. The jaeitsi aren't exactly going to get it from Miesarinda though, are they? I know Proserpina has brought Shigami with her, secreted away in the other realm. I watched her strap it onto her belt. Can Thrabr come into Miesarinda as easily as he can appear on Earth?

Perhaps it's nothing more than my proximity to Dominic, whose hand has come to rest on my arm, that makes me nervous. His breaths are shallow, focused, as if each one is practiced and he must remind himself to breathe. Have I not done the same when so close to him? I've felt as though he drew all common sense from me and had to remind myself how to continue, not just stand still and bask in his presence. Now he seems to be doing the same. And I dare to think what I have never allowed myself to before: Dominic's feelings for me match my own for him.

"Sis what's with your face?" Isabrand asks, overtaking us.

"Shut up," I reply, ducking my head, but I can still hear him laugh.

From ahead, I begin to hear the sounds of music and indistinguishable voices cheering and talking. The throngs overflow from the agora into the surrounding streets, a glimmering mass of beautiful dresses like insect wings, ephemeral and ethereal creatures, clustered together. The music grows louder as we approach and Dominic takes my hand, his own hot to the touch. This is more than I can handle right now.

"We should find the others," I say, finding I must call out to be heard over the ruckus. Bodies sway and crystal glasses slosh pastel drinks on the floor. All around us, the streets are buzzing with activity and joy. Dominic nods in agreement and pulls me through the crowd, but all we achieve is to lose Proserpina and Isabrand in a matter of seconds. "Should we go find them?"

"I think those two will be fine on their own," he answers, giving me a knowing look. He draws me to him and surveys the agora. I wonder if we're going to dance, but suddenly he's on the move again towards a gilt fountain in the middle of the open space. Set up all around it are tables laden with food and drinks. I can't even fathom eating or drinking anything else, but he grabs two glasses and hands one to me. "Cheers."

"Cheers," I reply, tapping my glass to his. He downs it quickly before taking another. "Is something the matter?"

"What?" he cries over the noise, leaning closer to me.

"Is everything okay?"

"Yeah, just looking forward to a drink is all."

Of course. After the hell he's undoubtedly been put through the past few days, a distraction will be much needed. I finish my own before taking up another.

"Let's find somewhere quiet to go," I say. "We should catch up."

He nods, following me as I weave back to the edge of the agora, to the streets that stretch from it like dendritic limbs. Finally, the crowd begins to thin, allowing us space to have more than a few centimetres between us. I wander away from him and lean against a nearby building, sipping my drink. Watching him, I find it suddenly seems Dominic is able to look anywhere but at me.

"So," I start. He nods, looking down at his already almost empty drink. Should I be concerned that his time with Diane was worse than his calm has made it seem? He's acted completely fine until now. I took her magic eventually, but she had it some of the time he was kidnapped. Who knows what torments he has been subject to. I'm about to ask if he's okay again when he speaks.

"They should make refills automatic, what with all this magic," he suggests, taking the last sip. I teleport another glass to my hand and pass it to him. "Thanks."

"Least I can do after you were kidnapped for me."

He winces and I know whatever was done to him is a topic off limits for now.

"You repaid the favour, saving my life and all. And after everything I did to try and keep you from this world," he mutters to himself, glaring at the ground angrily.

"Is that what's bothering you?" I ask, drawing closer to him without deciding to. It's magnetic, this pull when I'm with him. "If I had known what you were going through to keep me safe, I wouldn't have let you."

"I know. My stubborn girl," he sighs, and I detect the hint of a smile. *My stubborn girl.* My breath catches. This is the moment, if there ever was one, to find out. I must be bold. I close the distance between us and his eyes widen.

"Mallory!"

We spring apart and I glance all around, looking for who's calling my name. But I know who it is when a blur topped with black curls hurtles towards me, wrapping his arms around me

"Kyle!" I pull him close, pressing my face to his shoulder. I had forgot to look for them in the face of my aside with Dominic, but the relief I feel being back in Kyle's arms is overwhelming. I glance over his shoulder and, sure enough, Robyn and Aaron are approaching as well. I slip from Kyle's arms and hug Aaron, who lets out an 'oof' sound due to the force with which I hold him. Then I turn to Robyn, but she just raises her eyebrows. "Do we do hugs?"

"No, but you can get me a drink." I conjure five glasses, passing them around.

"I'm so happy to see you, all of you," I say, taking Kyle's hand in my own. The reality of what I was about to do with Dominic strikes me. Stupid Mallory. There's no way he feels the same about you. Thank heavens they got here when they did.

But he didn't draw away, did he?

Dominic takes a step back from the group, sensing he doesn't belong. I reach out and pull him forwards.

"This is Dominic. We went to the Academy together. He's the one who's been protecting me all these years."

"Ah so you're the one who got us into this mess," Aaron says, giving Dominic an appraising eye. And I realise he has read in me my feelings for Dominic since I first mentioned him. He sticks his hand out and shakes Dominic's. "Aaron Baeor."

"Got you into it?" Dominic asks, raising his eyebrows.

"After we met up again, Mallory found out you were taken and we all agreed to help rescue you. You didn't think we'd let her go alone, did you?"

"Why does this suddenly feel like a pissing contest," Kyle murmurs, and I laugh. "You look beautiful by the way."

My face lights up as only his praise could make it do. I do a little twirl for him before taking his hand again.

"You're looking good yourself for a man fresh out of prison."

"The bathhouse will do that for you," he assures me. "It's just a few blocks down."

"Mental note, try the bathhouse while here." And I know here is exactly where we will be for the foreseeable future.

After that, we drink and dance, Isabrand and Proserpina finding us eventually. I can see the curiosity on Kyle's face when I explain who Proserpina is and know he's dying to ask her a hundred questions only she can answer. I rest my hand on his arm, a gentle reminder that business can wait. Tonight, we celebrate Casey and all we've done to get her here. We're alive and together and, for the first time, there is no immediate danger. Hell, I may actually get some sleep tonight.

After some time, there's a sudden hush, followed by cries of excitement, and I know they've brought Casey out. We can't make her out over the heads of the crowd, but it seems an impossibility to get through as well.

"You should see her dress, she looks beautiful," I say to Kyle.

"Well come on then."

Leading the charge, Kyle and Robyn push their way through, the others following until it's just me and Proserpina. I drain my drink, but notice Proserpina has not touched hers.

"Not a drinker?" I ask.

"It clouds my visions," Proserpina answers. She's frowning, squinting at the crowd as though she can see through it to Casey.

"Everything okay?"

She doesn't answer, but runs her tongue across her teeth, still scrutinising. When I realise she's not going to speak, I glance around at the street that has now emptied out, everyone packing themselves forward to catch a glimpse of the caeletai umea. Empty except for one figure, that is, leaning against the wall.

"Killian!"

Proserpina nods to me, an assurance she'll be okay, so I lift the hem of my dress and dash down the street. Something possesses my limbs, which I throw around him as he leans away from the wall. He stumbles to catch me, but loses his balance, and we crash to the ground. I hear a low groan beneath me.

"I'm so sorry, are you okay?" I ask, sitting upright on the edge of the pavement to check he's alright. He sits up too, his face and body inches from mine.

"Beats being questioned by the Hirutere for hours," he says. He rubs the back of his head before his gaze slips down the length of me. He swallows, meeting my gaze. "You look breathtaking."

"Thanks. You look good too," I say, blushing furiously. "Bath-house?"

"I only bathe once a month, remember? And there was no time. I only just got released."

"But the others said they've been out for hours?" I ask.

"Funny thing. Being a bellatoja who helps a dragovik is a lot worse in the Hirutere's eyes than a dragovik loyal to its own kind."

"Are you going to be okay?" I ask, a flash of worry catching my heart. Of all of us, he's risked the most in allying himself with me. He shrugs.

"Helping bring a caeletai umea safely home wins you major points. They wanted to know the full extent of what happened, why I chose to stand by you, but won't be pressing any charges."

"What a shame, we both know how fond they are of doing that," I tease, prompting his laughter. "So, you're okay?"

"Internal bleeding from the fall aside, I'm fine. What about you, what happened?"

I glance over my shoulder, but none of the others have returned. The crowd has now gone quiet and I can faintly make out Casey's voice addressing them. There's time to fill him in now. I recount the day's events, leaving out Vaerdiexes and Proserpina swearing fealty. There's no need to tell him about my destiny. By the time I finish, the crowd has returned to dancing and chatting.

"Wow. Well thanks for coming for us."

"As if I'd let that pretty face rot in prison," I laugh. He grins, tucking a strand of hair behind my ear. He is gorgeous. His eyes are a whole forest to get lost in. So much like the beginning of a fairytale.

What am I thinking? It's Dominic I want. It's always been Dominic. I look down at my empty glass. I feel that familiar wooziness wrapping itself around me and know it would be best to stop drinking, but Casey was right. We deserve to party.

"Want a drink?" I ask.

"Sure."

I stand up. I could easily summon them to us, but something about Killian is making me nervous. I need to get away for a moment. I tap Proserpina on the shoulder.

"I'm just going to get more drinks," I say.

Pushing my way through the crowd, I think I spot the others' faces making their way back to us, all beaming smiles. Still, something urges me to get away, to get space, so I push on. Standing up has sent the alcohol straight to my head. I need to move. I need to get out of this crowd. Bodies packed tightly against me makes my skin crawl. My chest tightens and I hardly feel I can breathe. No, not here. My chest begins to heave shakily. With more urgency, I push people out of the way. There are some murmurs of discontent, but I ignore them. Finally, I emerge into another alleyway. Crashing against the wall, I slide down until I'm sitting on the cobblestones, trembling.

"You too, huh?"

I glance up and spot Dominic across the way. His hand is wrapped so tightly around a glass it's blanched white. I'm surprised the glass hasn't shattered in his grip. I can see the fog of drunkenness in his features, that distant look and parted lips.

"It's a bit much," I breathe, pressing a hand to my chest and willing myself to stop shaking. It's no use. But, of course, it must be worse for him, having hardly been around people since the Academy. No wonder he's been drinking so much. How had I not thought of this when I brought him here, the effect being around all these strangers would have on him? My heart softens and my breaths go steady.

Come poor thing, you're all alone.

I stumble to my feet, unaware of what I am doing until it's already been done. I hear his glass fall to the ground and shatter. His lips are sticky from the alcohol, his breath sweet and spicy at the same time. He puts his hands on my waist and crushes his lips against mine, sloppily. There's nothing rehearsed in it, just the urgency of two people who–

He pulls away, shaking his head and wiping his lips with the back of his hand. My heart drops.

"No."

"No?" I ask.

"Mallory. You are beautiful. And what every man wants. But we can't."

"Why not?" I mumble. My eyes begin to sting, drunkenness accelerating my embarrassment.

"It's not like I haven't thought about it too. For a time, I thought you were the only person in the world for me. Who else could understand what we've been through? But watching you strive to have a better life, a different life, at NYU, I realised something. When we love, it shouldn't be out of commiseration. We deserve something that will draw us from that darkness."

You deserve better than the darkness so many have tried to pull you into.

Killian's words come back to me through the haze of alcohol. I can remember them but, in this moment, I cannot rationalise them. If Dominic wants me and I want him, what's the problem? Unless he doesn't actually want me at all and he's just trying to make me feel better about myself.

I shake my head, backing away. I wrap my arms around myself.

"Mallory please don't hate yourself. This isn't a reflection on you," he assures me, but I don't want to hear it.

I dart back through the crowd, wiping my tears as I go, before

I stumble back out onto the street where my friends are. I wonder what they see? But it seems nothing is to be made of the shape of my recent humiliation. They scarcely glance at me before turning back to one another, laughing. Killian trots over to my side.

"No drinks?" Killian asks. "Don't worry, they grabbed some on the way back."

"Good." I throw the one he hands me back and take another from him.

"Okay, that one was mine, but go ahead."

"Sorry."

"No worries, you seem to need it more than I do."

"Mallory!" Proserpina cries, skipping towards me and dragging Isabrand after her. "We're going to go dance!"

One look at Isabrand's face tells me this is the last thing he wants to do. But it's exactly what I need. Senseless, I follow her. Aaron and Robyn come with us, leaving Kyle and Killian to talk.

"Hey," Aaron murmurs in a low voice just by my ear. "Are you okay?"

"Never better," I reply.

I study him, dressed in a white linen shirt and beige trousers. His stubble has grown out over the past few days.

"What?" he demands.

"You're a good person, you know that? Thank you for staying with Kyle when no one else did."

He takes my hand and spins me around. I giggle, eliciting a grin from him. *It will be fine*, I assure myself.

Chapter XXV.

It was, in fact, not fine.

The sunlight spilling from the window is what wakes me. That or the resulting pounding of my head, which is equal parts sunlight and hangover. Maybe it's more of a ninety-ten split. I groan, scrunching my eyes shut, but still the red of the light bleeds through them. There's no respite here. At least I don't feel like I'm going to be sick. All I want is to eat as much savoury food as possible and then a bit more. Rolling onto my right side, I stretch out my arms, only to come up against something soft and warm.

Oh no.

Opening my left eye as little as possible, I make out the vague and fuzzy shape beside me, its head topped with caramel coloured waves.

Oh shit.

I roll back over onto my other side, trying my best not to shift the blanket. I don't need to lift it up to know what my dress on the floor already tells me: I'm completely naked. The whole night comes back to me. Drinking with the others, dancing. Eventually Aaron and I went off to get drinks and never came back. We came back to the quarters the Hirutere had assigned to us and then… I don't want to think about and then. Not that it was bad, I'm just full of sheer embarrassment. How have I let this happen? I slip out of the covers and dart across the room, snatching my dress up.

"Now usually I'm the one off in a hurry after these things," Aaron says, making me jump.

I spin around, clutching the dress to my chest to obscure myself from view. He's propped himself up on one arm, the sheets tucked around his waist to reveal his muscular torso. It's the kind of body a god might envy. I swallow nervously. A lazy grin unwinds on his face, taking his usual pleasure in my discomfort. But this time is different. Where I have always rebuffed his advances before, here I've ceded territory. I pull the dress closer to me, as if it could wipe the image of my body from his memory. I might have to seriously consider a memory spell at some point.

"I'll spare you the trouble," I reply. "If you'll just kindly turn around while I get dressed."

He closes his eyes, still smiling, and I don my gown. Never thought I'd be doing the walk of shame in a ballgown, but there are all sorts of things life doesn't prepare you for.

"Are you decent?" he asks. "I wouldn't want to pervert my innocent self by sighting your mortal flesh."

I snatch a pillow from the bed and toss it at him. Even with his eyes shut he manages to catch it, his grin only growing as he opens his eyes.

"This isn't funny Aaron," I hiss, suddenly wondering if his room abuts any of the others. Oh shit, what if they heard us?

"Funny is definitely not the word I'd use to describe it." In one swift motion he's across the bed and on his feet, closing the distance between us. The sheets drop from his waist and that familiar blush creeps into my cheeks. I direct my gaze to the ceiling. "You weren't this shy last night."

"I know I wasn't, I was extremely drunk. And while at the time I definitely wanted this, I'm facing a severe case of regret this morning," I scowl at him.

"What, didn't enjoy yourself?"

He doesn't sound self-conscious at all, well aware that that is not the issue I am taking with last night.

"So not the point," I say.

"What is?"

"That this, as far as anyone else is concerned, never happened. Okay?"

"Okay," he says, shrugging. He laughs at the perplexed look on my face, surprised as I am by how easily he's agreed to keep last night between us. "Don't get me wrong Mallory, I'm glad last night happened and you're gorgeous, but I'm not looking to date you."

"Oh."

Of course he isn't. He'd never once implied that his interest was more than physical. Whatever feelings he may have had three years ago, much like Leo's, have long since dissipated. He cares for me as he does any other friend.

"Oh," I sigh again, with relief.

"You said that a lot last night."

He ducks as I swat at him, laughing as he stumbles back on to the bed. Catching me by the waist, he spins me around and lands on top of me. My breath catches and I'm suddenly struck by how very attractive he is, in a hyper-masculine sort of way. All muscle and nonchalance, he shifts his weight above me, his silver eyes piercing me through.

"So," he starts, dotting a kiss on my throat. "That's a no to telling anyone."

"Mhm," I say as his hand runs along my waist down to my hip and he kisses my neck, teasing it gently with his teeth.

"But would you happen to be free this morning?"

I feel fire blooming between my legs, begging me to be free this morning. My heart races as he slips his hand beneath my dress and runs his thumb along the crease between my thigh and abdomen, closer and closer each time. He stops, millimetres away from touching me, waiting for my consent.

"I don't think my hangover will allow me to get out of bed for at least another hour," I whisper. His eyes glint mischievously. He flips my skirts up and dips his head out of sight.

Oh shit, I think to myself again, taking in a deep, shuddering breath.

* * *

It's almost noon by the time Aaron falls asleep beside me, exhausted from our morning activities. I, on the other hand, feel more awake than ever, my skin buzzing with pleasure and energy. I climb out of bed and pick up my dress from where Aaron discarded it on the floor. I'm hoping the angeleru don't want it back; it took a while before it came off. Slipping the cool fabric over my head, I'm oddly comforted by the weight of the bronze rings on my shoulders, as if they're weighting me back down to Earth after a morning so distant from my usual life, from anything I could ever have imagined for myself. Though, then again, I suppose we're not really on Earth. Somewhere between it and Sundalev.

I sneak out the door, careful not to wake Aaron, and find myself back in the communal room of the suite the Hirutere has put us in. I can only hope the others were already up and out this morning, but, if they were anywhere near as hungover as me, they've spent the morning in bed. I pull the door shut and turn around, coming face to face with Leo. I start to smile, opening my mouth to say hello. But he hardly seems himself. His face is contorted in rage, his usually flat gold eyes lit up.

"Leo, what's the matter, are you okay?" I ask, dropping my shoes to the floor and rushing to him. I make to rest my hand on his arm, but he recoils.

"How," he starts, his eyes wide with fury. "How could you?"

"How could I what? I don't understand. Come to Miesarinda? I had to, to get the others out of prison. I had to do it to protect Kyle."

"Not that," he hisses, his eyes darting from Aaron's door to me.

Oh.

Oh.

"But, why do you care?" I ask, confused.

"Why do I care?" he asks, quietly before his voice rises to a roaring thunder. "Why do I care?"

"I believe that's what I asked," I say, cowering from him. Leo has never frightened me before, but he has also never looked angry before.

"You know. You know exactly how I feel. I all but spelt it out for you last time we saw each other."

I'm taken aback and the force of this realisation almost makes my knees buckle beneath me. After all this time, he still has feelings for me?

"Last time we saw each other we barely spoke," I say, running over the events of our last encounter. He had given no indication he was still interested in me.

"Not then, back in Aplin Hollow."

"That was three years ago!" I exclaim. "How was I supposed to know you'd still feel that way about me?"

His face flashes with pain and it's a feeling I am so unaccustomed to seeing on Leo's face, I can scarcely breathe. To think I've caused it. It's as if I've slapped him.

"I thought, I thought you felt that way too. But then you go and sleep with him? After what we shared?"

"Leo I'm sorry, truly I am. But it's been so long, I don't feel that way anymore," I whisper, dropping my gaze when I find myself unable to meet his.

"But I felt that way still."

My heart breaks to hear him so softened and utterly distraught.

"I didn't realise but, even if I had, I don't owe your feelings reciprocation. And I shouldn't be forbidden from doing what I want just because it's not with you."

I hear a creak of floorboards to my right and see Killian emerge from the hallway. His face is completely deadpan and I cannot gauge how much of our conversation he has heard. He stands a way's away and I assume he comes bearing news, else why stay for this awkward exchange?

"That's how you feel?" Leo demands, completely ignoring Killian.

"Yes, Leo. I am truly sorry for any pain I've caused you."

He shakes his head, looking at me in disgust. Without another word, he pushes past Killian into the hallway and disappears. I close my eyes, dipping my head and catching it in my palms. I know that I am justified in my response, that I am in no way beholden to Leo, but it doesn't make hurting someone I once cared about any easier. Folding my arms across my chest, I look up at Killian.

"You're not going to yell at me too, are you?" I ask.

"It's not usually my go to and I figure you've had enough of that. None of my business anyway," he says, but his face betrays disapproval. I can't stand to have him look at me like that too.

"Not you too," I sigh.

"What?"

"You're upset with me."

"No, Mallory, heavens no. I'm upset with Leo for speaking to you like that."

I swallow the knot of sobs in my throat and nod.

"Note to self, one night stands never work out well."

"Yeah, you mentioned that about the other guy you hooked up with. Funny how these things work out for men, but never women," he sighs.

"Too true. How come you can take a hundred girls to Brooklyn, but I hook up twice in my entire life and it ends badly both times?" His face cracks into a grin at this.

"One girl! I took one girl to dinner in Brooklyn."

"Two if you count me," I remind him.

"Damn you, skewing my statistics," he laughs.

"So, what brings you to this neck of the woods? I assume they haven't got you staying here too?"

"No, I've been allowed to go back to my place. They almost put me on house arrest though," he says, grimacing. "I came to bring this by."

He indicates the large cardboard box in his hands with my name on it.

"What is it?" I ask warily. "You're not going to put my dismembered body in there, are you?"

"Um, wasn't planning on it. It's just some stuff from your apartment, as you'll now be a fulltime resident of Miesarinda. We grabbed what clothes weren't lost in your suitcases and a couple odds and ends I thought you might want."

"You went to get my stuff?" I ask, taking the box from him and heading towards my room. He follows.

"A team of bellatoja were sent to retrieve personal effects for all of you. I offered to go with."

"Where's everyone else's?"

My room is spacious, larger than my entire apartment in New York. It has a balcony from which I can see the great glass rotunda and agora. The floor is covered in rich cream coloured carpeting, the fibres of which are unbelievably soft against my bare feet. Perpendicular to the door, abutting the left wall, is a massive king-sized bed with white linen sheets, unslept in. There's a vanity, desk, and wardrobe along the opposite wall, and a door leading into the bathroom. I set the box on my bed, but something stays my hand when I go to open it. What am I nervous about Killian seeing? He packed the thing.

"They're bringing the others by in a bit. I just thought I'd bring your stuff over and check how that hangover is. I didn't mean to, uh, interrupt your conversation."

Oh heavens. So, he did hear us. I sense his eyes trained on me, that soldier's gaze that perceives so much. I feel utterly humiliated knowing he knows about me and Aaron. But why should I care? And more so than I did when Leo found out.

"Don't worry about it. And the hangover's much better,

thanks," I lie. In reality, my head is still throbbing and Leo's yelling did little to assuage it.

"See and I was going to suggest getting breakfast if it was still bad. Coffee, crepes, bacon, the works. But I suppose if you're not hungry, I'll go alone."

"Oh sweet Mary and a muffin that sounds good," I sigh, and he bursts out laughing at the odd turn of phrase.

"Can't say I've heard that one before."

"Something my friend Wes used to say," I say. Using past tense to speak of Wes seems only right; I know now the likelihood of ever seeing him again is slim. We'll stay in Miesarinda until the war is won, one way or another. And, even if we do win, I don't foresee myself being able to go back to that life. I'll have to start over again.

"Wes was the hook up?" he asks, nonchalantly.

"No, heavens no," I laugh. "Just a friend from university."

A wave slips over my head, one of misery and loss. My entire life, the future Professor Baker and I had seen for me, is gone. Where there should have been grad school applications, now there will only be war tactics, manoeuvres, and strategy. Killian must read something of my misery on my face, because he nudges me playfully in the ribs.

"Hey, how about that food?"

"Sounds good."

I don't bother changing out of my dress. We leave the suite of rooms, going back down the hallway we came by. The apartment is in the same building as Casey's, albeit several floors down. We descend the stairs and emerge onto the street, which is full, but seems to move at a slower pace. It's as if a universal fog of hang-over exhaustion blankets the city and the only ones up are those who have to be. Killian beckons, leading me down the street to our right.

"So, you must have been up early today," I say, hoping to shift the awkward silence that seems to perch on both our shoulders.

"Yeah, they wanted me to lead the team given I know where you all live. I also think they're going to try and put me through the ringer over the next few months," he sighs.

"How so?"

"You know, sending me on all the worst missions, during the festival, in the middle of the night. It's their way of punishing me without out right punishing me. Algard knows I was helping you before I had any clue Casey existed, no matter what I told them."

"I wouldn't expect any less of him. I'm sorry you have to go through that because of me."

He shakes his head.

"Honestly don't worry about it. I'm not that big on those festival parties anyway."

"They are insane, all of this celebration over one person."

"The caeletai umeas are as close to our god communicating with us as it gets. It's his way of saying: hey I see you're in trouble and I want to help out. It's an honour to be one of them. Still, I would never want to live the way she's going to have to. Enshrined in a tower, only allowed to be with the other caeletai umea. Not that they'll ever find them."

"What makes you say that? Have they started looking?" I ask as we turn down a narrow street. He stops outside a café, the exterior of which is populated by half occupied tables. The waiter seats us with a smile and sets down two menus, which have too many options for me this early in the hangover cycle. "Should I even order for myself or let you do it again?"

"I'm honoured you trust me to order for you. Must have been those chilli cheese fries that did it."

"Actually, it was the tequila." He chuckles, skimming the menu.

He's dressed all in black, the same outfit Isabrand had worn the night before. I've seen a few people wearing it throughout the streets and wonder if it's the bellatoja uniform. It doesn't suit him as it had Isabrand. Where my brother is all shadow, Killian seems better suited to softness and warmth. He's something akin to the feeling of home. He nods at the waiter, who returns to the table.

"We'll have the truffle omelette, brioche French toast with caramelised pecans, chocolate crepes, and your largest plate of bacon," Killian says. "Oh, and two coffees."

The waiter scratches out our order then takes the menus, before disappearing into the building. It's a cute little place made of Cotswold stone, with a green awning and ivy snaking up the walls.

"Why did that all sound so good," I groan, falling back in my seat.

"Because you've had about two pints of booze and nothing to eat all morning."

"No but all the food here is insane. You should have seen the spread they put on at Casey's last night. I would have married the chef."

"That makes two of us. That will be the Hirutere's head chef who caters official events. I've tasted his slices of heaven occasionally. As for your question, yes, we're looking for the other caeletai umea, but it's hard to track one down. We can't find them unless they use their magic, but how are they to know how to use their magic if they don't know it exists? Caeletai umea aren't born to magically inclined parents, so they have no one to teach them what to do. It has to come to them naturally."

The coffees arrive and I take a sip. It's warm and earthy, not at all like the bitter, burnt coffee I get near campus. At least there will be some perks to moving here.

"Are they always male and female? And do they always end up together?" I ask.

"No to both. It's encouraged, regardless of sex or gender, that they stay together, as having children with anyone else could result in another group of jaeitsi, but nothing romantic is necessary." I nod, glancing at the café door to see if our waiter is on his way back.

"So, they're basically a gift from your god? I'm surprised there wasn't even more fanfare over her last night."

"Oh, there will be. Parties all week long. Not to mention after we win the war. She'll be a deity in the people's eyes."

"You say that so confidently."

"Which bit?"

"Winning the war," I say, setting my cup down. "Does it seem so easy to you?"

"You doubt us? We have you, Proserpina, and Casey. Not to mention an entire army of bellatoja."

"I've come up against two jaeitsi and, even with me and Proserpina fighting together, it was no piece of cake."

"I'm not saying it will be. But I have faith in my people. We've defended the portal to Sundalev against many foes."

"Including dragoviks?" I feel bad, probing him for information. But I need to learn what I can of the portal if I'm to one day return us to Sundalev as Vaerdiexes intends.

"You're not our enemy," he says, but doesn't sound certain. The Hirutere certainly don't see us as allies. Inferiors, perhaps.

"What would it take for them to let us through?"

Killian's eyebrows go up, just as the food arrives. I'm temporarily distracted by the heavenly smells wafting up, attacking an innocent piece of French toast with my fork. It's of such a light and fluffy texture it practically melts in my mouth. I think I've just found true love.

"Us? You want to go with them?" he asks, drawing me from my food reverie.

"You know what I mean," I reply, brushing him off. He doesn't seem convinced, but lets me get away with it, merely helping himself to a crepe. "What would it take for the Hirutere to finally let dragoviks through?"

"Honestly? I don't know. It's been so long, nothing's ever been enough."

My heart sinks as he says this. There were only ever two ways to get through that portal: by force or through an alliance. I had already thought the latter unlikely, although not impossible. Killian's making me rethink that though. If nothing has been enough until now, what could I possibly do to persuade the Hirutere to allow us through the portal? Killian opens his mouth, but just then I hear someone call my name. I turn around and spot Proserpina and Isabrand walking towards us. My brother looks embarrassed, while she waves vigorously at us, and I'm half wondering if they've been on a date. They certainly were getting very cosy last night.

"Oh, more food!" Proserpina squeals, pulling a chair over to our table. Isabrand tucks it in for her. She takes Killian's fork and begins to help herself to some caramelised bacon. "So yummy."

"Where have you two been?" I ask, noting they were coming from the opposite direction of the apartment.

"Isabrand wanted to go with me for a walk," Proserpina sings. She's clad in a knee length red summer dress I haven't seen before. Killian and I exchange a look. Definitely something datish going on here.

"I wanted to see the city," Isabrand grumbles, fully aware of what we're thinking. I smirk at him.

"Bro, what's with your face?" I ask.

"Shut up."

"How about you?" Proserpina asks, mouth full of bacon.

"Killian thought I might want some breakfast after last night's shenanigans," I reply, helping her with a crepe.

"Yeah, you were throwing them back sis. I didn't even hear you come back to the suite last night."

My face bursts into crimson flames. Thank heavens for that. I had completely forgot Isabrand would be in one of the other rooms. Proserpina giggles at the sight of my face and I have no doubt she knows exactly what's got me embarrassed.

"What did I say?" Isabrand asks.

"Nothing," Proserpina and I say at the same time.

She winks at me conspiratorially before taking a sip of my coffee. Killian says nothing, though his ears go slightly red.

"Okay," Isabrand says, looking between the three of us. "So, what have we missed?"

"Not much, I was just learning about how Casey's a gift from god."

"A god," Killian corrects. "Vaerdiexes may have made you but he didn't make us. Pritovis did."

"And therein lies all angeleru snobbery. *We were made by the oldest god,"* Isabrand says in a mocking tone. "I need some coffee."

Killian's eyes look to me, searching for something I cannot provide him with because I know not what it is.

"Come on, we need to order more food too," he says to Isabrand, and the pair head inside, in search of a waiter.

I turn to Proserpina who has gone utterly still, a bite of bacon halfway from the plate to her parted lips. Her eyes flash with amusement and surprise. She giggles before popping the last bite into her mouth.

"I knew I was right about him," she says.

"Who, Isabrand?"

"No, the bellatoja. I saw it last night in him. He's fallen for you."

Chapter XXVI.

After breakfast, Killian walks us back to the apartment, where we say farewell. He has more work to attend to before the festivities tonight. In the wake of Proserpina's comment, I'm grateful to part. It's not possible someone so kind, generous, and, let's face it, good looking as him could be interested in me. The thought sends a flush to my cheeks when I'm around him now, making me extremely embarrassed. I hardly spoke through the remainder of breakfast, though I noticed him looking at me frequently.

We head upstairs, and Isabrand and Proserpina loiter in the communal room, which is otherwise empty. They seat themselves cosily on one of the two velvet green sofas, where Proserpina kicks off her shoes, tucking her feet up beside her. I wonder what it is that draws two people, so different in their natures and experiences, together. So quickly as well. It has seemed since the moment they met at the jaeitsi's headquarters, something strung itself between them, a line of communication that cannot be broken. Nor do they wish it to be. But I am grateful for this, for Isabrand's sake, that he has so readily fallen to caring for someone other than just me. It reassures me that he cannot be the monster either Thaddeus or my mother thought he was. Not only does he have the capacity to care for people, but he wishes to as well.

I retreat to my bedroom to give them some time alone, which, it's quite clear from the way they sit with their foreheads centimetres apart murmuring to one another, is all they want. On my bed I find the box Killian had brought, still untouched. I hesitate a moment. This is all that's left of my life before now. I have lost the entirety of myself more times than I care to recall, have had to start from scratch to stay alive or keep others alive too many times. It's exhausting. What small pieces of myself will I be able to carry into the future with me? Prying up the tape, I peel it back and open the box. Inside are the few books I had left behind in my apartment, though my heart sinks to think of my precious annotated copy of Jane Eyre abandoned somewhere. I pull them out and arrange them on the desk. At least I'll have access to the Library Between. I wonder if there are any good bookstores around here.

Returning to the box, I'm about to collapse it when I spy the phoenix box my mother had left me nestled at the bottom. Only now, since Isabrand opened it, the phoenix is staring fiercely at the sun rather than the moon. Whoever picked it up has sealed it once more. Pulling it out, I stare at the beautiful but simple carving. Had Leo given away anything of his feelings when he'd brought it to me? I turn the thought over in my mind like a pebble but nothing comes to me. No, he had not given me any indication. Whatever I read into that interaction now will all be a retroactive projection of what he's told me. As bad as I feel for hurting him, I know I have a right to be happy without him.

Taking the box to the vanity where I intend to stow it away in a drawer, I hear something shifting around inside of it. I remove the lid and there I see what I had failed to notice after Isabrand opened it: an aged, folded piece of paper and something forming a lump beneath it. Extracting the paper, I lift the folded corner.

Dear Mallory.

I let the edge of the paper drop back down, my hands shaking. I look back into the box.

Beneath the paper is hidden a large pear cut diamond, the size of a bottle cap, hanging from a strap of black leather. I reach in and brush the gem with my fingers. Shivering, I set the box down before crossing to my bed and sitting down. How could my mother do this? Insert herself in my life like this after all these years? She had to know I'd only find the note when I remembered my childhood, when I remembered her. Did she want to try and argue her case for abandoning me at the Academy and Isabrand at his boarding school?

"Kaisma," I whisper, the pale flame growing in my hand. I hold the note over it, but cannot bring myself to drop it in. I want to know what she has to say for herself or how she'll justify her actions. I let the flame flicker out then unfold the piece of paper. Smoothing out the creases, I begin to read.

Dear Mallory,

How to begin to put into words a feeling with no certainty. But already I'm starting with a lie. I was certain, when I sent your brother away, that it was in your best interest. I see a darkness in him matched only by his father. But not in you. You were always the best of us, my little angel.

What I am uncertain of is what I am about to do. I am about to take you from myself, give you away to ensure no harm befalls you should Thaddeus find us. To do so, I know I must strip myself from your memory, be as a vessel: a face in memory with no memories to fill it. If you open this box, you will know what I have done and I hope the memories restored to you will give you enough love to forgive me. Not just for this but for all I did. I did it all for you.

My last gift, my love, is something of immeasurable power, something the gods themselves fear. The very source of the magic used to take from you your memories. It will ensure my spell will withstand my death. When you open this box, it will release them once more into the world, to their seat in their rightful home, your heart and your head. A Vaerdiexes stone given to me by your father on our wedding day. I have worn it every day since and hope you will keep it with you, always.

I love you, more than I thought I could love anything or anyone, more than I love myself. I know you are capable of greatness, as Vaerdiexes and the prophecy have foretold.

Love, always

Your Mother.

I drop the note, but gravity does not perceive it as having the weight it does to me. It flutters to the ground slowly, coming to a silent stop at my feet.

Forgive her? As if it is possible after all she has done.

Treading across the note, I return to the vanity. I take the stone and turn it in my hands. It feels cold, even after I clench it in my fist, but there's a trill of power coming off of it. I feel the sharp angles dig into my skin and know it could cut me so easily, if I just applied that last bit of pressure. But as with so many things, I fail to follow through. Instead, I clasp the choker around my neck. When I draw my hands back, the weight of the stone falls, resting on my throat. I despise my mother, but there's no question about it: I will carry this piece of her always because it is too dangerous to leave on its own. She has cursed me with another piece of her that I cannot leave behind.

Taking the Vaerdiexes sword, I attach the scabbard to a belt in the wardrobe that has been filled for me and strap it around my waist. I need to go find Kyle. Only he can tell me what to make of this. Snatching the note from the floor, I step out into our common room where Isabrand and Proserpina are speaking in hushed voices. Isabrand does a doubletake when he sees my ashen expression.

"You alright sis?" Isabrand asks, looking up.

He notices the worry on my face right away, but I know better than to tell him what I've found. Hearing about our mother would only upset him. Proserpina goes still in her seat, her eyes pinned on the necklace around my throat. Does she see it for what it is? She has seen the Vaerdiexes stones, so no doubt she recognises it, even after all this time. That's not the sort of thing someone forgets. But she doesn't betray me to my brother, remaining silent as I cross to Kyle's room. I rap on the door. It swings open to reveal Kyle, still in his pyjamas, his hair a curly mess.

"Mallory? What's up?" he yawns. He spots the sword on my waist and knows this isn't just a friendly visit.

"We need to talk," I urge. *Not here,* the look in my eyes says.

"Let me just change."

I wait outside while he gets ready, avoiding my brother's scrutinization. Finally, Kyle emerges, dressed in his jeans and sweater, despite the warmth of the day. We leave the apartment, heading outside. I wait until we've walked a few streets away before speaking.

"Kyle."

"I know what you're going to say. I'm sorry Mallory. You were right. I can't use what you did three years ago as an excuse not to trust you, because I do." I smile at him.

"That's not what I was going to say."

"Oh."

"But thank you. It means a lot."

"I'm just sorry I didn't own up to my wrongs right away. And then the Hirutere took us and we didn't get a chance to talk. I felt horrible. So, what's this about?"

I glance around before handing him the note. He slows, reading it once, then twice, before looking at me in bewilderment.

"Where'd you find this?"

"In that box she left me, the one that contained my memories."

"And that," he starts, nodding to the necklace. I place my hand to it. It's gone warm, pressed to my throat.

"This is it. I need to know more about it. What it does."

A couple passes us, eyeing our unusual attire and we go silent. I am still dressed in my gown from the party, not having thought to change. Pacing ahead, Kyle turns to me.

"Unsurprisingly, it's the memory stone. It's one of the four Vaerdiexes gave Illarion. It must have been passed down through the Thiel family tree in secret. It has the power to strip and hold memories, like a vessel. It can also entirely alter the memories of an individual. But its greatest power? It contains the entire memory of the universe, since its creation. Touch it and you can see whatever it is you want. If you have strength enough to channel those memories without going insane."

"I can see anything?"

"As far as I'm aware. I'm sure someone's found a way to obscure memory from it, but you could see how the universe was created if you wanted to," Kyle says and, if I'm not mistaken, I think he sounds jealous. Someone as inquisitive as him would love to get his hands on the stone. Where would I even begin using this newfound power?

"Honestly, the stone is the least of my concerns," he says.

"How so?"

"What concerns me is her mention of Vaerdiexes. Did you ever tell her about what happened when you died?"

"No," I say, "only you, Proserpina, and Isabrand know."

"Maybe she used a truth spell on you without you knowing?"

"I don't think so."

"Then the answer may be in this prophecy she refers to."

"Have you ever heard of it? A prophecy about dragoviks," I ask.

"No. But you said your mum met Diane in Miesarinda, right? Maybe this prophecy was documented in one of the Cadmus Codices and that's why she came to Miesarinda. She was looking for the prophecy," he says.

"Sorry, Cadmus? As in– "

"Aleia Cadmus," Proserpina interrupts. We both jump when she appears, clearly having trailed us using the Shigami scythe. She's overheard our entire conversation.

"Proserpina, what are you doing here?" I demand.

"You think you can just appear with a Vaerdiexes stone around your neck and I won't have questions?" she says, before her eyes brighten. "Hey! They're like friendship necklaces. Boop."

She touches the forever stone to the memory stone, elated as she does so.

"We're like best friends now."

"Um, sure," I reply. "Do you know anything about the stone?"

"Not much. It contains the memory of the universe, but it's not so simple as that. One cannot simply recall any moment, but requires a referent. Like, if you wanted to see the moment Isabrand took his first steps, you'd need to be near Isabrand. Or if you wanted to know how the first French toast was made, you'd need some French toast."

"Sure… So who's Aleia Cadmus?"

"My mother. Like you and me, she was blessed by Yima, though she was a far more powerful seer than either of us. She recorded each of her prophecies in what came to be known as the Cadmus Codices. Upon her death, the angeleru requisitioned them and they've been locked up in the Library Between ever since. They're in the most restricted section, known as the Vault."

"That's what I've heard too. Is there no way in?" Kyle asks.

"Magic won't work, it's protected by that. One misstep and the avikas on guard will trigger hallucinations that will lead you right into a waiting prison cell."

"Well, they're your mother's books, so surely they'll let you look at them?" Kyle suggests.

"When has the Hirutere let someone have something they wanted, just because that person has a right to it? Why do you think dragoviks are still on Earth?" Proserpina scoffs. I halt and the other two falter a few steps ahead of me.

"What is it?"

"I know how we're going to get in."

* * *

"You want me to help you break into the Vaults?"

Since we saw him, Killian has changed out of his uniform into a pair of black trousers and a green t-shirt. It suits him far better, bringing out the gold in his eyes and his tanned skin. His hair is damp from a shower and he's leaning against the doorframe of his front door, looking at us as if we've just suggested it's about time to assassinate the pope.

"Well would it really be breaking in? Don't you have that all access pass because of your dad?" I say hopefully.

He'll do it because he likes you. That's what Proserpina had whispered to me when Kyle couldn't hear. Suddenly I feel very guilty asking this of Killian. If he says yes, how am I to know he's not just getting himself into more trouble for me? He rubs his face, sighing into his hand, and mumbling under his breath.

"Fine. But only if you tell me why."

My heart skips a beat. Is this evidence that Proserpina is right about his feelings? Why do I feel so hopeful?

"We'll explain on the way," I promise.

Leaving the narrow building he shares with three other bellatoja, we trot down the street. We've already agreed between the three of us it's not safe to tell him about Vaerdiexes, so I start telling him the edited version of events. It's not that I don't trust him, it's just that this sort of information is extremely dangerous. It could easily get me locked up by the Hirutere and I don't think even Casey could save me.

"So, remember that box I was holding when you found me after Isabrand tried to kill me and I got my memories back, the one you brought for me?"

"My brother, my father, my sister," he says, alluding to how convoluted my statement is. "Yes."

"It was from my mother. I opened it after you left and found this note from her." His eyes widen and he looks down to the piece of paper in my hand that I'm offering him. "Read it, if you want."

"Absolutely not. That's private. Are you okay though?"

His face is coloured by concern, more than I deserve for what little grace I have shown him in exchange for his kindness. Proserpina's words float through my mind again. Damn her and her seer abilities.

"I'm fine. It's just, it mentioned this prophecy. About me. And Kyle and Proserpina thought it might be in the Cadmus Codices."

"You're asking me?"

"Well, I thought you might have read them?"

"Are you kidding? No one really knows what's in them, except for the five vyrium elected to read and track goings on for signs that one of the prophecies is about to occur."

"Vyrium?"

"They're the hyper intelligent faction of the angeleru. They intuit very well. My father's one of them, one of the council of five in fact." He sounds less proud and more wearied by the fact, as if he has been expected to live up to that all his life. "What I'm saying is, there's no way we can get through all the Codices to find out if there's a prophecy about dragoviks. There are at least a hundred, containing prophecies that may come true anywhere between the creation of the universe and the end of time. Each member of the council is responsible for twenty books."

"Dragovik prophecies are in books eighty-eight and eighty-nine," Proserpina intones.

"How do you know that?" Killian demands.

"My mum wrote them."

"Your mum is Aleia Cadmus?" he says, awe evident in his tone.

"Great so that's only two books we need to check," I say. "Think you can get us in and buy us enough time?"

He doesn't look away from Proserpina, just nods. One day someone really needs to write a book about this woman.

"Have you read them?" Kyle asks her. Both the boys fall back so they're standing either side of her, suddenly aware of the cornucopia of knowledge in our midst.

"Not all of them. She read them to me to help me sleep sometimes though. They were like poems. I actually wrote the last five out for her," she says proudly. "She was very ill by then and would foretell sugar gliders being the heralds of war." She frowns.

"Crazier things have happened," I sigh as we reach the library. I haven't been back since my arrest and the dirty looks I get from the librarians at the main desk tell me they haven't forgotten the disruption. Killian waves to the woman named Matilda, who was here during our visit with Alistair, and she beams back at him. "Another of your conquests?"

"Childhood friend," he says, looking away. Proserpina grabs me by the arm.

"Embarrassment over potential past flings? Seems a sign to me," she sings in my ear.

"It is not!" I hiss.

Killian looks to us, but I just smile back, hoping he hasn't heard anything.

We get into one of the overcrowded elevators and I wedge myself in next to Kyle, in front of Killian. He doesn't press any button, just waits, staring at the ceiling, as the elevator makes stops, letting people off. Once we're the last people left, he pulls out his metal card and slots it into a gap I had not noticed before. There's a low beep before the lights go out.

"You made it angry!" I say, turning around in the dark.

Hardly able to make out my own hands, let alone someone else, I bump into him. His arms go around me to keep me steady and I hold my breath. He doesn't let go until the lights come back on, green now, his hands dropping away just a second before the others can see us. Something about the smug look on Proserpina's face tells me she saw us even in the dark.

"It changes the light setting to go to the Vault," he explains, as the elevator begins its descent. "They're deep underground."

"Shame there's no music. I always like elevator music," Proserpina says after about five minutes. Still the doors don't open for another five. They glide apart, illuminating a three-foot radius, as if a halo, on the emerald green marble floor. Killian pulls back the grate over the door, coughing as he stirs the dust.

"When's the last time someone was down here?" I ask.

"The only time anyone is allowed down here is when a new member of the council is selected, so they can read the Codices."

"What if they need to refer back to one of them?"

"Vyrium have photographic memories. What they read once they retain."

We file out into the light but none of us walk forwards.

"Is there a light down here?" Kyle asks, squinting into the darkness.

"There are candles, but they only get lit when a member of the council is coming down," Killian sighs. "Can you do that fancy light thing?" he asks me.

"I'll do you one better."

Ignite.

Hundreds of small flames sputter into existence, flickering for a moment before they steady. Their shadows rise and fall against the black walls. Before us is a great hall, the floor a dark shade of green, the colour of a serpent. The front half of the room is empty, save for a large circular wooden table, with honey accents. The back of the room has several towering bookshelves, all full of identical massive tomes.

"Welcome to the Vault," Killian says, gesturing to the room. "Alongside the Cadmus Codices, it houses some of the greatest relics in possession of the Hirutere, including gods' weapons."

When he says this, I look at Proserpina. Her face has gone pale and there's a mist to her eyes. She sniffs, stepping forward. The other two understand as well, instantly. In this room is what is rightfully hers, her parents' greatest works, enshrined miles beneath the surface where no one will ever see them.

"I'd like to see them," she says.

Killian nods, placing a reassuring hand on her shoulder and guiding her through an arch made of black marble to the right. Kyle and I follow, and I cannot help but reach for his hand. My heart aches for Proserpina in this moment. In the adjoining room, there are three glass display cabinets. The one on the wall opposite us houses two weapons while the one to our left and right only have one each. That makes six if you count mine and Proserpina's. I wonder where the other seven are.

"They just keep them down here?" Proserpina murmurs.

"When a bellatoja comes to be in our ranks, they test them with each weapon to see if they'll pair," Killian explains.

"You didn't have any luck?" I ask. If there's anyone I would trust to wield one of these weapons, it would be him or Kyle.

"No thank goodness. They don't lend themselves to anonymity."

"You really don't like attention, do you?" I say.

"Not from the Hirutere, no."

No doubt, his father being the head of the library, he's had attention from the Hirutere all his life. He's had to live up to the expectations that such parental prestige demands of him.

"Wait, if your father is vyrium, how are you a bellatoja? Or is your mum a bellatoja too?"

"It doesn't work quite like that. Your angelic faction isn't like a genetic trait. No one's entirely sure why one faction's traits manifest and others don't. It seems to happen around the age of sixteen for everyone that they start showing signs of what faction they belong to. Though vyrium can present from an incredibly young age. Some council members have been found at age five even. And no, my mother isn't bellatoja. She's an ordinary angeleru, as most are. Not all of us are a member of a faction, but, when we are, it creates obligation," he says grimly.

Proserpina presses a hand to one of the cases.

"I remember the god who blessed this," she says, distracting us from our conversation.

I come up behind her and study the massive silver trident. Wound around the bottom of the shaft is a carving of a snake. It has a thick, painted blue body and a pale green underbelly. Protruding from its head are six great red spines on either side. A basilisk.

"This must be Alastor's," Kyle says.

"A fitting weapon for the god of water," Killian adds.

One by one, Proserpina takes the weapons in. There's a net, paired with a jambiya, a short, curved dagger. Vayna and Turoman. I remember Leo telling me about the two gods of chaos back at the Hadovachin temple. There's a massive, broad blade, the tip of which has five points. Kyeres. Lastly there are a pair of circles, with leather bound grips, and four protruding spikes. Ahiti. Another god of death.

Proserpina explains their powers and meaning one by one, the thought her father put into each one evident. Her face is an exquisite blend of pride and pain as she tells us. All the while she clutches at Shigami, as if it can somehow bring her father closer to her. I know that longing. I have carried it as an anvil in my heart since Inerea's death. I take her hand and she smiles at me.

"I haven't seen them since my father's death," she breathes shakily. "After Thrabr attacked, I never returned to our home."

"There are places we can't go back to," I say, as if it is some comfort to know what she experiences is not singular.

"Some people too."

"We find new ones."

She takes my hand, her eyes watery with grief. We walk back out into the main hall, surveying the books. The boys follow, careful not to say anything.

"Are they in order?" she asks Killian.

"Yeah, eighty-eight and eighty-nine should be over here," he says, leading the way. He pulls from the shelf, one by one because they are both immense, two dark leather-bound books. The base of each spine is marked with golden numbers. He hands one to me and the other to Kyle. "I'll stand guard."

We nod, sitting on the floor and cracking the groaning books open. They're covered in a thick layer of dust, which swirls up into the air when we open them. Coughing, Kyle wafts his hand through the air in front of him to clear it.

"Don't send it my way!" I exclaim.

"Sorry."

Hours go by and we only make it through half of each book. By now, night will be falling. But the candles flicker on, unmelting, imbued with my magic. I look up at Kyle, but he shakes his head. Still no luck. My shoulders slump forward and I rub my eyes.

Suddenly, a ping emits from the elevator. Looking around frantically, I catch Killian's eyes. He holds a finger to his mouth and disappears around the corner of the bookshelf. I hear footsteps.

"Killian?" a man's voice asks, hushed but strong.

"Dad?"

My body tenses and I peek between the space left by the two books on the shelf. Kyle continues to read. I can make out a tall man, almost as tall as Killian, dressed in a long black robe. He's holding a lantern, clearly having anticipated the utter darkness that greeted us.

"What are you doing here?" he asks.

"I, well, um."

His father's mouth sets in a grim line and I prepare myself for the oncoming admonishment.

"You came here about the prophecy."

Kyle's head darts up, his eyes wide. He points urgently at his book, but I wave at him to stop. How does Killian's father know about the prophecy? Killian's face sets into an equally mirthless look.

"Yes."

His father sighs, setting the lantern down on the table. He puts a hand on either of his son's shoulders.

"It's because of her, isn't it? That's what's got you thinking about it."

"How could I not? I just, I had to read it again."

I frown. It's evident now they're talking about something else, but what prophecy could he mean?

"Son, as long as I am the one in whose charge those books remain, no one will ever know. Now let's leave, before anyone starts to wonder why we're down here."

Killian doesn't look back over his shoulder as they get into the elevator, shutting the grate behind them. It begins to rise and they soon disappear from sight.

"What was that about?" I ask Kyle.

"Never mind that. I think I found it," Kyle says. Proserpina takes the book from him and reads over the page.

"That looks like it," she agrees. Before either Kyle or I can protest, she rips the page from the book.

"You just desecrated a four thousand year old book!" Kyle exclaims.

"And on that note, let's get out of here."

Part VI

Chapter XXVII.

Carrying the stolen prophecy through the street feels akin to playing the trumpet while on fire: someone's sure to notice. I feel as though every person might suddenly realise what we've done and call out to have us arrested for stealing from the Vaults. Of course, no one does. The slip of paper goes unnoticed in Kyle's pocket. The day has grown tired, and people are heading home to prepare for the festival. When we get back to the apartment, Isabrand is no longer on the sofa. I'm grateful not to find him there. I'm not yet ready to bring anyone else into the mix.

We slip into my room and lock the door before arranging ourselves on the bed. Kyle passes it to me to read first as I'm the only one who has yet to. The paper is thick and dried out, worn, as it is, by years. I being to read.

And when the first falls from favour,
of two will be chosen their ruler.
Sister, brother, one's fire the other's,
born again from ashes of death.

The god of fire will call upon his emissary
and she will be divine of body and mind,
all fire, he all ice, the first mortal being
blessed by not one but two gods.

Beneath her shall fall the infrastructure of old,
those who oppose the rise of the fallen ones.
Much will be lost, much will be shed,
blood of the innocent most of all.

The dominoes had been set long ago
knocked down by a power that rises
all to reclaim the throne of a lost king.

"Don't you love how these things are always in riddles?" I sigh. Kyle shushes me, taking the paper and reading it again.

"This has to be it, right? The throne of the lost king, that's got to be Illarion," Kyle says when he's done.

"I don't know," I answer. "That bit fits, sure. What about the rest of it? We still had half a book to go through each. There could have been something else."

"I don't know, I agree with Kyle," Proserpina interjects. "There's something in it. I liked this one when I was little. I liked any of my mum's prophecies that were about the gods or queens."

"What else did she write about?" I ask, as Kyle bites his nail and leans closer to the paper, as if to permeate it.

"Sugar gliders mostly."

"I'm surprised the fauna of Sundalev would be so similar to that of Earth," I murmur. "Are sugar gliders common?"

"I think it was the first line that tipped me off," he interrupts, still scanning the page. "When the first falls from favour. That's got to be– "

"Thaddeus," I finish for him, and he nods.

"Thaddeus was chosen by Vaerdiexes, or so he claimed. But when he was imprisoned and effectively failed Vaerdiexes, the latter abandoned him."

I bite my lip. It does fit with what I have seen of Thaddeus' past. Now more convinced that this is what we're looking for, I take the paper from Kyle and read it through once more, looking for clues.

"Sister, brother, one's fire the other's, born again from ashes of death. That must be me and Isabrand."

"From the first bit it would seem obvious, but what does the second part mean?"

"When my mother resurrected me, the spell she used transferred Isabrand's fire to me to give me life."

"So, it could have been Isabrand? The ruler of Dragovicia," Kyle asks. The idea doesn't seem to sit well with him.

"I don't know. It suggests he was an option, but then refers to the emissary as a she. I think it was always meant to be me. Vaerdiexes called me his emissary while I was dead," I explain. "So, it seems even a god's decisions are subject to prophecy."

"Mother said that once. She told me that fate is the god of gods, superior even to Pritovis in its divinity."

I half expect to hear a clap of thunder when she says this blasphemous comment. But the gods, it seems, are not interested in our doings today, letting it slide for the time being.

"Then there's the matter of divine, body and mind," Kyle starts. "You're blessed with Vaerdiexes' power, you channelled it when you fought Elias. But Yima also blessed your mind with the power of visions when she let you drink the water from her garden."

"And I suppose the rest is simple enough. In order to return to Sundalev we'll have to fight the war against the jaeitsi. Maybe once we've helped the Hirutere win that war, they'll allow us through the portal," I say hopefully.

"No, I don't think so," Proserpina interjects. "Beneath her shall fall the infrastructure of old. It's very specific. Something established will have to come to an end for you to rise to power. The jaeitsi are a new force."

Kyle stills. He scans the last few lines again.

"Oh. *Oh.*"

"What?"

"I knew I recognised this bit. *A power that rises.* Do you remember what Illarion said about the Onyevaras and Hirutere when we met him? 'In time, they will fall for what they've done. Not naturally of course. They will be torn down by a power that rises even now.' He was talking about you, Mallory."

I blink, thinking back to our conversation with Illarion. How does he remember these things? My face darkens.

"You're saying I have to wage war on the Onyevaras and the Hirutere," I whisper, afraid someone will overhear. The other two exchange a glance, before looking at me nervously.

"I think so."

I take the paper from Kyle, my hands shaking. *Much will be lost, much will be shed, blood of the innocent most of all.* How many will die for this cause, a cause executed due to a child's desperate promise?

"But I-I-I can't," I stutter, shaking my head and dropping the paper as though it burns my hands. I begin to climb off the bed.

"Mallory, I don't think you have a choice. You made a promise to a god. Besides, what's written in the Cadmus Codices will come to pass," Kyle says, putting his hand on my shoulder. I brush it off.

"I was a child! He took advantage of my predicament and now

I have to surrender my moral compass, become evil so we can live somewhere our people haven't been in millennia? People will die so that dragoviks can go to Dragovicia. How many of the dragoviks even care anymore?"

"Enough of them for the Vernis Lanin to have been a serious threat. And, Mallory, you are not evil. Fulfilling your destiny does not make you so."

"Doesn't it? Thaddeus has fulfilled his, one fallen from favour, and is he not evil? Destiny can make villains of us just as easily as it makes heroes."

"'It is not wise to assume this rising power is malevolent and must be stopped. You must let it run its course.' Do you remember Illarion said that, too?'"

"Of course he did. We're his people. I bet he would love to see a dragovik on the throne of Dragovicia. Besides, how am I supposed to do this? I don't have an army and I don't know how to wage war."

Kyle is uncertain of how to respond, both these things being true. Who would follow me into a battle I myself don't have faith in? Proserpina clears her throat, drawing our attention to her.

"I have seen many battles fought in my time. I would be honoured to serve as your advisor. As for an army, the Vernis Lanin were willing to follow Thaddeus, and he was quite insane. They would undoubtedly rally once more to your call."

"I don't want Thaddeus' army. They were needlessly violent. They made a puppet out of him. If I must do this, I'll do it on my terms, as myself."

They both nod in agreement. I begin to pace the room, before striding out on the balcony and staring out at the sorbet sky. Already, somewhere out there, Casey is preparing for another festival. All our friends are getting dressed, excited for another well-deserved night of relaxation. And here we are plotting the fall of everything they are putting their faith in. I turn back to Kyle and Proserpina.

"So, my mother knew, then, what I was to be. She had read the prophecy," I sigh.

"It seems so."

What does that mean? Is that why she loved me, because of

the power I could have afforded her? I wouldn't put it past her, not with all she has done. Perhaps she had plans for how the prophecy would come to be, but those are lost now. I'm not sure how to proceed. How do I go from one person to the downfall of an entire city?

"Vaerdiexes told me that, when the time comes, he would tell me what to do. There's no need for us to act or make plans until then. In the meantime, promise me you won't tell anyone," I plead.

"You're my queen, I'll do as you command," Proserpina agrees, bowing her head.

I turn to Kyle, expecting the scepticism and fear I saw the first day I told him about all of this in his family's house. Instead, I am greeted only by certainty and assurance.

"No one knows until you give the order," he says, walking out on the balcony and taking my hands in his own. This time, I let him hold me. "I will do everything in my power to keep you safe Mallory. You're my best friend and it seems you are now also my queen."

That shift I had felt between us when I told him about my destiny comes again, a widening fissure between us. I will not let this cost me him or anyone else I love.

It will cost you whatever price I demand.

This time, when I hear Vaerdiexes' voice, it is completely devoid of warmth. Despite the muggy spring air, I shiver.

Chapter XXVIII.

The party is already going strong as we make our way up the street to the agora. It's even louder than the night before, almost filling the whole city with music and laughter. I have managed to persuade Proserpina to change from her dress into something a little more festive. She prances ahead of us, dressed in a pale pink, shimmering gown. While hesitant to leave her dress behind at first, she's taken to the new one quite well. I won't be surprised if she wears it for the next four thousand years.

I have something of the war within me already in my choice of dress. A metal bodice engraved with flowers sits atop a blooming dusty blue tulle skirt. My shoulders and throat are protected by overlapping metal plates, strung to the top of the bodice by silver chains. The choker I had found in Regan's box just peeks out over the top of the collar. It is safer, I think, to keep it hidden, lest anyone recognises it. The skirt splits from the ground to the top of my thigh, opening with every stride to bathe my pale leg in moonlight.

"There you guys are. Where have you been all day?" Aaron asks, passing us each a glass of a pale pink liquid. Little bubbles rush up to the surface, breaking across it. I had all but completely forgot about him and last night in the wake of today's discoveries.

"As if you were awake to notice," Robyn says.

She looks beautiful in a simple green dress, her hair braided down her back and a gold circlet on her head. Aaron winks at me when she says this, but I look away. Whatever last night was, it was a one time thing. I'm not interested in revisiting it in memory or in side glances exchanged over drinks. No matter how good.

"We were just exploring the city," Kyle replies.

Luckily, he's so used to Aaron's flirty ways that he doesn't think anything of the wink. Robyn, however, is looking back and forth between us. I wonder if she overheard my shouting match with Leo this morning. If she had, no doubt she'd be much angrier than she is right now. Well, this is shaping up to be an awkward evening all around. I turn to Proserpina, taking her by the hand.

"Let's dance!" I call over the music.

I draw her away from the others into the thick of the crowd. We find a place nestled close to the food tables for easy snack access.

Snackcess, I whisper to Proserpina, but she doesn't get it. Back when I was with Lena and Wes, my puns were a constant source of amusement veiled by disgust. Now, when I close my eyes and dance, I can almost imagine I am with them again. We sway for an indeterminant amount of time, getting more drinks throughout, before the crowd begins to part. Through the opening, I spot Casey being led by a team of bellatoja guards through the throng. She waves demurely at people, who cheer and raise their glasses to her. She spots us and taps one of the guards, whispering something to him. He nods and they approach us.

"Casey! I wondered if you'd ever come down off that pedestal to see us again," I laugh, pulling her into a hug.

"I can't forget the one who put me on it. The past day has been so crazy I wondered when I'd see you two. They've had me training all day. I'm exhausted," she sighs, and I see signs of sleep-deprivation beneath her eyes. They've done their best to hide it, but they've clearly been running her ragged. I'll need to have a word with someone about how they're taking care of her.

"How about this: tomorrow morning I'll come to your apartment and check on you. Make sure they're treating you right," I say.

"Sounds perfect," she replies, before the guard murmurs something in her ear. "I've got to get going. More appearances to make."

We wave her off and the crowd closes around her.

"That will be you one day," Proserpina says, "revered."

"Please don't say that. I would never want to be treated like some sacred object, brought out at parties and in wartime to bolster people's spirits."

"No? Would you be the sort of queen helping the peasants plant potatoes?"

I laugh.

"Exactly. I'll be planting the fields while delegating to my esteemed advisor, the Lady Proserpina Cadmus."

Proserpina's eyes brighten at the prospect. She curtsies, before glancing over my shoulder.

"We have a visitor," she says, "or, rather, you do."

I turn around, my dress' hem sweeping across the cobblestone. There, behind me, is Killian. He's in a dark blue quilted jacket and black trousers. He's cut his hair since I saw him earlier today. I grin, walking over to him. Reaching up, I tousle his hair.

"I like it," I say.

"Yeah? Glad to hear it," he replies, grinning back at me. "Needless to say, you're a vision."

I study the man in front of me, of wilderness eyes and kind smiles, to whom my life is owed time and time over. I offer him my hand.

"Dance with me?"

He looks a little taken aback by my forwardness, but doesn't hesitate in taking up my proffered hand. Drawing me to him, he ropes an arm around my waist and we begin to sway.

"So, how much have you drunk tonight then?" he teases.

"Nothing. I'm giving up alcohol and the regrettable decisions it engenders."

"That seems wise."

We don't say anything more, continuing to dance until the song changes to something more fast paced. Our bodies don't yield to its rhythm, continuing to move slowly and at our own pace. I look up and see he's peering down at me. Has he always been this tall?

"Thanks for covering for us at the library," I say.

"Don't mention it."

"Dare I ask what your father was talking about? What prophecy?"

"You keep your secrets, I'll keep mine," he answers. Again, the song changes, but I realise we've gone still. I trust him, utterly. The spot where he touches my waist radiates warmth, awakening a fire in me I have been trying to subdue for so long. Looking into his eyes now, it seems an impossible feat.

"You show me yours I'll show you mine," I reply. He sucks in his cheeks, mulling over my proposition. Finally, he pulls on the hand he's still holding, taking me from the crowd back down a side street. I expect him to stop, but he keeps going, plunging deeper into the city. "Where are you taking me?"

"I can't explain, not here," he says.

We go further from the party, until the streets are empty, save for the green wrought iron lamp posts. Finally, he stops, glancing around nervously. Back at the party it had seemed more a playful proposition, but the look on his face makes me worried. Is he in danger from whatever this prophecy is?

"What's so bad we had to go all the way over here to discuss it?" I ask. He looks at me, a pained expression on his face.

"You really do look beautiful, you know that?"

"That's what you can't say in front of people?" I tease, my face flushing with pleasure.

"No that's not it. I just also wanted to tell you that. Before the other bit."

"Okay see now I'm worried you've complimented me in preparation for a vicious round of insults."

"I couldn't," he starts, but whatever he wants to say cannot be communicated through words.

He closes the gap between us, bending over me to kiss me. I feel his arms wrap around my waist, one hand running up the length of my back to knot itself in my hair. He stops, moaning against my lips and it takes me a moment to realise he's whispering my name, over and over, his lips tracing it like an invocation against mine. I press myself to him again. He has broken the barrier I have been using to keep back my growing feelings. I had once believed it impossible for someone who hadn't gone to the Academy to understand me. But I don't think that's true anymore. Proserpina and Isabrand are proof that shared experiences are not necessary when there is an innate bond between two people. Killian is the light Dominic believes we both deserve, the light I crave. He draws back, his breaths shaky.

"That was," he starts, but fails to find the words.

"Right," I finish, looking up into his eyes. They yield nothing. "Wasn't it?"

My heart pounds. Why does he look so unhappy? It's as if he got what he wanted, only to realise he doesn't want it anymore. Will he push me away, deeming me not enough? But he doesn't stir, lost as he is in his thoughts, his hand still on my waist.

"Fuck," he murmurs, running a hand through his hair. "Fuck."

He buries his face in the space between my neck and my shoulder, pressing a kiss to my skin. I wonder now why hate is spoken of in terms of fire, when what I feel for Killian burns so much stronger than my loathing for Diane or Regan. His hands tighten on my waist and I feel his laboured breaths, hot on my throat.

"What's wrong?"

"I wasn't supposed to do that," he says, taking a step back before changing his mind. He draws me to him by the shoulders, kissing me urgently. Our noses brush against one another's as he steps away again. "Or that."

"What were you supposed to do?" I ask, freezing. Has someone ordered him to get close to me? Have the Hirutere been setting me up this whole time? No. Killian wouldn't do that to me.

"I just meant," he starts, groaning. "I shouldn't be kissing you."

"Why not?"

He studies me and I see an explanation trying to unravel itself from his tongue. Try as he might, it doesn't come freely. Finally, he makes what he can of it.

"Because you're you, I'm me, we can't, we can't do this."

"Because I'm a dragovik?" I'm surprised by the hostility my voice contains. Killian never seemed the discriminatory type, choosing me freely over his own every time he helped me.

"Not like that," he says, reading my expression. "But in a way yes. Besides I told you, I'm not capable of relationships."

"Then why kiss me?" I demand, inordinately frustrated. "Just spit out what it is you want or don't want."

"I want you, but I can't be with you," he answers, as if it's any explanation. He groans in exasperation; whether it's at me, himself, or the situation I cannot tell.

"That's not an answer."

"I don't know how to answer, Mallory. How do you tell the person you want most that the universe has made it impossible for you to be together?"

"Has it? I didn't notice anything spontaneously combust when we kissed." The only thing at risk of that was my heart.

"You're the hero Mallory. You're always going to be the hero. And not just of your own story, of pretty much everyone's. It's amazing, an absolutely remarkable gift of yours, that you can help everyone. But what does that leave for the rest of us? I can't be the sidekick or the villain. I just can't."

The moon seems a gaping hole, a bruise, meant to illuminate the pain of this moment. If only it would swallow me whole. I stare at Killian in disbelief.

"I didn't ask you to be. You kissed me."

"But that's the thing about being around you. You're the hero whether someone wants you to be or not. You're the one who saved Kyle, Casey, Dominic. You're the one who brought Casey here to help the Hirutere. You're the one who thought of how to get us out of custody. You're the one thing that unites us. Don't you see, all these people who have fought by your side, they'd do anything just to brush against your greatness? I don't want to just be greatness' sidekick; I have to be my own person."

I nod, my lips set in a firm line, but I don't feel as though I'm going to cry. At this point, my heart is used to the sting of rejection. I don't need his acceptance to validate me, but I wonder why he says such hurtful things just after holding onto me like I was his only lifeline.

"Fine. What did you want to tell me?"

"Mallory," he pleads.

"No don't Mallory me. You just kissed me and then took an emotional shit on me. Don't you fucking dare demand I be okay right now."

He falls silent, his head bowed to the ground.

"What did you want to tell me?" I demand again. "Either spit it out or go back to the party."

I know I am being cruel, but I don't have it in me to try and wrap my head around what has just transpired. It's easier to bare my teeth than my heart. He looks down at me and I wonder if that is all he has ever been doing. Do I seem so inferior to him, something to be toyed with? Was that why he saved me all those times, getting some perverse kick out of saving the person he deems 'the hero'?

"It's nothing," he sighs, his shoulders slackening. "I suppose the same goes for whatever you were going to tell me too?"

"Yup."

"You won't tell me if you found anything in the library?"

"Why should I? I can handle it myself. I'm the hero after all," I reply bitterly. I bite the inside of my cheeks, in need of a distraction.

"Right. Of course," he whispers. "I'll just go then."

He turns, his shoulders squared almost up to his ears, and walks back the way we came. Now the tears come, but they're not for the loss of him. Is this the beginning of the price I must pay for my promise? If being perceived as a hero costs me my friends, what will being a queen cost? Do I have the strength to pay up or will I fall like Thaddeus? Wiping tears from my eyes, I turn to head back to the apartment. I'm in no mood for a party. Instead, I come face to face with a deabrueon.

Chapter XXIX.

"Shit," I hiss, dodging just in time as its tail, which has a mace-like protrusion at its end, comes crashing down. It cracks the stone of the pavement where it strikes. I spring to my feet and take the deabrueon in. It's not like any kind I've seen before. The creature is like a scorpion in appearance, with two massive pincers. Scuttling forwards, it snatches at me with one, but I leap back. Damn me, leaving my weapon back at the apartment. I thought we'd be safe in Miesarinda, but apparently not.

I hear the creak of one of the lamps as I draw the metal towards us. The light begins to flicker before the bulb shatters. Like a lashing whip, the lamppost comes down, thwacking the creature against its hard exoskeleton. It hisses, pausing for a moment. I take the opportunity to spiral the lamppost around it, drawing it tighter and tighter until the creature bursts. Hot, brown blood gushes into the street, sloshing the hem of my dress. Where on Earth did the thing come from? I hadn't even heard it approach.

I hear the screams then. Back the way Killian and I had come, terror rises in the voices of the many. Without a second thought for the corpse behind me, I lift the hem of my dress and start to run. The streets disappear beneath my feet. I've hiked my dress up around my knees, but I know it's only a hindrance. If only I had Proserpina's power to change outfits. The cacophony grows louder as I near the agora. People are streaming through the streets, running as fast as they can to get away from whatever it is that has reared its ugly head. Bursting into the agora, I see it with my own eyes.

An army of deabrueon, storming in from one side of the agora, quickly overwhelming the few guards that are on duty. Casey and her guards are nowhere to be seen, thank goodness. I can't see any of my other friends either. Finally, I spot, amidst the chaos of battle, the flash of Proserpina's scythe. I rush to her just as she fells another of the scorpion-like beasts. She leaps atop its corpse to survey what is to come.

"What happened?" I demand, taking a sword from a fallen bellatoja.

"They came from nowhere," she answers, disappearing only to

reappear astride a graemar's back. She crushes its windpipe with her scythe's handle until its knees buckle and it falls to the ground. Slipping off, she races back to me. "They took out the guards first and no one else was armed. They just started killing people after that, but it's a coordinated effort, clearly."

"It's the jaeitsi."

"Yes."

"Where are the others?"

"I don't know," she pants, shaking her head.

"I need to go get my sword," I say, wishing I could teleport it here. Damn me for not bringing it with me. I had felt so at ease in Miesarinda, I had seen no need for it tonight. Proserpina nods.

"I'll escort you."

She starts to leave, but I don't follow. I turn back to the onslaught of deabrueon and unleash a sheet of magic, sharp as knives, that slices through the bodies of the oncoming wave. But the next one keeps coming, crawling over the bodies of the deceased. I pray to Vaerdiexes, begging him to aid me, but no answer comes. Is this my punishment for questioning him earlier?

Proserpina and I dash through the streets, struggling to stay together amongst the crowd. We're jostled from side to side. There's a whoosh through the air and, suddenly, people halt, before skittering back. There's a great shift as they begin to hurry back the way they came. Proserpina and I look at each other. Whatever has them running towards the deabrueon can't be good.

"It's nice to see you again, Mallory," a voice calls over the tumult.

I look around and see what they're running from. Clara. Her grey wings are outstretched, having just flown in. I raise the bellatoja's sword, but Proserpina steps between us, armed with her scythe.

"Go, I'll take care of her."

"But– "

"I'll fare better with Shigami's scythe than you will with an ordinary sword. Besides, it's my duty to defend my queen."

I nod and take the side street. I hear the clash of steel on steel and know the battle has begun. Rounding the corner, my body collides with something warm and soft. Arms wrap around me and, for a moment, I think it must be Kyle or Killian. A relief. Or at least it should be. Then I recognise that smell. Like ash and death. I struggle, but the arms hold me fast, knocking my sword to the ground.

"Let me go," I order.

"But I've only just got you back," Thaddeus murmurs, his breath hot in my ear.

He presses his body to mine and for a moment I'm paralysed, torn between the memory of John and that of Thaddeus. He buries his face in my hair, taking a deep breath before murmuring my name over and over again. I scrunch my eyes shut. This isn't happening. I am not in the arms of my former lover. And yet I am. I can smell him and feel him as he plants a kiss on my neck.

I stomp on his foot and he stumbles away. Spinning around, I roundhouse kick him in the abdomen, sending him spilling across the ground. He drops his sword. When I lunge for him again, he catches me, flipping me onto my back. The stone is cold against my skin. He pins me down, wrestling my struggling arms.

"Now, now, old lover. You're breathtaking tonight," he says.

"Get off," I hiss, snapping at his wrists.

"Why would I do that? It's been so long. Let's catch up."

He's plucked from atop me by a gust of wind that I conjure, which blows him back a few feet.

"No time and not interested."

He tries to scramble to his feet, but I keep the pressure of the wind up to hold him down. Ripping a strip of fabric from my dress, I hit him over the head as hard as I can. He falls back on the street, unconscious. I drag him over to the nearest lamppost and pull his arms around it, tying the fabric tightly around his wrists. With one hand on the knot, I command it to be unbreakable by him. There will be time to deal with him later.

When I emerge onto the next street, there is no longer one cohesive crowd. It has fractured into groups, running every way imaginable. There is danger on every side. Sprinting, I spot, amongst the fray, Killian. He ushers a group of people forward, coming between them and a deabrueon. He's managed to get his hands on a weapon too. He catches the creature's attention before luring it away from the people he's helping escape. Then, with one swift move, he runs the creature through its soft underbelly. It howls as he draws the blade back out. Looking around, he spies me. Relief sweeps his face and he dashes towards me.

"Thank heavens you're alright," he pants. His shirt is black with blood and I am quick to rush to his side, our altercation already forgotten. My hands rest on his chest, feeling the dampness of the blood and searching for the wounds so I might heal them. He shakes his head. "It's not mine. You should stay with me."

"I need to get back to the apartment," I say. A pack of graemar crashes down the street, smashing windows and grabbing at everyone they can. "You have to help them."

He looks reluctant to leave me, but the sight of his people in peril is enough to drive him from my side once more. He charges one of the graemar, the others closing in on him, and I fear I've left him to his death. I uproot one of the lampposts and drive it through one of the beasts like a javelin.

"We've got him covered little sis."

"Isabrand!" I fling, my arms around my brother's neck. Spotting Aaron over his shoulder, I reach out and squeeze his hand.

"Have you seen Proserpina?" Isabrand asks.

"She's fighting one of the jaeitsi, Clara," I tell him. He doesn't look too worried, just draws the sword he has managed to come by.

"Girl can handle herself," he says gruffly, a look of pride on his face. He and Aaron dart forward to Killian's aid.

I turn right down an alley and emerge onto our street. I am almost back to the apartment when the air is stirred up around me. Spinning around, all I see is a single grey feather floating down from the sky. Then, I am plucked from the streets and Elias' great wings beat, drawing us into the night air.

"No magic, no sword to protect you. Just us," Elias hisses in my ear, digging his nails into the skin of my arms. I can't squirm now, we're already too high up. If I fall, there's no chance of surviving.

"What have you done?" I ask, staring down at the quickly disappearing ground. We've ascended to halfway up the apartment building. Where is he taking me?

"We've come for the caeletai umea. Can't have you keeping one of those around, can we? Speaking of which, can't be having you around either."

Suddenly I'm plummeting back towards the earth. I flail, screaming as I fall. The air roars beneath the sound of wings, a sound far louder than Elias'. I crash into a slick surface, which I quickly begin to slide down. Snatching at it, I try to get a hold before I fall. My hands finally dig into the meat of the whatever it is and I manage to hoist myself up and sit astride the thing. Looking around, I see glistening white scales, polished as ivory, beneath me. A mighty roar goes up into the night as the beast rears its head and comes to a skittering stop on the ground. Wings outstretched, it grabs a nearby lamppost with its massive bone like claw, as if it does not know how else to stop itself. The dragon's scaly neck curves itself like a thick rope, and I am greeted by its toothy mouth and ice blue eyes.

"Isabrand?"

The dragon growls again, before turning its eyes to Elias. What has my brother cost himself by transforming, here in the Hirutere's city of all places? Despite the deabrueon's attack, I have failed to notice any other massive airborne reptiles. They will not allow his ready breaking of the accords to go unchecked.

Suddenly, Isabrand is galloping forward. I lean close to his spine, clutching tightly to keep my grip. Pushing the bulk of his weight into his hind legs, he launches himself into the sky. His wings beat at an uneven rhythm, as he gets the hang of being in his new body. He bats at Elias, who is but a fly compared to him, but the jaeitsi dodges. Even from this distance I can see the fear on his face. He never expected the dragoviks to break the accords.

"Isabrand, I need my sword, then we have to get to Casey!" I cry, hoping he can hear me over the din of his wings beating a hurricane into the air.

With a mighty bellow, Isabrand takes another swipe at Elias. I see the burst of feathers where his talon makes contact with Elias' wing. The man plummets from the sky, every bit the fallen angeleru he is said to be. Isabrand groans, the effort of sustaining hovering too much. With little grace and much property destruction to the nearby shops, he lands. I watch as he rears on his hind legs, nodding towards the apartment building and turning around to stand guard. Elias lies motionless in the street.

Taking the stairs two at a time, I dart up to our apartment. The lights are out. It seems no one has returned yet and I can only hope they are all okay. I let out a sigh of relief when I spy my sword on the vanity where I left it. I was worried Elias and his deabrueon might have got to it first. I attach the sword to a belt and buckle it around my waist.

Back outside, Isabrand is batting a few deabrueon around. He tosses them in the air with his claw, then swats them with his arrowhead tail, knocking them clear from sight. I can only imagine how amusing he finds this. Spotting me, he lowers his body to the ground, his neck dipping low to allow me to climb on his back. I make myself as comfortable as possible, safe between his wings.

"Go to the Hirutere's headquarters. That's where they'll be keeping Casey. She's why the jaeitsi are here," I say.

He takes a running start before soaring upwards over the city. The people and the deabrueon become indistinguishable calligraphic marks in the streets as we rise higher. I survey the city, but it isn't until I can see over the city wall that my heart drops. Another army of deabrueon is on its way. Even if we manage to survive this first wave, there's no way we'll survive that one. And this, the power of only three jaeitsi. How will we possibly fend off all four of them?

Suddenly, I hear a tremendous boom from ahead and, turning, watch in horror as the glass rotunda shatters. Huge shards of pink glass fall to the ground, a mushroom cloud of dust rising around it.

"Shit."

We descend a couple streets over from the devastation. Coughing, I shelter my face behind my arm, but can make nothing out through the thick smog. I twirl a finger clockwise once and a small gust of wind blooms, spinning. It quickly grows before I hurl it forwards, clearing most of the dust around us. It sends a mighty gust, blowing my hair and dress. When at last the streets are clear, what I see makes me gag.

Bodies, bits of bodies, littered everywhere. Just as they had been at the Academy. They're scattered all over the place. The earth has a mighty fissure running through it where the blast went off. This is beyond the abilities of the jaeitsi, so how have they done it? Whoever took the building down is already gone, if they ever even came close. Likely a witch or several witches. I start to pick my way through the rubble in search of Casey, praying she is not among the dead.

But there's no time to find her. From across the newly formed clearing, I spot a wave of deabrueon coming in. I reach for my sword, but Isabrand lumbers in front of me and sucks in a deep breath, his chest swelling. I prepare myself for fire, for the reduction of all things to ash. But when he breathes out, a pale blue flame emits instead. There's a crackling sound as ice sets around the bodies of the deabrueon. The ones that have been lucky enough to evade his icy breath falter.

Isabrand does not attack immediately and he's clearly just as surprised by this development as I am.

She will be divine of body and mind, all fire, he all ice.

The prophecy comes back to me. This is the price of what he gave me the day I died. The result, a dragon unlike any other.

"I need to find Casey," I cry out to him, "but I think you can handle yourself."

He snorts, jets of mist coming from his nostrils. Turning back to the deabrueon, he charges, roaring out a cool fog on them. I turn back the other way.

"Casey!" I scream, stumbling amongst the bodies. She has to still be alive. I can't have failed her so completely. "Casey!"

"Mallory?"

A quiet voice reaches me from a nearby alley. I glance down it and, sure enough, cowering in a doorway, is Casey. I rush to her side, drawing her to me.

"Thank heavens, I was so worried. What happened?"

Her mouth opens then closes, a gaping wound of what she's seen. I can only imagine, if she was here for the explosion, that she has seen what I have.

"I can't do this. I can't save anyone," she whimpers, tears pricking her eyes. "I want to go home."

"Casey, look at me. I promise one day I am going to get you home. But we can't get there if we don't survive today."

"No," she whispers, shrinking back.

"I need your help, Casey. There's a whole second wave coming from the hills outside the city. We need you to fight this."

She doesn't answer this time, just coils her arms around a lamppost and hides her head. I stare down at her, uncertain of what to do. From behind us comes Isabrand's deafening roar, causing Casey to jump. I look behind me and watch as he decimates another swell of deabrueon. He smashes through the frozen ones with his tail, shattering them into glistening fragments. His power is great, but eventually they will overwhelm him. They'll overwhelm the entire city.

It would be so easy, to let it end like this. To not have to be the one to take the Hirutere and the Onyevaras down, but let the jaeitsi do it for me. Then I would only have the four of them to fight. But that is not the prophecy. The Hirutere's end does not come today and it will not come by the jaeitsi's hand. Suddenly, I have an idea.

"Come with me," I order, yanking Casey to her feet. She tries to fight back, but is no match for me. I pull her back towards the devastation of the collapsed building and she screams when she sees Isabrand, attempting to run back the way we came. "Don't worry, it's Isabrand."

She looks from me to the white dragon before her, disbelief colouring her features.

"No."

"We so don't have time for this right now," I mutter. "Isabrand, we've got to go."

With a final sweep of his tail, he takes out the last wave of deabrueon. Lowering himself to the ground, he waits patiently as we climb atop his back. I nestle Casey in front of me, wrapping my arms around her.

"This is going to work," I say, though her expression of incredulity matches my own. "We need to meet the second wave in the hills."

Once more into the sky, we cut like a sharp wind, rising into the inky black. Anyone could spot us from a mile away, but I'm hoping no one will think to look for us. Everyone's attention will be on the ground where the deabrueon are. Shutting my eyes, I attune my thoughts to Isabrand's.

Well, this is unpleasant, he thinks, my mind seeping into his.

Sorry, I needed to confer, I reply.

Sounds like you have a plan.

When we get to the army, I need you to fly low and drop me to the ground.

Are you nuts? There must be a thousand deabrueon out there at least. They'll rip you apart.

I'm counting on it being life threatening.

Mallory—

Resistance is futile. Get me there and I think I can stop this. Then make sure Casey is safe.

I pull back from his mind before he can argue more. I can sense his displeasure, but still he obeys, dipping down once we pass the city walls. The deabrueon have almost reached them, and there's a great din as the creatures howl and roar. They are all savagery, pure ferocity and no sense. It is only the jaeitsi's command that keeps them marching forwards. Above them, I see Elias hovering, somehow having survived Isabrand's attack. He grins at me, his eyes black in the dark. He thinks he's won.

Isabrand draws lower to the ground, shaking as we glide inches above it. I roll off his back, the landing undoubtedly bruising the shoulder I fall on. I groan, but am quick to spring to my feet. Already he has risen back into the sky, Casey safe with him. He soars forward, out past the deabrueon. The deabrueon draw nearer, howling with anticipation as they spot me. I'll be the first to fall beneath their claws.

What happens now?

His voice doesn't come to me as it has in past situations of peril. Instead, my mind is greeted only by silence. There is scarcely thirty feet between the oncoming army and me. They'll surely tear me to pieces.

Save me, I plead. But no god answers to such a simple plea. *Do you want me as a queen or not?*

The answer burns through my veins. I lift my hand and direct it towards the deabrueon. The answer is illuminated in the field in an instant, which roars to life with fire, consuming the army whole.

Yes.

I watch the deabrueon burn, a square mile of earth scorched to the bones. Vaerdiexes has once again upheld his end of the bargain, keeping me from death. I know now it is my turn and there is nothing I will be allowed to deny him.

Chapter XXX.

The enemy is already gone by the time we begin convening upon the library, but the bodies are still in the streets. The army has gathered itself by this time, too, but there is no one to fight. Just heaps of corpses to be moved and a burnt scar outside the city walls that may never heal itself to green.

I'm not sure how we know to go to the library, who decided it would be the new place to assemble with the Hirutere's headquarters blown up. But, when I return from outside the city walls, it is where everyone begins to head. I stagger, dizzy with the exhaustion of once again channelling a god's power, and on a scale such as I never have before. At first, I only see a few miserable people, trotting from the city limits, but, as we draw nearer the heart of Miesarinda, so thicker grow the crowds until we're an indistinguishable mass. There's something soothing about getting lost like that. Though my weakened body can hardly take all the jostling.

Outside the library are massive tents. Within, tables and makeshift beds are being set up for the wounded. I watch a man, aided by another, move slowly and shakily towards a bed on one leg. I see no one I recognise; there is no great white dragon out front. Isabrand and Casey should have been back by now. I just hope that the Hirutere hasn't captured him. As if they could when he's in that state. Hopefully he's transformed back into a human, his unidentifiable dragon form affording him anonymity. There's no reason anyone should know it was him.

I make my way into the library, which is densely packed. There's no space left on the rows of benches so I sink to the floor. I feel as if gravity wants to pull me deeper, yawn open the Earth and draw me down. I would let it, too. But every time I begin to close my eyes, a voice cries out from within me: *you cannot rest here.*

"Mallory."

I draw myself back from the edge of sleep and see Kyle's face swimming amongst the crowd. He kneels beside me and kisses my temple fiercely. I don't have the strength to return the small gesture of affection. He sits on the ground and rests my head on his shoulder. I fall asleep instantly.

Hands gently shake me back to consciousness, after a span of time too short to dream in. I grumble, pushing the hands away, but they persist. I open my eyes and see Kyle is rousing me. His lips are shaping out words, but I cannot make sense of them. His expression is one of wide-eyed panic. Behind him towers a tall figure. Killian. Crouching down, he scoops me up in his arms and carries me towards the back of the library. I see Kyle over his shoulder, following us. Bookshelves blur together until we finally reach a black door. Killian opens it.

It takes everything I have not to blink out of existence as he lays me down on a bed. The pillow is so soft beneath my head, the mattress yielding to my body. I want to tell him there are people who need it more, but speech is beyond my ability. He sits on the edge of my bed and runs his hand through my hair. It's all tangles and snarls. My eyelids flutter.

"Sleep," he urges me.

So, I do.

* * *

When I wake again, I feel much better. There is sensation in my limbs, where before there had only been a dull tingling. I manage to keep my eyes open, staring up at the black ceiling. I hear voices murmuring.

"This is her?"

"Yes."

"You don't think it would be wiser to stay away from her, given what we know?"

"I don't think that's a possibility."

They stop speaking when I turn my head. Killian is standing by a table, a man who I soon recognise as his father beside him. They turn to look at me and Killian approaches, kneeling beside the bed. His face looks gaunt with the shadows of exhaustion and battle. He is covered in grime and blood.

"You weren't out long," he assures me. I feel as though I've slept a lifetime.

"Where are we?" I ask, my voice hoarse.

"My father's office at the library. News of what you did travelled fast, though people haven't realised it was you yet. I thought you needed a place to rest."

I prop myself up on my hands and look around the room. It's surprisingly small for the head librarian's office, with just enough room for the three of us, the bed, and a desk. Killian's father smiles at me, though there are undertones of grimness in the gesture. I can't be surprised; we are at war after all.

"Thank you," I say to him.

"After what my son tells me you did, it should be me thanking you. Now, I believe they are gathering what remains of the Hirutere and the council of five, so if you'll excuse me."

He nods farewell and leaves the room. I fall back on my elbows, my body surprisingly forgiving of the sudden movement. I groan, closing my eyes for a second and letting my head loll back.

"Are you okay? Does something hurt?"

"Only my everything," I sigh, looking at Killian. His face is all concern, a worried brow and eyes that have thawed since our conversation at the party. "Where's Kyle?"

Killian swallows hard, looking down at his interwoven fingers.

"He is okay, isn't he?" He has to be, I only just saw him.

"Yes, it's just," he starts, scratching his head. "It's a subject best left for later."

I feel a chill come over me, though I don't press him. I'm too broken for bad news at present.

"Was it really you?" he asks, "who did that thing with the deabrueon army? Half the Library thinks it was a goddess, the other that it was Casey."

"But you knew it was me?"

"So, it was," he breathes, a look of awe overcoming him. "I knew from descriptions it wasn't Casey. How could anyone confuse you for someone else? Besides, fire isn't the magic of a caeletai umea. So, how did you do it? I've never heard of any dragovik with that kind of power."

I tell him then, though I'm beyond exhausted. Of the prophecy, of Vaerdiexes. I'm too tired to be the gatekeeper of my secrets anymore. He listens in silence, no interruptions. Finally, I finish and it's as if I've used up every last word in the English language. There are none left for me to speak.

"Are you going to tell the Hirutere?" I ask, after I'm done recounting my story.

"Mallory, I'd like to think you know by now that I would never turn you in. Besides, you saved the city."

I let out a harsh, derisive laugh and soon it overpowers me, rattling my entire body. Wiping tears of perverse amusement from my eyes, I turn to meet his curious gaze.

"I guess you were right," I say. "I really am the hero."

I don't mean it cruelly, but he flinches when I say it. He drops his head, staring at the ground.

"Mallory, please understand, I didn't mean it." Just then, the door opens. Killian's father re-enters, his face illuminated by a sense of foreboding. "What's the matter?"

"They want to see you. Both of you."

Killian doesn't ask why, nor do I. He helps me to my feet, an aid for which I am grateful, and we follow his father out the door. The bulk of my weight is on Killian, who has his arm wrapped around me. The library is even more crowded than before, if that's possible. We pick our way through the crowd, Killian holding me close to him so I don't get bumped into. People scarcely seem aware of where they're going, their faces vacant. Finally, we reach the elevators, but, instead of going down, his father presses the button for the topmost floor. Up we go and I feel as though I am rising on Isabrand's back once more, the library disappearing beneath us. Where is my brother?

The door slides open into a small lobby, which we cross. Through another set of doors, guarded by two weary looking bellatoja, there's a large square room. There's a big wooden conference table in the middle of it, around which sit four men and women dressed in the same black robe as Killian's father and five dressed in the green robes of the Hirutere. Algard is not amongst them. Is this all that remains of the Hirutere? I see Casey across the room, sitting in a large chair with a cup of tea being pressed into her hand by Proserpina. The latter sighs with relief when she sees me, beginning to cross the room. But Killian's father steps between us and there is no time to ask Casey where Isabrand is.

"Ronan," one of the men says, rising from the table to greet Killian's father. He nods to the two of us as well. "Is this the girl?"

"Yes," Ronan says, ushering us forward to sit down. Proserpina comes over, a mug of tea in her hand, but says nothing. She sits beside me, her hand resting over mine.

"You're Mallory Thiel?" the man asks.

"Yes," I croak, my throat still dried out as if by Vaerdiexes' fire itself.

"Master Ronan has told us what you did on the battlefield. The Hirutere are eternally indebted to you."

His words mean nothing. What's the promise of five people? Then again, I of all people should know the difference a promise can make, even that of a scared little girl. He turns back to the rest of the table. I recognise the old man who had slept through our trial. I find it oddly unsettling to see him as alert as he is.

"Our city is in shambles. Our government has been torn apart. May our brothers and sisters rest in peace."

Rest in pieces more like. I try not to snort, the absurdity of the morbid humour striking me. My head does not feel like my own anymore.

"It has been decided that, at this time, the council of five will join what remains of the Hirutere to form a council that will guide our people through this time of turmoil. We are fortunate that most of our army has survived this attack and we will be able to guard against future attacks from the jaeitsi. The question is, why did they attack? With only two of them they had to know they didn't have the power to defeat us, even if we were caught off-guard."

"Aside from their attack on the city hall? The Vaults were broken into it seems," Ronan says, clearing his throat. "The gods' weapons have been stolen, as well as some prized volumes, including volume eighty-nine of the Cadmus Codices."

I feel Proserpina perk up beside me. That's the one my prophecy was in. Did someone know or were they looking for something else? But there's something else more pressing right now. I clear my throat. The whole room looks to me, silent.

"I battled one of the jaeitsi," I say, "a man named Elias. He said they had come for Casey."

There's a murmur through the group.

"That makes sense. But why now, when they did not have the strength of numbers to attack? There are only two jaeitsi that we know of. Surely they would have been better off waiting until they had a third or a fourth?"

"There's a third," I say. I remember now that Diane had told me so.

"And you waited until now to tell us?"

"It slipped my mind?"

"Regardless, of course they'll attack now. Otherwise, they give us the chance to train her or find the second caeletai umea," a woman says, and I recognise her as the one who sat closest to us at our trial.

"Still, it doesn't make sense," the man replies. "It's a tactical miscalculation they're surely above."

"Stranger and stranger still," Proserpina murmurs. At first, she only has Ronan, Killian, and my attention. But as she begins to hum to herself, the group around the table turns to her. I take a sip of my tea, the heat blossoming in my chest, a panacea to soothe the soul.

"What was that?"

"It's strange that, if they came for Casey, I found her after an encounter with jaeitsi, very much unharmed."

Casey lets out a whimper, shrinking into her chair as if it could protect her from the thirteen sets of eyes that turn on her. Her gaze darts away and she begins to rock back and forth.

"What happened?" the man demands.

Casey shakes her head, rendered unable to speak by what's been done, by what she's seen. I feel Proserpina's fingers brush my throat, shifting the necklace with the Vaerdiexes stone. The memory of all things.

"I can tell you," I say. I hold the stone and summon to me that moment.

* * *

Casey watches as I roll onto the grass and spring to my feet. Illuminated as I am by the moon, I'm washed out to the paleness of a corpse. She watches me fade into the distance, gripping tightly to Isabrand as he plunges back into the sky, soaring high above the army that threatens us all. Here, at least, she will be safe.

She did not want this. She did not even want the revelry that came with being a caeletai umea, let alone the blood, the war. But here she is, on the back of a white dragon, sailing on the air through the harmless mouth of the sky. She hears the crack of fire roaring to life and sees the army burning. *Mallory has saved us again,* she thinks to herself, *and here I am, a coward despite all my power.*

Isabrand flies on, past the grey winged angel, at least a mile beyond the army that is already reduced to ash. He lands in the grass and bends his body to the earth so Casey can climb down. She stumbles a few feet before doubling over, spewing sick. It's not the ride on the dragon that has made her ill, but all of this. The bodies torn apart in the street. The screams as the building collapsed, the one her guards had rushed her towards, promising she'd be safe. They'd been set upon by some deabrueon, which had tore her guards to bits before she could recover her voice and call upon Pritovis' light to kill them. Then she had hid until Mallory had come. Like a coward.

She sways out in the cool breeze of the open field. The grass is a riot, rippling like a current that cannot unwrinkle itself to stillness. She doesn't hear them approach. Suddenly, her mouth is covered by a hand, grey wings wrapping around her to bind her tight.

"There'll be no lullaby from you little angel," a voice murmurs.

She doesn't recognise it, but it belongs to a man. A girl with a mane of blonde hair and peculiar green-blue eyes, not unlike a lizard's, strides forth. She closes her wings, having just landed on the ground. Beside her is a hooded woman with no wings.

Isabrand roars, swinging his tail to bowl them over, but the woman raises her hand and it stops, as if it's come up against an invisible barrier. Suddenly his body is low to the ground, a shimmering white net appearing around him. He thrashes, but cannot break its bonds. The woman walks right up to him, no traceable fear in her steady stride, and places her hand on his great snout. He tries to snap his maw open, but it is quickly bound too.

"Sleep," she commands.

His pale eyes, so like Mallory's, blink once before closing. A puff of mist comes out of his nostrils and he emits a mighty snore. There's a sickening sound. Bones breaking. His body writhes in his slumber, collapsing, folding, until he is human once more. His pale, naked body shivers in the cold. The woman kneels down beside him, stroking his hair.

"Time to go," she says to the others, walking away from Isabrand.

The man lets Casey go, grinning at her over his shoulder as he approaches the sleeping man. He knows she is too afraid to fight them and this amuses him. Her fear brings him pleasure. He scoops Isabrand up and slings him over his shoulder, his skin as white as his hair in the moonlight. Then the man's wings unfurl and he launches into the sky. The girl takes hold of the woman and soars after him. Casey shivers again, the touch memory of the man's hand over her mouth not fading.

"Casey!"

A voice cries out from the darkness, breaking the silence. Amongst all the things she has seen and heard this night, this is the first to startle her to action. She begins to sprint, not the way she and Isabrand have come, because that's where the voice calls from. Instead, she runs further into the field, full of itself. There is nothing on the horizon. There is nothing on her horizon.

"Casey stop, it's me!"

Mallory?

But when Casey turns around, she sees Proserpina, rushing through the grass, her scythe and armour smattered with blood.

"I tracked the jaeitsi girl out here. Where did she go? Casey?"

Casey falls to her knees, falls to weeping. What has she just allowed to come to pass?

* * *

The room is utterly silent and still as I finish recounting the memory. I cannot stand to meet Casey's eyes, nor she mine, but Proserpina gazes on her, all fire. Casey has allowed Isabrand to be taken, when everyone knows she could have stopped them or at least put up a fight. I bite the inside of my cheeks, occupying with pain the space tears should fill. My brother has been taken from me once more.

"I think to start we should discuss the matter of that stone and how you came to possess it," one of the men says coldly. Ronan and Killian stiffen.

"Of what I've just told you, you take issue with my having a Vaerdiexes stone?"

"That is a very powerful god relic, it should not be freely left in the hands of the people." I know what this man wants, his eyes glinting with a lust for power.

"It's a Vaerdiexes stone, it belongs with a dragovik."

"You like to hoard power, don't you?" he says, cocking his head to the right and studying the Vaerdiexes sword.

"No, I believe that's your tactic."

"Enough," Ronan interrupts. "We'll have none of your bickering here. The girl will keep what is hers by right, Tobias."

The other man seethes, glaring at me. It looks like it didn't take long for someone to fill Algard's shoes.

"An ice dragon?" the woman asks again. I simply nod. How could Casey? The only time she used her power last night was to defend herself and run away from Proserpina. "That's unheard of."

"It's a long story," I mutter, though I know it's one they wish to hear. To tell them would give too much away.

"He transformed despite the accords?" Tobias demands. My jaw drops. I notice the glances exchanged amongst the angeleru at the table, excepting Ronan, Killian, and that woman. They're all upset about this.

"That's what concerns you? He killed hundreds of deabrueon, is the only reason Casey is alive, and is apparently what the jaeitsi were really after, and the fact he transformed is what you have a problem with?" I ask, my voice rising. Before I know it, I'm on my feet. When will these idiots get it through their heads? My brother has been kidnapped. All the rest is not important. My hands feel hot, my blood boiling with rage. Proserpina's hand jumps from mine and she cries out.

"Mallory," Killian urges in a quiet voice.

Looking down, I see handprints on the table, scorch marks where I have touched it. Proserpina nurses her hand, the burns faint but there. Vaerdiexes purrs in my mind.

"I'm so sorry," I say to her, reaching for her hand to heal it. She flinches, her eyes wide. They say, *I'm angry too, Mallory, but why*? But then she yields, allowing me to wipe away the traces of my anger. Her hand heals swiftly with my magic.

"A fitting display of why dragoviks must be kept in check. You'll notice no other dragoviks took it upon themselves to decide what was right and what was wrong last night. Even during battle, the accords hold," Tobias replies, though even he looks frightened by my display of anger.

"If they had transformed, maybe fewer lives would have been lost. Isabrand would still be here. We are not the enemy."

Tobias' mouth curls into a lipless smile. *Oh, but you are*, his eyes say. We're just one he's learned to control. He turns to the others.

"This doesn't bode well. The enemy came emptyhanded and left with valuable weapons and an ally."

"He's not an ally to them!" I interrupt. Killian pulls me into my seat and I stare at him. Is he really condoning this?

"If this witch is powerful enough to force a dragovik back into human form, she may be strong enough to control one as well. Likely she is the one who blew up city hall. Under her control, he may bè an ally to them whether he wishes to be or not. And the jaeitsi will be able to summon another army. They could storm our gates with just as much force tomorrow if they wanted, tonight even. If the caeletai umea served as a deterrent before, she certainly doesn't now that they know she's afraid of them."

Casey hangs her head. Good. I'm surprised at the pleasure I feel swelling in me, knowing she's suffering. But what she thought of herself having failed my brother rings true. She's a coward.

"Morale will be low. The people know these facts just as well as we do."

"So, what do we do?" Ronan asks. The woman clears her throat.

"Rosalind?"

"A counter attack. We need to get to them before they grow any stronger. You could lead it, couldn't you?" she asks, turning to me.

"Are you insane? Leave our fate to a dragovik?" Tobias interjects.

"A dragovik who just decimated an army of deabrueon. Not to mention the fact she bears a gods' weapon and a Vaerdiexes stone. Could you do it?"

I don't hesitate.

"With a team of bellatoja and Proserpina by my side, yes." I have utter faith Proserpina and I will do whatever it takes to save my brother. The jaeitsi will be a necessary casualty. Proserpina said if I killed Elias the future would not come to be, but I am done playing by the rules of fate.

"It's out of the question. The girl is too unpredictable," Tobias says, shaking his head. "All in favour to veto Rosalind's plan?"

Of the group, only Rosalind, the old man, and Ronan keep their hands down. I turn to them, one by one, incredulous.

"You would risk your people's lives because of what I am? Tell me, were Casey to lead the charge, would it be okay then?" There's no answer. "I am better equipped than anyone to fight this battle. I've fought the jaeitsi three times."

"And failed to kill them. Not to mention you have a personal interest in the matter, that of your brother."

"I've fought the woman who leads them and took her isuazko. On my own."

There's another sharp intake of breath and I know immediately that I have said the wrong thing.

"A dragovik with no moral compass! What's next, blood magic? She would drain us for all the power we have my friends, if only to empower herself. She would have us weak, defenceless, snivelling in the street, begging for her protection. And only then would she let the jaeitsi rip our home apart."

"That's not Mallory," Killian interjects.

"Son," Ronan begins, but Killian cuts him off.

"She just saved the city at great personal risk. I was with her when she took the avika's power. She did it so we could rescue Casey and bring her here. She doesn't want this, these acts of heroism, these tokens of power. But they choose her, and you should take it as a sign that perhaps all these relics of gods are convening on one person because she is meant to lead and help us."

"While Master Killian has spoken out of place, I do believe he has a point," a woman in black robes says. She looks to Ronan for permission to go ahead.

"Yes, Anastasia?" Ronan says, clearly weary.

"It wasn't until you mentioned your brother, the ice dragon, that I put it together. As you know, volumes eighty to one-hundred of the Codices are my charge. One of the prophecies speaks of a dragovik, all ice, and his sister, born to rule. I believe it would be unwise to ignore the signs that Mallory Thiel may be this dragovik."

My heart clutches. She's realised the prophecy is about me, but has she realised the Onyevaras and the Hirutere are who must fall in order for me to come to power? If they put that together, surely they'll lock me up, if not kill me.

"Well then, let's see this prophecy," Tobias says. Anastasia shifts uncomfortably. "What's the matter?"

"The prophecy was in the volume stolen by the jaeitsi. Likely they know of the prophecy too, which is why they knew to take Isabrand."

"If the books are in your charge, how did they learn of the prophecy?" Tobias asks, leaning forward in his seat. "If the jaeitsi have managed to get access to the Cadmus Codices it is due to a grave failure on the part of the council of five."

"I'll thank you not to question the loyalty of my people, Tobias. We are at war out there, let us not be at war in here," Ronan replies coolly. "If the jaeitsi know of the prophecy, it is not Anastasia's fault."

Tobias studies her a moment, but says no more on the matter.

"Whether or not Mallory Thiel is the one in this prophecy is a matter for debate. As we don't currently have the prophecy, we can't prove that point. No, I have a better idea, one that will bolster morale."

I lean back in my chair, folding my arms over my chest. How can he be so blinded by prejudice?

"We're open to all suggestions," Ronan says, giving me a sideways look.

"We tell the people it was the caeletai umea who vanquished the enemy's army. Tell them she has protected her people and will do so again, as their new queen."

Now Casey objects. She stands up, her teacup shattering at her feet.

"I can't be a queen," she gasps, the panic attack she had been compressing in her chest now unfurling. "I can't lead."

"Of course you can't. Can't even protect yourself. You will be a figurehead only, a beacon to give the people hope."

"You can't just lie to them! It's Mallory that saved their lives," Killian objects, but his father raises a hand to silence his son.

"Go on, Tobias," he says. Killian fumes at his father, but obeys this time.

"We have captured one of the jaeitsi's advisors. We will interrogate him to determine their location and the jaeitsi's plans. We will be on defence only, countering every one of their attacks."

He leans back in his seat, looking very pleased with himself. There are some murmurs of assent amongst the other members of the council. I look to Killian, shocked. They can't be serious. This can't be their plan.

"That's a horrible idea," I say. "What about when the source dries up and you no longer know their plans? Will another advisor just fall into your lap? And how do you even know he'll tell you the truth?"

"You are not on our council, girl. While your efforts last night are commended, our patience will only extend so far. We will now put the plan to a vote. All in favour?"

Again, all hands go up with the exception of Ronan, Rosalind, Anastasia, and the old man's. He studies me, shaking his head and resting it in his palm.

"It's agreed, then. Send word to the prison. The interrogation of Thaddeus Velemir will begin shortly."

Chapter XXXI.

"Idiots," I snarl, storming out of the elevator back into the library. Killian and Proserpina rush out after me. "They're all prejudiced morons who are going to cost us our lives."

"Keep your voice down," Killian says, my loud voice drawing some attention. A nearby couple huddled together have their eyes on us, as does an elderly gentleman. I don't care though. I'm all wrath and fury as I storm through the crowd.

"I'm sorry, this is the natural volume my voice reaches when I'm furious and dealing with incompetent dunces."

"Okay well at least try not to incinerate any more tables," he suggests. I frown at him. How can he make jokes at a time like this? All of our lives are on the line and Isabrand has been taken.

Despite Casey's attempts to reach us before we left the meeting, we left the room without saying a word to her, though the look Proserpina gave her was just short of spitting in her face. The attachment between her and Isabrand has grown strong within the past couple of days and I wonder what a love so instantaneous and powerful must feel like. It is reassuring to me, as I know Proserpina will stop at nothing to rescue him and keep my brother from harm. Won't I too?

"I'm going after them," I say, spinning around to face the two of them. "They can't get away with what they did and they cannot take my brother from me."

"Agreed," Proserpina says, the Shigami scythe shimmering into existence in her hand. Her armour is already on from the battle. My dress is in tatters, covered in blood and grime, but I couldn't care less. "First, we go to question Thaddeus."

"Wait!" Killian says, but we ignore him, starting towards the door. "You can't just interrogate a Hirutere prisoner!"

"Watch us," I snap.

Unsure of what else to do, he follows us through the library. We're almost to the door when Kyle appears. His eyes are darkened and his face grave.

"What's the matter?" I ask, all fire draining from me. I have never seen him look so afraid or broken, not even after he lost his arm.

"It's Aaron."

My heart blanches like meat left in water over night. There is no blood, no colour, no life to it. I swear in that moment it ceases to beat.

"What happened?"

Kyle stifles a sob and I pull him into my arms. He trembles against my body, his face pressed to my shoulder.

"It's bad Mallory, it's really," he hiccups, "bad."

"Take me to him."

We push our way through the crowd, out the front door. In the courtyard outside are the vast white tents that were being set up when we arrived. They're now completely occupied, the beds full. Men and women rush to aid the injured and I watch as gold lights glow around wounds, attempting to heal as best they can. Kyle leads us into the tent in the far left corner. Weaving between beds, he glances over his shoulder.

"The Onyevaras set these up to tend to the dragoviks in the city after they were turned away from the Library, even once they had spare beds. If he had had medical attention sooner," he whispers, wiping his nose, which is snotty from crying.

Again, I feel my blood come to a boil. Those Hirutere bastards. If they cost Aaron his life, I will have no qualms tearing them down myself. I feel as if Vaerdiexes is purring in my mind, coaxing out my anger. He's enjoying this. The beginning of things.

We arrive at a cot and I scarcely recognise the mass of flesh and blood as the man I shared a bed with only the day before. Robyn is kneeling beside him, clutching his hand. She rocks back and forth, weeping. She's got more than a few scrapes on her as well, but has not healed them.

"It's no use," she whimpers, shaking her head. Her lower lip quivers. "Nothing I do works."

Kyle looks to me, utterly hopeless, and I kneel beside the body of my friend. I take his other hand in mine, raw knuckles, skin torn back and bloodied. He groans at my touch, though it's such a feeble sound.

"What happened?" I ask, looking to Killian. "You were with him last time I saw you two."

He looks utterly taken aback, his eyes wide in horror at what he sees.

"We got separated after Isabrand went to rescue you." He stops when he sees the look on my face. "No Mallory, that's not what I meant."

Rescue me. If Isabrand hadn't been with me, maybe he would have fought beside them and Aaron would be alive. Maybe the jaeitsi wouldn't have taken my brother from me. I look back to the mangled body before me and feel utterly helpless. His entire right arm has been flayed, revealing the slick red of muscle. The rest of him is drenched in blood, no doubt his own. He quivers, moans, then falls silent.

"You tried the usual healing spell?" I ask Robyn. She nods.

"Please, help him. You have Diane's magic, there might be more you can do that I can't."

I close my eyes. Where to even begin? I try to draw his skin together, but there is not enough of it to pull shut over the gaping wounds, Death's maw. I try to pour my isuazko into him, but his body rejects it, the pieces of myself I offer bouncing off of him as if he is wrapped and protected from it by Death's greedy hands. I plead with Vaerdiexes, beg for some of the fire he gave me, but this is not part of the prophecy. He does not care if this man lives or dies, so long as he gets what he wants. Slowly, I feel Aaron fade from himself. I try and reach out to catch him, but he slips away too quickly. I know exactly where he has gone. If Proserpina was to move between the realms of the living and the dead, she would see him now. I lower his hand back beside his body, shaking as I do so. Robyn must feel him go still too, because she raises her head, blinking in disbelief.

"No," she whispers, clasping either side of his face. "No!"

She collapses onto his chest though it is bloodied beyond recognition, weeping without restraint. Kyle crouches beside her, tears in his eyes, his arms wrapped around his sister's small, trembling frame. She looks up at me, eyes blistered with fury.

"What's the fucking point of you!" she screams. "What good are you, after all the times he saved your life?"

I open my mouth, but nothing comes out. There is no answer to the question *why* in the face of death. Instead, I place my hand on Aaron's forearm.

First, I draw the blood from him, empty of the isuazko that was his lifeforce, until his flesh is clean. I remove the excrement that has come out on his death bed, purifying the air so its scent does not reach us. I make for him new skin, his body now susceptible to my magic, hiding his bared humanity beneath its clean, tan swathe. No longer in the clutches of death but in the fields eternal, his body yields to my magic. I realise now there was no chance of healing him. His soul was already perched on his shoulders like a waiting bird, waiting for a god of death to come take it, by the time I arrived.

When I remove my hand, he appears to be himself once more, his eyes shut. He looks as he did in bed when I left him sleeping yesterday ,and the thought makes me whimper. Robyn and Kyle sit up, misery on their faces as they gaze on their friend's body, never to joke again, never to rush to their aid in the heat of battle. He is an open space they will need to reconcile the world to, a name they will wrap their tongues around by accident when the memory of his death rouses them from sleep.

"Thank you," she whispers, unable to look at me. Perhaps it is for hatred or perhaps it is because of her outburst.

I rise and leave them to their grief. Proserpina stays, but I hear Killian behind me. His footsteps are dulled by the blood roaring in my ears. The Hirutere allowed this to happen too. And every attack they allow to happen, only defending themselves instead of fighting back, there will be more dead. We have to prevent it all, stop the war before it starts. But that's foolish; it already has.

"Mallory," Killian starts, as if he can read my thoughts.

"You know I had him backed into a corner, Elias that is. Proserpina and I had him, and she told me it wasn't his time yet. I shouldn't have listened. Without him, Clara and the other jaeitsi never could have raised this army. Lives would have been spared."

"Don't," he says, grabbing me by the shoulders as we exit the tent. "You saved thousands of lives last night, whether the city knows it or not."

"Saving a life does not make up for the loss of one," I reply.

Now I am crying. Now, away from Kyle and Robyn's grief, I can exhibit my own pitiful manifestation. I didn't love Aaron, but he was dear to me. A friendly face always, someone to be counted on. He provided reassurance and stability through everything. When Dominic went missing, he was the first to spring to my aid. I can't imagine not seeing him anymore, waking up tomorrow and the day never knowing him. It seems too great an impossibility.

"But you didn't take his life. They did. If anything," he starts. His hands drop from my shoulders and he turns his blank stare to the sky, the morning sun rising steadily over the living and the dead alike. "If anything, it's my fault."

"Yours?"

"It's like you said, the last time you saw him he was with me."

"You're just a soldier, you can't save everyone."

It comes out harsher than I intend, diminutive even. He laughs.

"Not all of us can be the hero, right?" he says, throwing his words back in my face. "Sorry, I didn't mean that, it's just, you're wrong. I should have been able to protect him. If I wasn't so selfish."

He looks furious now, with himself most of all. He wanders a few paces away, kicking a piece of debris. I follow him as he meanders down a side street, seemingly oblivious to where he's going. I don't know why, but words seem impossible right now. It's as if he's in a bubble of grief and angst that I cannot permeate. We reach the next street over, which is utterly empty, before he turns around.

"I didn't mean what I said."

"Good, because like I said, it's not your fault," I reiterate. He shakes his head and looks down at the large slab of stone he stands on.

"Not what I was referring to. I didn't mean what I said about not being able to be with you because you're the hero. Or not how you thought I meant it."

"Oh?"

Why is he bringing this up now? Does it matter in the face of the night's events? Our kiss seems a ghost to me, almost as though it never happened at all. But Killian persists.

"Mallory, you're astounding. From the moment I heard about you, a complete outsider from the Academy helping strangers to bring down Thaddeus so she could save lives, I thought to myself, this is it. This is the paragon of altruism. When I saw you in the library that day, I knew I had to speak to you. You tried to be cold, hostile even, but it was so unnatural for you, I could tell. So unsuited to the kindness that you show every day. But then, just like that, you disappeared, not to be heard from for three years. Then I saw you again in Brooklyn, when I never thought I'd see you again, and what did you do? Rushed to Kyle's aid without a second thought for how it would disrupt your life. You saw a friend in need and gave up all you had worked to build for three years so you could protect him and others. You are selfless, good. No matter the villain you try to paint yourself as, I have always seen that. Last night you risked your life based on nothing more than blind faith in a god."

"Not that blind, he has penchant for saving my ass," I mumble.

"There you go again, diminishing what you've done. When the Hirutere formulated their plan just now, you didn't care that they were letting Casey take credit for saving lives. You didn't care that you were losing out on the glory that would have come with such an act of heroism. All you took issue with was the fact that they were risking the lives of the innocent by not fighting back. Not even your people, mind you. Angeleru, who have time and time again shown their worst side to you. You don't care about the power, just the good you can do with it. And it makes me feel like a failure."

I blink at the man who rushed into battle on his own last night, who rescued Kyle from the bellatoja three years ago on nothing more than the belief he was a good person; the man who stood by my side when he hardly knew me, fought for the people I care about, and I wonder how he sees failure in himself. How could he possibly be a failure when he's every bit the self-sacrificing hero he paints me to be?

"Killian, just because you don't have some great destiny prophesized four-thousand years ago, doesn't make you any less brave. It's not about how much power you have, it's about what you do with the power you're given."

"That's just it, Mallory, I haven't done anything with it. I could be doing so much more, but I've been a coward." He takes a deep breath, steadying himself for what comes next. "It's me. I'm the other caeletai umea."

My first thought when the words come out of his mouth are *of course you are.* Because who is better suited to be an angel on Earth than Killian? Perhaps Kyle. My second feeling is confusion. Why doesn't anyone know? Shouldn't he be groundlessly worshipped, like Casey? Shouldn't he have been enshrined and dragged out for parties like some idol? Last comes the anger. How. How has he kept his power to himself? Why didn't he use it last night?

Reaching down, I pluck my shoe from my foot and hurl it at him. He dodges it, his eyes widening in surprise. Why he's surprised I'm angry, I do not know. This is grounds for a good bludgeoning.

"You? You're the other one? You're a caeletai umea?" I demand, my other shoe already in my hand. He doesn't cower, meeting my gaze with his sorrowful eyes instead. But I have no pity for him.

"Yes."

"Why," I hiss, "why wouldn't you do something then? Last night, you could have saved lives, you could have saved Aaron's life. You have all that power and you did nothing last night but wave a sword around? Where were you when they took Isabrand? Where were you when Aaron was attacked? What the fuck are you playing at?"

I realise I'm screaming now. My body feels hot again and, without warning, Killian flies across the street, collapsing against a trash can. He looks up, extremely alarmed, and scrambles to his feet. He puts his hands up in front of him, ready for my next blow, though he can't counter it. Can't or won't, I don't care. Even if he is a caeletai umea I'll kick his ass. I don't care what he's done up until now to help me, he's kept all this power to himself when he could have been doing good, could have been saving lives. I feel as if my blood is boiling, as if it will burn through my skin.

"You're just as bad as her, Casey, cowering in a corner, hoarding the enormity of your power that could do good! You're selfish, whatever the reason for not telling people. You complain about not being the hero when you could be, when you could have helped stop everything that happened last night."

"But I wanted to," he interrupts.

I stop shouting, blood still pounding in my ears to a dizzying degree. I feel as though I could split the ground open, send him plummeting to the blazing centre of the Earth or wherever we are. But instead, I cross my arms over my chest, waiting for his explanation and pinning him with a furious look.

"Why didn't you?" I demand.

"You remember when we were in the Vaults and my father started talking about that prophecy, not your one, the other one? Well, I was going to tell you about it the other night, but then I kissed you and things were so confusing. You looked so angry already, I didn't know how to tell you."

He hesitates a moment, chewing his lip and studying me.

"Tell me what?" I ask, growing impatient in his pauses. He takes a deep breath.

"Well it wasn't your prophecy we were discussing. This prophecy… it's about me. It was in one of the books my father is responsible for, so he realised right away that it was me: first born, first to die, child of port wine stain, skin bruised by birth. Given by the angels so it will cost him his life, all for the woman who to his heart lays claim."

I frown, unable to make sense of what he's just said. It sounds exactly like the sort of gibberish that Aleia Cadmus would write, though glaringly absent of any mention of sugar gliders. My arms fall to my sides and I stop glaring. Could he be telling the truth? Could there really be some explanation for all of this?

"But, that's so vague, it could be about any caeletai umea, which I'm guessing what given by the angels is referring to. How can you be certain it's about you?"

"All things in the Cadmus Codices seem ambiguous at first or to someone who doesn't have all the facts. Are you saying your prophecy wasn't?"

He's right. I hadn't believed it was the right one at first. It wasn't until Kyle, Proserpina, and I analysed it that I realised all the pieces fit into place.

"I suppose you're right," I say, reluctant to agree with him.

"But you knew it was yours anyway, because there are signs we see in ourselves that others do not."

He lifts the hem of his shirt. Spread across his hip, running up to his ribcage, is a port wine birth mark, like a massive bruise that will never heal. I remember seeing the edge of it when he was sitting on my sofa, his shirt slightly hiked up. He drops his shirt back down, hiding the revelation.

"Child of port wine stain, bruised by birth. That's my birthmark. Given by the angels; that would be referring to my powers as a caeletai umea. And I'm the first, and only, born to my parents. First born– "

"First to die," I whisper, approaching him slowly. "So it will cost him his life."

I cross over to him and he keeps very still, as though waiting for a wild animal to approach. But my wrath has faded. Instead, I feel only the sinking of my heart. Killian is destined to die. We all are, but his prophecy implies an imminent and tragic death. I reach him and I slip my hand beneath his shirt and press it to the birthmark. His skin is hot and the place I know the mark to be feels no different from the rest of him, though it singles him out for a terrible fate.

"So, it says," he replies grimly. "All for the woman who to his heart lays claim. Guess the Codices mention you twice, huh?"

My eyes round out as I look up at him. How is that possible?

"You love me?" I ask, startled by his sudden declaration.

"Against my better judgement, in the face of my fate, I fell in love with a woman who was good and kind, and every inch of her was fire. How could I not burn?"

He leans down and presses his forehead to mine before kissing me. I feel the heat of his breath as it mingles with mine and his tongue flicks out across my own. It is not as urgent as last time, there is a softness and thoughtfulness to it. He's hesitant, worried, in the face of my angry outburst, that I'll reject him. Though my body is bruised, it doesn't hurt when he takes me by the waist and pulls me into his arms. He is just as quick to pull away though, brushing his forehead against mine. He lets out a small sigh, his eyes closed, and I study him.

"So that's why you never told anyone that you're the caeletai umea?" I ask in a whisper, as if he has not just taken my breath away. "You were afraid you would die?"

"No that's not why," he says, shaking his head. "Maybe as a child I was afraid of my fate, but since I've met you, I've learned to die for love would be a noble cause. No, I never showed anyone what I am because I don't have my powers anymore."

I frown, leaning back and looking up at him. His arms are still around me, keeping me safe against the cage of his body. I hear his heart beating, thundering on through life where fate has ordained it won't.

"How's that possible?"

"I first exhibited my powers at a very young age. Already my father had his suspicions about what I was, but after that he knew for sure. There were complications during my birth, bruised by birth, and my mother couldn't have any more children. My father knew losing me would kill her. It would kill him too. He didn't even tell her what he'd discovered, he didn't tell anyone. He was so afraid they'd take me away from him. So, he took me to a witch who bound my powers with an unbreakable spell. They're in me still, like a second heart, bound but beating," he explains.

"You don't tell anyone because it would do no good. You couldn't actually use your powers."

"Exactly. What good is a caeletai umea if I can't banish the deabrueon back to darkness? They would keep me like a trophy, as they do Casey, powerful in name only. Besides, there's the matter of being forced to be with the other caeletai umea."

"Because if you don't– "

"Any children I have would be jaeitsi. And the world can't take more of them. Not even on its best day." He traces the length of my cheekbone, pausing at its zenith. "I can't offer you a future. I can't offer you children. From the sounds of things, I won't be around long enough anyway. But I love you, Mallory, and I can give you the love you deserve."

I know he can, he has already given it over and over. In every action he has taken since we met in Brooklyn, he has proven his love. Yet he has never used these acts as a way to vie for my attention or demand reciprocity. They were given freely and unnoticed, until now. That thing he had asked for with his eyes at the cafe, I see the shape of it now, and understand that it is love, in return for his. I wasn't ready to give it, not yet, not then. It didn't even come in the paltry form as it had for Dominic, who I had believed I loved. But it has, at last. Some loves are the belly of a canyon, carved out slowly and tediously.

Part VII

Chapter XXXII.

After that, our kiss deepens and we are a flurry of haste to get back to his house. There is something in the kiss, a fire greater than my own or even Vaerdiexes', and I know I want to be consumed by it. I want to straddle Killian's lap and feel him, utterly and completely. We stumble up the stairs, unable to keep ourselves apart until he nudges me forwards through the door of his room. My gaze sweeps his room briefly when we enter, but it isn't long before he spins me around and is kissing me again. He kicks the door shut and tugs at my lower lip with his teeth. I moan and the sound is his undoing. He drags me across the room and bends me down over the wooden surface of his desk.

He pushes my dress over my hips and yanks my underwear down before leaning over me, his body flush against mine, and growling in my ear.

"You have my love, pure-hearted, but you still make me want to do filthy things to you Thiel."

"Do whatever you want to me," I breathe, twisting to look at him over my shoulder. His pupils dilate as I speak. He sweeps the hair from the back of my neck and kisses the exposed skin, grinding his hips against mine. He slips one hand beneath my chest, tugging the strap of my dress down to free my breasts. As he begins to trace the tip of his finger around my nipple, my breaths come out in sharp pants. He traces another lazy circle, pulling at the skin of my throat with his teeth, and I buck against him, begging for more.

"Anything?" he asks.

"Anything you want. Fuck me over this desk, bring me to my knees, make me scream your name, only don't stop touching me."

He pinches my nipple, a sharp biting sensation that makes me whimper and cave against his hand. His palm spreads for a moment to cup my breast, before he sweeps his thumb across it and clamps my nipple between his thumb and forefinger. He tugs on the sensitive skin until I whimper again and curl my head back, resting it against his.

"Are you begging?" he whispers, his hot breath tickling my ear.

"Yes."

"Even if this night lasted an eternity, it would not be long enough for me to do all the things I wish to. It would not be enough time for me to have my fill of you."

"I suppose we'll have to claim this eternity and the next then," I reply, pushing my hips back against his and squeezing my legs together, desperate for the friction.

His other hand slides down my backside and he slips from atop me onto his knees. I feel his hot breath on me and the growing wetness between my thighs. I clench my fists, resisting the urge to pull him to me, resisting every impulse to take his trousers off and straddle his cock. I can all but be certain he is smiling, enjoying the thrill of my desire, my anticipation. He moves his lips closer to me, his mouth millimetres from my sensitive skin. I twitch and he grabs my hips to stay me.

He doesn't waste time with gentle caresses.

His fingers slip inside me and I let out a stuttering gasp, curving my belly down against the table as he drags his tongue across my centre. His hand slides beneath my abdomen, stilling me. I push my hips back as he licks me again.

"Fuck," he murmurs against my body, his hand clawing at the soft flesh of my stomach.

He slides his fingers all the way out, teasing me, before pushing back in. Then his lips are back on me and he sucks on my clit for a moment, before sliding his tongue into me too. A curl of pleasure rolls through me and again I try to buck against his grip.

"Stay still," he orders, removing his mouth from me. "Stay still or I'll make you wish you had."

I nod, unable to string a single word from my mouth. He leans forward again, a series of unhurried, teasing licks turning me into a knot of nerves. I whimper as he flicks his tongue out once more. My thighs tense, drawing closer together, but Killian is quick to pry them apart again. His fingers pump in and out of me at a teasingly slow pace. It's not enough. In that moment I know, no matter what Killian does to my body, how many times he fucks me, I will never have enough of him. I push my hips back against him, driving his fingers deeper. I hear him chuckle against my skin, before running his tongue the length of me again.

"I didn't think you could possibly be as hungry for me as I am for you," he murmurs, pulling his fingers out to the tip before adding another and sliding them back in.

He strokes the inside of me, languishing with each touch. I feel release building, unlike anything I felt with Aaron or Thaddeus. Killian is coaxing a new beast out of me, something primal and utterly in need of him. He drags his teeth across me and sucks on my clit until pleasure draws itself over me like a blinding veil. I can see nothing, feel nothing but him as I let loose a cry and my body shudders against his mouth. My brain scrambles, searching for words, but I can't remember any, not in this language at least. No, I find myself crying out, as if in a language I never knew existed before, one wholly ours. Killian growls, unrelenting as he caresses me with his tongue. He keeps holding me steady, despite the writhing of my body.

"Fuck!" I scream, clenching my fists.

I feel Killian withdraw his mouth and suddenly he is standing over me again.

"Hold on to the fucking desk," he growls.

I reach in front of me and grip the other side of the desk just as Killian leans forward and pins my hands in place. His large hand easily encompasses my wrists. He nudges my legs apart with his feet, leaving me utterly at his mercy. He strokes the tip of his cock against the soaking apex of my thighs, teasing me. I try to push my hips back to take him in me, but he chuckles, drawing away. Then he pushes the first inch in and I gasp, shifting to accommodate his thickness. He leans forward and kisses my neck again.

"Beg again," he murmurs, though I know it is taking all his self-control not to fuck me senseless. I can feel my sensitive nipples exposed and tingling against the rough wood of the desk.

"Please Killian."

"Please what," he growls, biting my earlobe.

"Fuck me. Fuck me for days. Fuck me until I forget that time is fleeting and that there's a world outside this room that keeps turning."

He groans at my plea and pushes forward until he finally, finally sinks deep inside me. We moan at the same time, me burying my forehead against the desk and shuddering with the pleasure of being full with him. I can feel him throbbing inside of me. He's bent over me, one hand holding my hands in place while the other comes to clench my hip. He draws out at an excruciatingly slow pace, until only the tip of his cock is still inside me. I pant, trying to push back against him, yet he holds me fast with the hand on my hip.

Still he maintains his self-control, pushing back in slowly, though I feel him shuddering behind me. His hips are pressed against my backside as he sinks all the way into me. I writhe beneath him, curling my back and straining to break free of his grip. He pins me down with more force, before beginning to pound into me at a steady, deep pace that sends ripples of pleasure through me. I moan and at last he lets my hands go. I right myself slightly so that my back is pressed to his chest and our cheeks are side by side. He ropes an arm around my waist, lifting me onto my tiptoes before unleashing himself relentlessly on me.

He slams against me savagely and I may as well be sobbing in pleasure for the guttural cries that leave me. His fingers dig into my hip so hard that I wonder if he won't leave a mark, some reminder that he's claimed me. I'm barely able to hold myself on my toes for his frenzied movement now, grateful for his arm keeping me steady against him. Suddenly that veil that kept release from me lifts and I cry out again, tightening around him. I can feel the wetness running down my thighs, soaking me to the core, easing his way in and out of me.

"Fuck!" he snarls, his body tensing against mine and I feel his cock pulse in me as he climaxes. He tightens his grip on me, holding me as close as possible without ripping through me. I feel his cum running down my thighs as we stand there a moment. My body relaxes against his arm and he hoists me up easily, spinning me around in his arms so we're facing one another.

He gazes down upon me, trying to read my expression. His eyes burn, the gold accents in them lit up like molten metal. His chest is rising and falling quickly, as he pants. I start to reach for his face, but he catches both my wrists in one hand and uses the other to push me onto the bed. He pins my hands over my head and looks down at me. I've never felt more vulnerable yet comfortable in my own skin. He sees me not as something to mould, a half-formed thing, but a complete, an absolute in need of no one and nothing save for his touch.

I lift my legs and wind them around his waist, drawing him to me. Already I can feel him hard against me again. He pulls his hips back and thrusts into me.

"What have you done to me Mallory Thiel?" he whispers against my throat.

"Nothing. Yet."

I twist out of his grip and pull him down onto the bed, rolling on top of him. His hands find my waist but I grab them, weaving my fingers between his, and push them against the yielding mattress.

"My turn," I murmur, slowly rising up, teasing him all the way to the tip.

He groans, thrusting up into me. Curving my legs behind me, I use them to pin him down, stilling him as he did me, while I begin to ride him. I can feel his body tensing beneath me already, a mix of mounting pleasure and restraint, so as not to free himself from my grip and fuck me like a ragdoll. He grits his teeth taking a sharp breath as a I slowly draw myself down over him, tightening around his cock.

"Are you so hell bent on torturing me?" he growls.

"Say I am," I pant, back to the tip of his shaft, holding myself above him. "What would you do about it?"

He snarls, knotting his hand in my hair and throwing me down on the bed. He's on top of me again, pounding furiously into me and I cry out sharply. There will be no getting used to this, this exquisite pleasure. He could take me a thousand times and I would never tire, no never cease to be in rapturous pleasure as he fucks me. I wrap my legs around his waist again and he has his hands on my hips, pulling me to him so he drives himself as deep as possible into me. He tilts his head back, groaning before finding my gaze again.

"You're lucky, I'm more merciful than you. I'll always give you exactly what you want," he whispers as he leans over me, drawing me into a kiss.

"I just want you," I whisper against his lips.

He moans as he finishes, the throbbing of his cock inside me pushing me over the edge once more, so I cry out sharply. My body shudders beneath his. I knot my fingers in his hair, gasping as I see stars, as I arch my back before letting out a purring sound. He chuckles against my throat, kissing it again before dotting a kiss on each of my breasts. He lowers himself on the bed beside me, drawing me to him. I rest my head on his chest and shut my eyes for a moment. My body feels flushed and pleasant, still tingling with the delicious pleasure he's given me.

Slowly I become aware of other things. The pounding of his heart in his chest, the damp of sweat on the nape of my neck. I hear noise from the streets, joyous cries, and Casey's name is called out. It sends a curl of jealousy and anger through me. The woman who is meant to be Killian's lover, the woman who cost me my brother. I tighten my grip on Killian. They're out there, celebrating her impending coronation. How?

"How are they celebrating at a time like this?" I ask, listening to the cheers outside. The city is a riot of cheer and fanfare. Casey's coronation will take place tonight and, since the announcement, the streets have been full of joyous cries. Somehow, hope and happiness takes root in death. It seems so perverse, but I suppose how else are we to persist if good cannot come of the bad? I trace the length of Killian's arm with my index finger before intertwining our fingers and turning back to him.

"I don't know, how did we do what we just did at a time like this?" he questions in response. "Grief and war work in funny ways."

I study him, my hair splayed across the pillow like tendrils of the night reaching for him. His eyes are open to me, intricate and easily bruised with emotion. Right now, they bloom love and protectiveness. He will not let anything befall me and, in this cocoon of happiness, at least, I know I am safe. He brushes the hair from my face and draws me to his chest with an arm wrapped around me. I tuck myself against his body, feel his warmth radiating against my bare skin.

"Do you always sleep with girls on the first date?" I tease, resting my chin on his chest so I can still see his face. His body rumbles with laughter, shaking me, and I grin.

"I'm not counting this as a date."

"No?"

"Besides, we already had a first date. In Brooklyn."

"Ah-ha so you admit you take women to Brooklyn on dates!" I declare. He laughs again.

"I take *woman* on date to Brooklyn. One woman." He grabs my hand and kisses my fingertips. I purr to feel his lips on me again. "And then there's our second date."

"When was that?" I ask, breathing heavily as he rolls on top of me. I like the weight of him bearing into me, a blanket to hold me down when all the world wishes to pull me in different directions. Here, in the safety of his arms, I can draw my scattered mind back together, can think clearly, else fall apart in the most delicious way.

"Our hangover breakfast."

I wrinkle my nose.

"My brother was there. That doesn't count."

"So was Proserpina. Double date," he amends. I giggle, wriggling beneath him as he dots kisses across my forehead. I dart forward and steal a kiss quickly. He falls back on his knees, gazing down upon me hungrily. "What's it like being so marvellous a man would die for you?"

I know he's teasing, but the blithe reference to his prophesised death draws my breath short. I don't want to think about it.

"I don't intend on finding out," I say, sitting up and kissing him on his cheek. My prophecy can come true, but his I will thwart. Whatever the cost, whatever bargain I must make with the gods, it is already done.

He nips my neck playfully before sighing and rolling off of me. "We should probably get ready. They'll be expecting us there."

I groan, falling back onto the bed and drawing the covers over my head. I hear him chuckle.

"Never. If I don't leave, the Earth has to stop turning, right?"

"Technically Miesarinda isn't on Earth, so it doesn't turn. But I like your theory. Sadly, we can't put it to the test. The Hirutere will take it as a declaration if you don't go to Casey's coronation."

"Of what?" I ask.

"Of war. You have to remember the precarious position you're in right now. Your heroics in the battle last night will only earn you so much leeway. Tobias is clearly gunning for you. He'd love any reason to declare you an enemy of Miesarinda. Not to mention Anastasia seems to be putting together the fact that you're referred to in the Cadmus Codices. It's only a matter of time she realises the infrastructure of old it refers to is the Hirutere itself."

I hold my breath and close my eyes, taking a moment where he cannot see me. I am an enemy of Miesarinda. This is a city I cannot stand for, not as it is. How can he be so calm though, knowing that the Hirutere must fall for me to gain power? Does he think that he can spare me from my fate as I hope to spare him? Mine will not be so easily avoided, not with a god in the mix.

Killian tickles my ribs. He pulls back the covers, exposing me to the light, and ropes an arm around my waist. Brushing his nose against mine, he gives me a gentle squeeze.

"Where did you go?" he asks.

"The land of worry warts."

"You don't belong there. Come back to me."

"I'm right here," I promise, catching his cheek in my hand. I gaze up into his eyes and he smiles back down at me.

"Good. Because otherwise I'd be forced to tickle you."

"Such methods of torture. It's a wonder the Hirutere haven't enlisted you to question Thaddeus."

He doesn't laugh, just leans onto his elbow.

"How do you feel about that?"

"How do I feel about what?"

"Thaddeus being here?"

"If you're going to therapise me, shouldn't there be a chaise lounge involved?" I say, avoiding the subject.

The truth is, I don't know how I feel about Thaddeus having been captured. Thinking of him reliving the imprisonment that drove him insane makes me feel sick. I can only pray they're not torturing him as they once did. But he does belong there, behind bars, after what he's done. Even if they drove him insane, he still murdered. If only they'd put him there for the crimes he's committed rather than the ones he's accused of.

"I prefer a hands-on approach as a therapist."

Killian nibbles my ear and my thoughts of Thaddeus slip away. I am wholly here. He gives me another squeeze around the waist before hoisting me up. Heaving me out of bed, he carries me to the chair by the desk.

"That'll keep you from getting back under the covers," he murmurs, booping his nose against mine.

"Yes, because what's a few feet to a girl with the power of a god?" I tease, kissing him and drawing him to me.

"Hm, you have a point. How about this: if you stay there, I'll bring you some food."

"Deal."

He grins, pulling his trousers and shirt back on. I watch the birthmark, a blatant reminder of inevitability, disappear beneath his hemline. How can he be so calm in the face of his fate? How has he rushed so readily into scenarios that could have led to his death? He did it because he loves me, because he cares and wants to protect people. This, this is how I'll cost him his life. I try to smile at him before he trots out into the hall. My face falls.

While he's gone, I study his room to distract myself from the oncoming panic attack. It's not spartan, as I'd expect a soldier's room to be. It's full of life, books, a guitar. I remember he said he played. I wonder now if that music isn't the touch of caeletai in him, urging him to sing and call forth sleep. How much of who we are is rendered by our birth, by destiny? There are so many pieces of myself that I owe to what I've come to learn was inevitable. My death as a child for starters. I would never have met Vaerdiexes had that not come to pass. One misstep, one miscalculation of my own strength. I must be wary not to overestimate myself again, even as my power grows. I get up and wander over to his bookshelf, examining his books. There's not much here I've read before, mostly Russian novels. Who knew Killian would be into that? I hear the door open and he comes back in the room.

"I didn't take you for a Gogol fan," I say, plucking *Dead Souls* from his shelf.

"Are you kidding? I loved the short story *The Nose* growing up. I thought it was hilarious. Whose brain thinks like that, to come up with that kind of story."

I grin at him. Oh if he likes books we're going to get on very well. I spy the plate of cheese, crackers, and grapes in his hand and stick out my tongue at it.

"All we had, sorry. My housemates have ransacked my food while I've been away."

"This is what I stayed out of bed for?" I demand, walking over and plucking a grape from its stem. I hear the muted pop of it between my teeth, feel the plump flesh of it chill my gums as the juice runs over them.

"How about I make up for it with dinner after the coronation?" he asks, passing me my clothes.

"Deal. But I should warn you, I'm a ravenous beastie."

"All you've had since laying waste to an entire army is a cup of tea and a single grape. I'd say that's fair. And don't forget, I've seen you eat. I already know what you can pack away. You've got no secrets from me Thiel."

He's not wrong. And it is a relief to know he knows all there is about me. I never imagined someone could see those pieces I keep hidden, put them back together, see the shape they take when assembled, and love me still. Yet he does.

I slip on my tattered dress and grimace at it.

"Not really appropriate, is it?" I say.

"Could use a bit of a tidy up."

I use my magic to clean the blood and grime from it, and repair the damage where I tore a strip off to tie up Thaddeus. I don't feel right wearing it, wearing the dress I went to war in, but there's no time to go back to the apartment and change before the coronation.

The irony of Casey being made queen is not lost on me. How absurd to make the person who could have made a difference last night, but cowered instead, their queen. I glance up to see Killian's eyes trained on me.

"What?" I ask, walking over to where he sits at the desk and sitting in his lap.

"I was just admiring the woman I am extremely lucky to be with," he says, running his fingers up and down my spine. It sends a streak of warmth along my skin.

"None of that," I admonish, "or we won't make it in time."

"Fine," he grumbles, pulling me upright with him. "Let's go."

I follow him downstairs, through the kitchen, in which some of his housemates are relaxing. One of them blinks in disbelief at me, as if the mere fact of a woman's presence in the house is a miracle. I guess Killian can't really bring his dates back to Miesarinda. If seeing a deabrueon freaked one of them out, travelling to a different dimension for a hook up would be out of the question.

"You guys heading out soon?" Killian asks.

"Uh, yeah," the shocked one replies. "Who's your friend?"

"This is Mallory."

The man's eyes widen further. The other one stops eating and turns to look at me.

"As in Mallory Thiel?"

"The one and only," Killian answers, beaming at me. I'm not sure whether they look terrified or amazed.

"Hey," I say shyly. Probably best to be on good terms with the housemates.

As soon as I speak, the barrier goes down. They clamber out of their seats and surround me.

"Is it true you have a gods' weapon?"

"Is it true you've fought the jaeitsi?"

"Killian said you were the one who burned the deabrueon army last night. And you rode a dragon."

"Yes, yes, and that's not the official story," I reply, laughing.

"Wow. You're like a superhero. What made you settle for Killian?" one jokes.

"Hey don't make her think about her bad choices too hard. She might leave me."

They laugh at him, one clapping him on the back. Seeing him so at ease with his own friends warms me. It's nice to know his life isn't all saving my ass and my friends from life threatening situations.

"You want to know the truth? I'm with him for the access to the Library Between," I tell them.

"Badassery and a sense of humour? You're going to fit in around here just fine," the one with cropped brown hair says. I grin. It's refreshing to meet angeleru who don't hold my dragovik status against me but, then again, I'd expect nothing less from Killian's friends.

"Alright, if you're done hitting on her, we've got a coronation to head to. See you later," Killian laughs.

We head out on to the street, which is already streaked with people. Where the other events had been held in the agora, tonight it will be held in the courtyard outside the library. They don't want the reminder of war that the rubble of the rotunda provides. How quickly they brush their wounds under the carpet.

We make our way through the streets, Killian humming and grinning to himself as we go. I can't help but smile watching him; he looks so much like an overindulged child. I'm happy to be the one to spoil him. We reach the courtyard, which is filling up swiftly, and I spy Proserpina, flitting around the edge of the crowd, waiting for us. Her eyes jump immediately to our clasped hands and her face exudes delight.

"I was going to ask where you two have been, but I think I can assume," she whispers as we draw near.

I was worried us being together might upset her, what with Isabrand gone. But her loyalty is truly boundless, her happiness for me extending to us even in present circumstances. She is endlessly generous in her loyalty and I know it is a kindness I must still repay. I made her a promise after all. When this is all over, Thrabr will be slain.

"Where are Kyle and Robyn?" I ask, as we take our place towards the back of the crowd.

A large stage has been set up in front of the library doors. There are golden streamers hung from lampposts but, other than that, it lacks the fanfare and cheer of the two previous nights. There are no great tables of drink or food for us to mingle around afterwards. Despite the earlier cheer, there is solemnness in the occasion, even if the people are pleased to see their queen crowned.

"They decided not to come. Something about celebrating the coronation of the woman who failed to protect the city didn't sit right with them."

"I am right there with them," I grumble.

"The Hirutere have already disseminated the falsehood that it was her who defeated the deabrueon, and the angeleru are lapping it up. I bet the people would lick her feet if Tobias would let anyone near enough to her."

We get a filthy look from a nearby woman who overhears us. Proserpina sticks her tongue out at the woman, who scowls, turning back around. I forget sometimes, having seen Proserpina fight like a seasoned warrior, how childish she can be. It's utterly endearing.

"I don't care about that. Even as queen, Casey's power is effectively non-existent. I care about this Tobias guy having power. If we go against his command not to attack the jaeitsi, and rescue Isabrand, we could all be sentenced to death."

"Which we are going to do, right?"

"Of course."

"Well then all the better for the Hirutere to fall," she murmurs.

There's a bout of applause as Casey ascends onto the stage. They've dressed her in a white gown: pure and untainted. I want to laugh at the irony, of one whose hands are so bloodied by inaction being dressed so, but settle for a snort instead. Again, the woman glares at us, but I ignore her. Tobias follows Casey onto the stage.

"It is with great pleasure I present your new queen, the venerable caeletai umea, Casey."

There's a moment of silence before the roar of applause, a well of uncertainty everyone is trying to hide the depths of. Proserpina leans close to me.

"They doubt her already. This is good for us." I nod, clapping along with everyone else. But Proserpina doesn't clap. She doesn't look at Casey at all. "Do you see it now?" she asks.

"See what?"

"I thought with your gift for visions you would have read it in her by now. I noticed it our first night here. Casey will die if you don't assert your claim to the throne soon."

Proserpina's claim takes me by surprise, but I keep clapping. I remember at that first party, how Proserpina had stared through the crowd as if she could see through to Casey. I study the girl on the stage and swallow hard. Am I furious with Casey? Yes. Do I want her to die for what she's done or, rather, failed to do? Of course not. I trust Proserpina's gift to see the future more than my own, so I know what she says is true: I must do something soon to save Casey's life. But am I ready to make my move? I wouldn't even know where to begin.

Casey steps forward, nodding in gratitude to Tobias. Gone is the wavering slip of a girl from earlier today. She is all composure now. Her face is solemn, but it does not touch her eyes. Those are empty.

"Thank you. My people, last night we went through one of our darkest moments. Never before has the fortress that is Miesarinda been attacked so ferociously. The losses were great and will not be forgotten. But now, action must be matched with action. We cannot stand for the jaeitsi's attack on our homeland."

She continues but I'm too distracted by what she's just said to listen.

"Action must be matched with action? But Tobias said they weren't going to do anything."

"Lies spew easy and fast here," Proserpina intones. "When they are caught out in them, it will make it all the easier for you to win the people over."

"But how many more dead before then?" I ask.

"Shh!" the woman hisses. A few more people glance back.

"You 'shh' you dingbat!" Proserpina replies.

Casey finishes her speech and there's more applause. No doubt every word was written by Tobias, who has hovered by her shoulder throughout the whole speech. She leaves the stage with him and they re-enter the library. The crowd begins to disperse. There will be none of the jovial partying tonight.

We turn to leave as well, Killian's promise of dinner on my mind. From our right, the old man in the green robe who had slept through our trial approaches us. He has a plate and some ribs in his hand, his mouth sticky with the sauce, and I'm tempted to ask where he got them from.

"Kurtis," he says, wiping his hand off on his robe and offering it to me. There's a large red smear across his protruding belly.

"Pleasure," I say, taking his hand. I feel the sauce adhering to my hand where he failed to wipe it all off. My pale dress won't hide the stain so well.

"You've been summoned by her majesty to the clock room in the library. I'm to take you there."

He doesn't say it as a question. This is the command of a monarch. No doubt Tobias has orchestrated this, a demonstration that even we must bow to her leadership if we wish to stay in Miesarinda. Not that he'd let us leave; he'll want to keep his eye on us. The old man drops his plate in a nearby bin and strides across the courtyard. The three of us speed on to catch up with him. I hear the short huffs of breath he takes as he trots.

"Sorry, what's this about?" I ask, worried someone has overheard our conversation. It would be considered treason.

"I can't say. Just thought I'd make myself useful when Tobias, I mean Queen Casey, said she wished to see you," he replies, as we enter the library and he fumbles for the correct button in the elevator. "Ah."

Why do I get the impression it wasn't an accident he said Tobias' name first? I don't ask any more questions as we begin our ascent. He seems thoroughly preoccupied with massaging the bald spot on the back of his head and does not speak to us for most of the ride. I feel the others' eyes on me.

"Miss Thiel?"

"Yes?"

"I think it would be wise to keep our plans to ourselves at present," he advises me, winking.

"Our plans?" Is he conspiring with us?

He smiles as we arrive in the lobby and enter the room we came to earlier today. I'm greeted by the sight of the council and Casey, all sitting around the table. Casey looks utterly miserable now, her composure eaten up by the reality of her situation. Her chin rests in her hand and her shoulders slouch forwards. The day has drained her as I cannot imagine. Still, I find little pity within me.

"Ah you've brought friends I see," Tobias says. "Perhaps they should leave."

"Killian is my son, he will be permitted to stay," Ronan interjects. Tobias seems displeased at being superseded, but makes no further case against Killian.

"The girl then."

"Is my bodyguard," I reply hastily. "Where I go, she goes."

"You need a bodyguard?" he asks, raising his eyebrows.

"The power comes and goes. It's uncontrollable like that," I say, shrugging. "So, have I been summoned by her majesty or by you, Tobias?"

"Her majesty, of course."

I look to Casey, my gaze blank. I give her no opening through which she might interpret my thoughts or feelings. She gives me a pleading expression and I know she is desperate for allies, isolated as she is. But something has grown in me. No, I don't want her dead, but I won't serve her. I won't serve the woman destined to be Killian's partner, the woman who cost me my brother. Realising she'll get nowhere with me, she sighs.

"The prisoner Thaddeus Velemir has been thoroughly questioned," she says, but doesn't go further.

"And I'm guessing you brought me here because he hasn't responded to this thorough questioning?" I ask, directing my question at Tobias.

I will acknowledge the real power here. Casey clears her throat to get my attention, but I don't take my eyes from him. She looks around, as if for help, but there will be none here. None of the members of the council even look at her.

"Yes," Tobias finally replies. "He's been very tight lipped."

"Funny, it's almost like I told you he would be last time we spoke. But then, who am I to offer advice to such a wise governing body."

"Yes, you did say that. Do you know how we found him, Miss Thiel? Bound to a lamppost, unconscious, with a swathe of fabric that looked remarkably like your dress."

"If you're asking whether I was the one who caught him, you're welcome."

"Not where this is going. It's funny because now he says he'll only speak to you."

This shouldn't come as big a surprise as it does. Of course Thaddeus would manipulate the situation to get to me. He had tried speaking to me the night of the attack, hadn't he?

"Not too funny really, given I'm far more pleasant than the likes of you."

"Yes, I'm sure that's all this is, a madman's desire for civility."

He studies me, but I give nothing away, simply shrugging. There's something Thaddeus is willing to tell me and only me. Whatever it is may be the difference between saving Isabrand and losing him forever. He's played this well, I'll give him that. I'll get to Thaddeus at whatever cost.

"Will you act as inquisitor on the city's behalf?" Tobias finally asks, scowling. Mustn't seem too eager. I pause, as if mulling it over.

"I will."

"Very well. Bring in the prisoner."

Shit. I hadn't anticipated it being here and now. How am I to get the information I need in front of the whole council? But it seems Tobias has other plans.

"All but Miss Thiel and myself will leave the room at this time," he says, as the door opens and a bound Thaddeus is escorted in. He's in a strait jacket and he has a muzzle around his mouth. His eyes find me immediately and do not leave me the entire time they are directing him to his seat. I sit opposite him, Tobias on the side of the table to my left.

"Will you be okay?" Killian murmurs.

"I can handle myself," I promise.

Proserpina squeezes my shoulder before they leave with the others. The door closes behind them, leaving only the three of us.

"So, Thaddeus, you have what you want," Tobias sighs, removing the muzzle. "Miss Thiel is present."

Thaddeus licks his chapped lips. Now, in this light, I see he has aged a lifetime in the three years since I last encountered him. His brown hair is streaked with grey and there are wrinkles about his eyes. He looks more gaunt and wild than before, if that's even possible.

"Alone."

"What's that?"

"I said I wanted to meet with her alone," Thaddeus says to Tobias, not looking away from me for a second.

"That won't be possible I'm afraid. Your interview will be conducted under my supervision. Proceed." He takes his seat.

Thaddeus remains silent, clearly displeased with Tobias' presence. This is not how his reunion fantasy played out. I will have to coax him out of his shell.

"You wanted to speak to me last night," I say, quietly.

"And you knocked me unconscious. Last time I saw you, you almost died, is a moment too much to ask?"

"After everything you did?" I can't help myself, the words just slip out.

"Mallory– " he pleads.

"Let's try and stay on topic here please. You were going to tell us about the jaeitsi's plans." Thaddeus shakes his head.

"I already told you, I'm not kept in the loop."

"Don't trust you, do they?" Tobias muses.

"Their leader doesn't trust anyone." Diane, he means.

"They have a leader?" Tobias asks, raising his eyebrows.

"Yes. An avika. Or was an avika. Mallory took her powers away," Thaddeus says. "Thank you, for that."

I can tell from the glint in his eyes that he means it. She has enacted as much cruelty on him as on me. I nod my head. I am grateful to have provided the world reprieve from her particular brand of evil.

"And there are still only three jaeitsi?" Tobias asks.

"Yes. They think they're close to finding the fourth though. Your caeletai won't stand a chance against them, not without her mate."

"We've located her mate," Tobias replies hastily.

He's lying of course. If they had found out about Killian, he would already have been whisked away from me by now. What does Tobias gain from lying to Thaddeus? Thaddeus isn't in a position to communicate this information to the jaeitsi. Finally, Thaddeus heaves his gaze from me and appraises Tobias. Through his madness, he still sees so clearly and he sees Tobias' lie for what it is. He raises his eyebrows.

"You and I both know that's not true," Thaddeus says, grinning. "And the greatest weapon you do have you're too afraid to use. Scared the people will rally around her instead of your false queen."

Tobias and I both know he's referring to me. A look of displeasure flashes across Tobias' face, an admission of the truth in Thaddeus' claim.

"I'm not afraid."

"But you are. You're one of the unlucky few members of the Hirutere who have survived our attack. You will have to live long enough to see our plan come to fruition."

"I thought you didn't know the jaeitsi's plans," Tobias says, his voice shaking slightly.

"I know their ultimate goal."

"What's that then?"

"The end of you."

They can do it, I know they can now. Without Casey or Killian to defend the city, it will fall to the jaeitsi's will. Tobias must know this too because he quickly changes the subject and looks anywhere but at Thaddeus.

"The attack last night. Why did they do it?"

"They want her."

"Casey? But they had the chance to take her and didn't," Tobias says, confused. But I'm not. Holy shit. This has been their plan all along.

"Not the girl. She's ineffective. If she wasn't, the jaeitsi wouldn't have made it five feet through the door."

"Who then?" Tobias asks.

"Mallory."

Tobias stills, looking up slowly at Thaddeus.

"Why not take her then?"

He makes it sound as if he is offering me to them. Take her and leave us be. Thaddeus hears it in his voice too and laughs. He tilts his head back and his body shakes with the roar of amusement. When he's done, he is all smiles.

"And risk a god's wrath? We're not so stupid as to take her directly. No, we came up with a better plan."

Tobias freezes, as do I. Suddenly it is so obvious that Thaddeus is only here because it's exactly where he wants to be. I should have thought it strange how easily I managed to capture him last night, but there were more pressing matters at the time. He stares at me and it is without the invasive gleam of familiarity. No, he is looking at me as if I am a prize he's already won.

"Girl, reinforce the spell keeping him from transforming into a dragon," Tobias commands, but his voice lacks conviction. Whatever witch has cast this spell is not strong enough to hold him for very long. I can read it on Thaddeus' skin. But I ignore Tobias. I'm above taking his orders. Besides, I'm too intrigued.

"What do they want with me? The same as before?"

"What do you mean the same as before?" Tobias demands. "Answer me!"

"Yes," Thaddeus says, ignoring Tobias.

"So, they took Isabrand, knowing that I would come for him. Then, they sent you to deliver the message."

"That about sums it up."

"They used you. Knew you'd leap at the chance to see me like a dog."

"Of course I would, I love you."

The words from his mouth make me sick. They are not sweet, like a layer of protection that drapes itself around my shoulders as when Killian speaks them. They are possession, a desire to own.

"Guards!" Tobias cries out. The handle starts to turn, but I hold it shut with my mind. No one will get in here until I know everything I need.

"You told me once you were fighting to avenge me and Clara, but now you're fighting with Diane?"

"It was necessary at the time so I played along. There's a new power now."

"The woman who took Isabrand?"

"Yes."

"Who is she?"

"Can't say. We haven't met. But from what I hear, her goals align with mine. With yours. Annihilation of the Onyevaras and the Hirutere."

"You?" Tobias demands, turning to me. "You little rat, you've been plotting against us all along!"

"It's become a recent necessity," I reply coolly. He lunges at me, but I flick a finger in his direction. Vines burst into existence, rootless, and bind his wrists to his chair's armrests. I return to Thaddeus as Tobias begins to cry out. "So that's it, you expect me to just go with you to help someone neither of us knows, who kidnapped my brother, your son, after everything the jaeitsi did to Miesarinda?"

"I expect you to do whatever it takes to protect Isabrand. As I will you."

Damn him for being right.

"Are you saying they'll hurt him if I don't go?"

"Can't say," Thaddeus replies. Does he care so little for his own son?

Tobias rips free from my bindings and races across the room. He is pulling at the door, rattling it in its frame, when the roots I plant with my mind burst into vines. They bind him to the ground, wrapping around his body. I hear screams from the other side of the door as they try to push back through.

"Mallory, what's going on?" Killian calls, banging on the door.

Until now I have not considered Killian. What I want from him does not align with what I must do. And what I'm about to do will break his heart, but it is the answer to most of our problems. That's all I can afford to solve right now: most of our problems.

"We better get going," I say calmly.

Thaddeus' strait jacket undoes itself, dropping to the ground. I see the traces of a magic weaker than mine, which has bound him to his human form. With little more than a flick of my finger, I undo it. I see the cold coil unravel from around his torso, no longer constricting him, so that he might become his true self.

"You traitorous little bitch!" Tobias screams. I look at him over my shoulder as I begin to hear the creak and crack of bones snapping. Thaddeus' transformation has begun.

"I prefer to be called the Phoenix Queen."

The floor to ceiling glass windows on the opposite side of the room shatter to accommodate Thaddeus' true form. He flexes his wings as he has not done in years, smashing the windows either side of him. The ceiling groans, the wood beams splintering and falling around us. He drops his pale red belly to the ground, his gold eyes on me, waiting for me to get on his back. With one hand on his back, one on his neck, I hoist myself up and swing a leg over his spine. I nestle myself between his shoulder blades. He lets out a deafening roar into the sky, spews fire that draws screams from what remains of the crowd below. He leaps from the window and we plummet towards the ground. At first, he flounders, flailing his wings for a moment, but does not find his rhythm fast enough. I catch us on gust of air that sends us soaring upwards. Finally, he begins to beat his wings steadily, taking us over the city, where cries go up to see a dragon flying over Miesarinda. We soar past the field I had torched the night before, still charred by Vaerdiexes' power, and into the hills. I do not know if I have made the right decision or a smart decision in trusting Thaddeus. All I know is that I must save my brother and find a way to fulfil the prophecy. Miesarinda fades to nothing behind us.

Chapter XXXIII.

The city dips out of sight as Thaddeus' wings catch on the breeze and we glide through the air. What have I just done? Possibly make the stupidest decision of my life. And that's really saying something because I've done some very questionable things. But I know it's not that which bothers me. I've done idiotic things before and survived. No, it's that I am aware that this could be the answer to the many problems that have been accumulating: my need to fulfil my destiny, my lack of an army, Isabrand's kidnapping. But I am also aware of what I will have to leave behind and what I will be sacrificing by making the choice to leave with Thaddeus. And I hate to do so.

We fly through the night and the early hours of the morning. I'm surprised Thaddeus can sustain flight for this long, given he has not been in this form for such a long time. But I suppose this is what a dragovik's body was built for. Not fighting with swords and arrows, but for tearing enemies apart with teeth, for soaring through the sky and feeling the cool air on his back. Forbidding transformation was the true perversion of our nature. Yet another strike in the ledger against the Hirutere. After seeing Isabrand in battle last night, I don't doubt for a second that we would need no more than a handful of willing dragoviks to wipe the angeleru out.

It is late afternoon by the time we crest over a hill into a valley, Thaddeus dipping downwards into its belly. I feel exhausted, only having had a few hours sleep since the battle, but I keep my eyes open. My stomach is rumbling and I'm starving. I need to eat something as soon as possible, but my guess is there won't be time for that right away. I wonder where we are anyway. Loathe though I am to do it, I tune my thoughts into Thaddeus'.

Is this Sundalev? I ask.

No. None but the vyrium of the council of five know where the portal lies in these lands. It is a jealously guarded secret, even from the Hirutere.

So where are we?

The land between, between Sundalev and Earth. Miesarinda is only the gateway, but the lands extend well beyond it.

And this is where the jaeitsi are now?

After you discovered their location on Earth, they had to relocate. They were ready to make their move on the Hirutere, so here seemed best, he answers. I study the sweeping curves of the hills, the blue rivers that run like veins through the thick forests.

Why does it look so familiar? I ask.

This is where you were raised Mallory. In the years preceding your time at the Academy, you and Isabrand were raised one valley over by your mother and father.

Oh. One valley over, somewhere out there, is that river. The one that shaped my fate irrevocably. Could I go back to those waters, beg for my unencumbered life back, free of prophecy?

Thaddeus begins his descent, a somewhat shaky one, and I spy a great grey stone castle ahead of us. We land in a clearing not far from it and I am quick to slip from his back as soon as he comes to a stop. As I pace away, I hear the snapping of bones, his body stowing itself safely within its human form. Looking away, I'm surprised by the beauty I find in the place. It is all green trees dashed blue by the watery light of the sun. It is soft despite the brightness of the day and a part of me wishes I could stay here. The other part of me wishes it could return to Killian, but all of me knows this is the best decision I could have made.

"This way," Thaddeus says, motioning towards a path that leads from the clearing towards the great castle.

I walk along it, Thaddeus following behind me. I avoid looking over my shoulder. I'd rather not see him completely naked if I can avoid it, though he seems to have no shame striding forward. He's not being arrogant about his body, just utterly unfazed by the fact he's without clothes.

As we approach the castle, I see a lone figure standing outside. She's petite in stature and it takes me a moment to recognise her without her armour.

Clara is dressed in a simple white peasant dress with a brown leather belt around her middle. Sheathed either side of it are two daggers. Even at home she is battle ready. She approaches Thaddeus, brushing his cheek with her hand, a daughter's unearned love. Around his bare shoulders she drapes a grey wool cloak that seems too warm for the weather.

"Hello Mallory," she says, stepping back from Thaddeus and turning to look at me at last. Her eyes are the most peculiar shade of green and blue, streaked with gold that is highlighted by the sun.

"Hello Clara," I return.

She turns back to Thaddeus, smiling at him.

"Are you okay?" she asks.

"Don't fret, pet. They didn't hurt me."

He indulges her with a smile and I see some of his softness then. He loves her dearly, as a father would a child.

Looking up at the castle, I find it is smaller than I thought, smaller than the library in Miesarinda at least. It has one turret that stretches up into the sky, but it does not tower as high as I first thought. It is old and dilapidated, the stone full of cracks and the nature that has learned to grow despite the coldness.

"What is this place?" I ask. She beckons me to follow her, Thaddeus by her side, and we head in.

"Once it was the Ovira's family home, passed down for generations, much like that very stone you're wearing," she answers. I touch my hand to the memory stone around my neck. How did she know what it was? "Each of the three original families had one see: a stone and a house. The former was a gift from Illarion, the latter a token of respect from the Hirutere, back when they bothered to extend it to dragoviks. We all saw how that panned out. So, I suppose what I'm saying is, it's your home."

I look at the barren, dank stone walls on which hang sconces with unlit candles. There is no home to this house. I want no part of it.

"I take it your coming here means you're going to agree to help us take apart the Hirutere?" Clara asks.

"I don't think I have much choice in the matter."

That seems assurance enough for her. We cross the entrance hall and Thaddeus opens a door into a courtyard. In the middle is a fountain that does not run. The stones paving the floor are cracked and pock marked with weeds. Nothing else has lived here in a long time. I wonder why the jaeitsi chose the Ovira castle to be their base? Perhaps simply because it was abandoned and the Hirutere would not think to look in an old dragovik home for them.

"But I told you when we met in Aplin Hollow, you do have a

choice. I made mine and I do not regret it."

I study her. She hardly seems to have grown at all in the past few years. She still seems so childlike, but already she is touched by death. The massacre at the Academy, the attack on Miesarinda, whatever was done to her as a child. All of it reeks of death.

"You may come to yet," I advise her.

"And will you? Will you regret your decision to save your brother?" she asks, turning to me as we reach a door across the courtyard.

I can't answer that, not yet. It is something I will know only in hindsight.

"As I thought. Come, they're waiting for us."

Thaddeus throws open the doors and leads us into a great hall. Unlike the entrance, it has been cleaned and the candles lit. There is a roaring fire in the massive fireplace on the left wall. Again, it seems ill-suited to the weather outside. But inside it is chilled, the stone retaining none of the sun's heat. It is too cold for a creature of fire like me.

On the opposite end of the room are seven chairs. The three in the middle are set higher than the others on a dais. Unlike everything else in the room, these thrones seem new additions. The stone is not cracked and it is beige, rather than grey. Other than the thrones, the only furniture in the room is to our left. Around the fire are gathered a couple of chairs and a sofa covered in red velvet, which are occupied by Elias and someone else. Whoever it is sits too far back in one of the chairs for me to see their face. Elias rises when he sees me, but makes no move towards me.

"Sorry for our last encounter," he apologises. "I needed you out of the way."

"No hard feelings then, I suppose."

He grins, his black eyes glinting in the firelight.

"I'd like you to meet the third member of our group. I think you've met before though, back at the Academy."

A ribbon slim girl rises from one of the high-backed armchairs, its back to me. She is cast in shadow by the fire, but, when she emerges from its glow, I see her familiar face. Slanted almond eyes and short brown hair.

"Lena?" I ask, utterly confused by the sight of her here.

"What—oh my goodness."

"We can skip the whole shock and reveal thing," Lena sighs, before smiling at me. "Good to see you again. Shame we're both dropping out of college. Though I suppose it's a bigger shame for you. I was getting really tired of having to write those essays."

"You went to the Academy?" I ask, confused by what Elias has said. I don't remember a Lena from my days at the Academy.

"Yep. Same class and everything. Or don't you remember your old best friend?" she says, tilting her head to the side.

Those brown eyes, dappled with gold. They looked at me so kindly when I was afraid. They told me I would not be alone. Not when we cut throats, not when we were beaten into submission. Not even the night I cost us our one chance to escape by helping Elias. How did I not see it before? All these years had passed and I had not realised who was in front of me.

"Lilith."

I am not angry, nor am I surprised. In this moment, all I feel is relief for the friend I had long believed dead. I rush for her and she puts her hands up to defend herself, though does not arm herself with one of the weapons strapped to her hips. My arms wind around her and I pull her into a tight hug.

"You're alive," I breathe. "All this time."

She softens in my arms, reciprocating my hug. What anger had bided in her chest at my betrayal all those years ago yields to the familial love we shared.

"You really thought Diane would kill me? Aside from you, I was always her favourite. Sorry Elias," she adds.

He grimaces, but doesn't say anything. I lean back and take her in as if somehow, in light of this new information, she will appear different to me. She is one of the jaeitsi after all.

"But how? Your wings?"

She draws me to one of the couches and sits me down.

"Our wings can be hidden, as mine are. But I suspect you're more curious about how I'm alive. After we were caught, they took me to my room. Not my bedroom, but the one where Diane taught her lessons. Claustrophobia, that's always been my thing. The walls of the room were designed to close in slowly until there was not even enough room to draw breath. Anyway, Diane questioned me until I said it was your idea to escape; sorry by the way, we both know it wasn't. She told me she knew I was lying and I thought she was going to kill me. Instead, she set me free. After that, she withdrew me from the class and kept my training private. When she left the Academy, she took me with her."

"And she had you watch me?"

"Not at first, no. She used her powers to manipulate this couple into adopting me so I could establish myself. It was a pretty good gig to be fair. You saw how it was. When we found out you were going to NYU, she had me register and befriend you. I hated you at first, so self-deprecating, self-flagellating. But after a while I couldn't hate you because, well, you were still you. Mallory Thiel of the Academy," she answers, shrugging.

"A touching reunion," Elias says, taking a glass of scotch from the table beside his chair. "But now it's time for more important things. Are you or are you not here to join us in our fight against the Hirutere?"

They all turn to me, three of the most powerful creatures in the supernatural world and a madman.

"Where's my brother?" I counter, attempting to deflect his query for now.

"You'll see him soon enough."

"How about now?"

"How about you answer my question?"

There's a sudden clatter of heels across the stone floor. I look from Elias to see Diane making her way to us. She seems so out of place in the castle, what with her modern attire. Her eyes are brimming with rage, her nostrils flared. I have not seen her this angry before. It is an emotion she usually masks with cruelty and coldness.

"What," she demands, "were you thinking?"

"I'll deal with this," Elias sighs, rising from his seat once more. She comes to a halt a few feet away from him, placing her hands on her hips.

"Launching a full-scale attack on Miesarinda, showing them our hand? Do you have any idea the mess I've had to clean up back on Earth?"

"No, but I'm sure you'll tell us," Elias replies in a cool tone I would not expect him to direct at her. She doesn't either, clearly, taken aback as she is. She pauses, then moves forward, slower now, with the poised ferocity of a tiger.

"You bet I will. I had allies lined up to join us. But they view your attack as a failure in leadership. What's more, they question my authority. It made me look bad, it made you look bad, and now they're reluctant to join us."

"We don't need them," Elias says.

"Don't need them? How are we supposed to wage war on Miesarinda without them? This is just another example of your failure to obey me. First you send Isabrand after Mallory, after I explicitly told you not to. Then you went after her, again, only moments after we discussed her importance to the cause. Now you pull this?" Diane hisses, before narrowing her eyes. "You can't kill her Elias."

"I know I can't. That's why I've teamed up with her."

He swills the remainder of his scotch, nodding towards me. Diane redirects her gaze to me, shock taking hold of her face. She had not noticed me sitting beside Lilith on the sofa in all her anger. Her mouth is a small 'o' of shock. Fluttering her eyelashes, she lets the surprise bleed out of her expression, and it is taken over by that coy smile she always seems to offer me.

"Mallory! I'm so glad you've come to your senses. And you Elias," she says, beaming at him. He crosses to the fire, setting his glass on the mantlepiece. Resting his hand there, he plumbs its depths, his eyes darting back and forth, searching. What for?

"Yes. I have."

"Well, I don't know what's responsible for this one-eighty, only that I'm grateful for it. Now we can really get started with our plans. This will please our potential allies greatly, maybe even enough to rectify the damage your attack did."

"It's actually something Mallory said to me that made me decide it was better to fight with her than against her," he muses, as if he hasn't heard a word she's said. Diane's face flashes impatience, but she crosses her arms and waits to hear him out, willing to play along.

"And what's that sweetheart?"

"She asked me why I'm doing this. At the time, I couldn't quite answer. So it got me thinking: why am I fighting this war? The thing is, I didn't really know why, other than the fact you wanted me to. All that blood on my hands to satisfy your desire for power. Why? So, I talked to Clara, I talked to Lilith. They were clear in their goals. They wanted an end to the government that had let them so easily slip through the cracks, the one that would have imprisoned them simply because of what they were born as. They wanted the power they never had as children. The power you deprived us of. Like Mallory said, you broke my wings in the first place."

Diane looks agitated and, if I'm not mistaken, a little afraid. The only power she wields in this room is psychological since I stripped her of her isuazko.

"And then you brought her in. The witch. And when we were returning from Miesarinda the other night, I asked her why she wanted to do away with the Hirutere. Do you know what she said?"

"No," Diane whispers, before she clears her throat and tries again with more authority. "No."

"To protect the people she loves. That's why Mallory is here, isn't it? To protect her brother. So much more noble than me, enslaved to childish notions of approval. But Mallory was right, you don't love me."

"Elias, of course I do! Haven't I always said that?"

"No," he murmurs, turning to her at last. "You haven't. Not once."

He snatches his glass from the mantle and hurls it at the wall opposite. It shatters into a starburst, raining down as the mirror in that octagonal room had done on me, but, this time, the shards fall on Diane. She shelters her head beneath her arms, but I see the pinpricks of blood on her forearm as the glass falls. There's a movement in the corner of the room and the hooded witch steps out of the shadows. She's tall, tall as Elias at least. She doesn't come any closer. Diane looks to her.

"You're behind this insurrection?" The woman nods, drawing closer. "How could you? My oldest friend," Diane breathes.

"Elias already told you. I have to do it for the people I love," she says, and I swear I hear her lips curl into a smile as she speaks. Elias turns to me.

"You want in? Prove yourself."

I don't take his meaning at first, frowning. But then it's plain as the bright red blood beading to the surface of Diane's arms: he wants me to kill her. The woman that has brought us all together like pieces on a chessboard. The one who has been guiding our fates all along. It is time to take what we can of our futures back. I take a deep breath. She's defenceless now, surrounded by some of the most powerful creatures in the world, with no magic of her own. Can I really use her own magic, which seeps through my blood, to kill her?

Think of Isabrand.

Think of Kyle.

Think of Killian.

Think of Proserpina.

Think of Casey.

Just five of the lives I will save if I do this. There's no question. I will do what she taught me to do best. I rise from the couch beside Lilith, who squeezes my hand. Would that there were a hundred leagues between Diane and me right now. But the space between us is gone in an instant and I am confronted with that last moment to change my mind. No, better to do it quickly.

"Please Mallory," she whimpers, eyes wide.

I spare her the unfolding of Morvedae's curse, a complete reduction to ash. The fire roars to life behind me. I could kill them all right now. I could wipe them from the face of this planet and any other for that matter. But it wouldn't save me from the prophecy, unfolding liking crashing petals. The flames crack like the whip she brought down on my back, on my brother's. Her head hits the floor before the fire returns to the hearth. I watch, unmoving, as her body slumps to the ground, her neck cauterised where I have cut her head off.

I hear footsteps behind me and the clink of glasses. Elias appears by my side and offers me a glass of scotch. I take it, grateful for something to do with my hands other than deliver the will of death. He taps his glass to mine and downs the contents. It burns my throat when I swallow, but I have always been fire anyway.

"I'll be honest, I didn't think you'd do it," he laughs suddenly.

"You wanted me to prove my loyalty, there it is. Now, my brother," I say again, narrowing my eyes at him.

"Don't you want to celebrate your coming into the fold? Sit, have another drink. Trust me, Isabrand is fine."

"I'll believe it when I see it," I hiss. He shrugs his shoulders, walking back to an armchair and collapsing in it.

"Don't worry, I wouldn't let anything happen to your brother," the hooded witch says.

She walks across the room towards us and Thaddeus stiffens. I look over to him as his jaw goes slack. He lets out the sound of a wounded animal before crouching down to the ground. Grasping his head between his hands, he begins rocking back and forth, groaning to himself.

"Thaddeus, what's wrong?" Clara demands, kneeling beside him.

"I was wondering which of you would recognise me first. Seems cruelty forms a more solid foundation for memory than love," the witch muses. "Hello, my little angel."

She sweeps her hood back.

One eye green, the other brown.

"Who," I start, looking around at the others for some explanation. The witch catches me by the chin and turns me around to face her.

"Don't you recognise your mother?"

Chapter XXXIV.

I am standing in front of a full-length mirror that contains the image of me. But it is not me. It does not feel like me. I feel vacant. Absent, as though I am above my own body. Or maybe I'm somewhere else entirely. Maybe I'm already in hell. It certainly seems that way.

The two women who escorted me from the great hall in my shock, bathed me, and brushed my hair, are dressing me in a midnight blue gown with golden starbursts on it. But I am elsewhere. I am not sure where, but I am not here. I can't be. This can't be my reality.

Breathe.

I have to remind myself to do that now. How to keep breathing when the rest of your body stops? How to keep marching into the future when there are so many mysteries remaining in the past?

I hold the memory stone while they hem the dress and call back to me the events that led to this.

It's like this.

Once upon a time, there was a woman and she didn't love a man, but she married him anyway. They had a baby girl and they named her Mallory.

It's like this.

Once upon a time the woman's daughter died, unhappily, but not ever after, and her mother brought her back. In the delirium of her recovery, she told her mother about a god who had promised her a kingdom in exchange for her life. Such a promise from a god was not likely to have gone unforeseen by a seer. So, the mother went to Miesarinda, broke into the Library Between, and found the Cadmus Codices. There she read her daughter's fate: to become the queen of a fallen kingdom. The mother was attacked by one of the avika guards only to discover the avika had plans of her own. She wanted to educate and raise a school of supernatural assassins to take down the Hirutere. So, the mother made a deal. It wasn't unlike spinning straw into gold. Her daughter, in exchange for helping her escape the attack of a man she had once hurt brutally. The avika agreed.

It's like this.

That night, the one in the Thiel home just one valley over from where the daughter and the mother are now, the avika lay in wait. When the man had slaughtered everyone in the house but the mother and daughter, the avika needed only manipulate his and the daughter's realities to help the mother escape. They saw what she wanted them to see: the fallen body of the mother. Really, there was another door, there was another woman's body, and the mother escaped into the night. But see the mother never wanted to give her child up, not for all the spun gold in the world. She disguised herself and came to work at the Academy, where she watched over her daughter. She sang to her and brushed her hair, until one day it broke her. And she knew she had to make a better world for her daughter. She knew she had to create a world in which the prophecy could come true. If she didn't, Vaerdiexes would abandon Mallory, and her daughter would fall to madness like Thaddeus.

It's like this.

After many years, she was finally reunited with her daughter. And they lived happily ever after.

I withdraw my hand from the pendant as if it burns my skin, tears welling in my eyes. She had posed as my caretaker, stayed by my side all those years after abandoning me to Diane. She had watched and known exactly what was done to me, yet didn't intervene? And now she thinks I will sit on a throne on the dais beside her and all will be well.

And what of Isabrand? This fairytale doesn't mention him.

The young woman kneeling beside me finishes pinning the hem of my dress just as an older, slender gentlemen enters. He smiles, revealing the pointed teeth and forked tongue of a raika.

"Your mother desires your presence in the great hall," he announces.

I nod numbly, following him out the door and back down the dark stairway that brought me up here. After my mother revealed herself, she dismissed me to clean myself up. Not another word was exchanged. I was in too great a shock to speak, so allowed myself to be pulled away. I have no idea what awaits me downstairs, but they have allowed me to keep the Vaerdiexes sword and stones. I assume it will not be war. But the sense of comfort the sword once imbued me with has vacated my heart and I feel so utterly alone in this place. If only I could see Isabrand.

We reach the bottom of the stairwell, emerging into the courtyard. In the hours I have bathed and dressed, it has been repaired. The fountain now gushes water and the weeds have been picked. There are people as well, walking back and forth with plants, baskets of fruit, else piles of linen. Where did they all come from, I wonder. We make our way back into the great hall, where a large table has been set up with seven seats. I see the back of her first, the long curls of brown hair spilling down the back of the chair she's sitting in. She looks over her shoulder, her beautiful face beaming at me, and her familiar eyes twinkling.

"My angel," she murmurs, sweeping to her feet and walking over to me. She has changed now into a wide sleeved gown of emerald green, with a golden boarder around the neckline. "You look stunning, but you always have in blue. You looked beautiful in that dress the other night. Not surprising though, the angeleru sure do know how to make a dress. It's been a nightmare getting them from Miesarinda to the castle, mind you. Luckily, we have our spies in the city. Come, sit."

She nods to the man who has brought me and he disappears. With an arm around my waist, she leads me to the head of the table and draws back the chair for me. Picking up a carafe, she fills two goblets with red wine as I sink shakily into the chair. She takes her seat beside me and squeezes my hand, wrinkling her nose when she smiles.

"You must be hungry. I've ordered the kitchen staff to prepare dinner. It's been a long journey," she says, drinking deeply from her cup. She draws it from her lips, licking the red that stains them. Her eyes sweep over my face. "You're not asking how I'm alive, so I assume you've figured out how to use the gift I left you."

She taps the necklace and her touch sparks me back to life.

"Yes," I answer, almost mechanically. "I'm guessing you want it back."

"Of course not, it was a gift. Besides, it belongs to a Thiel." She runs a hand through my hair, tucking it behind my ear. Why do I want to press my cheek into her palm, feel her warmth? Why do I want anything to do with this horrible, cruel woman? "You really ought to put your hair up. You have such beautiful features. And those eyes. They're so like your fathers. Strange, your brother had them too after the spell I cast, though he wasn't your father's son. Perhaps it's something of the ice in him."

"You didn't love him, did you?" I say.

"Your father? Well, no, but it seemed a sensible marriage. He was ever so yielding to my every whim and he doted on you. He was a good husband and father, which was all he needed to be. Why do you ask? Are you in love?"

Does she really think we'll make idle chit chat after all these years?

"I just want to know the kind of person I'm dealing with. We haven't exactly had the chance to get to know one another, seeing as you abandoned me to a terrible and cruel fate as a child."

"As I said in my note, I did what I had to, for you."

"Funny how what you did for me seems to benefit you an awful lot."

She flinches, seemingly genuinely hurt by my comment.

"You think being separated from my darling daughter benefited me? You think I wanted to be apart all this time? I did what I had to to keep you safe from the Hirutere, from Thaddeus. They would have torn you apart if they found out it was you in that prophecy or what it meant for them."

"Why not take me with you then? When you left that night, you didn't have to leave me behind."

"I had made a deal with Diane. If she had turned me over to the Hirutere that day in the library, I would never have seen you again."

She has a counter for everything, such excuses that I cannot hope to rebut her.

"Where's my brother?" I ask suddenly. She sighs, drawing her hand away from my cheek.

"I've had them bring him down to join us for dinner. I never understood your attachment to that boy, he's a bad influence."

"Better than a rapist," I say.

She drums her fingers on the table, studying me. She cannot argue that point away. The door opens and I turn around, expecting to see Isabrand. Instead, six men carrying platters with various dishes file in. The table groans beneath the weight of them as they are served and I hear my stomach rumble. Everything looks as divine as the food in Miesarinda and I'm ravenous after a day's journey.

"Eat," she orders, and I don't disobey.

I load my plate with lamb chops and mint sauce, peas, and potatoes smothered in butter. I wolf down the plate before helping myself to seconds. It isn't until I'm halfway through my food that I realise she isn't eating, just sipping slowly on her wine.

"What, villainous witches don't eat?" I ask.

"You think I'm the villain?"

"Aren't you? You've moved all your pieces around the chessboard, even tricked Diane, and have us aligned against the Hirutere."

"That implies that they're the heroes of this piece and, when it comes down to it, we both know it's not quite so black and white. They have their faults as well as I. They have condoned worse things than you or I could possibly imagine."

Before I can ask what she means, the door opens again and Isabrand stumbles in. Leaping from my chair, I dash across the room to hug him. He looks startled, but pulls me close.

"Mallory, thank heavens," he says, holding me tight. "I knew you'd come for me. Let's get out of here."

I step back. He sees the table laden with food first. My dress is second. Why am I not armed for battle, he must wonder. Then, at last, his eyes dart up and he sees Regan.

He recognises her immediately. He was older than I when she faked her death and no doubt has a clearer memory of her. But despite believing her dead for over a decade, he doesn't seem surprised to see her.

"I should have known you'd slink back from the dead," he says, narrowing his eyes at her. He draws me behind his back. "If you think you're going to lay a hand on my sister– "

"Oh calm down Isabrand, as if I'd hurt Mallory. You should know better." She walks over to us, laying a hand on either of our shoulders. "All I've ever done is protect her."

It's what goes unsaid that I know stings him most. *But not you.* The silence rings with her admission. Isabrand has never mattered but as a means to get to me.

"But that's all bad blood that we're best washing our hands of. Come," she urges him. "Eat some of the food before your sister gets it all."

Suddenly, I'm devoid of any appetite. I follow Regan back to the table before I realise Isabrand is still standing by the door, his mouth gaping.

"What have you done to her?" Isabrand demands of Regan.

"Whatever do you mean? Have some more potatoes, sweetie," Regan says, loading more onto my plate. They smell heavenly, like warm, salty butter, but everything on this table seems tainted now.

"Mallory wouldn't do this. She wouldn't just come here and have dinner with you like nothing's happened. You cast a spell on her."

"Don't be ridiculous Isabrand. You really think I could hoodwink your sister? Have you seen how powerful she is?"

Isabrand looks to me for confirmation and I feel shame burn my cheeks.

"It's true Isabrand, I came here of my own volition."

"Mallory, if you came here for me, let's go. She can't stop us," he says, rushing forwards and kneeling beside my chair.

"He's right Mallory. There's nothing I could do to stop you from walking out through that door," Regan agrees, spearing a potato from my plate.

This only serves to confuse Isabrand more. He looks at me urgently, his eyes begging for a response.

"I can't," I say at last.

"What do you mean you can't? She just said you could."

"Not because of her. Because of Vaerdiexes, the prophecy."

His brows knit together. This serves as no explanation, because, though he knows of the promise to Vaerdiexes, I have not told him about the prophecy. Regan pours another goblet of wine.

"And when the first falls from favour, of two will be chosen their ruler. Sister, brother, one's fire the other's, born again from ashes of death. The god of fire will call upon his emissary and she will be divine of body and mind, all fire, he all ice, the first mortal being blessed by not one but two gods. Beneath her shall fall the infrastructure of old, those who oppose the rise of the fallen ones.

Much will be lost, much will be shed, blood of the innocent most of all. The dominoes had been set long ago knocked down by a power that rises all to reclaim the throne of a lost king," Regan recites. "Did I get that right?"

"What?" Isabrand asks, looking from one of us to the other then back again.

"It's in the Cadmus Codices. My destiny wasn't just a promise I made to Vaerdiexes; my destiny to become the queen of Dragovicia was set down four thousand years ago by Aleia Cadmus. I have no choice but to stay here."

"Yes, you do. You don't have to do it this way," Isabrand presses, holding both my hand so tightly I can scarcely feel them. "We can win this war without her."

I shake my head.

"I have no army of my own, no experience in waging war. The jaeitsi will help me win this war," I say.

"Please Mallory, Vaerdiexes wouldn't want it like this."

But he would. He has told me so by saying nothing. For the god of sun and flame, he is all coldness, unfeeling. He wants only his will executed and the means don't matter. This is how it will be done.

It starts with fire.

It will end in blood.

Isabrand rises, trembling, and I don't believe I've ever seen him look so afraid since he believed me dead that day by the river. He begins to back towards the door, his head shaking mechanically.

"How can you work with her? After what she's done? She's sick."

"And the sad part is, you're in this predicament because of him," Regan whispers in my ear. "So ungrateful."

"What's that supposed to mean?" Isabrand asks. I don't answer. I will not make him feel indebted to me. "Answer me."

I get to my feet and place my hand on the back of the chair.

"You should go, Isabrand. No one's asking you to come with us."

Of all I've said, this blow lands the hardest. He did not anticipat being unwanted by me. I want to wrap my arms around him, tell him I'm scared and nothing will bolster me like his companionship, but I also know I cannot ask him to fight beside our mother. I cannot ask him to turn his back on his morals as I must now do.

There's a great deal of noise from outside, the doors suddenly bursting open. Isabrand dives out of the way, rolling into a crouch position, prepared for an attack. I draw my sword from its scabbard, but lower it when I see who enters the room.

Proserpina, Kyle, Robyn, Casey, and Killian spill through the door. They are all dressed in the bellatoja uniform with the exception of Proserpina, who is in her armour and has the Shigami scythe drawn. I hear the shadows begin to shift and Clara, Elias, and Lilith emerge from where I had not seen them. They draw their weapons.

"Let her go," Killian commands, his sword raised and bloodied before him.

"Must we explain this again?" Regan sighs. "Kill them."

The three jaeitsi dart forth. Clara clashes with Proserpina, Elias with Killian, and Lilith draws her duelling daggers, facing Kyle and Robyn.

"Stop!" I cry out as they begin to fight, but no one hears me.

Proserpina dances through the room, cutting at Clara, who scarcely manages to avoid her blows. Lilith, on the other hand, is more than a match for the two siblings, snaking out a tendril of her dark manage to bind Robyn before she can speak a spell and disarming Kyle in an instant. She sends him skidding across the floor before pouncing on his chest.

"Stop!" I scream at the sight of my dearest friend moments from death.

Bodies go flying in every direction. The jaeitsi land in their thrones, bound by vines. The others skid towards the door. There's a roar and the fire leaps from the hearth once more, drawing a line between me and my friends. My chest heaves. Killian's eyes meet mine, confusion clouding the once clear green. I turn to Regan.

"You want me here, I'm here. But if a single one of these people is hurt, our alliance is over."

"Very well," Regan agrees.

"Alliance?" Killian repeats. Kyle gets to his feet. "Mallory, we thought we were coming to rescue you. What's going on?"

"You can't rescue me, I'm not in danger," I say. Well that's not true, I'm in serious danger of jeopardising my soul, but that's already well and truly corrupted. He starts towards me, but the fire bars his progress. He looks for a way around it, but there is none.

"You can't be serious. You're joining them? After what they did to the city, to Aaron?" Robyn demands.

I flinch. No, I have not forgotten Aaron. But I knew when I came here it would only solve some of my problems, not all. Besides, in the end, it was the Hirutere who failed Aaron by not helping him sooner.

"I have to," I answer. "The prophecy."

"Fuck prophecies!" Killian bellows. "You want to defy mine, why not defy yours?"

"It's not the same," I answer.

"Why not? Because you have to bear the burden of your curses but ours are escapable? That's bullshit Mallory," Killian replies. Proserpina, Casey, and Kyle say nothing.

"Because I made a contract with a god. You don't walk away from that alive or sane for that matter. Besides, if I don't," I pause, looking to Casey. She frowns at me. My heart softens at the sight of her. She came for me. Despite her fears and, no doubt, Tobias' objections, she came to save me, not knowing what she might face.

"If you don't what?"

But I will not tell them that Proserpina has read Casey's death in my failure to act soon. I will not let them feel guilty for what is destined to be. Proserpina catches my eye, nodding at me. Is she forgiving me or does she simply understand?

Isabrand rises to his feet. His face is cold and inaccessible, as it was a week ago when we were reunited. But now it is out of hatred rather than fear. I am becoming our mother and this has burned him more than any other blow I could deal.

"Mallory is staying here. You can't persuade her otherwise," Isabrand tells them, and I am grateful he speaks the words for me, because I fear I don't have the heart to tell them to go myself.

"I know I messed up," Casey starts, "but we can build a new government together, a better world. We can win this war, if only you fight with us."

I smile at her.

"I promised you one day you'd go home to your father and I

intend to uphold that promise," I whisper.

There seems nothing left to say. The chasm of silence grows until, finally, Robyn and Isabrand start towards the door. He reaches out to Proserpina, pulling her by the arm. She doesn't move.

"Come on," he mutters. "We should go back before my bitch of a sister changes her mind and kills us all."

I bite the inside of my cheeks, holding back tears. Proserpina does not budge.

"I swore my blade to you," she reminds me. "My fealty."

"I know. I release you from that oath," I whisper.

She holds my gaze. Is it my future or hers that she looks for in my eyes? If hers, I have just granted it to her. She is free to go back to Miesarinda with Isabrand if she wishes.

"That's not a promise I intend to go back on."

She pulls herself from Isabrand's grip. Clutching the Shigami scythe, she vanishes, only to reappear in front of me on this side of the flames. She kneels before me, offering up the scythe as she had once done in the forest, not long ago.

"You can't be serious?" Isabrand says. "She's planning on waging war on us."

Proserpina rises to look at him. I think I see a flash of pain as she undoes the bonds that hold him dear to her.

"She's my queen, Isabrand. What would you have me do? Go back on my word?"

He flounders, this as unexpected as my betrayal. I let the flames falter between us. I half want to tell her to go back to him, but am too selfish. I will need her by my side in the days to come. Isabrand's mouth sets in a grim line.

"Have it your way."

He walks out the door, Robyn following behind him. I may never see either of them again.

Killian, Kyle, and Casey remain, their eyes still on me as if they are waiting for me to reveal some trick. I don't. Kyle starts towards the door, but hesitates. He looks over his shoulder at me. Isn't this what we knew was coming, from the moment I told him about my promise to Vaerdiexes? That conversation in his library seems a lifetime ago, marred as it is by nights spent bathed in blood.

"But I could never leave you behind," he murmurs. He crosses the room to me, taking his place by my side. Between the two of them, some of the security I had lost in coming here has come back.

"So that's how it is? We have to choose now, you or good?" Killian asks.

"No one's asking you to choose," I say gently. I want so desperately to touch his cheek as tenderly as I had only a day ago.

"No, you're right about that. I guess you really are the villain."

"So go," I urge him. But he doesn't and neither does Casey.

"You know I can't. You'll be the death of me. My fate's as inevitable as yours."

The others look to us, confused. I shake my head. I won't cost Killian his life, nor Casey hers. And what I have to do next becomes so obvious.

"Come here," I murmur, extending a hand to each of them. As if bewitched by something in my voice, they approach. They hold out their hands, but I don't take them. "You promise to serve me as your queen?"

"Always," Killian says. Casey nods in agreement. Poor lost lambs, they know not what else to do in the face of a lion.

"Then let's bind the promise with blood."

They look confused, but do not protest. I summon one of Lilith's daggers to me. Slashing it across their flattened palms, I hear Casey's sharp intake of breath. Killian doesn't waver when I cut him though, holding my gaze all the while. I know what following me down this path will do to him. I also know his heart won't survive leaving me here. Not riddled with love as it is. I can fix that.

"Ciestor lista pervo tiesta suyakurava okhim, vrestir avot letai roteroka ni krestar isuazko."

As it had done with Diane, the spell incants a cluster of gold on the incisions I have made. Kyle gasps, recognising the spell instantly. An arch of light runs from their palms to me, streaming into the cut I have made on my own hand. I feel the enormity of their power sweeping through me, a match for my own, though neither knew how to use it. It seats itself in my heart, which has always been the true source of my power. The spell fades and both of their eyes are wide with horror. They feel their magic's absence.

"What have you done?" Killian whispers, clutching at his chest as if I have removed his heart.

"Now you are both free from your duties," I reply. "Casey, you can go back to your father and, Killian, you don't need to fear your prophecy."

He chokes, horror striking his features as I confirm what he already knew.

"You took our magic," Casey breathes. "We came to save you and this is how you repay us?"

If only she knew this was my way of saving her.

"It's not enough," Prosperina says, resting her hand on my shoulder. "You have to go all the way or not at all."

I know what comes next. I put my hand to the memory stone and rewrite their past. For Casey, it is a simple matter of rearranging the past week so that she will go home thinking she has been at a friend's house. Killian is harder. I build for him a whole new life, one on Earth, safe from visions of demons, angels, and dragons. I rearrange the universe's memories of him, slip him seamlessly into a new life. When I finish, they both slump to the ground, their eyes closing. I hear Kyle gasp beside me, but he doesn't object.

"Now, to send them home."

I kneel beside Casey first and, with my newfound power, send her back to her father's apartment, where she will believe she has been staying with a friend for the past week. I turn to Killian. My angel, who has already forgotten me, forgotten last night. I touch his cheek tenderly one last time. I will never hold him again, but he will be safe from me, safe from destiny. I send him on to his new life, far from this one. He disappears from beneath my touch. With them both gone, I rise.

"Well, that was dramatic," Regan sighs. "Oh darling come here. It'll be okay."

She pulls me into a hug as I undo the bonds that tie the three jaeitsi in place. They rise from their seats, rubbing their wrists. Regan lets me go, smiling sympathetically, before she turns to Kyle and Proserpina.

"I am delighted to see my daughter has made such loyal friends as you two. It will be a pleasure to have you in our court."

"Daughter?" Kyle asks, looking at me sideways.

"Yes, we've just spent the past hour catching up. But now on to bigger things." She takes my hand and leads me up to the dais. "Well, we won't be needing this anymore."

She flicks her wrist and does away with the third throne. It was meant for Isabrand, I know, a way of appeasing me. I seat myself on the throne as she directs. She steps back, admiring me as though I am a finished portrait, years in the painting. The three jaietsi, eyeing me nervously, join Kyle and Proserpina in front of me.

"Well, I present to you our new queen, the saviour of dragoviks," Regan says, "Mallory Thiel. Long may she reign."

They all kneel then, including my mother. I look out over their heads to where my friends had been moments ago. The table is still set for seven.

I am here, exactly where all the cataclysms of the universe have led me: the beginning.

Printed in Poland
by Amazon Fulfillment
Poland Sp. z o.o., Wrocław
21 October 2022

198d5899-d115-4e24-87b1-2951a558cc6dR02